THE
LAST
SNOW

Stina Jackson was born in 1983 and raised in Skellefteå, northern Sweden. In 2006 she moved to Denver, Colorado, where she lives with her husband and small dog. Her debut novel, *The Silver Road*, was an international bestseller and won The Best Swedish Crime Novel Award in 2018. *The Last Snow* is her second novel.

Also by Stina Jackson

The Silver Road

THE LAST SNOW

STINA JACKSON

TRANSLATED FROM THE SWEDISH BY SUSAN BEARD

CORVUS

First published in Sweden as *Ödesmark*
by Albert Bonniers Förlag, Stockholm, in 2020.

Published in hardback in Great Britain in 2021 by
Corvus, an imprint of Atlantic Books Ltd.

This paperback edition published in 2021.

10 9 8 7 6 5 4 3 2 1

A CIP catalogue record for this book is
available from the British Library.

Paperback ISBN: 978 1 78649 736 9
E-book ISBN: 978 1 78649 735 2
OME ISBN: 978 1 83895 219 8

Printed in Great Britain

Corvus
An imprint of Atlantic Books Ltd
Ormond House
26–27 Boswell Street
London
WC1N 3JZ

www.corvus-books.co.uk

For mamma and pappa

Where you come from is gone,
where you thought you were going to never was there,
and where you are is no good unless you can get away
from it.

Flannery O'Connor, *Wise Blood*

PART I

EARLY SPRING 1998

The girl moves through the night. A pale moon smiles down on her as she zigzags between the puddles left behind by the melting snow. The twenty-four-hour filling station casts its neon light over the desolate landscape and she goes in and buys a can of Coke and a packet of Marlboro Red. The assistant working the night shift has kindly eyes which make her turn away. She walks out and stands beside the illuminated car wash, lights a cigarette and blows smoke up into the night sky. Her attention is caught by the haulage truck parked beyond the pumps. A man is asleep in the driver's seat. He is wearing a dark cap and his head is nodding up and down in time to his breathing. She drops the half-smoked cigarette on the ground and crushes it with her foot. The pools of water glisten like oil in the arc lights as she makes her way over the tarmac. There is the hum of a few solitary cars in the distance but otherwise it is silent. The anticipation sends a shiver down her spine. When she reaches the truck she grabs the side mirror and heaves herself up the steps until her face is on a level with the sleeping man's. Close up he is younger than she first thought, with a shiny earring and cheeks shadowed by a stubbly beard.

She watches her own white knuckles move closer to the window. It is a gentle knock but even so the man wakes up with a violent start that knocks off his cap, revealing his thinning scalp. He blinks at her and it takes him a while to lower the window.

'What's going on?'

The adrenalin makes it hard to smile. Her hand gripping the mirror has already started to ache.

'I just thought you might want some company.'

He stares at her, open-mouthed. At first it looks like he's going to protest but then he nods towards the passenger door.

'Come on in, then.'

She walks around the truck, the expectation growing inside her. She turns her head to check for any eyes in the shadows but all she can see is the garage assistant and he's not looking out. It's nearly 2 a.m. and there are no other cars around. If anything should happen, there are no witnesses.

The man is breathing heavily through his mouth as she sits down.

'And who might you be?'

'Just a girl.'

The cabin smells of warm breath.

'I can see that.'

He seems awkward, rubs his eyes with the palms of his hands and gives her a sidelong look as if she were a strange animal he didn't want to annoy.

'And what makes you want to sit here with me?'

'You look lonely, that's all.'

She challenges him with her eyes, thinks he looks afraid. That gives her courage.

He laughs and his fingers play nervously with his stubbly beard as he continues to watch her out of the corner of his eye.

'So you're not one of those who wants paying?'

She places a hand over his. Her silver rings shine like tears in the darkness between them and she hopes he can't feel the blood pulsating through her veins.

'No, I'm not one of those.'

There is plenty of room at the back of the cabin. He bends her over a bunk and his hands are heavy on her hips as he thrusts himself inside her. They don't undress. Their trousers stay around their ankles, almost as if they are expecting to be discovered. She raises her eyes and sees a child smiling at her from a photograph. The child has its chubby arms wrapped around the neck of a chocolate Labrador and it looks as if they are both smiling. The girl lowers her eyes to the crumpled bedding instead. It isn't long before he cries out and withdraws – quickly, so all the sticky fluid lands on the floor. She bends over and pulls up her knickers. All of a sudden she is dangerously close to crying and she keeps gulping to smother it.

The man seems wide awake. There is a new kind of confidence in his hands as he fastens his belt, like a teenager who's just had his first lay. It amazes her how alike they are. The men.

They sit in the front of the cab, smoking. Beyond the massive windscreen the world is dark and damp. She feels sore but the feeling of wanting to cry has passed.

'Where are you going now?'

'Haparanda. And then back to Skåne again.'

His dialect sounds weird, almost like he's singing.

'You coming along?' he asks.

She turns her head to blow out smoke.

'I'm going further than Haparanda.'

His teeth gleam in the darkness. This isn't something he has done before. She can already see the guilty conscience taking shape in him. His voice is trying to smooth out what has just happened. He nods toward the filling station.

'I was thinking of getting myself something to eat. Do you want anything?'

'A cinnamon bun would be good.'

'Sure, leave it to me.'

He takes the keys from the ignition and smiles shyly at her as he opens the door and steps out. He looks slightly bow-legged as he walks and he ignores the splashes from the puddles. The girl watches him as he disappears into the shop, wondering whether to ride with him after all. She could get out at Luleå. She has heard it's a pretty big town. And you can disappear in a town.

Dusk was the worst. The realization that yet another day has been wasted. A day like every other. She stood in her place behind the till and tried to ignore the darkness as it edged its way across the shop windows. Standing under the harsh fluorescent lights was like being on stage. People who stopped to fill up could see her there in the light, the weary movements, the indifference. The thin hair that wouldn't grow beyond her shoulders and the false smile that made her cheeks ache. They could see her while she could just about make them out.

The filling station was in the middle of the community and she knew the name of practically every person who came through the door, but she didn't know them. Maybe they thought they knew her. But she was aware of the whispering, at any rate. Björnlund's daughter who'd had the world at her feet but never did anything about it. And now it was too late. Her beauty and her enthusiasm for life had begun to drain away. The song had gone quiet. The only thing she had achieved was the child, a boy, but how that had happened nobody could be sure as she'd never had a man in her life. Not as far as they knew, anyway. The boy had come out of thin air, and despite all the rumours that had circulated over the years it was never clear who the father was. It was an inconvenient concern that still led to disputes. The only thing the village could agree on was that Liv Björnlund would never be like other people.

They might even have felt sorry for her had it not been for the money. It was hard to feel sorry for someone who was sitting on a fortune.

She drank cold vending-machine coffee and stole a look at the clock. The seconds beat time inside her forehead. On the dot of nine she would step off the stage, anyway. If she didn't her brain would explode. But it was five past by the time the night-shift guy turned up. If he noticed how desperate she was he didn't make anything of it.

'Your dad's out there, waiting,' was all he said.

Vidar Björnlund was parked in his usual place by the diesel pump. He sat in his wreck of a Volvo, his claw-like hands painfully clamped on the steering wheel. In the seat behind him, like a shadow, sat Simon with his face in his mobile. She patted his knee before fastening the seat belt and for a brief second his eyes met hers. They smiled at each other.

Vidar turned the key and the Volvo coughed into life. The old motor had been born in the early nineties and was more suited for the scrapyard than the potholed country roads, but when she pointed that out to him he simply dismissed her.

'She isn't purring like a cat, but at least she's purring.'

'Don't you think it's time we bit the bullet and bought a new one?'

'No, I don't, dammit. Buying a new car is like using money to wipe your backside.'

Liv turned to Simon again. He seemed to take up the whole of the back seat with his long legs and his arms swelling under his jacket. The change had somehow taken place without her noticing. Suddenly one day there he was, a full-grown man.

His chubby face had gone, leaving only sharp-edged cheek-bones and a chin where a red-blond shadow grew thicker every day. There was no trace of her soft round boy. She tried to get his attention but he didn't appear to notice and carried on frenetically punching keys with his thumbs, lost in another world from which she was denied access.

'How was school?'

'Good.'

'School,' snorted Vidar. 'Nothing but a waste of time.'

'Don't start that again,' said Liv.

'They only learn three things in school. Drinking, fighting and chasing skirt.'

Vidar angled the rear-view mirror so he could see his grandchild.

'Am I wrong?'

Simon hid his mouth under his collar but Liv could see he was smiling. He was more amused by the old man than she was. He had the ability to laugh away the things that made her boil with rage.

'You're only saying that because you didn't get an education,' she said.

'What do I want with an education? I already knew how to drink and fight. And there was never any lack of skirt. Not when I was young.'

Liv shook her head and turned to look at the forest. She avoided the veiny hands and the old man's breath that scalded the air between them. Soon the tarmac became gravel and the trees thickened. They didn't meet any oncoming cars and beyond the headlights was only darkness. She undid the top buttons of her work shirt and started scratching her chest and throat. The itching always became worse on the way home, as if her body was trying to break free of her own skin in despair. The thousand ants in the roots of her hair and up her arms made her scratch until her skin bled. If Vidar and Simon noticed, they said nothing. Her behaviour was so familiar to them it wasn't worth mentioning. The boy's phone vibrated at regular intervals, demanding his constant attention. The old man sat with his trembling hands on the wheel, his jaws working. He preferred to chew on his words rather than share them.

When they reached Ödesmark the old familiar feeling washed over her, all the times she had jumped out of the car and run. Straight into the arms of the spruces she had fled, as if they could protect her. The village stood like a last outpost at the end of a road that no longer led anywhere. Twenty kilometres to the west it was swallowed up by the forest and the undergrowth, and the ruins of what had once been. If you drove a lap around the village you quickly got the feeling that the forest was biding its time before it swallowed that as well. The houses were a comfortable distance apart, separated by pine forest and marshland and the black eye of the lake that lay in the middle of it all, reflecting the desolation. There were fourteen farmsteads all told, but only five were inhabited. The rest brooded with their boarded-up windows and weather-beaten facades, well on their way to becoming overgrown.

Liv knew this land better than she knew her own insides. Her feet had worn tracks that snaked between the villages and she knew every fresh spring, cloudberry patch and forgotten well that lay slumbering out there. She knew the people too, even if she avoided them. She could identify the laughter and the smells carried on the wind, and she didn't need to look to know whose car was driving over the gravel or whose chainsaw was shattering the peace. She heard the barking of their dogs, the bells of their cows. They both suffocated and sustained her. The land and the people.

Björngården, her childhood home, stood on a hill safely surrounded by forest, and from her room upstairs she could make out the black mirror of the lake down in the valley. Vidar had built the house before she was born and here she had remained, well into her adult years, although even as a child she had sworn she would never stay. And not only had she stayed, she had also allowed Simon to grow up in the same godforsaken place. Three generations under the same roof, the way they lived in the old days, in times of hardship. But there was no hardship now, apart from that created by people who needed others to cling to. And the more time that passed, the harder it became to lift their eyes above the treetops and envisage being anywhere else. Then it was easier to be slowly swallowed up together with the rest of the village.

Vidar swung in at the barrier and cleared his vocal cords.

'Home, sweet home,' he said, staring at the dilapidated house on the hilltop.

They watched as Simon climbed out and leaned over the padlock. They hardly recognized him from behind, with his broad shoulders and neck like an ox. When he raised the barrier Vidar coasted in slowly and as soon as they had passed Simon lowered it and locked it again. Liv tore at her stinging throat with her nails as they drove up to the farmhouse.

'He's not a child any longer,' she said.

'No, and a good job too.'

She glanced at her father and noticed that time had left its mark on him as well. Vidar had shrunk with age; his weather-beaten skin hung loose over the angular features and gave the impression that he was slowly wasting away from the inside. But the spark of life still shone fiercely in his eyes, two unavoidable flames as he watched her. She turned her head and met her own empty gaze in the car window. The twilight had long since burned itself out, leaving only darkness behind.

✳

Liam Lilja studied himself in the broken mirror. A long crack in the glass ran like a scar right across his face, distorting his nose and cheekbone. The lower half was a scowl, the teeth white in the dark stubble. The upper half wasn't smiling. The eyes stared back at him, insolent, as if they wanted to cause trouble. If they hadn't been his own eyes he would never have tolerated anyone staring like that. Without looking away.

'What the hell are you doing in there? Putting on make-up, or what?' Gabriel's voice came from the other side of the door.

'Coming.'

Liam turned on the tap, put his hands under the cold flow of water and rinsed his face. A cut on his cheek stung and a tooth in his lower jaw ached, but he welcomed the pain. It gave the world more clarity.

Out in the illuminated shop the assistant's eyes were on him. An older balding man, blinking nervously. Liam felt the irritation rise in his chest when he looked at the man. He felt his face harden and time slow down.

Gabriel thrust a packet of crisps at his chest, hard enough to crush the contents.

'Breakfast,' he said. 'I bought cigs too.'

They sat in the car, ate crisps and drank ice-cold Coke. The sky was beginning to get light but the sun hadn't lifted above the treetops. Gabriel devoured the giant bag of crisps in less than ten minutes and moved on to rolling a joint with greasy fingers.

'I checked the plants yesterday,' he said. 'Two lamps are dead. We've got to get new ones.'

Liam crumpled up the crisp bag and started the engine.

'That's your thing now,' he said. 'I'm not a part of it any longer.'

'Fucking great plants,' said Gabriel, as if he hadn't heard. 'Best we've had so far. I think I'll ask more for them.'

Liam stared at the cars parked by the other pumps. One woman in a passenger seat painted her lips and then yawned widely. Her mouth was a dangerous red circle. He wondered what kind of job she had, whether she had children. Maybe a house with a garden and swings. The driver, presumably her husband, returned from the shop and sank down behind the wheel. He had nondescript glasses and slicked-down hair. Liam lifted his hand and patted his own bushy hair, but it wouldn't stay in place. It didn't matter how hard he tried, he would never look like them. Like ordinary people.

They left Arvidsjaur behind them, following smaller roads that wound away from habitation and deeper into untouched territory. Large mirrors of water on either side reddened along with the sky. Gabriel smoked his joint with his eyes shut, only breaking the silence with his rattling cough. It sounded as if his ribs had come loose and were tumbling around in his chest. He had a scar on his lower lip that pulled down the left corner of his mouth, the result of being caught by a fishing hook when he was a child. Although Gabriel always insisted it was a knife wound. That story suited him better.

When the lakes came to an end there was only forest. It stood dense and dark beside the cracked tarmac, and Liam felt his guts churn.

'Does he know we're coming?'

Gabriel coughed. The smell of unbrushed teeth and weed filled the car.

'He knows.'

An overgrown railway track appeared out of nowhere and followed them a short distance until it was buried again under the forest floor. They drove past an abandoned train station wrapped in the embrace of slumbering vegetation. Rusting carriages riddled with holes where plants and other life made their way out. Further on were the remains of a farm surrounded by empty paddocks, where ungrazed grass and dead flowers waited for the sun's warmth to grow again.

The tarmac became gravel and Liam turned onto a series of tracks, each one smaller than the other. In the beginning he had always gone the wrong way, in the days before he had a driving licence and the car they were driving was hot-wired. Then the route to Juha's place had seemed more like a labyrinth in the wilderness, and that was probably the whole point because Juha didn't want to be found.

Beside a black, rippling stream an unpainted log cabin protruded from the trees. There was no electricity or running water here. Liam parked some distance away and they sat in silence, preparing themselves. A coil of smoke rose from the chimney and settled like a blanket over the trees. It would have been a tranquil scene if not for the dead animals. Two carcasses hung from the branches, skinned and headless. Enormous slabs of meat, gleaming in the light.

When they opened the car doors they were met by the sighing of the spruce trees and the gurgling water. Liam carried the plastic bag with the coffee and the weed, trying not to look at the hanging meat. For a split second he imagined they were human corpses Juha had mutilated and hung there.

Juha Bjerke, the lone wolf who had turned his back on people and seldom ventured into the village. Rumour had it that a hunting accident in the nineties was the reason. Juha had somehow shot and killed his own brother during a moose hunt. The police were never involved but Juha's mother couldn't bring herself to forgive him, and there were many who said he had done it deliberately, that envy had taken the upper hand. It had happened before Liam was born and the only thing he knew for sure was that Juha shunned people as much as they shunned him.

A dog came hurtling out of the undergrowth and they stood still while it sniffed at them, hackles raised. A low growl came from its throat, although it should recognize them by now. Gabriel spat in the grass.

'I could shoot that fucking animal.'

The dog trotted ahead of them as they made their way to the house.

'You go first,' said Gabriel. 'He likes you best.'

Liam felt himself tense up as he approached the cabin. Visits to Juha always made him feel paranoid, even though they hardly ever saw the man. Often all he did was stick out his arm long enough to hand over the money and take the delivery. He wasn't much for small talk. But even so, Liam's muscles tensed every time the solitary building loomed up before him.

It was the same for Gabriel. He had fallen silent and lagged a few paces behind Liam. Perhaps it was the isolation that did it, and being on Juha's territory. Or else it was the tragedy that hung over the solitary man like a storm cloud. Despite the fact that many years had passed since the accident, the grief was etched deeply into his face. There was something frightening about a person who had lost everything.

A deer skull was loosely nailed to the front door and it juddered when Liam knocked. The dog panted at their feet and from the cabin they heard the sound of feet shuffling over worn floorboards. The door opened a fraction, revealing a skinny shadow in the crack. Inside, an open fire was burning and the shadows from the flames flickered in the dim light. Juha stuck out his head and grimaced at the dawn. He was old enough to be their father, somewhere between forty and fifty, but his body was hard and sinewy like a young man's. His long hair hung in a ponytail down his back and his face had been lined by weather and misfortune.

Without a word he took the bag from Liam, leaned over, and stuck his nose in the weed to convince himself that it was genuine before handing over the cash. Liam only had to look at the money to see it wasn't enough. It took him by surprise. Juha Bjerke wasn't the kind to give them grief about payments.

'This is only half.'

A peculiar light filled Juha's eyes.

'What?'

'You've got to pay all of it. This is only half.'

Juha glided back into the darkness with a catlike movement. He held one hand behind his back as if he was hiding something there. A weapon, maybe. Liam felt his heart begin to race.

'Come in for a minute,' said Juha from the darkness. 'So we can have a chat.'

Liam put the wad of notes in his pocket and shot a sidelong glance at Gabriel. He looked pale and confused. This was something new; Juha had never invited them in before. Once he got what he wanted he usually shooed them away as if they were stray dogs he couldn't afford to feed. This was the first time he had invited them over the threshold. The fire was burning inside. Liam could make out the hunting rifles in the firelight, hanging in neat rows beside the open fire. On the hearth stood a row of small rabbit skulls, gaping helplessly at them.

'Come in, then,' said Juha. 'I won't bite.'

For a few eternal minutes everything stood still. There was only the crackling of the fire and the wind in the trees. Juha's gappy smile challenged them from inside the room. Liam filled his lungs with fresh air before stepping in. The heat in the small space enveloped him, his nose was filled with weird smells and his eyes struggled to see everything that was hidden in the gloom. It was like stepping straight into a hole. A dark, quivering trap.

*

Liv was alone with the dawn. The light filtered through the naked birches and settled like a glowing crust over the black forest. She had the farmhouse behind her and avoided looking back at it. Her frozen breath was a shield against the world. She didn't see the lights go on or hear anyone call her name. Not until a scrawny Lapphund came racing out of the undergrowth and danced in circles around her did she hold the axe still and turn around.

Vidar was standing on the veranda, his eyes like black slits.

'Come and eat,' he shouted in his cracked voice.

Then he was gone. Liv brushed off her jacket and started to walk reluctantly towards the house, her footsteps like drumbeats in the silence.

The old man and the boy were in the kitchen, sitting in an aroma of coffee. Vidar's hands had locked during the night and when morning came his fingers were rigid claws that could hardly lift the cup to his mouth. It was Simon who sliced the loaf and spread the butter for him, with deep concentration.

'Have you taken your tablets, Grandad?'

Vidar carried on chewing his bread. He wanted nothing to do with medication and if it weren't for Simon lining up the tablets in a neat rainbow in front of him each morning, he would never take them.

'You're worse than an old woman, the way you nag.'

But Vidar swallowed the tablets one by one, and afterwards gave Simon a gentle pat on the hand which was a larger version of his own, and the boy smiled down at the table. Liv turned her eyes away, wondering where the boy got his goodness from, his inner light. It wasn't from her.

She went up to her room to change. The door to Simon's room was ajar and her eyes were drawn into the gloomy interior. The duvet had slipped from his bed and was lying in a heap on the floor beside islands of dirty clothes and books that wouldn't fit on the shelves. The blackout blind was pulled down and the only light in the room came from the old PC that hummed on the desk. She had bought it for him despite Vidar's protests, and the computer had become something of a friend to the lonely boy. A whole life went on in there that she knew nothing about.

She stood with her face in the gap, breathing in the smell of adolescence, sweaty socks and anxiety. She checked for their voices down in the kitchen before pushing open the door and going in. Her knees creaked as she picked up the duvet, and dust swirled around the room. Something glinted under the bed and when she bent down she saw it was a glass bottle without a label. The smell of alcohol was so strong she had no need to unscrew the cap to know what was inside. Homebrew of some kind, strong enough to make your eyes water. Vidar's maybe.

'Shit, Mum, what are you doing? You can't go snooping through my stuff.'

19

Simon stood in the doorway, his face black with rage. Liv straightened up, the bottle in her hand. The cool glass was smooth against her skin.

'I was going to make your bed,' she said. 'And found this.'

'It isn't mine. I'm looking after it for a friend.'

They both knew it was a lie, there were no friends. But she couldn't say that. Liv dusted off the bottle and stood it gently on the desk next to the computer. Thoughts flowed in time to her pulse. He was seventeen years old, there was no point in arguing about it. It might even be a good sign that he was doing typical teenage things.

'Which friend?' she asked.

'None of your business.'

They looked at each other for a long time. A furrow had formed between his eyebrows and it made him look like Vidar. Even so it was herself she saw in the boy's face. Defiance, the hunger for something else, for freedom. If it hadn't been for him she wouldn't be standing here, in the house where she was born. She would have been somewhere else, far away. Maybe he knew it, that he was the reason. Maybe that was why the distance between them had grown wider. She wondered if he had actually found friends, maybe the worst kind, kids who drank and got into fights. Or whether he sat alone in the blue light of the computer, drinking all evening. Either alternative made her feel weighed down.

Simon reached out for his backpack. The angry flush had run from his cheeks.

'I'll be late for school.'

She nodded.

'We'll talk about it this evening.'

'I don't want you in my room while I'm out.'

'I'm leaving now.'

He waited until she had left the room and made a show of shutting and locking the door before going downstairs. Liv followed him; she looked at the downy boyish neck and thought of all the times she had buried her face there and filled her lungs with his smell. All the nights she had wrapped her body protectively around his, rested a hand between his delicate shoulder blades just to reassure herself that he was breathing, that he wouldn't die and leave her. That was so long ago now, another time.

They stood at the kitchen window and watched as he walked to the bus. Liv and the old man. They kept their eyes on the boy's gangly figure until the forest swallowed him up.

'I reckon he's got a woman,' Vidar said.

'Really?'

'Yep. I can smell it. He smells different.'

'I haven't noticed.'

Vidar put a sugar cube between his teeth, sucked coffee through it from his saucer and gave her a meaningful look.

'He takes after his mother, you mark my words. Soon he won't be coming home at night.'

It was hard to breathe in Juha Bjerke's cabin. Liam and Gabriel sat at an unsteady table while the skinny man paced the floor in front of them. Small clouds of dust and pine needles whirled around his boots and the smoky air stung their eyes. His gaze went from one to the other but they couldn't catch his eye.

'You'll have to forgive me,' he said. 'I'm not used to folk.'

Liam tried to hide the uneasiness that was pulsing through his body. He glanced at Gabriel. His brother seemed amused. There was the hint of a smile on his lips and his eyes were taking in the cabin, absorbing the strange contents and the hunting trophies. A knife was stuck in the tabletop and dried blood had left a dark shadow on the scratched surface. The head of an animal hung like a curtain in the only window and it was hot and stuffy in the crowded space. Juha stood to one side of the log fire and his eyes seemed to burn as he looked at them. His voice was hoarse, as if the vocal cords had started to go rusty in his throat. That must be what happens when there's no one else to talk to.

'You're the kind of lunatics who hunt foxes on snowmobiles,' he said. 'I can tell just by looking at you.'

'You don't know what you're talking about,' said Liam. 'Do we look like freaking hunters?'

'But you hunt money, don't you? That's what your life consists of: drugs and a quick buck.'

Liam felt the vibration from Gabriel's legs as he drummed them on the floor. Neither of them spoke.

'You don't turn up with coffee and a smoke for an old man out of the goodness of your hearts, do you? You want paying for your trouble.'

'We don't do charity, if that's what you mean,' said Gabriel. 'Fair's fair.'

Juha cackled. Out of the corner of his eye Liam saw the

knife. He would only have to reach out his hand and it would be his. That made him feel calmer.

Juha suspended the coffee pot over the fire.

'You're hungry,' he said. 'And I like that. I was hungry too, once. But if you've been starved for long enough, you don't hear your stomach complaining any longer. It goes deadly quiet.'

Despite his rusty vocal cords his voice had a melody to it, as if he would rather be singing the words.

'I knew your dad when I was younger,' he went on. 'We were at school together. He was one hell of a man. Evil-tempered as a badger, he was. Slippery too. But if you were in trouble, he'd lend a hand.'

'The old guy's dead,' said Gabriel.

'Don't I know it. No one escapes cancer. Once it gets its claws into you it's thank you and goodbye.'

He had mentioned his friendship with their father before, the first time he wanted to buy weed, in an attempt to win their trust. Liam had a feeling the same thing was happening now, that Juha was using their dead father to win their confidence.

Juha scratched his sunken chest and his eyes were on the flames as the smell of coffee filled the room. Liam and Gabriel looked at each other, waiting.

'I've got a job for you,' Juha said at last. 'If you're interested.'

'What kind of job?' Gabriel asked.

Juha smiled as he poured out the coffee and carefully placed two steaming mugs on the table in front of them. A massive axe had pride of place against the fireplace, its blade glinting in the firelight. Liam's stomach began to churn. The stifling heat and the smell of the animal heads was making him feel sick.

Juha stood at one end of the table, rocking backwards and forwards. He made a whistling sound as he blew on his coffee.

'There's an unworked gold mine not far from here. It's just sitting there, waiting for some poor starving creatures like yourselves.'

His jumper lay like a loose skin over his torso and was discoloured by time and sweat. His trousers had long rips in the fabric and pale flesh showed underneath. He gave off an odour of pine needles and damp leaf mould. With a sudden movement he tugged the knife out of the tabletop and began cleaning his nails with it. Liam glanced at the door. Only three paces and he would be out in the fresh air again.

'We'll have our money,' he said. 'You've had your weed and like my brother says, we're not running a charity.'

'I had a brother as well, once,' said Juha. 'We were exactly like you two, always together. Unbeatable, we were, my brother and me, with the whole world at our feet. But then the son of a bitch went and died, and that's when I realized there weren't any rules. Fate laughs in your face.'

He grimaced, as if in pain, and said nothing for a long time. Everything was still. There was only the fire, living its own life behind his back, flaring and crackling. It was hard to read his face in the dull light, hard to keep one step ahead. Gabriel's foot found Liam's under the table and gave it a kick.

'Tell us more about this gold mine,' he said. 'Where is it?'

Juha's smile was like a scowl.

'Do you know a Vidar Björnlund from Ödesmark?'

'Everyone knows that old skinflint.'

'He might live like he's as poor as a church mouse but he's got money all right, and then some. He's accumulated piles of it through the years, the tight-fisted bastard. And he doesn't trust the banks, neither. Most of it is stashed away in a safe in his room. He's old and worn out. Robbing him would be as easy as taking sweets from a baby.'

Gabriel raised his eyebrows.

'How come you know all this?'

'I know it because we did some business together way back. At a time when I was still too stupid to realize that he tricked decent folks out of their land and sold it on to the logging companies. A greedy bastard, that Vidar. No one wants to do business with him these days. All he's got is his daughter Liv, though servant would be a better name. Never had a life of her own, poor girl. Still living with her dad out there at Ödesmark, even though she's got her own kid to look after. Or maybe that's why.'

Juha turned his head and spat into the fire. The colour had deepened in his cheeks and his voice shook as he went on:

'Vidar is the only one with the code to the safe. When it comes to his money he doesn't even trust his own family. The daughter and grandchild dance to his tune, both of them. No say at all as long as he's alive. They won't stand in your way, I promise you that. So you leave them alone, you hear me? There's no reason to lay a finger on the daughter or the grandchild. All you've got to do is catch the old man unawares and the cash is yours.'

Liam took a look at Gabriel. His nostrils were flaring, his dull eyes had taken on a new lustre.

'Why don't you go there yourself, if it's that easy?'

A painful expression crossed Juha's face and made him look older.

'I can hardly get myself to the village these days. Can't bear to see people, let alone go and steal money. Better to give two capable young lads such as yourselves the chance. I know you can do it.'

'You've run out of money, haven't you?'

'No, dammit, I manage all right. Let's just say I'm heartily sick of Vidar Björnlund. That fool has had his own way long enough. It's about time he learned a lesson or two.'

The old man fixed his eyes on Liam and drew an imaginary knife across his own throat. It looked comical but Liam felt a shiver run down his back. He looked at Gabriel, saw the new light in his face and knew he had already made up his mind. It didn't take much to arouse his hunger. The constant dream of easy money. As for himself, he wasn't so easily convinced. An image of Vanja came to mind, all the dreams he had woven for her even before she came into the world. Dreams of normal life, a house with many rooms, all the surfaces clean from shame. He thought of the incubator she had been in for days after her birth, a blind little bundle with tubes in every opening while the drugs pulsed around her tiny body. He hadn't been allowed to touch her, only to look on as she lay there, fighting. That image would always be his driving force.

'What do you want from us?' asked Liam.

'What do you mean?'

'You're telling us this because you want something in return, right?'

'I don't want a penny from you. All I want is to see Vidar Björnlund brought to his knees once and for all. I want to see him lose the fortune that should never have been his in the first place.'

Liam pushed his chair back and stood up. Juha stood staring at him, weighing the knife in his hand.

'And you're sure there's a safe?'

'As sure as I know the sun comes up in the morning and goes down at night. Wait, I'll show you something.'

Juha faded into the gloom, turned his back to them and began rummaging in a chest that was standing on the floor. Clouds of dust flew up like smoke around him and filled their nostrils. Eventually he grunted and held something in the air, a yellowing piece of paper marked by time and greasy fingers. With a triumphant movement he put it on the table between them.

'What's this?'

'You've got eyes, haven't you? It's a chart.'

It looked like a rough floor plan – hall, kitchen and one room, shakily captured in black ink. Doors and windows meticulously marked, black arrows leading to the room. There, in a corner, someone had put a thick black cross. Juha leaned over the table and stabbed the knife so hard into the centre of the cross that the shaft vibrated.

'There she is,' he said. 'The answer to your dreams.'

*

Liv drank her coffee standing by the sink to avoid sitting next to her father. Vidar was staring out through the window, watching for signs of life on the desolate gravel road. He was warmly dressed and had his knife in his belt, even though his hands rarely let him use it these days. He never watched TV or read books, never did crosswords or bet on horses. His days consisted of drinking coffee and keeping watch on the village. Even if he refused to have anything to do with the neighbours, he had to know what they were up to. He kept them under the same ruthless scrutiny as he did his own family. Nothing slipped past the old man. His cloudy eyes still saw everything.

Liv didn't mention the bottle she had found in Simon's room. Vidar would discover it all in good time, anyway.

A car drove by down on the road. Vidar raised himself out of his chair and his joints creaked. He craned his neck, hungrily.

'Look at that. Karl-Erik's out and about again. They should take the bugger's driving licence away from him.'

'Sit down and stop staring.'

'He's never sober long enough to drive a car. He'll end up killing some poor soul, you wait and see.'

Liv looked down at the muddy gravel road and the sun reflecting in the meltwater. She heard Karl-Erik's car disappear out onto the main road. She knew Vidar's hatred of the neighbours was on account of his loneliness. He no longer knew how to approach people. Their proximity scared him, made him toxic.

'There's a problem with the chainsaw,' she said.

'There is?'

'I don't intend chopping all the logs by hand.'

'The lad can help you. He's got to do something with those muscles he's built up.'

Vidar chewed his bread slowly. He only used butter in the mornings, and nothing else. Fillings had to wait until lunch.

Liv poured out more coffee and studied the miserable pile of logs outside. The bright red handle of the axe was like a piercing scream in the greyness. A chainsaw was another superfluous item, and if she wanted a new one she would have to buy it herself. A man who denied himself a slice of cheese would never allow himself a new chainsaw.

With a calloused hand Vidar smoothed the newspaper that lay on the table in front of him. The houses for sale she had circled with a red pen stared back at him. She did it for his sake, so he would understand that they were on their way out of here, she and the boy. When she started doing it, many years ago now, he used to get annoyed, but now he only made a joke of the whole thing.

'You don't want to be living in the town. It's all exhaust fumes and litter and empty-eyed people. Out here you can at least see the stars at night.'

When he got up to fetch more coffee she made her escape to the bathroom. She peed in the rusty toilet and afterwards stood with her hands on the cracked basin for a long time. The mirror was also damaged, a spider's web of cracks in one corner. She avoided meeting her own reflection; the tired mouth and the sad eyes just made her more tired and sad. It wasn't only the house that was falling into ruin; her face was also full of cracks. She heard Vidar humming in the kitchen. He was the one who was old, he was the one who should be thinking of death, yet she was the only one who did. Every day she thought it couldn't be long, that she only had to bear it for a few more years. Then life would start.

When she returned to the kitchen Vidar was sitting in his

chair again. It was like an unspoken agreement they had, a kind of dance, so if one was sitting at the table, the other stayed by the sink. If one was moving about the floor, the other stood still, almost as if the house couldn't tolerate too much movement at the same time. Despite the fact that they had lived under the same roof since the day she was born, the distance between them had only grown.

A quad bike drove along the road and Vidar ducked behind the curtain. A dayglo jacket flashed between the pines.

'Well, what do you know?' he said. 'Old Modig's gone and bought himself another new toy. The man hasn't got change for a bus but it doesn't stop him buying more things.'

'How do you know it's new?'

'I've got eyes in my head, haven't I? The old one was black. This one's red.'

Liv walked over to the window. Douglas Modig had stopped by the barrier and was raising his hand. She waved back.

'Maybe I can borrow his chainsaw,' she said. 'Until we get a new one.'

Vidar started to cough. The catarrh rattled in his lungs.

'Like hell you will,' he said, when he had recovered. 'I'm not having that bastard on my land. I'd rather chop the wood myself.'

She was soon back at the chopping block. The spring sunlight was so bright she had to close her eyes each time she lifted the axe, and when it fell it was her father's head she split.

SUMMER 1998

The girl walks along the cracked road. The sun is beating down and the smell of the pines is strong in the heat. Horseflies have chased the reindeer from the forest and they watch her inquisitively as she walks on. Their antlers sway proudly against the sky and she feels secure in their presence. She imagines she belongs to them.

She is wearing a white dress and it billows in the wind like a flower and feels pleasant against her legs. When a car approaches she hides in the ditch and huddles there until she can see the colour and make. Only then does she stand up and hold out a hand.

An old Merc whines to a standstill. The reindeer move indifferently across the centre line. Perhaps it is because of them that he has stopped. But the man behind the wheel nods at her to move closer. She brushes moss and pine needles from her dress and walks over to the opened window. His eyes are concealed by large sunglasses and all she can see is her own reflection. The dishevelled hair and the mouth trying to smile.

'Where are you going?'

She shrugs.

'Anywhere.'

He laughs a little as she gets in. His top lip bulges with tobacco. The car stinks of tobacco and sweat, and the seat burns her bare legs. Men like it when she doesn't give a straight answer, it excites them. She can practically see him getting aroused as he looks at her out of the corner of his eye.

He starts the engine and manoeuvres cautiously among the reindeer. The air blowing from the fan is deliciously cool and she waves her arm out of the window, her fingers outspread in the stream of wind. She keeps her eyes on the wing mirror to make sure no one is following.

'You're not going into the village to meet some guy?'

She shakes her head. The village is too close, she is going further. The man breathes heavily.

'You look bloody gorgeous in that dress,' he says. 'Are you going to a dance?'

'Nope.'

'It's a long time since I had such a stylish woman in this old heap, I can tell you.'

'Have you got a cigarette?'

But all he has is tobacco. She takes the tin he is handing her and kneads a good-sized ball which she wedges under her top lip. He laughs again, that nervous kind of laugh they often have. That is precisely what she likes about the men, the fact that she scares them a bit. That they view her as a wild animal, capable of anything. Something dangerous.

Then the questions come. He wants to know her name, where she lives, who her parents are.

'Who cares?' is all she says.

His smile dies. As they drive through the village she sinks low in the seat. Everything is in blossom and the trees are coming into leaf, the sun glitters on the lake and laughter filters in through the dirty windows. She wonders if he is going to stop, but he doesn't. He drives on past the shimmering birches and the shops.

'How about a shot?' he asks, nodding towards the glove compartment.

Hidden inside is a bottle with no label. She unscrews the lid and the smell of alcohol is so overpowering it makes her eyes water. She swallows a couple of mouthfuls and he laughs again. He won't have any himself, he's driving of course. They come across more reindeer, and this time he rests an arm on her seat back while they wait for the animals to scatter. He doesn't swear at them or sound the horn.

'Damned fine, aren't they?'

That decides it. She reaches out a hand and strokes his cheek. He's done a bad job with the razor and missed some stubble. It scratches the palm of her hand. At first he flinches at her touch, as if it scares him, but there's a gleam in his eyes as he looks at her. Dark patches of sweat spread across his shirt.

'Who are you, really?'

'Just a girl.'

That's how she always answers. *Just a girl.* Because it's good to be nothing, to blot out the heavy ache in her belly and start over. It doesn't always work but at the moment – when she sees the apprehension in the man's eyes – she feels as if her body is floating above the seat. The alcohol has helped, of course, and made her feel weightless. The man rests his rough hand on her thigh and moves his fingers higher under her dress. She hooks the tobacco out of her mouth and opens her legs slightly. That's what they always want, these men. They never surprise her. There's comfort in that.

33

They are parked in a lay-by when a car appears out of nowhere. Dust flies as it skids to a halt and gravel patters onto the Merc like a hail of bullets. The man beside her swears and fumbles with his jeans. She can't seem to find her dress. They had tumbled onto the back seat, among the reindeer skins and the fishing boxes. She is only wearing her knickers when her father flings open the door and hauls her from the car.

'Can't you see she's just a child?' he shouts at the man. 'She's underage – I could have you locked up for this!'

The man blinks rapidly, his face blazing behind the wheel. He looks like a cranberry as the father drags her away with him. His fingers are rough against her skin as he propels her over the gravel and into his own car. He is yelling at her. She can see his lips moving and feel the spray of saliva on her cheeks, but his words don't reach her. Her ears have closed up. And the moment the car door slams shut her whole body starts to itch.

Liv tied her trainers and chained up the dog so he wouldn't run after her into the forest. There was a smell of meltwater in the air and the ground had turned to mud which spattered her trouser legs. When she reached the village school on the crown of the hill she stopped and rested, leaning over with her hands on her thighs. Her lungs were burning and there was a metallic taste in her mouth. Below in the valley was the lake, its water black where the ice had retreated. She glanced back at the abandoned school. One window was broken and a yellowed curtain flapped between the remnants of glass. The building ought to be demolished but no one wanted to pay for it. The plot of land had been advertised for sale from time to time but there had been no takers. No doubt the forest would eventually reclaim its old timber. She continued running past the neighbouring farmhouses until there were only spruce trees, an ancient dense forest that would be slow to relinquish its snow. She didn't stop until she caught sight of the last house in Ödesmark. It was so far out of the village that it was hardly a part of it. She stood in the undergrowth, hesitating. The white walls looked other-worldly against the grey forest. Last year's leaves were raked into neat piles and two dogs lay outstretched like dark pools on the grass. If they noticed she was there they gave no indication, and not until she began to move towards the house did they summon up the energy to lift their heads. Their tails wagged in time to her heartbeats and she crouched down and stroked their rough coats before going up the steps to the veranda. They had barked at her in the beginning but now they were used to her, now they knew she wouldn't harm them.

She didn't bother to knock but left her shoes in the porch and folded up her trouser legs before going in. The sweat prickled on her back as she padded through the dark rooms. The house had belonged to an old widow and the contents testified to a forgotten time: dark varnished wood, chenille tablecloths and crocheted doilies. The bed in the bedroom had a colourful valance that collected dust, and the only object that seemed out of place in the house was the man lying in it. She could see the body's outline under the duvet and the shadow of hair spilling across the pillow. The air in the room was heavy with sleep and the smell of warm body. Liv pulled off her top and tracksuit bottoms, removing everything before slipping in beside the sleeping man.

His hands woke first and began feeling their way over her skin, as if he had lost his sight during the night and wanted to make sure it was her. He smelled strongly of timber and tar, and the widow's old bed creaked precariously as their bodies moved towards each other.

Afterwards, while he lit a cigarette, she lay staring at the moose head that protruded from the far wall. She thought she could see reproach in the shiny, porcelain eyes.

'Did you know she died in bed?'

'Who?'

'Widow Johansson, who lived here.'

36

He handed her the cigarette.

'I have actually changed the sheets.'

They laughed, sending white smoke up to the ceiling. Laughed until their eyes ran and the dogs began to howl outside the window.

'Are you hungry? Shall I make some food?'

'Has the food also been here since 2008?'

'Nope. Freshly bought.'

The bed creaked in protest as he got up. It was a miracle that it took his weight at all and didn't collapse under it. She lay in the stillness, smoking, while he clattered with cutlery and china on the other side of the wall.

The first time she saw him the Northern Lights had been flashing over the village. He had been driving all day and it was easy to tell he was from the south. He wasn't wearing proper clothes. He stood there in trainers and a hoodie and held out his hand. Liv had made coffee and Vidar had given him the key to the widow's house, the house Vidar had picked up for almost nothing even before the widow was cold in her grave. Liv guessed it was his need for control that made him buy the ramshackle old place, rather than his desire to own the place, because he let it stand empty for over a decade.

No one had wanted anything to do with the house until Johnny Westberg showed up. That was his name, the man she was sharing a bed with. He was forty-two years old and worked at the sawmill in the neighbouring village. The first time they met he had answered her questions evasively. When Liv asked if he lived alone all he had done was nod in the direction of the car where two black beasts sat panting in the winter night.

'I've got the dogs.'

Perhaps she knew even then that she would end up in old Widow Johansson's bed a few weeks later. Perhaps Vidar sensed the same thing, because after Johnny had driven off, leaving behind a cloud of fine snow, he had turned to Liv with a serious expression and said:

'You keep away from that one.'

'Why?'

'Because he's not to be trusted, I can see that clear as you like. He's hiding something.'

Liv stubbed out her cigarette and got up. She turned her back to the moose head while she dressed. In the kitchen, candlelight flickered over the widow's wax tablecloth and Johnny had put out two beers and a plate with cheese and ham. Even so, she couldn't sit down.

'Nothing for me.'

'You can stay for a while, surely?'

'It's late. I've got to get back.'

His face was sad in the light from the candles. It made her feel ashamed and she swore to herself that this would be the last time, before they were discovered and the neighbours started talking. And before Vidar got a whiff of it and chased him out of the village. She walked towards the hall and the whining dogs outside. She felt his gaze burn her back as she tied her shoes, and when she straightened up and tried giving him a smile there was none in return. She wondered what would happen if she took him home, if she held hands with him and introduced him to Vidar as the man in her life. She tried to imagine Vidar's reaction, what he would say. But she couldn't. It was impossible.

The night swept its cold membrane around her as she made her way home to Björngården. She was already longing to be back in the warmth with the man. Quietly she slipped in and out of the shadows surrounding the barn and the woodshed. By the garage door she came to a standstill. Fluttering on the washing line was a dress she hadn't worn for many years, the white fabric like a ghost in the corner of her eye. The sight made the darkness throb around her. She ran over and violently tore down the dress, so that the washing line bounced and the clothes pegs flew to the ground. She ripped the delicate material into strips and let them fall into the dustbin, then she stirred the contents around with her hand to convince herself it was beyond saving.

He was sitting in the darkness when she walked over the threshold. It was the smell she noticed first, the liniment and the fumes from his homebrew. One candle was alight on the table but he sat outside its glow, skulking like a phantom in the shadows.

'Why are you sitting here?'

'I'm waiting for you.'

'It's the middle of the night.'

'I'm sitting here with your mother, thinking how damned alike you are.'

Liv took a few steps into the room. She saw the photograph on the table and could just make out Kristina's smile in the flickering light. She felt the dizziness overtake her, her legs so unsteady she had to sit down opposite Vidar in the darkness. They kept their faces outside the circle of light and couldn't see each other clearly. It was only when he drank that he talked about Kristina. In his drunken state she became alive again, and he could see her and hear her. The alcohol turned him into a mouthpiece for everything she would have said if she had stayed. If she had lived.

'Mum's dead,' said Liv.

But the words drifted past him, soundless wingbeats that disappeared into the night, all too easy for him to dismiss. Vidar poured out more homebrew, pushed the glass across the table and told her to take a mouthful. His eyes were like warm pebbles in the glow from the candle.

'Do you know what she said when we got married?'

'Don't talk so loudly, you'll wake Simon.'

'"Don't let the darkness take me," she said. "Make sure my head is always above water. Don't let me sink, whatever you do."'

The alcohol had smoothed out his voice. The words ran in a gentle melody that sent shivers through her body. Liv raised the drink to her mouth, held her breath and drained the glass. Flames shot down her throat and set fire to her belly.

'It was me who got her pregnant,' Vidar continued. 'I was set on having a child, but I should have known what it would do to her.'

His chin trembled and his nose ran. Liv stared into the candlelight, wishing she was somewhere else, anywhere at all except right here. Shut up, she wanted to say, I don't want to hear any more. But she sat there, feeling him push the black guilt across the table and put it where it belonged, on her shoulders. It was an unimaginable burden to bear.

'From the day you were born, she was lost. She disappeared into herself, cut herself off from us. The doctor told me to have patience, that it would get better. But it didn't get better. She was already gone. She might as well have died in childbirth.'

The words fell like stones from his mouth and reverberated through her. She had heard them so many times before, the truth that seeped out of him when he'd been drinking, but even so they never lost their power. The knowledge that it was her fault her mother was dead. Suicide due to postpartum psychosis, the medical notes said. After childbirth. Those were the key words. That was where the blame lay. That's what she'd had to bear, in spite of being only a few months old.

Vidar reached for his pipe and the sound of his smacking lips filled the room. The crying had given way to a kind of stillness, almost contentment, now that he had reminded her of the way things were. About the life they bore on their conscience.

She grasped the neck of the bottle of homebrew, poured out half a glass and drank so fast the liquid ran down her chin. She tried to keep her hands from shaking.

'You can't see it yourself,' Vidar said. 'But you carry the same darkness as your mother. I know it's got its claws into you, trying to coax you away from this world.'

'I don't know what you're talking about.'

'I can't force you to stay here any longer, you're too old for that. But I'll never take my eyes off you, believe me. Not as long as I live. There's no chance I'll let you disappear into the arms of one of those monsters you run to at night. I'd rather die.'

He leaned across the table so she could see him better, the ageing body's sagging contours. The loneliness in his eyes bored deep inside her and stirred up everything she wanted to suppress. She twisted her face to the window, to the night outside. When she was younger the darkness had suffocated her, but now she could disappear into it, and take cover. She saw her own face in the glass, the unhappy child hiding there, pleading with her.

The flame from the candle flickered in the draught as she stood up. The alcohol had already reached her bloodstream and made her unsteady on her feet. Only when she had her back to him did she dare to protest.

'I am not Kristina.'

She got as far as the doorway before something crashed behind her. When she turned round the glass lay in splinters on the floor. Vidar's outstretched hand fumbled in the air, reaching for her.

'If you leave me, I don't know what I'll do.'

She lay between the cold sheets and heard his heavy footsteps on the stairs. He hissed and wheezed on the other side of the door. She held her breath and waited, slid a hand under the mattress, searching for the knife. His shadow filled the gap under the doorway, those restless feet wanting to come in to her. Every muscle in her body tensed. She watched as he tried the handle, cautiously at first then tugging so hard the door shook on its hinges. Her skin felt clammy as she hugged the knife to her chest, both hands tight round the shaft. But the lock didn't give way and she heard him let go of the handle with a drawn-out whimper. He remained outside the door, alone and restless in the night. It was a long time before he left her in peace. Before she dared to close her eyes.

*

Vanja spread cloudberry jam with precision. She did the same with the cream, before painstakingly rolling up the crispy pancake, making sure nothing bled out of the sides. She took a huge bite and pulled a face at him.

'Grandma says you've got to get a house. She says no one can live in a garage.'

Liam dropped a knob of butter in the pan and poured in more pancake batter.

'Grandma's right,' he said. 'Only cars should live in a garage. But I'll build a brand new house for you and me, just you see.'

Vanja's lips were shiny from the jam.

'Can we paint it green?' she asked.

'Green?'

'Yes. Like the Northern Lights.'

Liam flipped the pancake in one quick movement and smiled at her.

'Of course we can. Our house will be Northern Light green.'

She smiled her gappy smile, the one that made everything skip and sing inside him. Like midwinter ice, or spring. He had lived above the tractor garage since he was seventeen, mainly to get away from his mum and the dogs. The sofa bed fitted in at one end, but when it was opened out the bed took up most of the space. At the other end was a hot plate, fridge and a kitchen table for two. The only window was draughty and overlooked the dog pen. Their barking and howling at daybreak jolted him from his sleep most mornings. And then there was the smell of diesel that came up through the floorboards. It was no place for a child to grow up. Vanja needed her own bed, her own room. And he would make sure she got it. That was all he really thought about. Building a home for her.

They had just eaten the last pancake when the door flew open and Gabriel lurched in. His unruly hair was squashed down under a cap and below its peak his face was a mass of dark shadows. Vanja rushed over to greet him and he swept her up, light as a bird, and sat her on his shoulders. She held his ears and laughed. The ceiling was so low it looked as if she would bang her head any second. Liam turned away, listening to their affectionate chatter.

'How's the snotty kid today?'

'I'm not a snotty kid!'

'Oh yes, you are. You're snot-green all over!'

Vanja laughed so loudly that the dogs began barking out in the yard. Gabriel only had to open his mouth to make her laugh. He only had to look at her.

Liam picked up his phone and took a photo, capturing their smiles without them noticing. It always turned out best that way. Then he took a Coke from the fridge and put it on the table. Gabriel dropped onto one of the kitchen chairs with Vanja in his lap, and combed her long flyaway hair with his clumsy fingers.

'No beer?'

'It's not even ten yet.'

'But it's Saturday so it's allowed, isn't it?' He put his face close to Vanja's. 'What do you say, Snotty? You can have a treat on a Saturday, right?'

Vanja nodded. Of course you could. Liam put back the Coke and replaced it with a Norrlands Guld. He leaned against the fridge door and watched Gabriel spray beer as he opened the can and offer a sip to Vanja, who wrinkled her nose. Liam clenched his hands and tucked them tight under his armpits, digging his nails into his palms until it hurt. He didn't know where the rage came from, only that it was something to do with Vanja. Vanja and his brother. He didn't want Gabriel's twisted view of the world to rub off on her. All that crap about how you had to numb the human brain with substances or in the end you would go mad. People have always taken drugs, Gabriel said. We wouldn't have survived otherwise.

Gabriel took a couple of swigs and stifled a belch. He was playing with a cigarette but knew better than to light it. Liam put out drawing paper and pens for Vanja and asked her to draw the house they were going to build, the Northern Light house. Above her head the brothers exchanged a look.

'Why have you come?'

'Does there have to be a special reason? I wanted to see my niece.'

'I can see you want something.'

Gabriel grinned, lifted his cap and pulled a hand through his hair before putting it back on again. The skin on his face looked sickly in the fluorescent light, as if he never saw the sun.

'I can't stop thinking about that old guy.'

'What old guy?'

'The one down in Ödesmark.'

Liam looked at Vanja as she leaned over the drawing paper. She was changing between a blue and a green pen, licking her thumb and wetting the paper to blend the two colours. Just as he had taught her.

'We'll talk about it later.'

Gabriel's eyes twitched.

'I know you need money,' he said. 'So you can get out of this dump once and for all.'

'I don't trust Juha.'

'Me neither, but it can't hurt to go and look.'

Liam stood in silence in the corner. It was true he needed money; the market garden had never generated much, neither had that other shit. That was the problem with easy money; it disappeared as fast as it came. A harsh spring wind scoured the walls and silenced the dogs. He poured coffee and looked out of the window. The forest was battling against the blast. One of the dogs, a bitch, stood sniffing the air. Her coat rippled in the wind. The others lay in their kennels. Only the bitch seemed unaffected by the approaching storm.

'So what do you say?' insisted Gabriel. 'Shall we go and have a look?'

Liam slurped his cold coffee, grimacing at the bitter taste. His eyes wandered to the dog with her regal bearing in the storm outside. She was standing still and determined, as if nothing would make her move. The wind sang through his veins, bringing with it a warning cry that made the hairs on his arms stand on end. He looked at Gabriel, then at his daughter's bent head.

'OK,' he said as last. 'No harm in having a look.'

Gabriel's smile sent shivers down his back. He watched as his brother lifted Vanja off his lap and stood up. The empty beer can wobbled on the table.

'Give me a kiss, Snotty. I'm off now.'

Vanja pursed her lips and put them to his.

'I'll tell you when it's time,' he said, giving Liam a long look.

As the door slammed Liam sank to the table, suddenly exhausted. He caught sight of Vanja's drawing. In one corner she had coloured a sun that was sending out long rays towards a big blue-green house. Outside the front door stood two smiling figures, hand in hand. Vanja followed his gaze and pointed.

'That's you and me, Daddy. And that's our house.'

✶

Simon's door was always shut. Only the blue glow from the computer seeped out to her. Liv liked resting her ear to the cool wood and listening for him on the other side. His fingers tapping on the keyboard, the muffled snores as he slept, or that insistent rap music that Vidar hated. Sometimes he laughed in there behind the door, and it made her want to laugh too. She didn't know what at. A film, or one of his secret friends behind the screen. They lived all over the place, those friends. Spread across the globe. The very thought of it was astonishing. She understood it was his way of getting away. He could travel far without ever having to leave his room.

When she knocked it went silent immediately. She held her breath until he called to her to come in. A cold blast from the open window met her as she held the door half-open.

'Aren't you cold?'

'Nope.'

A Japanese film was paused on the screen. Simon had always dreamed of going to Japan. He had talked about it ever since he started school, how he wanted to see the cherry trees in bloom and eat real sushi. I'm not going to be like you, he used to say. I'm not going to live in Ödesmark my entire life. *As soon as I'm eighteen, I'm off.*

He looked at her dismissively.

'What do you want?'

Liv considered, standing there in the doorway. Pack our bags, she wanted to say. Let's do it now. Let's go to Japan.

But all she could manage was a shrug. She ran her eyes under the bed where the bottle of alcohol had been, but it was too dark to see if it was still there. Simon followed her gaze.

'You don't have to nag. I've given the bottle back to my friend.'

'Which friend?'

'Just a girl.'

'A girl?'

'Yep.'

She saw the colour rise in his face. It struck her that Vidar's guess had been correct. As usual, nothing escaped the old man.

'Anyone I know?'

'Maybe.'

A knowing smile spread over his lips, startling her. The joy and anxiety felt like electric shocks under her skin. Seventeen years had flown by; soon he wouldn't be sitting here, soon he would leave her. For Tokyo or Lofoten and all those places he talked about. She walked into the room and closed the window, ruffling his hair on her way back.

'Don't tell Grandad,' he said.

'Of course not. But can't you tell me who she is?'

He shook his head, not wanting to say. Liv had never seen him with a girl before, not since primary school, when only girls asked him to their birthday parties. He had been like a puppet in their hands, silent and compliant, letting them brush his hair and put him in dresses. Just so he could be with them. The boys had been merciless after that.

She hesitated in the doorway, looking at him pleadingly. There'd been a time when he'd told her everything. She would sit on his bed and listen to the clear voice with all its questions and ideas about the world, and there had been no barriers or distance between them. She wondered when they had appeared, the barriers and the distance. All of a sudden, there they were.

'Why are you so secretive?'

'That's good, coming from you.'

Suddenly he had adopted Vidar's tone.

'I'm not the one who goes sneaking around the village at night.'

*

The mist floated out from between the trees and turned the road into a deathtrap. Liam drove the car slowly. The reindeer had returned from their winter pastures and he detected

49

their shadowy figures between the pines. They were thin and blue-skinned, shedding their winter coats. Gabriel sat in the passenger seat, staring down at his phone with the picture of the plan Juha had given him. His dirty nail hovered over the screen.

'Where do you think he got the plan from?' Liam asked.

'He's done it himself, right? He says he knew the guy, after all, back in the day.'

'Wouldn't surprise me if it was bullshit, all of it.'

'Could be, but everybody knows Vidar's sitting on this fortune. He hasn't made that up.'

It was true. Everyone knew Vidar Björnlund's history, though no one really knew him. Liam tried to remember when he had last seen the old man. In his memory he was only a blurred face behind a windscreen, an almost mythical figure everybody talked about but who rarely showed himself in the village. He was something of a hermit, bordering on crazy, and there was a rumour he would threaten people with his shotgun if they so much as stepped onto his land. But it hadn't always been that way. In his youth he was hungry for life, had done a lot of smart deals and made a hefty profit. But everything changed after his wife died. That was when he sold the forest, gave up his business dealings and retreated. The official explanation was that she hanged herself from a tree in their garden, but there were many who said it was Vidar himself who'd strung her up. That he'd lost control.

Gabriel handed over the joint.

'Want some?'

'No.'

'Why not?'

'Because I promised Vanja.'

Gabriel gave a laugh, as if his brother had said something amusing.

'Vanja doesn't know any different.'

'Yes, she does.'

'Who are you trying to fool? You've talked for five years about giving it up, but you've done fuck all about it. Just because you've got a kid you think you're better than me, but you're as clueless as you always were. You'll *never* stop, and the sooner you get that into your thick head the better.'

Gabriel waved the joint in the air. Liam couldn't be bothered arguing. He wound down the window and leaned out. The sweet aroma of marijuana blended with the sour smell of meltwater. They passed a couple of farms with horses standing in muddy paddocks, flicking their tails. Liam looked longingly at the red wooden homes with their white window frames and veranda rails that lit up the greyness, and small fruit trees with knobbly branches where solitary swings moved in the wind. He could picture Vanja there, on one of those swings, smiling her gappy smile up at the sky. *Faaaster, Daddy!* she would shout. *Faster, Daddeeee!*

'There it is.' Gabriel elbowed him.

'Where?'

'Ödesmark five kilometres. Didn't you see the sign?'

Liam checked the mirror.

'I didn't see anything.'

'You're too busy bloody dreaming. I know you.'

They had to drive for almost two kilometres before they saw a side road where they could turn round. Two ravens were perched on the sign that pointed to Ödesmark, and turned their heads after them as they passed. Liam felt the unease in his gut. The road was in a bad state. Water-filled holes and muddy wheel tracks seem to suck down the tyres. On the left they saw a gloomy lake. The mist hung in thin streaks over the still surface. The first house they passed was abandoned and stood with its back to the water. A carpet of moss had grown on the roof and the chimney was a ruin of blackened bricks.

'Why would a millionaire live in a hellhole like this?'

'Because he's too mean to move anywhere else,' said Gabriel.

The road was lined with spruce trees and naked birches. Stubborn patches of snow jutted out from under the low skirts of the spruces and the forest steamed and glimmered in the dawn light. It was a season suited to their purpose, with the chance that any tracks they left behind would melt away or be snowed over. No one day was like the other when winter and spring were in combat with each other.

Yet another uninhabited house on their left appeared between the trees. White sheets hung from the windows and brown withered plants clung to the walls. The bumpy gravel track made their heads hurt.

'With his money he could live anywhere,' Liam said.

'Folk get stuck in their ways. When the money starts rolling in it can be too late. You can't leave.'

'Sometimes I swear you're smarter after a smoke.'

Gabriel grinned.

'Over there. See the barrier?'

Liam slowed down. The ground sloped up to their right and at the top sat a house painted a faded red. A yellow barrier blocked the driveway, keeping trespassers at a distance. A metal postbox was attached to a pole. Streaks of birds' droppings covered the name plate, but there was no doubt they had found the right place. This was where the treasure was hiding, if there was any.

'So what do we do now?' asked Liam.

'See if we can park down by the lake, then reach it on foot.'

They coasted past two large farmsteads before they found wheel tracks leading down to the water. The forest grew right to the shore and the trees hung over the lake, scraping the shiny surface with their branches. A few remaining ice floes formed islands further out in the water. Liam drove the car in as far as he could, to camouflage it under the branches.

'What if they see the car?'

'Who the hell's going to see it? No one lives here. The old guy's surrounded by a ghost town.'

Gabriel took the binoculars from the glove compartment and got out of the car. Liam walked behind him, warily. They moved in a wide arc and approached the house from the north side. They were wearing the wrong kind of clothes. The snow was damp and heavy and in no time their trainers were filled with icy water that numbed their feet. Liam wanted to protest but Gabriel was way ahead by now, as determined and focused as a hunting dog on the trail. A hundred metres or so away from the house he slunk in among the spruce trees and raised the binoculars. Liam crept up behind him and waited for his turn. Vidar Björnlund's house had seen better days. Pale streaks ran down the exterior where the seasons had peeled away the red paint, and on the driveway stood a Volvo from a forgotten decade. On the shady side a snowmobile was half-buried in a dirty snowdrift, still clinging to winter.

Liam peered at the dark windows but saw no sign of life.

'The guy could at least treat himself to a new car, if he's as rich as people say.'

'That's exactly why he's rich, because he doesn't buy himself anything.'

Gabriel handed over the binoculars. Liam aimed them at the yard, trying to take in the details. On one side of the house was a rotary clothesline where faded jeans and a pair of blue overalls flapped in the wind, a sign that someone actually lived there in spite of the sorry state of the house. He scanned the cracked facade and there, in one of the windows on the ground floor, he glimpsed a man's face. Despite the distance he could tell the man was old, from his fluffy white hair and stooped body.

'I can see him. Vidar.'

'Where?'

'In the window. Ground floor. There's someone else in the room too. The grandson, I think.'

'Shit, they're up early.'

It looked like they were eating. Liam could see their mouths moving and coffee cups glinting as they were picked up. The boy was bigger than his grandfather, more a man than a child. That worried him.

'You know he molested his own daughter, right?' hissed Gabriel. 'That's how the lad came into this world.'

'That's just talk.'

'Maybe. But there's something wrong with that lad, so I heard from reliable sources. Not the sharpest tool in the box, if you know what I mean.'

Liam watched the two as they ate. It looked so normal. Commonplace, even. There was nothing to indicate things weren't as they should be. They lived in a crappy house, but they weren't the only ones. All he had was a pathetic garage to offer his daughter and he knew the way others talked, the looks they gave him, hinting that he was a useless dad. That he wasn't up to the job. People liked jumping to their own conclusions but that didn't mean it had anything to do with the truth.

'Well, if he's stupid, it certainly doesn't show,' Liam said. 'But he's bigger than I thought. A head taller than the old guy and at least ten kilos heavier.'

'That's cool,' said Gabriel quickly. 'We'll surprise them when they're asleep. He won't stand a chance.'

Three against two, and one of them a teenager. It didn't feel great. And it became perfectly obvious as they stood there watching that it wasn't going to be as simple as Juha said. Liam passed the binoculars to Gabriel, slid his phone from his pocket and took a few pictures of the house, the junk and the forest that surrounded it all. There were more openings between the trees, paths that came from all directions and converged on the house. The escape routes were many, should they be needed. He took the photos so he wouldn't have to commit everything to memory. Water dripped and glistened from the knotty branches where the sun was stripping them of winter. He felt himself perspiring under his jacket, as if he had also started melting.

'Shall we check out the other side as well?'

'Not now. Better to come back at night. When they're all asleep.'

Gabriel turned back to the lake as Liam took a last look at the house. He couldn't see their faces without the binoculars but he knew they were sitting there, Vidar Björnlund and his grandchild.

Cradled in their false sense of security.

✳

They were sitting in the kitchen when she came down, their heads bent over the table as if in prayer. The tin of liniment stood among the breakfast food. They were speaking in soft intimate voices and for a moment she felt an outsider.

'About time too,' said Vidar. 'Most people have done a full day's work by the time you see fit to get up.'

He pulled out a chair for her but Liv didn't want to sit down. She preferred to drink her coffee standing by the sink. But the rank smell of the liniment got in the way and spoiled the taste. Vidar's claw-like hands rested on the table while the boy massaged life into them. It looked both tender and brutal, the blotchy old hand and the soft young one, the creases of pain in Vidar's face as he gritted his teeth. The coffee tasted of sickness, but she drank it anyway. Drank, and wished she was somewhere else.

Simon went over and stood beside her to wash his hands, but it was impossible to get rid of the smell of the liniment. It would accompany him all the way to school. Their eyes met over the dirty dishes and he winked at her, as if they shared a

56

secret, and suddenly the blood surged in her veins again. Her boy was in love and he had confided in her, not Vidar. The distance between them was narrower than she thought. And one day she would tell him everything, just as it was. If only she could find the right words.

'What's the matter?' he asked her. 'You look weird.'

'Nothing. I'm only looking at you.'

She saw she was embarrassing him, but she couldn't help herself. Her eyes needed to see him constantly. His damp hair, the dimples each side of his mouth. Even if he seldom laughed out loud these days, she could make out the small hollows. The light that surrounded him wherever he went gave life and colour to the bleak room.

'You're so annoying when you stare at me,' he said, and reached for his backpack.

But he didn't sound angry. When he headed towards the hall she felt the itching flare up on her back. She held her breath, listening as he pulled on his jacket and shoes.

'Bye!' he called, before the door slammed shut.

Bye, echoed their voices. They gazed after him as he disappeared under the barrier and out to the main road and the bus stop. Vidar's gurgling breathing filled the silence. The itching spread between her shoulder blades. The village lay bloated and dying out there and she could see the smoke from a neighbour's chimney coiling above the treetops, or was it mist? The forest glared back at her, grey and brooding.

One day she would explain to her boy why she had stayed. That it wasn't only Vidar's hold over her but the actual land, everything that had been buried over the years that she felt she had to protect. She surveyed the rowan with its naked branches splayed against the sky. On some days she could see her mother there, although she couldn't possibly have any memory of her. In her imagination Kristina was wearing the same white dress as in the wedding photographs, the filmy lace fluttering in the wind and her hair falling thick and glossy around the contorted neck. It was Vidar who had cut her down, so the report said, and when the ambulance arrived she was lying on the sofa. At first they didn't understand what had happened, they thought he had strangled her. And in his shock he had forgotten the child. It was a police officer who had found Liv upstairs, who had heard her wailing. It had taken many years to fit the puzzle pieces together. Not until she was an adult and given access to the records and reports did she understand how it had happened.

Her skin felt sore as they sat in the car. She had buttoned her work shirt up to the top so no one would see any traces of the scratching underneath. Vidar was leaning over the wheel. His glasses weren't strong enough. Even with them on his sight let him down. A milky veil had fallen between him and the world and it was off-putting looking him in the eye. He drove too fast and too close to the ditch. She shut her eyes, not wanting to see. The road was imprinted on her mind; she didn't need eyes to know they were getting close.

She found the job at the filling station the winter after Simon was born, a first tentative step towards something of her own. Vidar hadn't objected — she had to earn some money, after all — but he insisted on driving her there every day. For sixteen years he had taken her and collected her as if she had been a child at nursery school. Would you deprive me of my only pleasure? he used to say when she protested. Taking her to work was all he had. Besides, they only had one car and there was no question of buying a second one. He wouldn't tolerate that kind of extravagance, not even if she bought a car with her own money.

She never knew how much he got for the forest. Several million, or so the rumour went. She had seen the money in the safe when she was a little girl, thick bundles of notes held together with elastic bands. These days he never opened the safe in front of her. She never so much as caught a glimpse of the fortune. A few thousand kronor a month, that was all he allowed himself to live on. Enough to cover essentials, but never enough to really live. The fortune was like a distant relative, someone whose name she had heard but never met.

Many people had asked her why she wanted to work at the filling station, of all places. After all, you're rich, they used to say, their eyes glittering. But Liv always dismissed it. I'm not the one who's rich, it's my dad.

Vidar swung off by the church and parked. That meant he had something to say. The yellow wooden exterior shone against the sky. As a little girl she had thought it the most beautiful building in the world, like a castle in a fairy tale, but now it hurt her eyes. She put a hand on the door. The filling station was only a stone's throw away; if she opened the door and ran he would never catch her up.

'I start in ten minutes.'

Vidar stared out of the windscreen, studying the naked birches.

'I think we've got to get rid of our tenant.'

'What do you mean?'

'Johnny Westberg. There's something not right about that man.'

The fear struck her like a knife in the guts. Liv looked away at the filling station. A film of condensation spread across the window as she breathed.

'He hasn't been any trouble.'

'I should have known better than to let it to a stranger from down south. He's taking us for a ride.'

'What are you talking about?'

'A letter addressed to Johnny Westberg landed in our postbox recently. From the bailiffs.'

Small white drops of spittle landed on the dashboard and he scowled as if the very word disgusted him. The Debt Enforcement Agency the most despised authority of them all. Liv tried to work out if he was lying, making things up simply to cause trouble, but he took out the letter and waved it in front of her face. Held a filthy fingernail against the words. *Debt Enforcement Agency, Stockholm*, they said, loud and clear. Liv shrugged and tried to look unconcerned. She pictured Johnny, his face in the glow of a cigarette, his rough hands against her skin. She half-opened the door and leaned out into the cold.

'That doesn't have to mean anything. So long as he pays the rent we've nothing to complain about.'

The sky was low, and tiny pointed flakes whirled in the air

before landing on the ground and vanishing. Vidar leaned closer, close enough for her to smell his stinking mouth.

'I'm going to keep an eye on him. One foot wrong and he's out. People in debt can't be trusted. And I've got you and the boy to consider.'

'I think you're exaggerating.'

He seized her wrist and held her back with surprising force.

'It wouldn't be him you run to at night, would it?'

'Let me go.'

'Because if it is, I'm evicting him right now, do you hear? He'll be gone before you get home.'

Snowflakes eddied outside and through the white haze the filling station looked like a safe haven. Liv braced herself and pulled away, rushing blindly through the spring snowfall. She could hear him wailing after her but she didn't turn round once.

AUTUMN 1998

Her father's gaze makes the back of her neck tingle as she walks down the road. Two rifle shots ring out over the village. The hunt has begun in the valley. The thought that a stray bullet might hit her is terrifying, but when the bus arrives she's still standing upright. And just like every morning, only the driver says hello. He doesn't notice she wears the wrong clothes, does the wrong things. She hides at the back in the sleepy silence and watches the pine trees flicker past outside. When they pull into the village the bus is full, but no one is sitting beside her. They would rather stand in the aisle.

She comes to a halt outside the school entrance and begs a quick smoke from two boys loitering in the shadows. They are wearing black clothes and eye make-up. One of them is so short he barely reaches her shoulder, but he tries to compensate for his lack of height by spraying his hair to make it stand on end. The other one wears a long overcoat and always carries a battered paperback with a boring title. At break, when he isn't smoking, he usually sits with the open book to his face like a butterfly, hiding his loneliness. They don't care that she always wears the same jeans and the knitted jumpers that belonged to her mother. They just assume she's like them. That she's trying to make it clear she doesn't belong.

Inside the school building she walks with her eyes on the shiny floor while the voices and laughter split the air around her. She hasn't got a book butterfly to hide behind. The fluorescent lighting hurts her eyes and she walks on her toes so the heavy boots don't attract attention. They are at least two sizes too big to ensure they last for a couple of years while she grows into them. The heavy soles make it impossible to walk quietly. Her solitariness echoes through the corridors.

At lunch break they meet in the toilets. He never says anything, he only presses her up against the graffitied wall and squeezes her breasts and runs his tongue over her lips and cheeks and in her ear. His moustache tickles like an animal as he moves. He never kisses her properly. Everything has to go quickly, so quickly. A finger inside her that he wants to sniff while she puts her hand in his trousers. He supports himself against the wall and his hips thrust hard and fast until it's over. Then she hands him toilet paper and waits while he breathes onto his glasses and puts them back on. He doesn't want to look at her, he simply nods towards the door and whispers: *You go first.*

Afterwards, as he stands in the classroom booming out in German, he never looks in her direction. Not even when she puts up her hand.

Vanja watched television while he packed his things. The balaclava, the Glock and a roll of silver duct tape. The worn leather gloves were too tight on his fingers. Vanja's shrill laughter filled the room and made his heart ache. Liam knelt beside the backpack for a few moments and bent his head as if in prayer while his thoughts and his blood raced in tandem. He ought to call Gabriel and tell him it was off, it was too big a risk.

'What are you doing, Daddy?'

'Nothing. Just resting.'

'Why have you got your gloves on?'

'Because we're going now.'

He hoped she would protest, but Vanja merely switched off the TV and reached for her outdoor clothes. Her hair was so long it swept the floor as she bent down to tie her shoes. She didn't need his help any longer, not with her shoes or her zip. Before he knew it she wouldn't need him at all.

Liam hung the backpack over one arm and took her hand as they walked over the gravel. The dogs panted and whined behind the bars, their eyes shining yellow in the moonlight and staring longingly after them as they made their way towards the big house. The dog thing had started after their dad died. First one new puppy, then another. Older dogs in the free ads, needing a new home, and rescue projects from

Greece and Denmark. Fighting dogs that should in theory be put down padded around wearing muzzles, whimpering for attention. The old man would have killed them, every last one, if he had still been alive, but Liam was pretty sure the situation was his dad's fault anyway. It was a kind of gap that had to be filled – in a world full of unreliable people the dogs had become her security. If it hadn't been for his mum, he would have lost custody of Vanja long ago. She was always there, as steady as one of the old pines he used to rest his head against when he had done something stupid or disappointed her. She had always been there to save them both.

She was sitting in the kitchen when he stepped in. The tabletop glittered with stones and crystals in all the colours of the rainbow. Vanja quickly dropped his hand. She loved those stupid stones. The healing stones, as Grandma called them. Liam stood in the doorway and watched as Vanja climbed onto one of the old chairs, still wearing her hat and jacket, and started sorting among the brightly coloured nonsense.

'I was just hoping you would look in. I need someone to help me distribute the energies.'

She was wearing a long blood-red kaftan and stuck in her frizzy hair was a feather from a bird of prey she had found somewhere. Her right eyelid drooped as she looked at him, a memento from her life with his dad.

'Aren't you coming in?' she asked.

'There's this thing I've got to do. Can you look after Vanja?'

'Where are you going?'

'Just helping Gabriel, that's all.'

A flash of her eyes closely followed by that sideways smile meant she didn't believe a word of it. She got up from the table and approached him, her narrow bracelets rattling as she moved. A smell of thyme and wet dog followed her across the room. Liam backed into the hall, hugging the straps of the backpack. She came up close and studied his face, as if she expected to find something among the pimples and acne scars. He stood perfectly still and let her continue. The Glock, the balaclava and the tape turned to lead as she scrutinized him.

'It isn't worth it,' she whispered. 'Whatever you're thinking of doing, it isn't worth it.'

'Give it a rest.'

She raised her hands to his face, cupping them gently over his ears, as if she was trying to block out all other sound. Her eyes, as grey and alive as the meltwater outside, looked right into him.

'You're not as weak as you think,' she said. 'You don't always have to run with the pack. You can choose your own direction.'

He gripped her wrists and shoved her away, using more force than he actually intended. She fell against the wall, stopping herself with one hand, and a shift in her expression revealed the fear that had overtaken her. She was staring, wide-eyed. Liam saw it and felt ashamed. He turned his back and walked out into the night. Something was dangerously close to welling up inside him, something he knew he would be unable to control.

'Look after Vanja,' he said. 'And don't fill her head with all that magic crap.'

*

Liv pressed her ear to Simon's door and held her breath to hear better. The faint blue light ran over her toes but she couldn't hear a sound. Nothing to indicate whether he was sleeping or awake.

Sometimes he caught her out, standing there listening for him. Occasionally the door flew open so suddenly they crashed into each other. He looked so like Vidar when he was angry. Ugly and contorted. But still she couldn't stop, she had to convince herself that he was at home, that he was safe. And that he wasn't lying there on the other side of the door listening as she walked quietly away.

It was gone midnight when she stole down the stairs and past Vidar's room. The dog's tail thumped on the floor as she passed, but otherwise no one noticed her disappear into the night. Vidar's snores resonated through the ground floor, but even so her hands shook as she put on her shoes and reached for her jacket.

Outside, the moon brushed the forest with silver and illuminated the wet path for her as she ran through the village. She felt a burst of freedom as the cold hit her cheeks, and she smiled into the night as if she had been yearning for the darkness.

Widow Johansson's house looked better in the dark when the shabbiness couldn't be seen. There was no light on inside but the dingy rooms were bathed in moonlight, giving the old furniture an eerie lustre. Liv removed her shoes and trousers in the hall and continued undressing as she made her way to the bedroom and the man, leaving a trail of clothes behind her.

He was lying on his back in the dead woman's bed, breathing through his mouth. She stood for a moment at the end of the bed and looked at him. At the unshaven cheeks and the scar like a white smile across his throat. She felt the thudding start between her legs as she saw him there, defenceless and unaware. An unexpected wave of uncertainty went through her as she got closer. In reality she knew nothing about him, or about his life before this one. She talked herself into believing that it was best not to know, best not to get too close.

She pulled aside the duvet and straddled him. His body woke to life before he did, as if it had been lying there waiting for her. His eyelids fluttered when she guided him inside her and soon his hands were clasping her hips. They made love silently and furiously, with only the worn bed groaning beneath them, and when he opened his mouth to say something she laid a hand over his lips and shut her eyes tight until she climaxed.

Afterwards they lay side by side on the bed while he smoked his cigarette. They had still not said anything to each other, but she could tell from his breathing that there was something he wanted to say. Several times he tried but stopped, and she kept her eyes on the moose head hanging on the wall to avoid looking at him.

'I saw your boy today,' he said eventually.

She hadn't been expecting that. Her heart began pounding so hard in her chest she could see the duvet moving.

'Yeah?'

'He's bigger than I expected. Looks almost fully grown.'

'He's seventeen.'

'He looks older.'

Johnny stubbed out the cigarette and laid a hand on hers.

'Who's his father?'

'I don't know.'

He turned his head to look at her.

'You don't know?'

'He's not from round here. Simon has never met him.'

'Bloody hell, that's sad. Everyone needs a dad.'

'He's got Vidar, hasn't he?'

It felt like he was judging her, so she started to tell the story about the German. The German with the curly hair who had circled her on the ice the first time they met. The car was covered in dark cloth to hide the make, and he drove much too fast and too close. To impress her. He was a test driver for Audi and had a fiancée at home in Dresden, but of course he didn't tell her that before it was too late.

She was fishing through a hole in the ice when he circled her like a predator around its prey. The January sunlight was so bright she could only make out his smile behind the wheel, but she had understood by then what that smile would lead to. They had driven to the top of a hill, she had wriggled out of her snowsuit and he had thrown himself over her inside the secret car, and it had been so dark and cold she neither saw nor felt anything. When spring came and she discovered she was pregnant, he had already left for the season.

Johnny rested the ashtray on his chest as he listened. It rose and fell with his breathing.

'It can't be that difficult to trace him,' he said. 'You knew where he worked, after all.'

'But what do we want him for?'

'No, you're right.' He glanced at her. 'And I've heard that your old man is well off, so I guess you and the kid don't go without?'

She held her breath and avoided his gaze.

'Where have you heard that?'

'What?'

'That we're well off?'

He stubbed out his cigarette, an unreadable smile on his lips.

'Everybody talks about it. They say Vidar has money but doesn't know how to use it. But he'll make sure you're all right, I hope? His own daughter.'

Liv disappeared under the duvet, keeping her eyes tightly closed.

'People talk too much,' she said. 'I wouldn't listen if I were you.'

She waited until he had fallen asleep before she reached for her clothes. Then she left the widow's house and ran through the forest without looking where she was putting her feet. The dog met her in the hall and she held her breath as she stole through the rooms. Vidar's bedroom door was ajar. She hurried up the stairs into her own room, crept under the cold covers and kept watch on the door for a long time before she dared to close her eyes. The wind howled against the outside walls and as she lay there on full alert she thought she heard voices outside. She got up and walked to the window. The night was on the move; the moon slid in and out of the clouds and the forest trembled in the gale. It was hard to see anything clearly. She listened for sounds of people but all she heard was the howling of the wind. It sounded almost human, like a cry of warning.

✳

'So what work will you do when you become an everyday guy?' Gabriel asked.

'I don't know. Anything.'

'It's not so easy to earn money legally.'

'I know.'

'You won't get rich that way.'

'You don't get rich doing this kind of crap either.'

'Not yet, maybe, but you will.'

Gabriel was holding a smoked reindeer heart, slicing off thin pieces and placing them on his tongue. It didn't matter what they were doing, his appetite never failed him. Liam parked by the lake and switched off the engine. In the moonlight they could see the steam rising off the water like frozen breath. They sat there for a while, wary about the darkness outside. Gabriel swallowed two tablets before pulling on his gloves.

'You ready?' he asked.

'Yeah.'

'You don't look too good.'

Gabriel held out the pack of tablets but Liam shook his head. He wasn't going to deaden his feelings in spite of the fear that was choking him and making it hard to breathe. It was a completely different experience, not being intoxicated. Nothing came in between and there was nothing to hide behind. All his senses were as sharp as knives, the world hard and shiny around him.

He put on his gloves and his fingers throbbed inside the leather. Everything seemed to be hammering and writhing under his skin. Gabriel put a hand on the back of his neck and pressed their foreheads together. His breath was sweet and Liam could feel the tension vibrating through him.

'This will change everything.'

Liam shoved him away and pulled the balaclava over his head. The fabric was warm and damp and irritated his scalp where the sweat was already surfacing. The feeling that he was suffocating grew stronger.

'What do we do if the old guy makes trouble?'

'We'll put him in his place.'

Gabriel winked before disappearing into the night. This wasn't the first time they had robbed someone. In their early teenage years they had taken the bus to Pite Havsbad at the weekends and pocketed money from drunks who were on their way home through the night. Gabriel had called it their summer job. It had been so easy. The following summer they had robbed the Finnberg's supermarket in Glommersträsk. It was after closing time and there were no customers in the shop, and not much cash either. Gabriel had been the one to stand by the till, wave the Glock about and do all the talking. Liam had kept watch by the stockroom door. The shop assistant hadn't even seen him, but he had recognized Gabriel.

A week later the police came to get Gabriel, who later grassed on Liam because he couldn't handle taking the blame alone. It ended with them both being put on the at-risk register.

Everything was dark and cold. The only sound was the water lapping on the pebbles. Gabriel went first, lighting the way with his phone. A layer of ice made their feet unsteady on the forest floor. If they needed to run they would be in trouble. The path climbed steeply at the end, the spruce branches grabbed at their clothes and their lungs burned. The forest was so black it was hard to see where they were putting their feet, and everything snapped and creaked. Gabriel stopped several times to cough and spit. All that smoking had drained him of his fitness.

'Shit, listen to you!'

'Shut it!'

The house appeared on the hill, a single window on the top floor glowing in the night. They stopped at the boundary so as not to trigger any security lights. Liam raised the binoculars and scanned the house and the lit window. A lamp was on inside but he couldn't see anyone.

'What can you see?'

'Nothing.'

They stood perfectly still in the shadows and listened. White clouds from their mouths filled the raw air, and apart from their own breathing there was no other sound. No birds, no dogs, not even the wind in the trees. Only a deadening, dormant silence.

All of a sudden she was standing there like a wraith in the lighted window. A thin woman in a white nightdress, staring hollow-eyed into the night. She seemed to be searching for something. Liam lowered the binoculars and put a finger to his lips. Gabriel had also seen her. He took the binoculars from Liam and put them to his face.

'It's her,' he whispered. 'The daughter.'

They recognized her from the filling station. She was the shy girl behind the till who would never look you in the face. She had a soft voice that always rang a little false, that betrayed the fact that she would rather be somewhere else. She wasn't like the other assistants, who watched them like hawks as they moved between the shelves, convinced they would steal something.

Liam slid his phone from his pocket and took a couple of pictures, being careful not to use the flash. On the screen she became a strange, light figure, more a phantom than a person.

She was gone as suddenly as she had appeared. The light in the window went out and only the approaching dawn was reflected in the dark glass. Gabriel lowered the binoculars.

'Do you think she saw us?'

'I don't know.'

'Come on, let's get out of here. This isn't our night.'

∗

When Liv walked into the kitchen at dawn Vidar was staring out of the window with the binoculars. On the table, beside the empty coffee cup and the daily paper, lay the hunting rifle, ready for use. The black muzzle pointed directly at her. She stopped abruptly in the doorway.

'What are you doing?'

He didn't seem to hear her at first, his old body motionless on the chair, but reluctantly he lowered the binoculars and turned to face her. His eyes glistened.

'I want to see what the hell is prowling around on our land.'

'What do you want the gun for?'

He laid a protective hand over the weapon as she came into the room.

'I think it's wolves,' he said.

'Wolves?'

'I saw them in the night, at least two of them. Maybe more.'

She walked to the worktop and measured fresh coffee into the machine, pouring out the rest of the cold as she waited. Vidar went back to peering through the binoculars. His fingers were like rigid twigs round the black plastic. They wouldn't bend properly. There was a faint smell of gun oil in the room.

She went into the hall to let the dog out. On the steps Simon was sitting shivering in his pyjama bottoms. Liv grabbed his jacket from the hook and put it tenderly around his shoulders.

'What are you doing? Why are you sitting out here?'

He lifted a hand red with cold and pointed into the distance. Liv followed his direction and thought she could make out movement in the shadows, two nervous forms among the fir trees. The wind carried on it the chime of a single bell.

'It's reindeer,' he said. 'But I scared them off.'

'Why?'

'So Grandad wouldn't shoot them, of course.'

'He's sitting in there talking about wolves.'

Simon threw a dark glance over his shoulder.

'You know what he's like. He only sees what he wants to see.'

They chopped the logs by hand, Liv and the boy, while the old man sat in the window and watched them. It was the kind of day when the snow fell and the sun shone alternately. Dressed in only base layers they took it in turns to swing the axe, and it surprised her that Simon didn't complain once.

When they paused for coffee they sat on the pile of logs with their faces towards the sun, and although her shoulders ached from exhaustion she was glad for this time they were having together, just the two of them. He wore a bracelet she hadn't seen before, painstakingly plaited in red and yellow threads. She stroked the handiwork. You could tell from the brightness of the colours that it was new.

'Did your girlfriend give you that?'

He nodded and hid it with the cuff of his damp top, a blush spreading under his soft stubble.

'Does she like cartoons?'

'Anime, it's called.'

'Of course, Anime. That's what I meant.'

'She prefers reading books.'

'Can't you invite her here?'

'To you and Grandad? I don't think so.'

He gave a laugh as if it were a bad joke, something unthinkable. Liv ran her hand over his hair and rested it on his sweaty neck. She thought of the Houses for Sale ads, the red pen, all the possibilities she had circled through the years, the life they could have had together. Just the two of them.

Simon spat into the sawdust.

'I lied to her,' he said.

'What about?'

'I told her I usually go to Germany over the holiday. To see my dad.'

There was a numbness in her chest as she looked at him, the sudden insight that he had made her lies his own. She nodded and gulped, trying to get rid of the stinging in her throat. Melting snow fell from the trees. It sounded as if someone was walking in circles around them, waiting to attack.

'Well, that could be true,' she said at last.

They had almost finished when there was a sound of whistling from the forest. They dropped what they were holding and exchanged questioning glances, standing still and listening. Nobody in the village would willingly walk on their land, quite the reverse. Neighbours would take long and circuitous routes to avoid coming face to face with Vidar. But now a clear, light-hearted tune carried over their property and the shadowy figure of a man was visible between the trees. When Liv saw who it was she sank down on the woodpile, afraid to go and meet him.

Johnny was wearing thin running shoes that squelched on the sodden ground, and a smile that revealed far too much when he saw her.

'Christ, don't tell me you're chopping logs by hand?'

Liv took a quick look at Simon. His eyes had narrowed in suspicion. He raised the axe above his head and brought it down on the chopping block with such force that the handle went on quivering for many seconds. He wiped the sweat from his forehead with his damp sleeve. Liv did the same.

'It's good exercise,' she said.

'You're damn right it is. You look like two drowned cats.'

His Stockholm dialect reverberated over the yard and she felt every muscle tense as he approached. Perhaps he noticed, since he stopped a short distance away and held out a white envelope, not touching her or in any way indicating that they shared a bed most nights.

'Next month's rent.'

She took the envelope and threw a look over her shoulder. Inside, in the kitchen, Vidar was on his feet with his forehead pressed against the glass, watching them like a starving dog in a pen. Johnny saw it too and raised his hand in greeting. Heavy, wet snowflakes appeared out of nowhere and she thought he looked different in the daylight, bitter and more determined than he seemed inside Widow Johansson's gloomy walls. He kept his eyes on the house and Vidar.

She held out her half-empty cup, for something to offer him. He stood close beside her, sipping the coffee, and Simon sat down on the log pile, hunching his shoulders. From time to time she glanced at Johnny and she could tell the stranger touched something in her son. They chatted about logs, whether the bark should face up or down, and the weather, the snow that seemed as if it would never relent. Johnny smiled at Simon and asked if he liked ice hockey, saying he could fix a couple of tickets to the final if he was interested. Simon became as shy and monosyllabic as when he was a little boy, mumbling under his fringe that Luleå was his team but he had never been to a match. It was too expensive and too far away. Liv felt ashamed to hear that because it was something Vidar would have said, and she heard herself laugh as if he had said something funny. Of course you must see the final, she said, now you've got the chance. Simon only shrugged but she could see him smile with his head down, happy to have the opportunity. She wrenched the axe from the chopping block, in spite of her exhausted, trembling shoulders, and said they had to finish the logs otherwise it would never get done. She could see Vidar's restless form behind the glass, and although his voice did not reach out to them she could hear the obscenities coming from between his gritted teeth.

Johnny thanked her for the coffee and said he had to go home and feed the dogs, but before he left he reached out his hand and stroked the snow from her hair. She stood frozen to the spot and let him continue, knowing very well what the consequences would be. They stood and watched in silence until he had disappeared among the trees. Simon's nose was running and as fast as he wiped it away, more appeared.

'He loves you,' he said.

'Do you think so?'

'You can tell it a mile off.'

When they stepped into the warm kitchen, worn out and stiff, Vidar was sitting with his pipe in his mouth, waiting for them. He had laid the table with boiled potatoes and herring, and when Liv handed him the envelope with the money he insisted on counting the notes not once but twice, before cramming the bundle into his breast pocket. The clumsy movements confirmed that he had been drinking. There was an evil gleam in his eye when he looked at her.

'I certainly hope you set the bar higher than this mother of yours,' he said to Simon. 'Before you get too cosy with people.'

Simon's cheeks were full of food and he kept silent, stabbing the fish with his fork and eating as if he hadn't seen food for days. That was the way he usually reacted when Vidar decided to be spiteful. He drew himself into his shell where nothing seemed to touch him. But Vidar wouldn't give up.

'Let me tell you, when she was your age she went off with a different man every other day. If I hadn't kept her in some kind of order you'd have a whole pack of brothers and sisters by now. More mouths than we could feed, believe me.'

Liv gripped her knife and fork and felt the itching spread over her back. She slid a hand under her top and began to scratch the burning skin.

'That's enough now,' she said, glaring at him. 'We're tired.'

'I'm only saying how it was. No point in hiding the truth, is there? If it wasn't for me the poor lad would have a new dad every week.'

Simon reached for the milk, filled his glass to the top and then drained it. This was nothing new, he had heard it a thousand times. Vidar's comments about her bad choices and her incompetence. His nagging about how grateful they should be for the roof over their heads and a permanent place to live.

Simon wiped the milk from his face with the back of his hand and looked steadily at Vidar.

'A new dad every week would be better than none at all.'

'Oh, you think so, do you?' said Vidar, raising his eyebrows, surprised that the boy had spoken out. 'I'm not so sure about that. Because when you were born she couldn't have cared less about you, and that's the truth. I was the one who fed you and wiped your backside. She was too busy offering herself like a cat on heat to the first available man. She didn't have time for a kid.'

'Shut your face!'

Liv brought her knife up to his throat, holding it to his quivering skin. The dusk was reflected in its blade and threw angry flashes of sun onto the walls. But Vidar merely mocked her, leaned back and nonchalantly blew smoke rings over their heads. Rage filled her, black and hot, challenging her to stick the knife in once and for all, but she saw the fear in the boy's face. He had stopped chewing although his mouth was still full of food. She let the knife fall and pushed back her chair.

'Perhaps you should tell the whole truth,' she said. 'While you're at it.'

Her skin never itched during working hours. She stood on her stage in the spotlight as twilight settled over the petrol pumps. The floor was a mess of brown sludge dragged in by the customers. When the after-work rush was over she got out the mop and tried to clean up the worst of it. Hassan, one of the local police officers, hopped lithely over her newly washed floor towards the coffee machine and began to fill a mug.

'Have you only got yesterday's cinnamon buns?'

'I've saved you a fresh one. It's behind the counter.'

He had the kind of smile that was like a punch in the guts, and if it hadn't been for the uniform she would almost have liked him. She propped the mop against the wall and went to get the bun for him.

'I thought you'd given up sugar.'

'That's what my girlfriend thinks too.' He winked at her. 'But when I'm on duty I eat what I want. Believe me, no one wants to be around a hungry police officer.'

He brought out a card to make the payment, but she waved it away. Police and lorry drivers got their coffee free, and she might as well include the bun in that.

'Is everything all right?' he asked. 'You look pretty tired today.'

'It's Dad. He drives me crazy at times.'

'Parents usually have that ability. You've never considered doing what everyone else does and leave home?'

'He wouldn't manage without me.'

Hassan lifted the lid and blew on his coffee.

'Of course he would. Give it a try, you'll see.'

Liv shook her head. He wouldn't understand.

'The only consolation is that nothing lasts for ever. One day he'll be gone,' she said.

'You mustn't say that.'

She shrugged and felt her face blush. It was always like this when she tried to have a conversation with people. Either she said the wrong thing or she said too much.

They parked by the lake at the deepest hour of the night, that silent, blind moment before everything wakes up. Misgivings swirled in Liam's head and a heavy feeling filled his chest as he looked across the dark water.

'We won't have enough time. It's nearly light.'

'We don't need much time. This'll go fast. In and out, that's it.'

It was Gabriel's fault they were late. Liam had waited for him for several hours before he finally turned up, off his head on benzos and whatever else he took to numb his feelings. His eyes were empty as he pulled the balaclava over his head and nodded at Liam to get going. Liam stayed where he was for a brief moment, looked at the darkness outside and heard his mum's voice echo in his head. *You don't have to be like Gabriel. You can go your own way.* It wasn't too late. He could still turn round, go home to Vanja and forget the entire thing. Find a normal job and try to get a loan for a house, like everyone else.

But when Gabriel banged on the car window with the Glock he climbed out and followed him. Just as he had always done.

The stretch up to the house felt shorter now they knew the forest. The trees gave off a cold, dank air but he sweated in spite of it and couldn't seem to catch his breath. Gabriel walked resolutely ahead of him. Nothing could stop him now. The way he moved showed he was capable of anything.

The house lay in hushed darkness when they reached the top of the slope. They crouched in the shadows by the woodshed. Liam felt sick, shivering and sweating in turns. When he was younger he had liked the fear. The adrenalin that pulsed around his body made him feel alive. He had liked the colours and the clear contours. But the fear was different now, it made him weak.

Gabriel put his lips to Liam's ear and his breath sent shivers down Liam's spine.

'I'll go in first. You wait ten seconds and then come after me.'

Liam nodded. He felt the need for a shit as they began to move towards the house again. His body threatened to let go of everything. He pictured Vidar, saw Gabriel drag him from his sleep and put the weapon between his shoulder blades. He breathed deeply to blot out the image.

Gabriel hadn't gone far before he hurled himself to the ground. Liam did the same, lying flat with his cheek against the chilly earth. The ground shimmered with frost in the bleak moonlight and their thin layer of clothing quickly soaked up the cold. Liam hadn't heard the door open but illuminated in one of the yard's lamps was a figure, walking towards them. It was moving fast, despite the darkness, and the frost crackled under its shoes. It was Vidar and it looked as if he was coming directly towards them.

Liam shut his eyes tight and braced himself. Beside him Gabriel had stopped breathing. Neither of them made any attempt to move. The only sound was the old man's shoes on the grass.

The plan had been to tie them hand and foot, the daughter and the grandchild, and put tape over their mouths. The old man would lead them to the money. Juha said the safe was in a wardrobe in his room, and only Vidar knew the code.

Liam watched as Vidar changed direction practically in front of him and was swallowed up by the forest. He stayed with his face against the freezing ground until Gabriel got to his feet and nodded silently towards the undergrowth where Vidar had disappeared. Liam was so cold he could hardly form the words.

'What do we do now?'

'We go after him.'

SUMMER 1999

They come from Norway and they don't know who she is. The flames leap up to the sky and she is sitting with them, warm in their company. A bottle is passed round and everyone puts it to their lips and swallows. They come from Bodø, four boys and two girls. They have cycled across the border and will continue all the way to the coast, cycling all summer. No parents, no pressure. The girl sits between the two other girls, enveloped in their suntanned shoulders and the happy language that sings in her ears. One of the boys has hair over his eyes and a guitar in his arms. They lock eyes in the firelight and he sees right through her as he plays.

At midnight the lake calls to them. The night sun is hanging low and throwing a pathway of gold across its surface. The girl swims towards the light, the boy with the guitar comes after her, his dark hair disappearing under the water. They swim close together towards the gold. Close, but not touching. He talks about his favourite band that is playing at the Piteå music festival. That's where they are heading, that's the goal of their long cycle tour. He sings the chorus, his voice husky and subdued, but she recognizes the song. Who doesn't?

'Come with us,' he says. 'All you need is a bike. We've got plenty of room in the tents.'

She is grateful for the blinding sun so that he can't see her going mad with joy. Despite that, she shakes her head. It's no good. She splashes him with water to stop him asking her any more questions, and hides behind the laughter and tumult that follows. His invitation rings in her ears as they return to the fire again, all of them, hair dripping and bodies close together. The two girls also want her to come with them, and before long they are shouting in unison that she has to come, she has to come. And eventually she lifts up a hand and agrees. The bottle does another circuit as they cheer and give a toast to their new recruit.

Morning is drawing close and they steal off to their tents, one by one. Only one of the Norwegian girls remains by the embers and she plaits her hair, combing it gently with her fingers and making her skin tingle with pleasure. She sits perfectly still, thinking this is what it must be like to have a sister. Or a mother. She isn't tired, not in the least. Her head is too full of plans to think of sleeping. She will steal a bicycle from the village so she won't have to go home to her father. And she must convince them to choose side roads on their ride to the coast, roads where cars aren't allowed.

The bottle is empty and the fire burned down when the Volvo comes cruising through the campsite. She hears from the squeal of the brakes that it's him, long before she sees the car. Her hair is twisted in small whipping plaits down her back as he drags her from her new friend. It happens swiftly and quietly, a couple of paces, that's all, and there she is in the back seat again. The Norwegian girl, the only one who is still awake, sits with a hand to her mouth as they drive away.

Her father drives fast with the sun visor down, the mirror turned so he can keep an eye on her during the journey.

'I should lock you up, damn it,' he says. 'Lock you up and throw away the key.'

Liam crouched among the spruce trees. The sharp dawn sun rose over the treetops and made his skull throb. Vidar had stepped out into the clearing. The ground sank under him and his meagre body swaggered as he walked. His shoulders were hunched and his hands were tight fists held in front of his body, as if he was preparing himself for a fight. There was a self-confidence in his movements that spoke of past strength, before age had crept up on him and made him easy bait.

Liam scanned the forest that encompassed the marsh, searching for Gabriel. He was the one who'd insisted they split up and before Liam had time to protest he had vanished in among the shadows. And now he was gone. All that remained were Liam and Vidar, and the sun that probed ever deeper into the trees where Liam was hiding and would shortly reveal him. Following the old man into the forest had never been part of the plan and the impulsive act scared him. They always screwed up when they improvised.

Vidar swore loudly into the silence and Liam held his breath at the sound of the rasping voice. The spiky needles of the spruce were in his face and sweat was running down his neck. Everything prickled and itched. Vidar had come to a halt. The soaked ground was steaming around him and the hair on the top of his head stood on end in the wind and made him look even frailer. Suddenly he dropped to his knees in the moss and began digging with his hands, as if searching for something. He had his back to Liam and his neck was red from exertion. His fingers, black with earth, alternately dug and felt over the ground. Perhaps he had stashed something out here, something he wanted to keep well away from his daughter and grandchild. Liam raised his phone and took a few pictures. He wanted to capture the hiding place, if that was what it was. At last the old man stopped digging and got to his feet, wiped his dirty hands on his trousers and squinted at the rising sun. He swore and spat repeatedly, his body unsteady as if the digging had exhausted him. He put a hand to his forehead to block out the sun before he started walking. Liam sat where he was in his hideout, too tired to follow. He began tapping out a message to Gabriel about meeting up by the car, but had no time to send it before everything exploded.

The shot came from nowhere and hurled Liam out of his shelter. Suddenly there was only soil, pine needles and the taste of blood on his tongue. He landed face upwards and saw the light arc of the sky fill with silent black birds. His eardrums screamed as he managed to sit up, one hand on his chest as if to reassure himself that his heart was where it should be, that he was still alive. All he could feel were the hard contours of the Glock inside his jacket.

He kept absolutely still until his blood stopped racing, crouched in the thicket, out of sight. He saw a bundle on the wet ground, Vidar's body writhing and jerking in the loose earth, a hollow rattling sound rising up from its throat. Then everything went quiet.

Liam kneeled in the moss, the ground swayed under him and the forest disappeared from his sight. The only thing in his field of vision was the dying man. The body that slowly became still, the hungry earth that eagerly drew the body into itself, wanting to swallow it up. There was a trail of black dirt across the lifeless face. Liam was rooted to the spot in his hiding place like one of the forest's wild animals. He couldn't move, couldn't take his eyes off the dead body. Time stood still.

A shadow broke away from the bushes on the other side of the marsh and two skinny legs sped across the ground, spraying up meltwater. It was Gabriel. He rushed towards the old man with such speed that he stumbled and fell flat onto the cold ground, then staggered to his feet and carried on, his clothes drenched and clinging to his scrawny body. His face was as white as the patches of snow nestling under the trees. He stopped beside Vidar and bent over the lifeless body with one arm over his face, as if to protect himself. He emitted a sound that jolted Liam out of his paralysis. Feelings returned and he became aware of the coldness rising from the earth, working its way in between his clothing and his skin and making him shiver. His teeth were chattering as he stood up and headed for Gabriel. The marsh was full of brilliant pools and he had to jump from one icy tussock to the next. Under thin shards of ice lay bottomless bog holes that could suck the life out of someone in a matter of minutes. That must have been what happened. Vidar had slipped in the uneven terrain, hit his head and passed out. But Liam had heard the shot and he could taste the explosive on his tongue as he drew nearer, his eyes on Gabriel and the firearm half-hidden under his jacket. The sight made his stomach turn and his body fill with cold, black fear.

'What the fuck have you done?'

Gabriel didn't answer but stood leaning over the dead man, his gloves rummaging inside his clothing. Dark blood seeped from Vidar's nose and mouth and trickled down his chin. His eyelids were partly open and the whites showed in the gap. The back of his head was low in the ground and the water came up to his ears. His throat bobbed yellow and sagging below the surface and didn't seem to belong to the face.

Liam's legs gave way and he sank onto a rotten tree stump and coughed up something sour that landed in the moss and splashed over his boots. The world spun around him and he found it hard to fix his eyes on anything. He tried to focus on Gabriel, on the hands that pawed the old man's body, unconcerned about the blood. On the fingers that searched under the fabric, inside every pocket and secret compartment, and then took out Vidar's knives from his belt and studied them in the daylight. There was a serenity to his face that reminded Liam of their father, the controlled stillness that always took over once the madness had subsided. When Liam could put his ear to the bathroom door and listen for his mother's sobs to make sure she was still alive, while his dad sat in the armchair and finished off the beer.

Liam staggered over to the place where Vidar had until recently been digging in the earth. He bent over the uprooted tussocks but saw nothing apart from the traces of the man's fingers and the water leaking from the ground. He supported himself against a grey tree trunk when his legs would not obey him, and tried to avoid looking at the dead man.

Gabriel stepped briskly over the body and splashed towards Liam. He stood over him and inhaled deeply, thrusting out his chest. Liam waited for the blow. But Gabriel didn't hit him. Instead he grasped him by the neck and propelled him along in front of him.

'Move, for fuck's sake! We've got to get out of here!'

The birds screeched above their heads as they started to run. A grainy morning light filled the forest and Liam felt exposed and hunted. It astonished him that his legs held him up, that he had the strength in spite of the fear that thudded in his body. The taste of bile filled his mouth, but he didn't slow down. He noticed that Gabriel was lagging behind and couldn't keep up. Liam ran faster. His only thought was to get away as fast as possible, away from the dead old man. Away from Gabriel.

∗

He came to her at dawn. A warm honey-coloured light fell over the walls of the girl's bedroom and the pines outside her window cast restless shadows into the room. The howl of the wind, like the distant cry of a child through the old planks, made her sink deeper under the duvet. She could feel his shadow behind the door, the agitated feet that wanted to come in, that pursued her. She shut her eyes tight and behind the lids she saw them both. He was young and her mother's dark hair flowed around his head; they smiled over each other's shoulder as they danced, his arm like a thick belt around her waist. They swirled round and round until her mother dissolved and vanished like a flower in the wind, and instead there was the child in his arms, pressed hard to the sunken chest. He rocked her as he paced over the creaking floorboards, his face as red and crinkled as the baby's. She saw the child slowly grow in his arms, take the shape of an adult woman. She swivelled her face to the rising sun and opened her eyes. She didn't want to see any more.

The house was holding its breath when she woke. It was that delicate time between night and morning, when dreams and reality wore the same shimmer and it was hard to tell them apart. She headed for the closed door, treading quietly on the cool boards. Slowly she lowered her hand to the door handle, at once afraid to pierce the silence. The hall was in darkness. She glanced towards Simon's room. A pool of dawn light leaked out from under the closed door. Her bare feet moved soundlessly across the red mat that ran like an umbilical cord between the two rooms, and she put an ear to the doorway and listened for him as so many times before, resisting the impulse to open the door a crack the way she had done when he was younger.

Vidar hadn't woken yet either, even though the kitchen was filled with a milky dawn light and the birds in the birches had come to life. She drank a glass of water and looked at the frost that was slowly evaporating in the daylight. The dreams had left her with a heavy head and she was about to return to bed when she heard a car down on the road. She stood on tiptoe and watched it skid in the gravel, black and shiny, an unfamiliar car that did not belong in the village. It drove dangerously close to the yellow barrier, and for a second or two she thought it would stop there, outside their driveway, but then it accelerated fast and roared away, leaving deep grooves in the mud. She went back to bed and let the birdsong lull her to sleep. And this time she could dream in peace.

✳

Liam couldn't feel the wheel under his fingers. He saw the road in front of him but had no idea where it was leading. Everywhere there was the smell of blood. Gabriel was sitting in the passenger seat, shouting at him, but even so his voice sounded distant and the words didn't go in. Without warning Gabriel leaned across Liam and grabbed the wheel, trying to control the driving. The car lurched over the gravel and came alarmingly close to sliding into the ditch.

'Pull over by the house.'

'What?'

'We're getting that money. That's why we're here, isn't it? Stay by the barrier.'

Liam pushed him off and accelerated. Up on the slope was Björnlund's house. It looked even more run-down in the watery morning light.

Gabriel pulled on his balaclava, snorting like a mating bull under the black material. He had the Glock in one hand as he tried to take over the wheel with the other. Liam hit his hands away, strong from adrenalin and fear. He was filled with a feeling of doom; it felt like he was lying in a hole while someone shovelled earth over him. Burying him together with the dead man.

He passed the yellow barrier and the decrepit house on the hill, cowered under the blows but kept his hands on the wheel. The money didn't mean anything, not any more. It had all been a mistake; someone was dead and it was their fault. The sweat ran into his eyes and he found it hard to tell the forest from the road. Still he drove on, determined to get them away. Insanity burned in Gabriel's eyes, two black fires in the holes of the mask, and all Liam knew was that he mustn't stop whatever happened. He mustn't give in, not now. Not even when Gabriel lifted the Glock and pointed it at him.

When she woke up again it was still quiet. The sun shone brightly behind the blinds and she let her head sink back against the pillow as she listened. But she heard nothing – no radio, no crashing of plates or pans, no swearing – merely a grave-like hush that made her get out of bed and peer into the hall. Simon's door was closed and when she listened in the direction of the kitchen all she heard was the humming of the fridge. Her head was pounding as she went down the stairs, and an odd feeling filled her chest when she noticed that Vidar hadn't made the coffee or brought in the newspaper. Only the dog came to meet her. It was delighted, as if it hadn't seen anyone for a very long time.

'Dad? Are you awake?'

Her voice sounded eerie in the silence. She pictured him lying in his room, grey and rigid, his eyes staring.

But his room was empty and stale. When she switched on

the light she saw he had pulled the cover over the crumpled bedclothes to make it look as if he had made his bed, as usual. Vidar always made sure to give the impression of neatness and order, even if there was chaos beneath the surface. It was the same with his hygiene. He hardly ever washed, maybe a few quick showers a year, otherwise it was the forest and the firewood that cleaned him in between, meaning he hardly ever stank of his own bodily odours.

It was a long time since she had been in Vidar's bedroom and the sight of the small room made her gag. The shabby old bed with its sunken mattress which was too wide and spilled over the sides – it was impossible to think that two people had once shared it. On the bedside table the yellowing wedding photograph stared back at her. Only Kristina was smiling.

Vidar's work trousers and a pair of stained socks hung over the end of the bed, but otherwise there was no trace of him.

'Dad?'

She took a couple of steps into the room, chasing a few large balls of dust over the floorboards before she reached the wardrobe. She opened the door and pushed the few item of clothing aside to get at the safe that was hidden behind them. It was bolted to the floor and the black eye of the code lock stared back at her. Vidar had never given her the combination. As far as his fortune was concerned, he didn't trust anyone.

She shut the door and called him once again. The only response was from the dog, which got up from its sleeping place in the kitchen and padded over to Vidar's room. It stopped in the doorway and looked at her submissively.

'Where's your master?'

There were a few half-hearted wags of the tail and ears to attention, but no answers. Liv felt her panic grow as she looked at the dog. Vidar seldom went anywhere without it.

His outdoor clothes were gone. She half-opened the door, stuck out her head and called his name so it echoed over the village. The dog slunk past her and trotted off to the edge of the forest to pee, and when it was finished Liv pointed to the forest and ordered it to look for its master. The dog was old and had never shown any particular tracking instincts. All it did was look up at her, mournfully.

When she returned to the kitchen Simon was standing there with his bare feet on the threshold.

'What's up? What are you yelling for?'

'Grandad's gone.'

'What do you mean, gone?'

'He hasn't made coffee, he isn't in his bed. It's like he's gone up in smoke.'

Simon looked around the kitchen, as if he expected Vidar to be hiding somewhere, as if he would find him if he searched more thoroughly. Outside, the dog barked and they stood squeezed together by the window, watching as it ran in wide circles over the dead grass.

'Raja's outside.'

'I just let her out.'

'Grandad wouldn't go anywhere without Raja.'

Liv made coffee and watched Douglas Modig's 4x4 glide past on the gravel road. She raised her hand but couldn't see if he returned her greeting. Simon was sitting at the table. He had showered and his hair dripped onto the tabletop. For once he didn't sit with his face glued to his phone but kept his eyes on the forest as he gulped down his coffee. They saw the dog come back from the undergrowth and flop down on the veranda. Still without its master.

Maybe the spring had tempted him out into the forest. Vidar had always had a weakness for the changing of the seasons – cracks in the ice, the return of the birds, the sun's height above the top of the tallest pine. Everything was observed, and he kept the same constant eye on the land as he did on her. The forest was as much his beloved child as she was. But even so something disturbed her as she looked at the bushes, like a cold hand in her chest, clenching and unclenching.

Simon chewed his nails. The sun flooded into the room and warmed his skin. He had a cut from shaving where the blood had coagulated.

'Where do you think he can be?'

'He must be in the village somewhere.'

'Do you want me to look for him?'

'You've got to go to school. He'll be here in his own good time.'

Simon frowned but didn't argue with her. She went with him into the hall and watched as he tied his laces.

'What will you do if he doesn't come back?'

The boy's concern warmed her heart. Despite all his talk about leaving as soon as he was eighteen, he still wanted to keep the family together.

'Then I'll go out and look. He can't have gone too far and the village isn't that big.'

He seemed content with that and gave her a quick hug before he left, just like he used to. Liv ignored the morning chill and went out onto the veranda to watch him go. Vidar's pipe lay on the railing and she lit it and blew flimsy smoke rings to the sky as if she was calling to him. The forest was bathed in spring sunshine, light and alive. She peered at the track that ran down to the lake. Here and there the snow had melted away, leaving the ground dark and steaming. It would be easy to find his footprints if he had set off through the trees. Child's play for her and the dog.

But she closed her eyes and sat motionless, enjoying the silence.

✳

Liam stood beside the fire, his teeth chattering. Shafts of sunlight fell between the pine trees and landed on his skin but he didn't feel any warmth. Gabriel poured more petrol on the rusty bin and flames shot up.

'Chuck your shoes in as well.'

'But they're the only ones I've got.'

'So what? You should have planned it better.'

'Planned? How the hell could I have planned for this chaos?'

'Do what I say and take off your shoes, before I burn you too!'

Gabriel put a hand round his neck and held him close to the fire, so close his skin scorched. Liam yelled and struggled free. Reluctantly he pulled off his shoes and socks and tossed them in the bin, making sure to stand well back. The smoke smelled toxic, like burned plastic, and he ran on tiptoe over the wet ground towards the car where there was a change of clothes.

He pulled on a top and a pair of jeans. The fabric was cold and rough against his skin. In the car he found a pair of boots and shoved his frozen feet inside them.

Gabriel was stark naked and shaking drops of petrol over the fire, making it splutter. His dick had shrunk against his thigh like a terrified animal. Liam would have laughed at that, if everything had been normal. But nothing was normal. They had messed up badly this time. Despite the cold his scalp was dripping; the drops of sweat came from nowhere and ran down his back. He bent over the moss and vomited uncontrollably, then stood for a long time, spitting. His legs trembled as he walked back to Gabriel and handed him a change of clothes. He kept an eye on the gravel road at the same time, paranoid that someone would drive by and catch sight of them.

The world had taken on a film of unreality; contours were cold and unstable. Liam found it hard to focus; his thoughts were spinning and gave him nothing to hang on to. He saw Vanja's face, heard her trembling voice calling for him in the dark, her forehead wet with perspiration when she had a nightmare. He saw Juha stab the knife into the table and could hear it vibrating. Felt that suffocating sense of being used.

They only meant to rob him, no one was supposed to die. The plan had been so simple: surprise them while they were sleeping and then disappear as quickly as they had arrived. Take the money and run, in and out, that's all, before anyone came to any harm. He wanted to scream it at Gabriel, roar with his whole body that he had wrecked everything. That their life was over now. But his vocal cords wouldn't obey. Nothing was working the way it should.

Gabriel was staring at the fire, apparently not noticing Liam's panic. He didn't seem to be cold either. He just stood there, naked and still, not looking at his brother. Liam hunched as he got nearer, cowering like a dog afraid of a beating. Gabriel flung out an arm, releasing a blast of warmth from the fire.

'Give me your gun.'

He had assumed their father's voice now, low and unyielding, the one that said his reality was the only one that mattered. They were his rules and if you wanted to survive you had better comply, play along. Liam took a fleeting look at the Glock lying on a rock beside him.

'What are you going to do?'

The blow came from the side. A slap on the head, that was all, but enough to make him lose his balance.

'Shut the fuck up and do as I say! Give me the gun.'

Gabriel was standing behind him, breathing over his shoulder like a god, or a devil. Liam reached for the gun, forcing himself to keep his hands steady, taking care to point the barrel at the ground. Gabriel held out his hand, beckoning impatiently with his fingers, but Liam didn't want to give in. He slid further away, keeping the weapon out of sight, a voice screaming inside him that he mustn't hand it over.

A few pulsating moments and then Gabriel was over him, pressing an elbow against his head until his ears rang, and the gun was wrenched out of his hand.

'Go and sit in the car. I'm sick of the sight of you.'

Through the smeared car window he watched as Gabriel wrapped both weapons in plastic and hurled them far out into the water. The river had freed itself of ice and was rushing swollen with snowmelt towards the sea. The weapons would travel far before being washed ashore, if that ever happened. He found no consolation in the thought.

Liam took two tablets from the bag on the seat and let them dissolve under his tongue. He couldn't handle it any longer; he needed something to deaden the tumult, relax his body. Outside, Gabriel started getting dressed at last, in black trousers, jacket and boots. His face was a white mask against the dark clothes as he walked towards the car, his eyes hard and blank. He slid into the passenger seat and pulled the door closed. The smell of bonfire spread through the interior and his madness lay like a fog around them, making it hard to breathe. Liam's muscles ached from the tension. It felt as if he was hanging over a sheer drop and the only way out was to let go.

Without warning Gabriel slammed his fist against the dashboard and cried out. He hit the plastic over and over again until the glove compartment came loose and the fixings broke. Only then did he stop and take hold of Liam, dragging him close, his eyes filled with a crazy gleam. Liam tried to twist out of his grip but Gabriel was stronger. He had always been stronger.

'I don't know what's wrong with you,' he hissed. 'Either Mum dropped you too many times or you were born that way. Whatever, I don't give a shit. But I'm not letting you fuck up our life. I'd rather kill you.'

'Go on then, do it. Kill me.'

Gabriel made a move as if to head-butt him, but stopped himself at the last moment. Liam shut his eyes tight, made an effort to relax, to let his body go slack. Gabriel always lost interest quickly if there was no resistance. Liam tried to hide the fear pumping through his body, putting severe pressure on his bladder.

'You got scared, right?' Gabriel said. 'You got scared and your finger slid onto the trigger. That's what happened.'

His mouth was too close to Liam's. It sucked the oxygen from him. Liam shook his head, feeling a new fear take over as he understood what Gabriel was trying to do. Just like he had always done since they were kids – when the crystal bowl fell on the floor, when their dad's snowmobile went through the ice, when Mum's weaving loom burned up and when the neighbour's radio-controlled car was found in their cellar – on every occasion he had stood there, pointing a finger to save his own skin. *Dad, come and look at what the spaz kid has done!*

'That's what happened,' Gabriel said again. 'It's my own fault, basically. I should have known better. You're not cut out for this life, the smallest thing and you freak out. And it's got worse since you had the kid.'

Liam pushed him away, hard, so that he fell against the car door. Gabriel said something he didn't hear; his head was buzzing. He looked at the river surging past. The fire had gone out but the bin was giving off a vile black smoke that clung to the trees. There was nothing left – the guns were gone, the clothes burned. All that remained were the images in his head, what he had seen on the marsh. But no one would believe him. If it was his word against his brother's they would both go down. He put a hand to his eyes, pictured Vanja, felt her arms around his neck as he gave her a piggyback. Her laughter ringing in his ears.

'I'm not doing time for this,' Gabriel said. 'And I'm not letting you do any either.'

He was calmer now. Liam heard him light a cigarette and draw deeply, heard the rattling cough that followed. They sat in silence for a while, leaving each other alone. The tablets had started to work and Liam felt the chemicals being carried along in his bloodstream, slowing everything down. Enough for him to be able to start the engine. He had to get home, home to Vanja. Everything would be all right if only he could hold her in his arms.

The sky and forest blurred into one as he drove, a bleak grey veil covering everything. Gabriel sat with his eyes shut and his fists clenched. When they reached Arvidsjaur it felt as if everyone was staring at them, as if their failure was written all over the paintwork. Liam drove slowly between the buildings and parked outside the block of flats where Gabriel lived with his girlfriend. Only then, when they had come to a complete standstill, could he unblock his throat.

'I'm done with this.'

Gabriel didn't seem to hear. The sun poured in, radiant and ruthless. Morning was long past. Liam shoved him, suddenly impatient.

'Did you hear what I said?'

He saw the tendons stand out in Gabriel's neck.

'You're not done until it's over.'

'I don't want you coming over any more. I don't want you anywhere near Vanja.'

Gabriel regarded him sleepily, a hint of a smile on his mouth, as if the situation suddenly amused him. Liam waited for him to attack, thump his head against the window, head-butt him. But nothing happened. There was only the air, vibrating between them.

'No problem. I'll leave you alone.'

'Good.'

Gabriel had his hand on the handle but didn't move.

'Can I trust you?' he said.

'What do you mean?'

'You're not thinking of doing anything stupid?'

His bad tooth was aching. Liam opened the door and spat. There was a taste of blood in his mouth.

'Don't you worry, I won't say anything.'

He wasn't sure if it was true, but it was enough. Gabriel gave him a long, final look before leaving, a mute warning. Liam sat and watched until he disappeared through the front door. The daylight was so blinding it hurt his eyes and made them water. All the way home the sun burned through the window, yet he was so cold he was shaking.

*

Vidar still hadn't returned by the time she had to leave for work. Liv sat in her uniform shirt with her eyes on the undergrowth, waiting for him to emerge from the trees. He had never missed an opportunity to give her a lift, not even when he was feeling rough, and it seemed unthinkable for her to get behind the wheel. But as the minutes ticked by she understood he wouldn't be coming. The realization should have alarmed her, but the only thing she felt as she clenched the car key in her palm was elation.

As she swung onto the main road she had Laleh's voice in the loudspeakers, and all the way to the filling station she sang along at the top of her voice. When she parked behind the stockroom Niila was there, throwing rubbish into a container. He looked startled when he saw her climb out of the driver's seat.

'I didn't know you could drive!'

'There's a lot you don't know.'

He grinned.

'So where's your dad?'

Liv shrugged. There was a foul smell from the container but she stayed to help him throw in the rubbish sacks. Once Vidar had seen her standing there laughing with Niila, and had snarled all the way home.

How many reindeer does he own?

How would I know?

If you're getting together with a Lapp you need to know how many reindeer he's got.

Niila held the stockroom door open and looked puzzled as she walked past him.

'Has something happened?' he asked.

'No. What do you mean?'

'You look so happy. Your eyes are really glowing.'

*

Liam walked into his mum's house and said he was ill and needed to lie down. Vanja had that look of fear in her eyes, the one that got him in the gut every time. He tried to smile. *Daddy's got a bit of a temperature, that's all.* She helped him lie down on the sofa, fetched a duvet and a pillow and soft toys to tuck under his arm. He was overcome with shame and the realization that he didn't deserve the good things in life, least of all her.

He drifted in and out of consciousness, small pockets of daylight, and the sound of animated films and Vanja singing. He tried to hide his shivering and sweating by pulling the duvet up to his chin, but he dared not relax, afraid of sleep and what it would do to him.

At twilight his mum was leaning over him; he could hear her rattling bracelets and anxious breathing. She laid something on his forehead, one of her stones. It weighed nothing and lay there like a cool kiss until he could no longer feel it. Liam wanted to shout at her, shake her off, but his body wouldn't obey and he could only lie there, incapable of resisting. On one occasion she lifted his head and held a teacup to his mouth. The smell of pine needles and mint filled his nostrils. He clamped his lips shut, unable to drink it.

'I thought you'd stopped,' she said.

'I have stopped.'

'And you really want me to believe you're ill?'

'I don't give a shit what you think.'

She ought to throw him out, like she had done with Gabriel. She should know better by now. No herbs or stones had any effect on her sons. Not love, either.

Vanja's breath was soft in his ear.

'Are you really, really poorly, Daddy?'

'It's just a temperature. Sleeping will make it better.'

But he couldn't sleep. Vidar's face was hiding behind his

closed eyelids. He felt the marshy ground sway beneath his feet, felt the frozen moss and the fear explode in his body.

When he opened his eyes Gabriel was sitting on the edge of the sofa, a younger Gabriel with his hair in a ponytail and one of their dad's roll-ups behind his ear. In his hand was a can of Lapin Kulta, stolen from a neighbour. The television flickered in the corner, the sound off so as not to wake anyone. The night was their time. When the arguing was over they sat in the moonlight letting themselves relax at last. Gabriel became silent when he'd been drinking, turned in on himself. Still, Liam could tell he was in turmoil, all the thoughts attacking from nowhere, the kind of thoughts that multiplied and spread and had to be shared. Before they ate him up.

Gabriel lit the cigarette and blew smoke up to the ceiling. He studied Liam from under his heavy lids. 'Have you ever wondered what it would be like to murder someone?'

Liam shook his head.

'Have you?'

'I think about it a lot.'

He spoke in a low voice, no more than a whisper, but still the words echoed between the walls and kept on echoing inside Liam's head. It was an admission, the kind of thing you couldn't laugh off or forget. Liam didn't know what to say so he closed his eyes the way his mother did when everything was too much, when she didn't want to be there any longer. Gabriel elbowed him.

'Some bastard that deserves it, I mean. I wouldn't kill just anyone.'

When he woke up Vanja was sitting on the floor beside him, watching television. Darkness had fallen outside and her body glowed strangely in the dim light. She must have felt him looking at her because she turned her head and smiled her gappy smile that made the ground give way under him. Suddenly it became clear what he had to do. He had to forget. For her sake.

Six hours behind the till and the excited butterflies in her chest were still fluttering. By the time she finished spring had been defeated and large fluffy snowflakes were tumbling to the ground. But the snow only had time to give the asphalt a wet kiss before it melted away. Even so, she drove slowly and by the time she turned off onto the village road she was feeling nauseous.

Simon was sitting on the veranda but he wasn't alone. Someone was sitting beside him, and it wasn't Vidar. It was a slimmer figure, dressed in a light blue denim jacket and with long hair dyed a vibrant blue. Not until Liv got out of the car did she recognize Felicia Modig, their neighbours' daughter. The surprise hit her like a punch in the stomach.

'Grandad isn't here,' Simon called. 'The house was empty when I got home. Only Raja was here, whining in the hall.'

As she drew closer she saw they were holding hands. Felicia's nails were painted black and she was dangling one jeans-covered leg over Simon's. Liv turned to look at the forest and felt her cheeks burn. It was the first time she had seen him like this with a girl and the sight embarrassed her. So this was the secret girlfriend whose name he hadn't chosen to reveal. She didn't know what she had expected, but it wasn't the neighbours' daughter from the other side of the lake. Simon tried to catch her eye. His dimples were deep in his cheeks as he smiled, his eyes full of joy. See, Mum? his eyes said. She's here. *She's my girl.* And Liv thought of that party when they were younger, of him sitting among the girls like a wide-eyed doll. So happy to be included at last.

She smiled at their intertwined fingers, smiled and nodded and thought that at last the pieces were falling into place for her own son, too.

'Felicia,' she said. 'So you're the one Simon is seeing.'

It sounded idiotic and she regretted the words the instant they were out. She saw Simon look embarrassed. But Felicia seemed amused.

'Surprise, surprise,' she said. 'That was a shock, right?'

'A bit, I have to admit. How are Douglas and Eva?'

Felicia pulled a face.

'Okay, I guess. Dad's stressed, as usual.'

'Is he?'

'He says those cows will be the death of him.'

Douglas Modig's farm was on the other side of the lake. He was a fourth-generation dairy farmer, but his wife did most of the work. Eva came from Wilhelmina and was the only person in the village to win Vidar's respect. She was taciturn and hard-working, two qualities he valued highly. Douglas, on the other hand, he couldn't tolerate, and the feeling was mutual. They hadn't exchanged a word since midsummer 1998 when an old grudge about a strip of land had led to a fist fight. Alcohol was a contributing factor, but there had never been a reconciliation. Every time the wind carried the smell of Modig's cows or the sound of their bells, Vidar became even more foul-mouthed. Felicia was their only child. She and Simon had grown up on opposite sides of the lake but they might as well have been at opposite ends of the country, because Liv couldn't remember them ever playing together when they were younger. The adults had put a stop to that.

Liv had seen her down by the lake a month or so earlier. The ice had broken up and was floating in jagged pieces on the swollen water. Felicia was quite far out, her body hardly more than an illusion as she jumped from one ice floe to another, with her arms outstretched and her hair like a shiny veil in the wind. The ice floes were unpredictable under her feet; she twisted and swayed to keep her balance, her fingers splayed in the air. Liv stood with the sun in her eyes and panic in her chest, but her shouts didn't carry. If the girl fell in there was nothing Liv could do, other than stand there and watch the lake take her. The freezing water would suck the life out of her before any rescue was possible, if she didn't drown first. Liv sank onto a stump and waited. It was all she could do.

When the girl finally grew bored and came closer to the shore with a few breathtaking jumps, Liv got to her feet again.

'You'll kill yourself.'

Felicia was red in the face and breathing hard. She stood with her legs wide apart on the bobbing shard of ice.

'So, who cares?'

Liv recognized the indifference, that same weariness with life she had felt before Simon was born. It was his arrival that had brought her face to face with her own mortality and made her cling tightly to life.

And now here he was, holding this nonchalant girl's hand in his, and the sight filled Liv with the same dread she had felt down by the lake. She walked past them and began to open the front door, but she only had to put her foot on the threshold to know the house was empty. She could feel it in the air. Vidar was missing. Despite that, she checked the kitchen, where yesterday's paper lay open on the table. The coffee she had made that morning was cold in the jug. There were only two cups in the sink. The tin of liniment was still on the windowsill. It was unusual for him to set off so early. Often it took a few hours before his fingers were flexible enough to tie his shoes.

She looked into Vidar's room, running her eyes over the untidy bed and the filthy work trousers hanging over the end. Everything looked the same as when she had left for work. Vidar had not been home all day. She felt the stirrings of anxiety at the reality of it.

She went back to the veranda and looked at the youngsters and the sunset spreading like fire over the treetops. Felicia's eyes were black with make-up and she had a glittering stone in one nostril. Liv's heart beat faster as their eyes met.

'Shall we call the police?' Simon asked.

Liv leaned on the loose veranda rail and gripped it so hard her fingers hurt. The shadows lengthened over the dead grass and soon the forest would be in darkness. She thought of Vidar and wondered if he was lying out there somewhere, calling for them. He was eighty years old with a body as tough as resin and a head that refused to accept old age. If he had taught her anything through the years it was that nothing could touch him, not people or time.

'If we call the police he'll never forgive us.'

CHRISTMAS 1999

On Christmas Eve morning there is a circle of licking flames around the rowan tree. The photograph of her mother is on the kitchen table between them, her dark eyes watching their hands as they pour coffee and spread butter on their bread. The grief etches deep furrows in her father's face. The silence is thick and paralysing, just their jaws are moving. The girl eats even though she is not hungry, eats because it's the only way to remain unnoticed.

Midwinter smothers the sun and only a fleeting twilight marks the difference between day and night. But still he insists they go out to the tree. To her mother. He lugs a reindeer skin outside and digs a hollow in the snow for a fire. They will sit there until the embers have all but died away and they can no longer see each other. He always tells the same stories, how they met at the dance in Malå and how her mother tripped him up to get his attention. He spilled beer on her dress, and that's all it took. One look at those dark velvet eyes and he was lost. They danced through the night and maybe that was enough for her, because after that she'd had her fill. She didn't want to see him again. He spent a whole summer chasing her until she agreed to go out driving with him. He had pursued her as doggedly as he had pursued the forests. In the foolishness of his youth she was merely one more piece of land to capture.

'It took three years. Then I hooked her.'

He makes her mother come alive, describes the way she pirouetted in the kitchen, how she tipped her head back when she laughed so every single tooth in her mouth was visible. All her feelings intense and unconfined. But darkness was always lying in wait on the threshold. She was sensitive to the fickleness of the seasons and other people's stares. Spring was the worst, when everything came into bloom and winter clothes were discarded and the pitiless light filled every corner and cranny. So it was unfortunate the girl was born in the spring, when the birds clamoured all night long and her mother was already so fragile. It was like watching her gradually bleed to death after giving birth. She had no physical injuries but even so he noticed the lifeblood run out of her. And it went fast.

'Your arrival was the final nail in her coffin.'

The girl wants to run away more than ever as she sits and stares blindly into the flames, but her father's hold on her is tighter than winter's grip. He drinks more and more, his lips shiny with alcohol. When the embers have burned out he can't get up. She considers leaving him there in the dark, in the freezing cold that penetrates the bones and takes a life before you know it.

She goes indoors and puts on the coffee, enjoying the warmth and silence. The morning is almost over but daylight is slow to arrive. The snow crust will show no sign of a sparkle until lunchtime. She puts a cube of sugar between her teeth and sucks the coffee from the saucer as she looks at the darkness embracing her father. It wouldn't be the first time someone had drunk too much and frozen to death. Nobody would raise an eyebrow. Quite the reverse. Poor kid, they would say, now she's lost her mother and her father. Now there's no one to look after her.

She only has time to enjoy the first cup of coffee before the fear takes over. There is something about being alone that she can't handle, the way it sits on her chest and sucks the air out of her.

She pulls the sledge to the rowan. Her father is lying wrapped in the reindeer skin with his boots in the blackened fire, crystals of snow in his beard and nostrils but otherwise no indication that the cold is about to take him. The ash whirls like rain around them as she forces him onto the sledge and takes him to the house. He only opens his eyes once, when he is lying in the bath. He makes a grab for her hair and looks at her with the gaze of a younger man. Her mother's name echoes around the tiled room. It is a mistake he makes only when he has been drinking. Believing her to be his wife.

They split up. Simon and Felicia took the southern part of the village, the road that led to Modig's farm, and Liv the north. Darkness fell fast and the track that circled the lake shone treacherously in the light from her torch. Snowmelt froze to a skin of ice over the tree roots and carpet of pine needles and she was careful not to slip over. Everything was brilliant and shimmering. She could hear the water slapping between the ice floes and see the eager black waves in the moonlight. The joy she had felt during the day was gone.

Vidar had left tracks on the path; she recognized the heavy footprints, the same ones that criss-crossed the yard back home. He liked taking walks, checking the movements of the villagers, and the changing of the seasons. He was in the forest almost daily, returning with a report of what he had seen. He didn't miss a thing. He knew this land better than the back of his own hand, far too well to allow it to swallow him up.

A house took shape among the trees. A weak light coming from the window made her switch off the torch and hang back among the trees. She could not recall ever knocking on anyone's door, not even as a child. There was no outright animosity, no unresolved dispute, not as far as she was concerned. But even so, Ödesmark had its own well-defined territories and she had learned early on not to trespass onto them. It was a truth Vidar repeated often, that the Björnlunds weren't much for company. We have solitude in our blood, he used to say, when midwinter spread its cloak over the land and the coldness and silence forced people indoors. But he never offered an explanation as to why that was so.

Liv walked slowly towards the house. A smell of birch logs hung in the air and the birds sang loudly, as if a great flock had settled in the pines and was warning her not to come any closer. She hesitated for a long time before finally tapping her knuckles on the door. The impulse to run came over her as soon as she heard footsteps behind the door, and by the time it opened she had pulled back into the shadows.

Serudia Gunnarsson became more birdlike every year. Her head jutted forward on her long neck and loose skin flapped under her chin.

'Who's there?'

'Only me, Liv Björnlund.'

'Vidar's girl? What are you doing back there in the dark? Come out so I can take a look at you.'

Liv took a hesitant step up to the porch and her voice trembled as she explained why she had come. Serudia peered up at her and seemed to read Liv's lips as she spoke, as if her hearing had begun to fail her.

'Vidar? I saw him this morning,' she said. 'It looked like he was on his way up to the marsh, and in a hurry, too.'

'Do you know what time that was?'

'It was early, I can tell you that much. The sun was still behind the trees.'

It was obvious from Serudia's cloudy eyes that she couldn't see much. She reached out an aged hand, feeling for Liv. The skinny fingers held on with unexpected strength.

'Come into the warm, you poor child. Don't stand there freezing.'

Soon she was sitting at the old woman's kitchen table, looking out over the lake. Lights from Modig's farm shone on the far side, and she thought she heard voices coming through the forest and penetrating the warmth of the room.

Serudia didn't stop at coffee. Cheese, cloudberry jam and three different kinds of biscuits quickly appeared.

'You shouldn't go to all this trouble.'

'Of course I must offer you something. It isn't every day I set eyes on Vidar's daughter.'

She seemed genuinely happy for the visit, insisted Liv ate and drank, and stared wide-eyed at her as if she couldn't quite believe Liv was sitting at her table.

'I can't stay long. I've got to find Dad.'

'Vidar was here yesterday,' the old woman said.

'What, has Dad been here, to see you?'

Liv looked around the sparsely furnished room as if she expected to see Vidar skulking in one of the dusty corners. The old woman blushed like a schoolgirl and touched the silver plait that had fallen over her shoulder.

'He was here having a look at my wood burner. It's been playing up all winter, but Vidar got it working in no time. He's clever at mending things, your father. Always has been.'

'He never told me he'd been here to help you.'

'Bless me, if it wasn't for Vidar my house would have fallen down years ago. And he didn't want anything for it, either, though a woman likes to pay her way.'

The cheese stuck in Liv's throat as she tried to take in this piece of unprecedented information. The old woman's eyes looked even cloudier in the light from the kitchen lamp and Liv wondered if she saw only what she wanted to see. She couldn't believe Vidar had been there and helped Serudia about the house without asking for payment for his trouble. It sounded like something she'd made up, or from a lost age.

'Are you absolutely sure you saw him this morning?'

Serudia directed her gaze to the window. They could see the movement of the trees in the moonlight, the delicate evening light reflected in the lake.

'He ran past here at dawn. It was barely light, but there was no mistaking Vidar.'

Something in the woman's voice made Liv catch her breath.

'I haven't seen Dad run for twenty years.'

'Well, he was running right enough. He ran like the wolves were at his heels.'

✳

As soon as he fell asleep he heard the shot. The darkness was no protection, the bullet hit him anyway. In his dream he ran deep into the forest. The spruce branches whipped his face and the warm blood ran like sweat down his neck. Liam couldn't see where the forest ended and the sky began; all he heard was Gabriel's cough, reverberating in every direction, and he knew he was running in circles. When the shot came he felt only relief that it was all over. That he could wake up.

Their father had always set one against the other, ever since they were little. Early memories floated through Liam's head, from the mornings when Dad was hungover and feeling sorry for himself. Sometimes he wanted them to come and sit with him. He asked Liam to open the window, even in the winter, so snow gusted in and lay like a sparkling cover over the cactus from the Arizona desert that his mum had imported. It was like sitting in a snowdrift without either clothes or a fire, and when Gabriel and Liam's teeth started chattering their dad told them to come and cool him down.

'Come here, you little brats, before I burn up!'

And they had to lie beside him on the sofa while he smoked Gula Blend and sweated out yesterday's vodka. His armpits stank, but Liam had liked those times all the same. It had felt grown-up and slightly dangerous, being so close to their dad. Like lying in the bushes and watching an enormous animal close up. An animal that any minute could turn round and attack.

Gabriel was allowed to hold the lighter. He cupped his hand round the flame every time their dad put another cigarette between his lips. Liam had to be content with the ashtray. He balanced it on his thin chest, right between the ribs, and every time the wind blew through the open window he got ash in his eyes.

Dad never used to cuddle them, but at times he would scrape his stubbly cheek against theirs, scratching their faces.

'Lucky there are two of you,' he said. 'Because every king must have at least two heirs when he dies. I haven't got a favourite, believe me. When I'm gone you can fight for the throne between yourselves. I won't interfere in who gets what.'

Gabriel and Liam had looked at each other over their father's hairy chest, and it was clear even then that a battle was going on between them.

＊

She could hear the cries from the other side of the lake. Simon's voice riding on the wind, clear and unflagging.

The forest thickened on the north side of the village. Trees scratched and grabbed her, and the ground had a fresh cover of ice that looked dangerous under her feet. Shadows crawled and shifted in the light as she swung the beam from her torch. When she called Vidar's name she didn't recognize her own voice.

All the memories flickered past, small flashes in her head from another time when she had scabs on her knees and tangled hair, and she could disappear into the safe embrace of the forest. Vidar had tried to frighten her with stories of trolls and other unearthly beings, to keep her at home, but they had only driven her deeper into the shade of the spruce trees.

She was breathing so heavily she didn't hear someone catch her up. A sudden hand on her back made her spin round so violently that the torch fell in the moss and went out. The figure of a man stood on the path in front of her and all she could see was the rough outline and the clouds of frozen breath. He gave off an odour that blotted out the smell of pine needles. As she bent down to fumble for the torch she felt the damp chill rising from the ground.

She shone the light directly into his face and saw him flinch at the brilliant light.

'Karl-Erik, you almost scared me to death!'

He protected his face with a woollen fist. She could see the lined face behind it, the long beard down to his chest.

'You're all shouting so loud I can hear it over at my place. Anyone would think the village was on fire, the way you're carrying on.'

'We're looking for Dad. He's been missing since this morning.'

'Well, I'll be damned. Vidar isn't the kind to get lost.'

Karl-Erik Brännström was the village bachelor, younger than Vidar but never married. They were related but Vidar liked to keep that quiet. He always said Karl-Erik was a bad loser, the kind of man you couldn't bring indoors. When she was a little girl Liv had been fond of Karl-Erik, despite the fact that he smelled of beer and sang love songs out of tune. Sometimes he cried like a child although he was a grown man, and Vidar had said you had to watch out for such weakness, it was infectious.

But Karl-Erik looked anything but weak as he stood on the path before her, shifting his weight from one foot to the other.

'You haven't seen him?'

'Last time I saw Vidar he was behind the wheel with you sitting beside him, like you always do.'

Liv moved the torch so they could see each other better. Karl-Erik stepped back when he saw her, and gave a whistle. A sweet smell of alcohol filled the darkness around him.

'Sometimes you are so like your mother it's frightening.'

She hadn't expected that. There were few who remembered Kristina, and even fewer who spoke of her. At times she even imagined her mother was a figment of Vidar's imagination, one of many. A weight to hang over her head.

The sound of Simon's voice broke through the forest, and this time he was calling for her. She couldn't see him but could just make out the beam of torchlight slicing through the sea of trees.

'I have to go now, before they think I've got lost as well. But you'll keep your eyes open?'

Karl-Erik's teeth shone in his beard.

'If you're lucky he'll be gone for good.'

OCTOBER 2000

The father disappears into the dusk with his rifle over his shoulder. The girl sits in the window, seeing her own eyes in the glass. She can breathe again, her shoulders can relax. She doesn't switch on the lamp, there is only the glow of the cigarettes reflected in the windows. She lights a new one with the old, considers putting on some music and dancing. Or calling someone to ask them to come over, making use of the freedom. But she doesn't call anyone. She has no one to call. She sits in the darkness with her loneliness.

Towards the small hours she begins pacing the creaking floor. She looks constantly out at the night but all she sees is her own face and the fear that is burrowing into her, her eyes growing large and black. She lights a candle and places it in the window. The flame dances to her breathing. Maybe he won't come back. The cigarette smoke has settled like fog in the room and her eyes sting. She doesn't think of dancing any more. It's as if all the feelings of freedom have blown away.

The house creaks in the wind and she lies in bed and thinks it is her father. She hears his hushed footsteps on the stairs. But the door stays closed.

By dawn she has still not slept. She drinks coffee and breathes patterns onto the frozen glass of the window. Hoar frost glitters in the trees because it's cold out there, too cold for a person to survive. The thought arouses her interest. She thinks about what she will do now, the bags she will pack with only the lightest clothes. Where she is going there is no winter. In the still daylight she feels almost excited again. She puts on the music, turns it up until the walls throb.

The music is so loud she doesn't hear him return. It's almost lunchtime and the moose is lying butchered in pieces on the flatbed truck. Mixed feelings of disappointment and relief hit her as he comes into the hall. They sit in the kitchen and eat as they look at the huge antlers he has left on the grass. He tells her about the night, the cold, and the long hours before daylight arrives. About everything that moves in the dawn fog and the weight of the rifle. She asks if he killed it with one shot and his eyes glitter. The most important thing is patience, he says. Not to be too keen.

He asks about her night and she looks down at the table, embarrassed.

'You weren't afraid of the dark?'

'I want to come with you next time.'

He nods and smiles. Of course she can go with him. Next time.

But next autumn comes and then the next, and each time her father takes the rifle alone. He leaves her with her fear and freedom, and the stirring of the old house in the wind. It isn't until much later that she understands he is also afraid. Far too afraid to put a weapon in her hands.

She made her way to Widow Johansson's house without switching on the torch. A single porch light welcomed her and so did the dogs, their chains rattling in the stillness. The black glass of the windows stared back at her. No lights were on. She opened the door a crack and called his name, and although there was no answer she stepped inside. She walked quietly through the hall as she had done so many times before, past the kitchen and the sitting room with all the worn furniture. In the doorway to the bedroom she stopped. The bed was made and only the shiny eyes in the moose head met her inside. Johnny wasn't there. When she put on the light she saw the floor covered in trails of muddy footprints, as if he had forgotten to take off his boots.

She went to the kitchen and lit one of his cigarettes. Perhaps he was working late at the sawmill; she didn't know his shifts. They didn't have the kind of relationship in which they knew what the other was doing. She had never had that kind of relationship. She walked to the window and noticed the car was gone. Then she opened the fridge and found food inside, not a lot, just a six-pack of beer and an opened jar of hotdogs, a tub of butter and a jar of pickled beetroot. The remains of the cheese he had offered her. She went back to the bedroom and was overtaken by a sudden desire to look through his things. With the cigarette in her mouth she opened drawers and wardrobe doors. There wasn't much: a sorry collection of faded jeans and dark flannel shirts. T-shirts with rock bands from the eighties.

She pulled out her phone, thinking she would text him. I'm in your bedroom, she would write. Dad's missing. She squinted at the screen and realized she didn't have his number. She had nothing apart from Widow Johansson's house and everything that had taken place in the dead woman's bed. He worked at the sawmill and drove a Ford, that was all she knew. She had never asked any questions, hadn't felt the need. And now she regretted it.

They were still calling Vidar's name on the other side of the lake. The anxiety in Simon's voice distressed her and she started running, even though her body protested. Everything ached. By the time she reached Modig's farm the group had split up. She saw the light from their torches flashing between the trees. Voices seemed to be coming from all directions, carried on the wind.

She ran into Douglas first. He was moving clumsily, his stomach bulging over his belt. When she touched his shoulder he whirled round as if she had scared him.

'Liv, here you are! Where the hell has your father got to?'

'That's what I'd like to know.'

'Simon tells me he's been gone all day.'

'I'm sure he'll be back shortly.'

Douglas blinked.

'Vidar's not as young as he used to be.'

'Dad's fitter than any of us.'

'Fit, maybe, but that's no guarantee.'

Her rage flared up from nowhere. Douglas Modig was no stranger to bad luck. His farm had burned down ten years earlier and the business had never recovered. He had inherited the dairy unit from his father and if local rumours were to be believed he was on his way to losing the lot. Now here he was, delighting in someone else's misfortune, glad that the bad luck had abandoned him for somebody else. A woman appeared out of the darkness behind him and locked her arms around Liv, giving her a hug so hard it winded her. Eva Modig was short and sturdy with cropped hair, and she didn't miss a thing. Vidar used to say she was more man than Douglas would ever be, and if it hadn't been for her the farm would have gone under long ago. She held Liv at arm's length and looked at her in amusement.

'Usually it's Vidar running about looking for you. Now it's the other way round.'

'There's always a first time.'

'We see Simon practically every day, but Vidar hardly ever shows his face on this side of the lake.'

'Serudia says she saw him from her window this morning.'

'That old girl is as blind as a bat,' said Douglas. 'I wouldn't rely on anything she says.'

Eva put a finger under her lip and hooked out a wad of tobacco.

'We might as well wait until it gets light. It's as dark as the grave out here.'

'I'm not really worried,' Liv said. 'Dad's always known how to look after himself.'

It was true. If anyone knew how to survive without a roof over his head it was Vidar. Neither cold nor darkness touched him. He knew the forest better than he knew people and there was nothing out there that would harm him. Even so, the unease filled her chest when she looked at the worried faces of Eva and Douglas in the torchlight, as if they could see something she couldn't.

'If he's not back by tomorrow, call us,' Eva said. 'We've got dogs and four-by-fours available.'

'Thanks, but that won't be necessary.'

There was a rustling as the two youngsters came out of the bushes, their shadows so tightly entwined it was hard to make out if it was one person or two. They scowled when she shone her torch in their faces. Their noses and cheeks were red and Felicia's make-up had run in the cold. She didn't look like either Douglas or Eva. The blue hair and belligerent expression made her entirely her own person. Liv found it hard to take in that the girl was nineteen. Old enough to leave *Ödesmark*.

'Have you found him?' Simon asked.

'Not yet, but we might as well go home. It wouldn't surprise me if he's been sitting waiting for us all this time.'

It was almost midnight when they entered the hall and hung up their clothes. Vidar's dog wrapped herself round their frozen legs and the room was still dark and silent. In Vidar's room the badly made bed was the same as before. Simon went over and opened the wardrobe door, as if he expected Vidar to leap out. As if it had all been a bad joke. The black lock of the safe stared back at them.

'He's not here.'

'No, I can see that.'

'What shall we do?'

'If he's not back tomorrow we'll call the police.'

'You said he'd never forgive us if we got the police involved.'

'That can't be helped. We've got to find him.'

Liv made a pot of tea and lit the fire. Neither of them wanted to go to bed so they sat close together in front of the flames. They were so seldom alone that it felt odd, almost awkward. Despite the worry that hung in the air neither of them wanted to talk about Vidar. They sat in silence and looked at the crackling flames and the darkness pressing up against the windowpanes. Simon rested his head on her shoulder and Liv stroked his hair in a way she hadn't done for many years. She stared blankly into the fire, drunk with exhaustion.

'So Felicia is your secret girlfriend. I would never have guessed.'

His head felt hot under her hand.

'Why not?'

There are so many other girls, she wanted to say. The whole world is full of them. Why fall in love with the only one who lives in Ödesmark? But she didn't want to destroy the moment between them, didn't want to stop combing his hair with her fingers.

'I don't know. I thought you'd met someone online. Someone who lived further away.'

'You didn't think I could meet a real person, did you?'

'I didn't mean that.'

He twisted his head away, shaking off her hand. It was so

hard these days knowing what to say. She tried all the time to find the right words, the ones that would bridge the gap and bring them closer.

'Felicia isn't like anyone else,' he said. 'She doesn't care what other people think. She doesn't believe the bullshit. She makes up her own mind.'

'That's good.'

'But Grandad doesn't like her.'

'Grandad doesn't like anyone.'

He turned to look at her.

'Why do you always do as he says?'

'I don't know,' she said. 'Maybe it's easiest that way.'

'You're an adult, you can do what you like.'

'It's not always that straightforward.'

He looked smaller in the darkness. Younger. It had been so easy to answer his questions when he was little, easy to be evasive when she didn't know the answer or wasn't able to tell the truth. But that time had gone. Now he could see right through her, see the lies that lay twisted up inside and threatened to choke her.

'You never drive even though you've got a licence. It's pathetic.'

'I drove today.'

'Yeah, only because Grandad's not here. Otherwise you'd be sitting in the passenger seat like you always do.'

Liv looked at the fire. It sounded as if the flames were laughing at her. This was something new, questioning her lack of confidence. He used the same spiteful voice Vidar used when he wanted to put her in her place. She wondered if he was aware of it, how alike they were.

His eyelids flickered as he drifted into sleep. She sat perfectly still and felt him glide away from her, leaving her alone with the night. She watched the fire die down to embers while listening for Vidar's steps outside. She didn't know what frightened her most, never seeing him again or hearing him come striding in through the door as if nothing had happened.

*

His body was restless in the night. Liam sat in the darkness, listening to Vanja's breathing as she slept. He didn't want to sit too close, afraid his own anxiety would transmit itself to her and pull her out of her sleep. He was sensitive that way — he soaked up the feelings around him and made them his own. And his own feelings affected others, all his shame and failure became hers. That was the realization he couldn't live with. He must be better, there was no other way.

His nightmare had always been that he would end up like his dad. His dad, who had laboured at the sawmill since he was fourteen, paid his tax and bought alcohol at Systemet like a dutiful citizen, only to die before he was fifty. He had poisoned their existence with his rage and his despair, and on his deathbed he blamed the job. He put everything he had into the sawmill but got nothing in return, and had nothing to leave at the end of it. *Do something with your life,* he spat at them from his hospital bed. *Take whatever you damn well can.*

Liam crept out into the night to smoke. The dogs moved behind the bars, their eyes shining in the dark. Their wagging tails sounded like whispering. Two lights were on in the main house. He pictured his mum inside, her mass of hair and her flowing clothes, floating like a moth in her lonely fortress. She slept badly, often only for a few hours before dawn. There's too much going round in my head, she used to say. Liam knew what she meant. They hadn't made it easy for her, either of them. And it made no difference that time had passed and their father had gone, because all the bad memories still lingered in the walls, hanging over them all like an approaching storm. Liam pressed himself closer to the wall so she wouldn't see him and wondered what would happen to her if the truth ever came out, if she found out her older son was a murderer. She would lose her mind, once and for all, and all the dogs and stones in the world wouldn't be able to save her.

He was woken by Vanja pushing bread into the toaster. She was standing on one of the unsteady kitchen chairs with her hair like a glossy cloak down her thin back. The coffee was brewing. Five years old and she could make coffee already, a shameful reminder of all the mornings she had tried to look after him when he was flat out. She was like him, poor girl, with a birthmark like a raspberry under her ear. He had a similar one on his shin. At first Jennifer had screamed at him that Vanja wasn't his, but now no one would think to say that.

He didn't like thinking about Jennifer. The last he heard she had discharged herself from rehab and headed south, still doing drugs. The hard stuff. She had been gone so long Vanja had stopped asking about her, almost as if she had never existed.

He got out of bed and went over to her, pulled up the blind and let the sun stream in.

'I'm getting breakfast.'

'I can see, that's great. Why don't you sit and draw and I'll take over?'

They ate toast and jam and listened to the chaos that broke out in the dog pen when his mother went in to feed them. It sounded as if they would rip her to shreds.

'Your eyes are ever so big,' Vanja said.

'Are they?'

He went into the bathroom and saw that his eyelids were swollen and the whites of his eyes a sickly pink. He took time rinsing his face with cold water and when he had finished Vanja was sitting on the toilet lid, watching him.

'Are you still poorly?'

'No, I feel better now.'

'Am I going to preschool today?'

He met his own reflection in the mirror. The bloodshot eyes scared him; he didn't look at all well. A pack of tablets in the bathroom cabinet cried out for attention. He was close now, he felt it, felt himself going downhill. His hand shook as he opened the bathroom cabinet and took out a razor, trying not to look at the tablets.

'Yes, you must go to preschool today because I'm going to look for a job.'

'With Gabriel?'

'No, not with Gabriel. I'm looking for a proper job, so we can build our Northern Lights house.'

She gave a little shout of joy and threw her arms around his legs, clinging on to him while he shaved. After he had finished he brushed and plaited her hair. He had struggled through numerous YouTube videos before mastering the technique, determined to impress the preschool staff from day one. He didn't want to give them a single reason to believe he wasn't a good father.

They stood side by side on the bathmat and brushed their teeth, spitting into the handbasin at the same time and grinning widely at each other. Her laughter triggered small sparks inside him and filled him with life and warmth. When they left the garage and went out into the sunshine he realized he hadn't thought of Vidar Björnlund once. The night in Ödesmark seemed only a bad dream as he walked beside her. Almost as if it had never happened.

Liv was six years old when the police came to Ödesmark. They walked in without taking off their jackets or shoes and their voices boomed in the room. She had sat under the table and watched them leave wet footprints in the dust. Handcuffs gleamed in their belts and Vidar's knees shook under the table. She had put a hand over the rip in his jeans and patted the damp skin that was exposed. They accused him of poaching and it was the first time she had seen him really afraid. His voice was as frail as the snowflakes that landed on the windows, and when the police went to check the outhouses he had reached down under the table and seized her hand.

Are they going to put you in prison, Daddy?

Not me, I won't let them. Over my dead body.

But all she heard was fear and soon it had run from his hand into hers, down into her stomach where it crawled around like a blind animal. When one of the policemen leaned over Vidar and shouted in his ear, the fear was so great her trousers filled with pee.

Her bladder contracted again now when she saw headlights between the trees. Simon stood by the window and watched the patrol car drive through the open barrier and pull up in the drive. The grave expression made him look so much like Vidar that she forgot to breathe. Ever since the puppy fat had rolled off him it was clear he had inherited Vidar's cheeks and chin, and the sinewy body with arms so long they seemed to be in the way. When she looked at him it was her father she saw. The likeness shocked her.

Simon knew nothing about the poaching gang of the eighties that had threatened their whole existence and almost driven them crazy. The police officers were fixed in her memory as faceless monsters in official uniforms. The terror that they would take Vidar away from her and put him in prison was worse than anything she had ever experienced. He was all she had, after all. If she lost him she wouldn't survive. At least that's what she had thought as a child, and perhaps still did. That was why she had never managed to leave him and Ödesmark.

She had paced the floor all night and when the first light of dawn arrived she phoned the police, despite her memories and her fear of Vidar's wrath. Now she was standing full of suspense beside Simon, watching as a large man stepped out of the car. His uniform was tight across his body and he was alone. Simon had to go and open the door while Liv stood immobile in the kitchen, clasping the liniment tin so hard her knuckles turned white.

When the policeman stepped into the kitchen she exhaled deeply.

'Is it only you?'

Hassan looked around the room.

'Only me? Actually, I've been called Arvidsjaur's finest cop at least twice.'

He smiled and took in the room — the shabby cupboard doors, the dog, the empty chair by the window where Vidar should have been sitting.

'So this is where you live.'

'Do you know each other?' Simon asked.

'Not exactly. Hassan sometimes buys things from me at the filling station.'

Liv brought out an extra cup and invited him to sit down. He sat opposite Simon and reached across the table to shake his hand. She was pleased it was Hassan, a familiar face, yet his presence made her feel unsettled. Her voice was shrill as she started to tell him about Vidar, about the empty bed and the morning paper that hadn't been collected from the postbox. He couldn't have driven anywhere since the car was in the driveway, which meant he must have gone into the forest. There was nothing unusual about that — he did it all the time — but he had never been away for more than twenty-four hours without saying anything, unless it was hunting season. And it was still cold at night. Far too cold to be wandering about the countryside.

Simon told him about the search the night before, how they had shone their torches into the darkness and called his name without getting an answer. They had walked right around the lake, him and Felicia, but hadn't found anything. Liv told him about her conversation with Serudia and how the old woman had seen Vidar run past as if he was being hunted by wolves, but that had to be taken with a pinch of salt. You only had to look at her to realize she couldn't see much these days, other than ghosts in her head.

He listened attentively. His broad hands rested on the tabletop in front of him and he didn't bother to write down what she said. Something in his look got under her skin and irritated her.

'How old is Vidar?'

'Eighty.'

'Is he in good health?'

'He's not as young as he was, of course, but otherwise he's as fit as a fiddle. He's never ill.'

'Apart from the stiffness. That gives him trouble,' said Simon.

'Stiffness?'

'Yeah, his body seizes up when he's asleep, especially his hands. He can't bend his fingers in the morning, they're like claws.'

Simon held up a hand and demonstrated.

'He takes stuff for it.'

'Any trouble with his memory?'

'Never,' said Liv. 'Quite the reverse. He doesn't forget a thing.'

'Has he expressed or shown any signs of being tired of life?'

'No,' they said together.

Outside, the rowan swayed in the wind. It looked as if the old tree was laughing at them.

'He would never commit suicide,' said Liv. 'He thinks it's the most cowardly thing a person can do, getting rid of themselves before life is finished with them.'

Hassan's jacket creaked as he stood up and walked into Vidar's room. Liv and Simon waited in the doorway and watched as he pulled out bureau drawers and opened the wardrobe. Liv felt her stomach begin to ache as he stared at the safe.

'Do you know what he was wearing when he left?'

'His winter jacket has gone,' said Liv. 'And his boots. I don't understand how he managed to tie the laces that early in the morning.'

The dog lay curled in its tail and watched them intently. Liv wished she could do the same. Curl up and hide, like that time ages ago when Vidar squeezed her hand under the table so hard she thought her fingers would break.

Hassan went through the house room by room and continued outside in the barn and outhouses. They stood in the window and saw him being buffeted by the wind as he crossed the yard. The forest rippled, trees swayed and leaves chased each other over the dead grass. Beside her Simon was growing impatient.

'This is such a waste of time,' he said. 'I'll find him myself.'

He walked into the hall, put on his shoes and started tying his laces. Reluctantly Liv followed. When they met Hassan on the driveway it had started to snow, small wind-lashed grains that stung like pins and disappeared as soon as they had landed.

'I've requested a dog handler,' Hassan said. 'But they're coming from Piteå so it will be a while before they show up.'

'We'll search on our own,' said Simon. 'We can't just sit here, doing nothing.'

He was as tall as the police officer, but thinner. His voice had taken on a hostile tone that made her feel ashamed. Simon pulled up his hood against the snow and set off towards the edge of the forest, gesturing impatiently with his head for her to follow.

'Are you absolutely sure he hasn't gone off somewhere?'

'The car's here, isn't it?' said Liv, nodding at the Volvo.

'Someone could have picked him up down on the road.'

'And who would that be?'

'A friend or colleague?'

Liv looked in Simon's direction but he had already vanished among the trees.

She shook her head.

'Dad hasn't got any friends.'

He felt his courage desert him the second he dropped off Vanja. The news droned on the radio as he drove through the village, still not a word about Vidar Björnlund but it wouldn't be long now before all hell broke loose. But he couldn't just give up, he had to keep going. It was now or never if he was to get his life into some kind of order. They would take him on at the sawmill, he was sure of that — Dad's boss had promised him at the funeral. My door is always open, he had said, and Liam and Gabriel had exchanged glances that said they would rather die than take up the offer. It still felt like that. The very thought of putting on the blue overalls left a bitter taste in his mouth. It was a principle they had developed through the years, never smoking the same brand or drinking the same beer or putting on the same blue overalls as their dad. The day you did that, you were finished.

Anything at all so long as it wasn't the sawmill. He turned off at the filling station instead, parked by one of the pumps and sat there. He looked for Vidar Björnlund's daughter through the large window, hoping she would be sitting there as a sign that everything was normal, that the night at Ödesmark had been a bad dream. But she wasn't there. The owner himself was behind the counter, a short man with deep laughter lines. The relaxed way he moved showed he was a person who was content with life, somebody who always thought the best of everyone and could look them in the eye without triggering an argument. The kind of person Liam wanted to be.

They had pocketed stuff from the filling station more times than he cared to remember. Gabriel still did it when the mood took him, and hid a Snickers bar under his jacket more from habit than hunger. But it was a long time since they'd been caught. Not since the summer Liam was fourteen and they had tried to steal cigarettes from the stockroom. The filling station had a different name then. The assistant had chased them all the way to the church, tripped Gabriel up and put a knee between his shoulder blades as he lay on the ground. He threatened to kill them both until the police turned up and talked sense into him. The punishment was a thrashing from their dad and a few conversations with social services. Their dad had lost all his hair by this time, but it didn't stop him beating the shit out of them. He was mainly angry because they'd got caught and made him feel ashamed.

Liam twisted the rear-view mirror to look himself in the face. A thought struck him: this was where he would work, at the hub, the heart of the community, so every lousy person could see how he had changed. He ran his fingers through his hair, suddenly enthusiastic. There was no chance they would employ him, but it was worth a shot. He looked down at his clothes. His jeans were clean and whole and his shirt looked new despite being a few years old, a Christmas present from his mum before all her money went on dog food and worming tablets. He had never worn it until now. The shirt hadn't suited his former life. The eyes that met him in the mirror looked agitated. He attempted a smile but failed. He looked more like a terrified dog baring its teeth.

He felt sick as he headed towards the entrance. An old man was standing by the till when he walked through the door. The owner laughed loudly. It sounded like they were talking about ice hockey, something about a transfer from Motala. Liam recalled how he had begged his dad to be allowed to play, nagging until his dad said he'd had enough and shouted that no way could they afford the skates and helmets and jockstraps and all the other crap they'd need. *Do you have to bloody well choose the most expensive sport there is? Can't you kick a ball instead?*

The old man bought what he wanted and nodded at Liam as they passed. Liam nodded back. The shop was empty of customers now, it was just him and the owner. He felt the rush of adrenalin as he walked to the till, as if he was planning to rob the place instead. There was a twinge of pain from his bad tooth as he clenched his jaw and he wondered if people could see what a piece of shit he was, that everything under his skin was black and rotten.

The owner's smile faded as Liam put his hand on the counter.

'Can I help you with anything?'

'I think so.' Liam hesitated. 'I mean, like, I wanted to see if you needed anyone.'

'You're looking for a job – here?'

'Yes.'

The owner blinked and there was silence. Liam glanced at the name badge, *Niila*. The name meant nothing to him. He couldn't recall if their paths had crossed somewhere else, but you could never be sure. He hid his hands in his jacket sleeves to hide his tattooed knuckles, but then changed his mind and put a hand back on the counter. If he was going to do this he couldn't keep hiding his hands. You couldn't lie your way to an honest life. He watched Niila studying him, taking in his scarred face and the shirt that was new and unfamiliar against his body.

'Can you work weekends?'

'I can work any time.'

'Have you used a till before?'

'No, but I'm good at adding up and stuff.'

'We don't actually add up much these days.' Niila patted the machine where the change spewed out. 'This does most of it for us.'

Liam's body was boiling under his shirt. He fought the impulse to turn and go.

'Sure, of course. Stupid of me.'

'What kind of work have you done before?'

He sounded genuinely interested; there was nothing unkind or patronizing in his voice. Liam swallowed. He had planned to tell some story about gutting fish in Norway. It wasn't totally untrue, he had gutted fish a million times, just never in Norway. And he had never been paid for it. He didn't usually have a problem being economical with the truth, but now it was as if his brain had locked. It wouldn't let any lies through, not now.

'I've never had a proper job. Other things sort of got in the way. But I'm good at lots of things and I'm a fast learner. I've got a daughter – she's nearly six – and she hasn't got a mum because her mum prefers drugs. She's only got me and I've promised to look after her. In the right way. I need a job and if you give me one I promise you won't be disappointed. I'll work my balls off.'

It ran out of him, all of it, and maybe there was something in his voice because he saw Niila's expression change, and he didn't laugh or tell him to leave. But before he had time to answer the door swung open and two young girls came into the shop. Liam stood aside to let them get past. They spent a long time browsing the shelves and Niila said nothing until they had paid for their sweets and shiny magazines, and left.

'I know who you are,' said Niila. 'You and your brother. The Lilja brothers from Kallbodan.'

Liam held his breath. The sense of defeat came like a punch in the stomach. Of course he knew, everybody knew. He would have to go further than Arvidsjaur to look for work.

'You're the ones who sell grass and pills to my cousins.'

'Not any more. I don't sell anything any more.'

'Do you take drugs?'

Liam shook his head. His face felt hot, shame and anger pulsed in his body, and he felt an impulse to reach out and grab Niila by the throat and slam his head into the shiny counter until it was pulp. Give him the answer he was looking for. But he pictured Vanja and her big, serious eyes, and he stood completely still and let everything go over his head.

Niila scratched his neck pensively. A tattoo was visible under his starched collar.

'We do actually need someone at weekends,' he said. 'But I can't give you more than ten, fifteen hours. At least to start with.'

'No problem. I'll take anything.'

'Come here at ten on Saturday morning and we'll see what you can do.'

They shook hands over the counter and Liam felt a lump in his throat. All he could do was smile and nod. As he went out through the door it started snowing again and he lifted his head to the sky and let the flakes land on his face. A shout was forming in his throat but he didn't let it out until he was back in the car. Only then did he slap the wheel and yell out loud.

His gaze fell on a man standing by one of the diesel pumps, watching his behaviour. He had his collar and hood up against the snow, and his pallid face showed inside the dark material. Liam froze. For a split second he could have sworn it was Vidar Björnlund standing there. The living image.

*

The forest echoed with their shouts. It had stopped snowing, the sun was streaming between the trees and the ground steamed, leaving a layer of moisture on their faces. They followed the track that circled the lake. Simon went first and Liv found it hard to keep him in sight, suddenly afraid she would lose him. Vidar's dog ran in and out of the bushes, joyfully unaware of what was going on, as useless at tracking as a lapdog. Liv was surprised that Vidar had let it live. He had never had much time for stupid dogs.

The ground was wet and the tangled undergrowth twined itself round their legs. Liv picked up her feet and shuddered at the sound of the fragile branches cracking and breaking under them. It felt as if they were trampling over bones, a whole forest of bodies cradled in the leaf mould. And Vidar's face everywhere, leering from behind the trunks of the pine trees, smacking his thin lips. With every step she expected his clawed hand to reach out of the moss and grab her.

Simon's voice broke into her thoughts, his shouts drifted over the black mirror of the water and multiplied through the village. It didn't take long for the neighbours to attach themselves to the group. Serudia came first, her crooked form so camouflaged among the spruces that nobody noticed her until she started calling out Vidar's name with the same forceful voice she used to round up a herd of cows.

The Modigs came too, with their cheerfulness and smell of manure. Felicia's eyes were thick with make-up and her blue hair flapped defiantly in the wind. A smile flickered on her lips when she saw Liv, as if something about this distressing situation amused her. Eva had come equipped with long ski poles which she used to prod deep into the loose earth. Douglas struggled behind her, red-faced and out of breath.

'Have you phoned for help?' he asked.

'A dog handler is on the way.'

'On the way?' He spat into the grass. 'We'll have sniffed him out before that, I'm sure.'

They reached the marshes that extended beyond the lake. Eva led the way, directing them and pointing with her poles. Douglas kept closely behind Liv. All she could hear was his panting and the water that squelched under the clumps of moss. Johnny joined them too, wondering what all the commotion was about. He looked as if he had just woken up. He needed a shave and his hair was on end. He gave Liv a pained look when she told him Vidar had gone missing.

'Why didn't you come to me?'

'I tried, but you weren't home.'

She asked him to take the outer flank, furthest away from her. She didn't want him to touch her or get too close. Not now.

The person who didn't offer to help was Karl-Erik. He stood at the edge of his land with his arms crossed, grimacing at the sun and their efforts. When Douglas called him he turned his back and disappeared into the bushes as if he had heard nothing. Simon picked a stick from the ground and waved it threateningly at him.

'Why doesn't he help?'

'Because he's a lazy bastard,' said Douglas.

'Let him be,' said Liv. 'Dad wouldn't have looked for him if it was the other way round.'

Douglas spat and moved closer to her. His face twitched, betraying his eagerness. He thought the search was exciting, that much was clear. Vidar's disappearance had put new life into him.

'Someone could be lying out here, dying,' he said. 'It's a scandal he won't help, dammit.'

Liv turned away and concentrated on the ground in front of her, the wet earth and the false illusions. Everything looked sharper in the clear light, less threatening, but even so she saw Vidar beneath her feet, the whites of his eyes gleaming from under the dead branches and the moss. His voice echoed through her like a cold wind. He was everywhere and nowhere.

By the time the dog handler turned up, their shouts had fallen silent. They were resting by one of the village's abandoned houses and Serudia was passing round a thermos of coffee. The empty house had belonged to a butcher, but now no one was interested in taking on the greying planks. Only the wind and the voles whistled and scuttled through the old wood.

The garish patrol car looked out of place in the undergrowth. A German shepherd was in the back, drooling in anticipation. The dog handler introduced herself as Anna Svärd, and asked the same questions Hassan had already asked. Simon stood with his arm around Liv as she answered, and they pointed out the tracks and paths they had already searched. Anna wanted something that smelled of Vidar so Liv led them back to Björngården where she took the old man's cardigan from a hook, the cardigan he often wore but seldom washed. Before she handed it over she buried her nose in the wool to convince herself it was still there, the rank odour of her father like rotten fruit in the itchy yarn.

She stood watching them from the window when they left. The black dog tugged and strained on the leash as if it had already picked up the scent. Tension vibrated in the air. Simon's voice hovered somewhere behind her.

'They'll find him now. The dog will find him.'

Liv didn't answer. She couldn't even turn round and meet his eyes. Because she was sure he would see right through her and all the shameful thoughts she was hiding. The thoughts that it was better like this, without him. Better that he never came back.

SEPTEMBER 2001

An old wreck of a car pulls up beside her with its windows down. There is a man behind the wheel, with unruly hair and a gaping mouth. Stubble covers half his face and his clothes are ripped and faded and covered in moss and twigs. Without taking his eyes off her he reaches across the seat and pushes open the passenger door.

'You getting in?'

The girl stays where she is with one foot in the ditch. Autumn is on fire in the birches, and clusters of dancing leaves swirl around her legs and the rusted chassis of the car as it waits impatiently on the gravel. This is the first time she has hesitated. The sound of another car on the hill makes her mind up for her and without a word she jumps in and slams the door shut. The man accelerates so abruptly she slams her head against the seat. A trail of exhaust fumes chases after them. He swings off onto a smaller road without asking where she wants to go. The girl raises the volume of the radio, mainly to mask her fear. Inane dance-band music that makes him whistle.

'Do you know who I am?' he asks.

She nods.

'You're the guy who killed his own brother.'

He snorts as if she has said something funny. The road is rough and full of holes, old rainwater splashes over the windows. She has no idea where they are going and she doesn't care. He turns off the music and glares at her.

'I didn't kill him, it was an *accident*.'

She glares back. His eyes aren't on the road even though they are driving fast. A spider crawls over his beard, in and out of the coarse stubble. She stretches over and squashes it between her thumb and forefinger, holds it up triumphantly before flinging it out of the open window. There is an odd look in his eyes.

'That was unnecessary.'

She smiles. He mustn't see her fear, that's the most important thing. Men are like wolves, they smell their way to fear and attack it.

The narrow road begins to climb uphill. The birches are small and bent and the wind tears their leaves from them. The car is about to give up; it rattles and coughs and there is a strong smell of burning. Not until they reach the top does he let it rest. Heather shines between the sparse pines and way below in the valley she sees a solitary house. She plays with the door handle. He'll catch her up if she starts running. The forest can't shield her from someone like him.

With a quick, catlike movement he throws himself over her. She shuts her eyes and clenches her teeth, but he's only after the glove compartment. He pulls out a pipe and a lighter, and a bar of chocolate which he holds out to her. The heat has got to it and the chocolate is soft in its wrapper.

'This is all I've got to offer you.'

She eats the chocolate and watches as he fills the pipe. The black under his nails smiles up at her, his arms are suntanned and veiny. A sweet smell fills the car as he lights the pipe; her fingers are sticky as she reaches for it. He hesitates before he hands it over. She draws the smoke deep into her lungs, then lets it run slowly out of her nostrils. Before long her body feels heavy and she sits still and watches the wind making waves in the trees and the gold leaves raining down over the forest.

'Is it true you live in the forest?' she asks.

'Don't we all?'

The laughter bubbles up inside her. All her fear has drained away; she can tell by looking at him that he's not going to touch her. He's wild and dishevelled and his eyes scream loneliness, but he doesn't mean her any harm.

'I know who you are, too,' he says. 'I know who your dad is.'

She drops the pipe on her lap. The tobacco burns her jeans and she's not laughing any more. The man doesn't get angry. He brushes her jeans gently, as if she were made of glass. Chocolate shows in his beard.

'Do you think your old man will give me a reward if I drive you home?'

'I'm not going home.'

'Right. Then where are you going?'

She points towards the shadows lengthening and flickering in the dusk.

'I'm going with you,' she says. 'Into the forest.'

'Can you come over? We need to talk.'

'I can't. I've got to pick up Vanja.'

'Just a quick chat. It's important.'

Gabriel was using his caressing voice and that meant there was a problem. Liam ended the call, the joy over his new job replaced by a gnawing uneasiness. He wanted nothing to do with Gabriel, but at the same time he felt forced to keep an eye on him to make sure he didn't make things worse.

The block of flats was only a couple of roads away from the filling station. It couldn't have been more central. Liam sat in a visitor parking space and looked up at the red balcony. A dead Christmas tree hung over the railing, still with a strand of glitter in its yellowing branches. The balcony door was slightly open and the faint light from a television flickered inside.

Gabriel had left home when he was sixteen. He wasn't given a choice – their mum had had enough of his drugs and his temper, and had thrown him out. Something she was never able to do with their dad. She had slung his things out of the window in her anger and the whole yard was filled with his jeans and stolen trainers. Gabriel had pushed her down the stairs, held an arm round her throat and tightened his grip. Their mum had sunk her teeth into him and bitten hard. It could have ended badly if Liam hadn't intervened. He had wrenched them apart at the last minute, before they murdered each other. He was convinced his brother would come back, but he hadn't.

Gabriel had never had his own home, but he managed somehow. He lived with his mates or girlfriends. One bitterly cold winter he had even slept on the sofa of an old wino who had taken pity on him. Anything to avoid going back to Kallbodan.

Currently he was living with Johanna, a young girl who was always asleep, or so it seemed. Even when she was awake her eyelids drooped as if she would pass out any second. Her voice drawled on the few occasions Liam had spoken to her. Gabriel said they were getting engaged. He had given her a ring he had stolen from a jeweller's. It was the wrong size so she had to wear it on her middle finger and every time she showed it to people it looked like she was making an obscene gesture.

Liam took the stairs two at a time. He had his knife in his belt and he pulled his shirt across to cover it. He had never been afraid of Gabriel before, not really. Not like now. The flat was on the third floor and a nauseating smell of marijuana and oven chips seeped out from under the door. He had to ring three times before Gabriel opened. He was naked apart from a pair of jeans that hung loosely from his hips. His chest and cheeks were white and sunken.

Gabriel smirked when Liam walked into the hall.

'What the fuck are you wearing?'

Liam looked down at the long-sleeved shirt. The stiff fabric was sticking to his skin.

'I've been looking for a job today.'

'No shit. I thought it was only talk.'

Gabriel scratched his bare chest. His eyes were restless. The flat was in darkness behind him, apart from the light from the television screen. A glowing cigarette smouldered in an ashtray and the air was thick with smoke. Johanna was lying on the sofa in her underwear and didn't answer when Liam said hello.

They went into the galley kitchen where crisp packets and pizza boxes were scattered among empty bottles and pieces of foil. Everything was covered in a film of ash. There were no chairs to sit on so Liam leaned against the wall. Gabriel pulled up the blind and peered outside. Both of them found it hard to look each other in the face.

'I didn't think you'd come.'

'What do you want?'

'I just want to see how you are.'

'I'm still alive.'

Liam undid a couple of top buttons. He was finding it hard to breathe in the stale air.

'Jesus, you look a nervous wreck,' said Gabriel.

He pulled a bag from his jeans pocket.

'Here. Take as many as you like. Before you crack up.'

'No way.'

But Gabriel threw the bag at him anyway. Liam caught it and slid it into his pocket. He knew he shouldn't — he already had stuff at home and anyway he wanted to stop — but he couldn't summon up the energy to argue with Gabriel. He peered into the flat. In the corner was a mattress with blankets flung over it, and cushions in various sizes and colours. The sofa was shabby and patched up with gaffer tape where the filling had started to come out. Johanna's pale legs were splayed on the rough fabric and there were angry red marks on the insides of her thighs. She didn't seem to be breathing. Liam looked away. He hadn't a clue where Gabriel found his girlfriends. They were always young, considerably younger than him, and he was only nice to them at the beginning.

'So why did you call?'

Gabriel glanced into the room where Johanna was lying and leaned closer to Liam.

'I thought we should, like, go somewhere.'

'Why?'

'To get rid of what's left, that's why. Before they find anything.'

'It's too late, don't you get it? It'll be crawling with people out there by now.'

'Not in the middle of the night. We'll go tonight and take care of it.'

'Have you lost your fucking mind?'

Gabriel ran a hand over his shaved head and the scar tissue on his knuckles gleamed in the dim light. He attempted a smile but one half of his face was slower than the other and couldn't keep up.

'I worry about you, bro,' he said. 'It keeps me awake at night.'

'I'll be OK.'

It was true. For the first time in his life he felt there was a distance between them, something keeping them apart. For as long as he could remember he had let Gabriel go ahead and take the lead. It had been easier letting someone else make the decisions. Even if it nearly always went belly up, at least there were two of them, someone else to share the blows. Not even after Vanja was born had he managed to go his own way. It was only now, when his world had collapsed, that he realized it was possible. Whatever it was that had taken place on the marsh, it had liberated him.

Perhaps Gabriel picked up on the change because he was more cautious now, almost pleading.

'So when do think they'll find him?'

'I'm amazed it's taking this long.'

Gabriel took out two cigarettes, put one in his mouth and handed the other to Liam. His pupils were like pinheads in the flame from the lighter. Tiny drops of sweat shone on his chest, betraying the torment inside him. But his face gave nothing away and his voice was steady and placid. Gabriel had always been like that, kind and easy-going one second, ready to explode the next.

'You've deleted the photos, right?'

'What photos?'

'The ones we took when we were checking it out, remember?'

Liam inhaled the smoke deep into his lungs and almost choked. His iPhone was burning a hole in his pocket. He pictured the marsh, relived the damp filling his throat. The old man swaying in the dawn light had looked so small when the sun rose above his head. So small and insignificant. Just a fraction of a second from death. The thought of the pictures made him feel sick.

'What's going on?'

Johanna was standing in the doorway, looking at them sleepily. She pulled her camisole down to cover her knickers. Gabriel pointed the cigarette at her.

'Get back to bed.'

Johanna looked at Liam, blinking her heavy eyelids.

'Hey, Liam. It's been ages.'

'Get back to bed, I said!'

Gabriel lurched towards her. He tried to grab her but only caught a strand of her hair. Johanna screamed and broke free, hurried back to the sofa and disappeared under a blanket. Gabriel scowled at her.

'Liam's come to talk to me and I don't want to hear a sound out of you, get it? I don't even want to hear you breathing.'

Her thin body hardly showed under the blanket but the cover shook as if she was crying. Gabriel had turned out exactly like their father. He treated the women in his life worse than a dog, worse than anyone else. The realization made Liam feel drained.

'I've got to make tracks.'

'You've only just got here. Stay and chill.'

'I must collect Vanja.'

Gabriel followed him out to the hall. He had never been one for hugs but now he put an arm round Liam's neck and drew him close, so close his lips brushed Liam's ear.

'You've deleted the pictures?'

'Yep.'

'Show me.'

'There's nothing to show. They've gone.'

'Good.'

Gabriel twisted his head so their foreheads met. His mouth gave off a metallic smell.

'Forget the old guy,' he whispered. 'Forget the whole fucking thing.'

*

The night fell dense and heavy but Liv couldn't sleep. Her body ached after the day in the forest. It cried out for rest but she couldn't calm her thoughts. Things moved in the dark, shadows crawled and roamed in the undergrowth. The temperature had dropped to minus six. She thought of Vidar lying out there, freezing. She saw his hands, the claw-like fingers, and she knew he wouldn't survive many nights.

The police dog hadn't found anything despite seeming so confident. The handler had handed back the cardigan with an apologetic expression. The cold, damp wool no longer smelled of Vidar when Liv put it to her nose. Hassan wanted to know if he could have travelled somewhere – had he taken his passport? Cash?

'Dad hasn't got a passport. He's never travelled anywhere in his life.'

He asked her to open the safe but neither she nor Simon had the code. The fortune wasn't theirs, it was Vidar's. Hassan asked a lot of questions about the money, how much he could be carrying if he had chosen to go away. He wanted the name of Vidar's old business associate and every contact who might have some information. Liv wrote a list of those she could remember, but Vidar hadn't done any business for over twenty years so it was short and incomplete.

'He hasn't gone anywhere.'

'How can you be so sure about that?'

'He would never leave me and Simon. We're all he's got.'

OCTOBER 2001

She spends that autumn with the lone wolf from North Forest. His car stands idling in the lay-by whenever she can get to the main road. Not until she is almost level with the car does he switch on the lights and start the engine, giving her a smile that warms her heart. He smells strong and wild, and that fills her with a sense of freedom. They drive along narrow roads through the mist, eat meat he has hunted and dried, and talk about the kind of things they never talk about otherwise.

He tells her about his brother and what a couple of rogues they were before the fatal accidental shooting. The kind of life they led together.

'I held him in my arms until help arrived, but it's all a blur to me. The only thing I remember is Mum refusing to let me in when I got home. She locked the door for good. That's how I ended up in the forest.'

He still has the bloodstained clothes, in a chest in the hut that has become his home. He takes them out sometimes, buries his face in the stiffened cloth. Grief and loneliness have aged him; he's not even thirty but the lines are deep. And his parents have never forgiven him.

The girl tries to imagine what it would feel like if her father locked the door for good, leaving her outside. She can't think of anything better.

'Your old man's a bastard,' says the loner. 'But you, you glow.'

She picks forest debris from his clothes and tells him about all the places they are going to see, palm trees and cobblestoned alleyways, green water pounding on rocks. We'll go together, she says, and he smiles that indulgent smile which means she is too young to understand the world. He is ten years older but he keeps his hands to himself and never attempts to touch her like all those other men. Sometimes he smokes too much and she has to take over the wheel. He sleeps with his head in her lap and a happy smile on his cracked lips.

When the first snow falls they park on a hilltop and watch the flakes clothe the forest in its winter robe. In a few exhilarating moments the world is achingly white, and the solitary man weeps as he looks at the valley spread out below them. He won't say why he is weeping. They exhale white air and soon all they can see is the condensation. When he climbs out into the cold she follows, and they raise their faces to the sky and take greedy mouthfuls of snow. His beard is stiff and sparkling when he turns to her and points over the pine trees.

'All of North Forest would have been mine,' he says. 'If it wasn't for your dad.'

His voice pulsates with anger. Wet flakes land on his eyelashes and she is glad they can't see each other clearly. She has heard about her father's craving for land since the day she was born, but she doesn't understand what it's got to do with her.

'He came to my parents after my brother died, when they were grieving and vulnerable. He offered to buy the land so they could start a new life somewhere else, away from the memories. Land that has been in our family for four generations. They sold it without a second thought.'

The girl takes his hand and they stand for a long time watching the snow slowly weave a blanket over the valley. The river's frozen breath rises skywards and he opens his jacket and lets her step into the warmth and hide there. From his pocket he takes a shining piece of jewellery, a silver heart and chain. Wordlessly he lifts her hair so he can fasten it around her neck.

'It's no coincidence we met,' he says. 'We were meant to throw in our lot together. So we can put things right.'

She saw restless shadows to the right and left, and her eyes flitted between the road and the trees. Liv still expected the forest to open up and release Vidar's wiry figure. Any minute he would appear, walking towards her as if nothing had happened. He would step into the hall and see the intruders' footprints and curse her for letting outsiders into his home, his sanctuary. She envisaged him lifting his head and sniffing the stale air like a dog. His gruff voice rebounding off the walls: *What have I told you about bringing people home?*

Perhaps he wanted to teach them a lesson. Test their loyalty once and for all by staying away. It wouldn't surprise her to find he was standing out there, at a safe distance, keeping his watery eyes on them. But she couldn't tell the police that. They wouldn't understand. Not even Hassan.

'Are you OK if I head off to Felicia's?'

Simon was standing in the doorway, his voice hoarse after all the shouting, his face grey from crying and lack of sleep. She wished she could open her arms and let him run into her embrace, like he did when he was younger. She wished she could ask him to stay.

'Why don't you come too?' he asked, as if he could read her thoughts. 'Eva's always telling me to bring you with me.'

'Someone has to be here when Grandad gets home.'

She sat on Vidar's chair by the window and watched him go. Before the trees swallowed him he turned round and waved. She resisted an impulse to open the window and call him back, into the warmth and security where nothing could harm him, and settled for raising a hand to the glass, feeling the coldness that was shrouding the house.

The dog was lying in the doorway to Vidar's room, and every time the wind swept past the old house walls it lifted its head and smelled the air, still waiting. She had left the door partly open, as if to convince herself that it really was empty inside.

She was on the verge of sleep in the chair and didn't see the figure moving along the road. Not until the dog got to its feet and let out a low snarl from its skinny body. Liv peered behind the curtain. She could make out the contours of a man moving in and out of the shadows. He walked close to the woodshed as if he didn't want to be seen.

The dog's snarl turned into barking. Liv hurriedly removed the extra cup that was still on the table, the one Hassan had used. She hissed at the dog to be quiet and went silently into the hall. She kept a hand on the wall as she moved, needing something solid to lean against. It was too dark to see anything out of the hall window, but she heard him step up to the doorway. The old planks creaked and groaned under his weight.

'Dad, is that you?'

Her voice cracked and there was no answer. She walked backwards, burying herself in the winter jackets hanging on their hooks as thoughts raced in her head. It was over now, the game was over. Vidar was back, ready to step in and take charge again. She glanced at the shotgun hanging on the wall and imagined raising the weapon and shooting right through the door. One of the jackets had a fur trim and it was tickling her face. The shiny fabric smelled of him, of pipe tobacco and old unwashed skin. His words rang in her ears, the cruel remarks he used to throw at her when he was in that frame of mind.

'When I'm dead you'll be rich,' he used to say. 'That's for sure. The only way you won't get your inheritance is if you kill me.'

Then he had laughed, the way people do when words become too vicious.

A sudden knock on the door sent the barking a few octaves higher. Liv held her breath among the jackets and waited. Vidar would never knock on his own door; he would sooner rip it off the hinges. Three gentle knocks and then the handle moved. Darkness and cold air came in with a sigh as the door slowly opened.

It wasn't Vidar standing there. The shoes on the doorstep were thin and muddy, and the dog dropped its tail between its legs. A man's face took shape in the gloom and a mild smell of cigarette smoke reached her, mixed with that other smell, the one she could never get enough of.

'Johnny?' she whispered. 'What are you doing here?'

'Liv?' He peered through the gloom. 'Where are you?'

Slowly she emerged from the winter jackets, her knees weak with relief.

'You almost scared the life out of me.'

'I didn't mean to. I just wanted to see how you were. Have you heard from him?'

Liv reached for the switch and the hall was flooded with light. The dog padded up and nosed Johnny's wet trouser legs. Liv threw a look towards Vidar's bedroom, as if she couldn't quite trust the fact that he wasn't there.

'Come on,' she said. 'We'll go up to my room.'

He allowed himself to be led up the creaking stairs, past Simon's closed door and into her room. They lay on the bed, careful not to touch each other. She couldn't distinguish his face but felt the warmth coming off him. It was strange to see him here, in the room she'd had since childhood. She found it hard to imagine him anywhere else but in Widow Johansson's house, as if he was one of the old pieces of furniture left behind. Liv kept her eyes on the closed door, imagining someone pulling at the handle.

'I've never had a man in my bed before.'

'Don't take this the wrong way, but that's pretty hard to believe.'

'Dad doesn't like me bringing strangers home.'

He froze when Vidar was mentioned, and ran his eyes over the walls.

'So where do you think he is?'

'I don't know. We've searched the entire village, the police sent a dog handler, but he's nowhere.'

'Maybe he's gone away.'

'But the car's still here.'

'There are buses.'

'You don't know my dad.'

She thought of all the times she had stood there on Highway 95 with her thumb in the air, thinly dressed since it was never planned. Sometimes with money in her pocket, often not, and always prepared to jump into the ditch if she caught sight of Vidar's Volvo coming round the bend. And frequently he was the first to drive past, as if he had some kind of telepathic ability to know when she was getting ready to run.

Johnny's gruff voice caught her attention.

'There's something I've got to tell you,' he said. 'I didn't want to say anything while we were out in the forest, searching with the others, because it doesn't sound too great.'

'What?'

'Vidar came round the other day, started accusing me of this and that. In the end he told me to find someone else's house to rent. He said he didn't want me in his village.'

Liv shut her eyes tight.

'He gets ideas sometimes, about other people. This doesn't concern you.'

'It sounded like it concerned me. He's got a godawful temper, your dad. Must be hell to live with.'

'I'm used to it, I suppose.'

He reached out for his jacket and she was afraid he was going to leave, that it was all over now, but then she heard the click of a lighter and saw the end of his cigarette like a glow-worm in the darkness.

'Can I ask you something?' he said.

'Ask away.'

'How come you still live with your dad?'

This was it, the question she always dreaded. The panic flared in her chest like a fire.

'That's just how it is. I was so young when I had Simon, I couldn't manage on my own. It was Dad who helped me. So we just stayed.'

'But why? He suffocates you.'

'You don't know anything about us.'

'I know you sneak about at night like a teenager, and that he drives you to work as if you were a school kid. Christ, Liv, that's not normal. And everyone around here talks about you, you and Vidar and the kid. You should hear what they say as soon as I tell them I'm renting from him.'

'People love to talk.'

'And do you know what they're saying?'

Liv curled up in a tight ball with her head on her knees. She heard him pace up and down beside the bed, the weary sigh as he exhaled.

'Do you know what they say about you?' he repeated.

Her heart was thumping so loudly she felt sure he could hear it.

'I want you to go now.'

'What?'

She lifted her head and tried to look at him in the darkness.

'I want you to go now.'

She saw him droop as if under a heavy weight as he pulled on his jacket, but he didn't argue or try to stay. Ash from his cigarette flew around him as he opened the door.

His footsteps resounded in her head long after he had disappeared down the stairs. She stayed where she was under the duvet, her arms cradling her body as if afraid it would break into pieces. She shook from loneliness until sleep took over.

NOVEMBER 2001

The hoar frost shimmers on the birch trees when she and the loner drive off. Snow fills the forest with new light and they can't go anywhere now without leaving a trail. It turns colder and he holds her hands in his and gently blows life into them, then puts them under his jacket, inside his layers of clothing, so that his own warmth becomes hers. With him she never has to feel cold and it doesn't take long for her to realize she loves him. Not as a man but as a brother. Someone she can rely on. The first.

'I've got something for you,' she says.

'You have?'

She waits until they reach the top. He parks in the same place, where they first met. Now the mountain is theirs, the world is white at their feet. The girl takes the piece of folded paper from her pocket and feels the pulse in her fingertips as she hands it over. He gives her a long look before unfolding it. She holds her breath as she waits. The loner lifts the sheet of paper to the light and reads her shaky lines.

'What's this?'

'You can see, can't you? It's a plan.'

It is a plan of her father's house, but she doesn't need to say that because the loner's eyes have already become alert and his lower lip is trembling. She moves closer and indicates the cross that marks the centre of the house.

'There's more money there than your family's land was worth,' she says.

Carefully, almost reverently, he refolds the piece of paper and tucks it into his breast pocket.

'What do you want in exchange?' he asks.

'Nothing.'

'Come on, you must want something.'

'I only want you to take me away from here.'

They make a fire and sit on opposite sides of the flames. He has a guksi cup in his belt and they drink from it as the sun rises in the sky and melts the frost from the trees. He rolls a joint and smokes it slowly, and after a while his face stops twitching. He strokes his beard and the tension throbs between them, a kind of significance that wasn't there before. She sees in his eyes that he loves her too. In that miraculous way that can't be described in words.

When he drops her off at the lay-by her father's car is there. They get out, all three of them at the same time, and her father has a curious smile on his lips.

'Well, here you are,' he says. 'I'd almost given up hope.'

His eyes are as leaden as the sky as he pats her shoulder and gives her a look that makes her shrivel up inside. The loner says nothing. He merely stands beside her, breathing steadily.

'Go and sit in the car,' her father tells her. 'So I can have a little chat with your new friend here.'

His voice is as soft as moss, yet she doesn't dare to protest. She sits in the back seat and watches through the window as her father walks up to the loner. They stand together, speaking quietly. Her father does most of the talking, and his hands flap in the air. The loner's face changes colour, but in the end he nods. When he turns around to go she leans closer to the window, waiting for him to send her a look, mouth a few words, give her something to hold on to. But he gets in his car, puts it in gear and drives out onto the main road without looking in her direction.

Her father grabs her when he returns to the car, and thrusts his hand inside her jumper. It's the necklace he's after, the shiny heart that is nestling there. With a swift movement he tears the chain from her neck and drops the necklace into his pocket.

'You'll never see him again,' he says. 'Not while I'm alive.'

All through the winter she returns to the lay-by, trudging through the darkness and the snow, standing for a long time under the Northern Lights, waiting. The spruces are heavy and silent around her, keeping her company. The cold eats into her bones but she doesn't notice, and the loner never comes. She thinks of the plan she gave him, his words about them putting things right. The road so quiet and deserted.

They are alone again now, each in their own place. But she refuses to believe he has gone for ever.

She was woken by Vidar calling her, the cracked voice ringing over the frozen gravel. Half-awake, half in her dream, she left Björngården and followed the lonely voice luring her into the forest. She stumbled among pines turning red in the dawn light, the path uneven and slippery all the way down to the water. The sun had not yet lifted the mist from the lake. She couldn't discern the farm on the far side, only the shadowy signs of life. A single bark reverberated off the trees and seemed to come from all directions. Fresh frost crunched under her feet and Vidar's voice no longer echoed inside her. The night chill rose up from the ground and found its way under her clothes, and she froze and sweated alternately. She was wide awake now, but still she couldn't let go. He was out here, she knew it.

Suddenly Serudia's house appeared by the path, making Liv slip between the trees. Vibrant birdsong filled the glade and as she came nearer she saw the nesting boxes and bird feeders hanging from the branches like Christmas tree decorations. The ground was covered with spilled seeds, and birds were everywhere, flapping and hungry. Her approach made them vanish into the canopy of the trees.

The voice came like an unexpected gust of wind.

'Who's that prowling about, scaring my birds?'

Serudia stood like an angel fallen to earth among the

spruces. Her white hair flowed from underneath her hat and loose strands whipped around the weather-beaten cheeks and amazingly light eyes.

Liv stepped out of the bushes.

'It's only me. Liv. I didn't mean to scare your birds. I'm out looking for Dad. I dreamed about him last night.'

The old woman's eyes tried unsuccessfully to locate her. She stopped close to Liv but just out of reach, and raised a veiny hand into the air. She held it there for a second or two before opening her fingers and letting more seed rain down onto the moss, coaxing the birds to her.

'Vidar will come when he comes,' she said. 'That's what he's always done.'

The old woman was only wearing her nightdress under her coat and the flimsy material dragged over the wet ground. But it was the hat on her head that made Liv stop in her tracks. It sat low over her forehead and was several sizes too big, and there was something about the red wool that made Liv gasp.

'Where did you get the hat?'

Serudia touched her head and slowly patted it with her fingers. The birds were singing hysterically.

'I found it,' she said. 'It was lying there waiting for me in a glade.'

'It's my dad's hat. Mum knitted it for him years ago.'

The fear made her voice harsh. She snatched the hat from the old woman's head and pressed it to her hammering chest. Serudia blinked at her mutely, her mouth gaping in terror, but she didn't protest. Liv lifted the hat to her face, smelled the damp and the forest and Vidar's liniment. An odour so powerful it was as if he had come back and was standing beside her.

Liv gave the old lady a last look, turned her back and ran.

PART II

The timber harvester extended its long black arm among the trees, hesitated for a couple of seconds and then gripped one of the trunks. It held the tree in a powerful embrace before the bark stripper got to work. The surrounding pines trembled in the draught. A watery sun looked down on the destruction and when it was at its highest the machine stopped and the man behind the controls climbed out. He hung his ear defenders around his neck and shook himself like a dog as he clambered over the timber he had just felled. As he unzipped his trousers and peed in the bushes his attention was caught by the abandoned house nestled among the trees. The faded walls looked sad in the sunshine and the front door was half-open and creaking on its hinges. Shrivelled hop vines clung to the drainpipes.

The man sat down on the veranda steps and the old boards creaked disturbingly under his weight. He took a flask and some sandwiches wrapped in cling film from the bag slung over his shoulder, and as he ate he listened to the wind stirring in the old house. Now and then it carried with it a smell that made his food taste foul. The man unscrewed the top of the flask and inhaled the hot coffee aroma. He could see the logging machine over in the bushes where it stood waiting for him, and immediately he wished he had chosen to eat his lunch there instead, in the sun-warmed cab.

He swallowed the last of his sandwich and stood up. As he waded back through the overgrown grass the stench grew stronger. Whiffs of it reached him and made his stomach turn. He looked back at the house and the gaping windows and imagined someone was lying inside there, a dead body in a forgotten bed. He turned back to the forest, tripping over his feet in the wet grass as he started to run. But the smell went with him into the undergrowth and led him towards an abandoned well visible in the moss. He stopped a short distance away and covered his face with part of his shirt to protect himself, but filled his nostrils with his own fear instead. He didn't want to go any closer. His insides screamed at him to return to the safety of the harvester's cab, but his body would not obey. Slowly, slowly, his feet approached the well. A lid of greying wood covered the hole and when he lifted it off a cloud of flies rose up from the depths. He held his breath as he leaned over the opening. There was a rusty chain hanging down into the well and it disappeared in the shadows. He couldn't make out any water, only an impenetrable blackness. When he tugged at the chain he felt an unyielding weight. Whatever had been lowered into the hole would not be retrieved by him. The stench was so overpowering it was making him nauseous, and with a sudden need to retch he crouched in the moss and vomited up the food he had just eaten. When it was over he caught sight of the blood, dark patches that had been absorbed by the white lichen and spread over the stones. He recoiled so violently that he fell backwards onto the wet ground. Then he jumped to his feet and started running. By the time he reached the machine the sky was filled with black birds.

EARLY SUMMER 2002

She can already smell her new life. In the evenings, when she sits opposite her father at the kitchen table, everything is only pretend. Nothing gets to her any more. Her head is full of the future and she contemplates the wall of forest and counts the days and nights until she can be on the other side. Her father's pale eyes are already searching for her over the rim of his glasses, as if he senses she is leaving. That her head is full of freedom.

He searches her room while she is at school, rummaging through her storage boxes and secrets, leaving traces of his hands among her clothes and notebooks and in the concealed diary where she only writes things she wants him to read. Meaningless things.

The real secrets she keeps hidden in the forest. She walks in misleading circles before reaching the marshland, the springy ground a kind of protective moat to keep people out. In the shadow of the moose observation tower she sinks to her knees and crawls the last few metres. The anxiety throbs in her body as she hauls herself up the old ladder. Like a child in a treehouse she sits behind the gaping planks, waiting for her breathing to calm down. She shuffles over to the firing slot, peers out over her father's open countryside and imagines him walking there with his back turned to her. An invisible weapon rests in her hands and she raises the barrel and fires a shot in his direction. He drops to the wet ground. The wiry body jerks and thrashes like a fish on dry land. She shuts her eyes tight and sees it all play out in front of her until the carefree thrushes begin singing in the branches, gradually drawing her back to reality.

She looks for the loose plank in the wall, finds it and pushes her fingers under the dark wood. She prises out the treasure hiding there. She feels her heart pumping all the way to her fingertips as she undoes the tightly wrapped plastic – three bags in all to keep the moisture out. Inside are the bundles of notes. She weighs them in her hand and counts every single one as she has done so many times before. The blood is racing around her body and her fingers are trembling with longing for the outside world. Soon it will happen. Soon.

But the summer passes and the bundles still lie in their observation tower hideaway. Some kind of illness has overtaken her, an overwhelming tiredness and nausea that turns her inside out and robs her of her strength. Every night she makes the decision to get away at dawn, but when morning comes she is once again lying on the bathroom floor with the world spinning around her. Her father's shadow hovers outside the locked door.

What's wrong with you?

Working was like acting. Liam stood behind the till, sweating in his uniform shirt. He had buttoned it right to the top and the collar rubbed his newly shaven throat. In the dirty mirror of the staffroom he had almost looked like one of them, a normal person, but when he was standing behind the counter he found it hard to look customers in the eye. It sounded as if was repeating a line when he wished them a nice day. And he imagined they sneered at his scrubbed face and his outfit. They shouldn't let themselves be fooled so easily.

But Niila seemed satisfied at least and after the morning rush he came with coffee in a china mug.

'You learn fast.'

That was all he said, but Liam felt his throat contract and he took a gulp of scalding hot coffee to disguise how the praise had affected him. The work itself wasn't difficult, it was the people he wasn't used to.

It had all gone so quickly. He worked a trial weekend and on Monday morning Niila had called to ask if he could also work on weekdays. One of my staff has found herself in something of a crisis situation, he had said. Her old father has gone missing. Sure, said Liam, his heart in his throat. I'll come.

So here he was, sweating under the fluorescent lights and trying unsuccessfully to blend in. After lunch the customers were few and far between and most of them only wanted to pay for fuel. Niila showed him how to keep an eye on the pumps and make a note of the number plates. There were cameras but a pair of eyes was better. Niila had a calmness that spread to others. His voice was like the tranquil sigh of an ancient forest; it brought his pulse rate down.

'Do you smoke?' Niila asked.

'Sometimes.'

'You can take a cigarette break if you like, so long as you tell me.'

'I'm giving it up anyway.'

Niila pulled a face that suggested he didn't believe him.

'Don't be so hard on yourself, it won't work. We've all got to have some vices.'

He disappeared into the office leaving Liam alone behind the till, a simple gesture that confirmed he had passed the test. That he could be relied on.

She must have entered through the stockroom because he didn't hear her arrive. He was standing with his back to the counter, refilling the cigarette shelves, when suddenly there she was beside him, Vidar Björnlund's daughter. She was wearing a shabby jacket several sizes too big, and her face shone white above the collar. He could see the blue veins below the surface. She didn't look quite alive. A porcelain doll with empty eyes.

'Who are you?'

'I'm Liam. I work here.'

'Since when?'

'Since now.'

She didn't resemble her father, not at all. His eyes took in the shiny forehead, the lips, the thin hair she had tried to pull back into a ponytail. Not a hint of the old man. Maybe you couldn't compare the living with the dead.

She held out her hand. He fumbled with the cigarette packets, in a hurry to put them down. Her hand was freezing cold in his and the touch sent shivers down his spine. He had dreaded the moment when he would be forced to look her in the face, the fear that she would see everything he was keeping hidden inside.

'Liv Björnlund. But you knew that already.'

'Niila said you wouldn't be working this week.'

'Did he?'

'He said something about a crisis in the family, that your dad was missing.'

He saw her sway, lose her footing for a millisecond. But she recovered fast and leaned closer to him. Too close.

'I know who you are,' she whispered. Liam threw a look at the stockroom door behind her, searching for a way to escape. Her face was next to his as she stared right through him, and at every pore and scar in his flushed face. Fear took hold of him, fear that she might have seen him at Ödesmark when he was snooping around the run-down dump that was her home.

'You come in here and shoplift things with your brother,' she said.

'That was a long time ago.'

There was the shadow of a smile on her face.

'Don't worry, I won't cause any trouble. Niila has a weakness for things that need mending, and that includes people. Why do you think I ended up here?'

They smiled tentatively at each other. He looked down at her feet, her heavy men's boots, bigger than his own and covered in forest debris and mud. Her jeans were no better. The legs were wet and filthy and she smelled bad, a mixture of sweat and rotting hay. She really was a person in crisis, no mistake about it, and his guilty conscience was like a weight on his chest.

Perhaps she noticed, because she started to say something, but the sirens came out of nowhere and interrupted her. Through the streaked window they saw the two patrol cars with their blue lights flashing go past at such a speed the meltwater flew up like curtains around the tyres.

'What's going on?' Liv asked.

'I don't know.'

But she had already turned away. The boots squeaked against the floor as she ran to the door. Liam watched as she stopped by the pumps and squinted towards the church with her hand over her heart. The rain had turned the world dark and she looked small and pale under the lowering sky. She staggered as if she would collapse any second.

Niila came rushing out of the office.

'Holy shit, what's going on?'

Liam watched as Niila ran to the pumps and put a protective arm around Liv. She leaned against him heavily. But he stayed behind the till as a feeling of doom filled him. The police were driving north, towards Ödesmark, and deep inside he knew the waiting was over. The game was up.

He leaned on the counter and squeezed his eyes shut. Vidar was hiding behind his eyelids. Liam saw him clearly, the bloodless flesh and the black hole of the mouth that stuck up out of the moss, gaping at him. Maybe predators had got hold of him, ripped him to unrecognizable shreds. He knew it was impossible to lie out there untouched for any length of time. The forest looked after its dead.

He stood immobile as Liv and Niila came back into the shop. Niila led her gently between the shelves and held the stockroom door open. Before she left she turned to Liam and gave him a long, meaningful look, as if they shared a secret. As if she knew.

Her shoulders trembled with exhaustion each time the axe fell, yet she lifted it again and again. She split the logs with a fierce anger that echoed over the village. She didn't see him approach, not until he had come level with her and shouted at her to stop. A cold rain had started to fall but she hadn't noticed that, either. It was only when she let the axe fall for the last time that any feeling came back, the smarting in her back and the frozen rain on her neck. Simon laid a jacket around her shoulders and began to steer her towards the house and the warmth, as firmly as if she was an animal being locked up safely for the night. She limped over the wet gravel.

'I've got to do something while I'm waiting.'

She had already phoned Hassan from the filling station. He had a tone to his voice that suggested something was wrong, but he didn't want to talk about it over the phone. We'll come to you, was all he would say. But the minutes ticked by and they didn't come.

They sat in the kitchen in the dark and looked at the forest. There were no words, only anxiety hanging in the air between them. Liv went into the sitting room and filled a glass with Vidar's vodka. Back at the kitchen table she swallowed a few large mouthfuls and then pushed the glass over to Simon. He drank more greedily than she had expected. She wished he would say something, feel sorry for himself, call her pathetic – anything at all so long as it was something. The silence thudded unbearably against her eardrums and her heart was beating so wildly she thought her chest would explode.

The barrier was up and the rain fell like silvery spears in the headlights of the patrol car when it finally rolled up the drive. They met in the doorway. Hassan had removed his hat and his hair was dripping. A younger colleague stood like a shadow behind him. Their faces were stiff masks of grief; there was no need for them to say anything.

'He's dead, isn't he? Dad's dead.'

'It's probably best we come in,' said Hassan. 'So we can sit down.'

His words were almost drowned out by the rain and she took a deep breath. *This is it*, she thought. *This is really it.* As she stepped aside to let them in her legs threatened to give way. She leaned heavily on Simon, who was also shaking. She found it hard to keep her eyes focused, hard to stand upright, but she didn't want to sit down. She wanted to scream at them to go away, they didn't need to say anything, she didn't want to know. She already knew.

'Have you found him?' Simon asked.

'We have found Vidar,' Hassan said, and his voice sounded

distant. 'We have found him and I'm afraid he is dead. A forestry worker came across him at lunchtime, just over five kilometres north of Ödesmark, in the village of Gråträsk.'

His hair dripped as he spoke. Liv felt her throat thicken and her tongue glue itself to the roof of her mouth. Gråträsk, what was Vidar doing there? That couldn't be right. She looked at Simon. All the colour had left his face and his chin was trembling. She reached for his hand while the news sank in, pictured Vidar lying out there in the forest with his eyes facing to the sky and his body dusted with snow. She pictured the birds standing on his head, picking out the dead eyes.

'What happened?' she asked. 'How did he die?'

'We can't go into any details yet, but there's no question someone took his life.'

She nodded. Her throat felt oddly tight, her body heavy. She threw an arm around Simon, felt him shaking, heard his teeth chattering in the silence. The floor felt spongy under her feet as she got up to fetch a blanket from the sitting room. She draped it round his shuddering body. The police followed her movements, as if they were afraid she would do something unpredictable. She stroked Simon's back while the fear gnawed in her stomach and made her angry.

'Can't you see what you're doing?' she said to the police officers. 'You're scaring my boy.'

Vidar was gone. He was dead. The words rang in her ears but she couldn't take them in. The moon was shining over the forest and she found herself staring into the trees, still searching for him. She could see him there, behind the sombre police officers, deep inside the forest, smiling at her.

'Is there anyone you want us to call?' Hassan asked. 'A friend or relative?'

'We haven't got anyone else. There's only us two.'

The words saddened him, she could tell, and it was clear he was feeling sorry for them. Calmly he explained what the police would do, how they would look for the scene of the crime and try to establish Vidar's last movements. Although she felt confused Liv nodded, trying to hide the chaos inside her head. When Simon went to the bathroom she had nothing to hold on to. The floor rocked under her feet, the pine table floated. She looked at Hassan and his colleague and made an effort to show she was taking in everything they said, so they wouldn't notice the exhilaration inside her.

Naturally she couldn't say she didn't believe them, that she still expected him to walk into the room any second. She tried to recall the farms in Gråträsk – Big-Henrik's and Granlund's, the only two remaining – but she couldn't picture Vidar there however hard she tried. Her gaze fell on the rowan tree. She thought she saw an empty noose dangling in the wind.

'Did he hang himself?' she whispered, while Simon was still out of the room.

Hassan merely shook his head.

'As I said before, his death was not self-inflicted.'

She understood the words but couldn't take them in. She didn't want to.

'My mum hanged herself,' she said, nodding towards the rowan and its branches reaching skywards.

Hassan followed her gaze but she knew he didn't understand. He was too young, it had happened long before his time. It was 30 April, Walpurgis Night, when Kristina Björnlund hanged herself from the rowan. Liv couldn't remember, yet the image was burned into her brain. The bridal gown trailing in the snow and the rotting leaves, the wind tugging at the long dark hair. The many times she had wished it was Vidar who had left her and not her mother.

Simon was in the bathroom for a long time. Hassan asked if there was any medication in there, something that could harm him. Liv shook her head.

'He wants to cry alone.'

Vidar never had any time for boys who cried. From when he was a kid Simon learned to take himself off when things got too much. But she didn't say that. The police officers thought she was mad. She saw their look of concern, their worry that she hadn't properly understood. Because it wasn't about a hanging. Vidar hadn't taken his own life, someone had killed him. The room spun when the reality hit her.

'I want to see him,' she said finally. 'Can I?'

*

The patrol car drove slowly past the filling station window, glided in between the pumps and pulled up. Liam looked around for quick ways of escape. Niila was piling up a display of apples, his cheeks as shiny and red as the fruit. When he looked at Liam his face broke into a smile.

'How's it going over there?'

'Good.'

'Just ask if there's anything you want to know.'

He was too kind, almost as if he was planning to hurt him somehow. A distraction technique before revealing his true self. Liam felt the hairs on his arms stand on end. It had been a mistake to think he could work here.

A police officer got out of the car. Liam recognized him; he was one of the younger officers, one who still had something to prove. He raised a hand to Liam and waved, as if they knew each other. Liam returned the gesture stiffly, trying to remind himself that he was one of them now, one of those people who worked and paid tax. One of those who could trust friendliness.

The customers could tell by looking at him that he didn't quite fit in, but they were kind and encouraging anyway. He was like a child learning to ride a bike – the best thing was to do it and not think about it too much. Even so, that's what he did. Think too much. He had counted seventy-five paces to the stockroom door, to the car and freedom. He could overturn shelves as he ran, make an obstacle course of tins and shiny apples. Nobody would catch up with him if he set his mind to it, not Niila or the police. The old hideaway in the forest was there, waiting for him, the one he and Gabriel had built at a time when there was a lot they needed to hide from. Before they grew up and realized that everything would only get worse as the years passed.

The seconds became minutes, an eternity passed before the officer replaced the nozzle. He paid by card and made no attempt to come into the shop. He simply took a last look at Liam and then slid into his seat and drove off. That was it. Over by the fruit display Niila was whistling, unaware of the tension filling the air between them. How close it had been.

His phone vibrated in his pocket, demanding attention. He was worried that it could be his mum calling to say something had happened to Vanja, but between customers he sneaked a look and saw it was Gabriel. He called over and over again, as if it was crucial. Liam didn't bother answering.

'Is that buzzing coming from you?' Niila asked.

'No.'

'Is it the girlfriend?'

'I haven't got a girlfriend.'

'You can take a break if you want to answer.'

'Thanks, there's no need.'

'Don't forget to take a break, will you? It's important to clear your head every so often.'

But by the time his shift finished Liam still hadn't taken a break. As he walked through the stockroom his head was muzzy from all the new impressions. He passed a shelf of car batteries and found himself wondering how much he could sell them for. Then he felt ashamed. He lit a cigarette and undid the top buttons of his shirt before opening the door. The stink of rubbish met him as he stepped out into the dank evening.

The blow came before his eyes had adjusted to the dark. A blinding pain on the bridge of his nose, quickly followed by warm blood. He fumbled for the door but it had already slammed shut behind him.

When the next blow fell he had already put up his arms to protect himself. Two hands gripped his neck and smacked his head against the rough brick wall. Thick blood ran over his mouth and chin and down his throat.

✳

They would be allowed to see Vidar but not to hear how he had died. The police didn't want to give away any details because of the investigation, and Liv thought perhaps it was for the best. The critical thing was to see him, to reassure herself that he really was dead.

She clasped Simon's hand in hers and felt his body shaking on the seat beside her. Or was she the one shaking? The darkness stung her sleepless eyes but she hadn't shed any tears.

The forest thinned out and the town took over. The street lights and signs were intrusive and blotted out the stars. They drove over a bridge and she saw the river snaking below. A single walker huddled under an umbrella and on the other side the neon lights of a fast-food joint dazzled her. She clouded the window with her breath and thought to herself that he couldn't be here. Dead or alive, it didn't matter – Vidar Björnlund hated the town.

They drove into an underground car park and got out. A sluggish lift sucked them between floors and Simon still hadn't let go of her hand. His face was ashen and impassive under the harsh lighting. They walked out of the lift and down a long corridor lined with closed doors. Their footsteps echoed and the smell of sickness and disinfectant grew stronger and more suffocating. They stopped outside a pair of white swing doors.

Hassan led them into a room full of gleaming surfaces and stained tiles that made the walls look like they were bleeding. A long row of small square doors ran along one wall and the sight made Liv choke. Her fingers ached around Simon's, their damp skin was welded together.

'Are you perfectly sure you can handle this?'

'I want to see Grandad.'

A dark-haired woman in blue scrubs appeared.

'Follow me.'

Liv felt every muscle in her body tense up as they went through a door. There was no smell in there and that surprised her. She wondered how they had managed to eradicate the stench of death. Vidar lay stretched out on a trolley of stainless steel. She held her breath when she saw him. It was a husk rather than a body, the skin grey and bloodless, but there was no disputing the fact that it was Vidar. His face looked damaged, full of small cuts and scrapes that hadn't been there when he was alive, as if a wild animal had got its claws into him. A white sheet covered his abdomen and legs but she imagined she could see the damage underneath – peeled-back skin and a dark hole where his heart had been.

His hands, covered in a web of blue veins, lay soft and still at his sides. Cautiously she reached out a hand and touched his fingers. They were no longer painful claws. Death had straightened him out, made him flexible and compliant. Made him better.

Simon began sobbing beside her, uncontrollable sobs that rang between the sterile walls, and it made her heart break. She pulled him close, held his face to her chest so that he didn't have to see the body, although she couldn't take her eyes from it. She didn't cry, scream or curse. She merely stood there with her eyes on her dead father, feeling a silent jubilation building inside her. She nodded at Hassan.

'That's him,' she said. 'That's Dad.'

✻

'So this is where you work,' hissed Gabriel. 'Of all places, you chose this one? With her?'

'It was Niila who gave me the job. It's got nothing to do with her.'

There was the backdraught of another blow but this time he ducked and fell into a lingering snowdrift. He felt the cold penetrate his clothes. Gabriel stood over him, his jerky movements proof that he was speeding. Liam pinched his nose to stem the flow of blood and glanced at the stockroom door to make sure they hadn't been heard. If Niila saw him now, in this condition, he would have second thoughts and sack him for sure.

Gabriel kicked him.

'Get in the car,' he said. 'We're going for a little drive.'

Gabriel navigated Liam into the forest, away from people, along potholed roads that no longer led anywhere. The trees gave off a raw dampness that covered the car in glistening condensation, erasing all sharp contours. Gabriel drummed his fingers on his jeans, casting thoughtful looks at Liam.

'I can't trust you,' he kept repeating. 'You never think. You never use your brain.'

Liam pictured the old man. It had gone so fast, like snuffing out a candle. A few seconds, that's all it took, and a life was over.

He kept an eye on Gabriel's jacket and whatever was hiding underneath. On Gabriel's hands resting on his thighs, the itchy fingers that kept returning to his pockets, getting out cigarettes and a lighter. Every time he did that Liam's heart lurched.

'It was a shock, get it? Going past, seeing you standing there in her place.'

'It's got nothing to do with her.'

'Guilty conscience giving you trouble now? You feel sorry for her.'

'I don't know what you're talking about.'

Liam drove too fast and had trouble taking the bends. The road sloped upwards, the forest thinned out and the trees became stunted, making room for the sky that opened out dark and starless above their heads. It was past Vanja's bedtime. He wouldn't be able to say goodnight to her.

They reached the crest where the road ended. Night swallowed up the view and they could only imagine mile after mile of forest and lakes and felled land below them. They could just as easily be surrounded by a lake, black and still. A few lights in the distance showed evidence of life, otherwise there was nothing. Liam recognized the place. They had come here when they were little, the times their dad had put them in the car and told their mum it was all over and he was taking the kids and leaving, once and for all. A six-pack of beer on the bonnet as his dad flung out an arm. *You could build a house up here,* he'd said, *and no bastard would ever look down on you.*

Liam parked and they simultaneously opened the doors and let the cold air flow over them. He took a quick look at himself in the rear-view mirror, a moustache of blood on his upper lip but no major damage done.

'What are we doing here?'

Gabriel didn't answer. When he opened his jacket and brought out a packet of cigarettes he didn't try to hide the firearm. Liam fixed his eyes on the valley below and tried to assess the distance to the edge of the forest, persuading himself he could flee when the time was right. Darkness would hide him.

The dull throb of an engine interrupted his thoughts. After a while they saw a tired old car driving up the slope, a cold white light between the trees. Liam recognized the car, the broken headlight and rusted body. It was a miracle it still worked. Darkened windows hid his view but he already knew who was concealed behind them.

'What do we say?'

'You won't say shit, you've done enough already.'

The driver's door opened and the figure of Juha slowly appeared in the darkness. He left the headlights on and his catlike body walked in a wide circle towards them, approaching from the side. The wispy beard hung down over his chest and he was dressed in bulky clothes with room to conceal a great deal. Gabriel got out of the car and signalled to Liam to come after him. The pain from his rotting tooth was excruciating.

Juha stood with the blinding headlights behind him so they couldn't see his face. His skinny legs were restless on the gravel. Gabriel walked over and handed him the goods, keeping one hand in front of his face to shield his eyes from the lights. Juha snatched the bag and stepped back. He didn't bother inspecting the contents the way he normally did. His movements were swift and unpredictable, and the whites of his eyes glowed in the darkness.

'I want to know what happened,' he said.

'What are you on about?' Gabriel asked.

'Out at Ödesmark. I want to know what happened.'

Juha took a step forward and spat in their direction. The wind tore at his hair and filled the night with the sour smell of him. Liam kept to one side, the fear turning his guts to water as he watched Gabriel flex his muscles. He was nervous about what would happen if Juha said the wrong things, if there was trouble.

'There's two months' supply in that bag,' Gabriel said. 'Then you find someone else to supply you.'

Slowly Juha slid a hand inside his jacket. Time stood still while he took the notes from an inside pocket and held them out to them. He drew his hand back as if he was afraid he would be bitten.

'I'm a solitary man,' he said. 'But I can't avoid the birdsong, however hard I try. And now the birds are whispering that Vidar Björnlund is dead. They're saying someone killed him. And I'm guessing you two know something about it?'

Gabriel counted the notes and pretended not to hear. Liam stayed just outside the circle of light, looking out over the forest and the sky and the black valley below. He wanted to tell Juha to get in his car and drive away before it turned nasty, before Gabriel lost his patience.

'Unbelievable,' said Gabriel. 'This evening he's parting with the whole amount. We're honoured.'

He stuffed the money into his jeans pocket and nodded mockingly at Juha.

'Those are some of my best plants. They'll soon kill any paranoid ideas you've got in your head, I promise you. And now I think you should piss off home to your stinking hovel and forget we ever existed.'

But Juha stood his ground, swaying on the gravel. He was breathing as if the night air was suffocating him.

'It was me who sent you to Ödesmark,' he said. 'And now I want to know what happened. You owe me that much.'

Gabriel laughed and the hideous sound rang over the valley. He looked at Liam and gestured with his head.

'Get in the car,' he ordered. 'I want to talk to Juha alone.'

Unwillingly, Liam went back to the car. His pulse was racing and a feeling that the ground was giving way under him made his legs unsteady. He got behind the wheel, wanting to drive away and leave them there, but Gabriel had taken the key like he always did, almost as if he knew Liam was only one step away from turning his back and fleeing. He slammed the door and wiped his hands on his jeans. He felt for the knife tucked under the seat, but left it there. If there was a fight he would stay out of it.

He watched as Gabriel walked up to Juha. They put their heads so close together he could no longer see their faces. There was only Gabriel's hand waving in the air as he talked, his white fingers like moths in the darkness. Juha's head moved as if in agreement or understanding. Liam opened the window a crack and leaned closer but he couldn't make out what was being said.

Finally, Gabriel took a step backwards and patted Juha's

arm. Juha pulled off his hat and scratched his head before putting it back on. He seemed considerably calmer now. He took a long look at Liam before raising his arm in a wave. Liam jerked back as if he had been lashed with a whip, and waved clumsily in return. He saw Gabriel and Juha shake hands, all the tension and enmity between them gone. Whatever they had said to each other, they had made a deal.

By the time Juha eventually walked back to his car, Liam's ears were screaming.

*

Hassan and his colleagues repeated their questions over and over again and were still not satisfied with the answers. *Did Vidar have any enemies? Was there anyone who wanted to harm him? Had they had a row?* Liv and Simon had to sit in separate rooms and answer the same questions until the words became an unintelligible muddle. Everywhere there was the jangle of keyrings. The house had become a prison with doors that were not allowed to be closed. Light had to be shone into every corner, every key had to be handed over. The police wanted access to the car, the gun cabinet and the outhouses. Strangers' hands searched cupboards and shelves, everything was exposed to the merciless spring sunshine – every photograph and valuable document, and Kristina's nightdress that still hung, ghost-like, at the back of Vidar's wardrobe. Liv sat with her arm around her son and together they created a small unassailable island of tranquillity. With no key.

As soon as the police left Felicia was there, like a wedge between them. She slipped through the front door and headed for the stairs to Simon's room, ignoring Liv completely. Like a restless spirit she moved through the unlit house and Liv played along, pretending not to see or hear. Then she stood for a long time on the dark landing, listening for their voices behind the closed door, the feeling of loneliness like a heavy weight.

When she couldn't bear it any longer she knocked on the shabby door and before they had time to answer she opened it slightly. Inside, Felicia was sitting with her back against the yellowing wallpaper and Simon's head in her lap. His blotchy face was turned towards the computer and Felicia was running her fingers through his hair. Liv coughed to attract their attention.

'Felicia,' she said. 'I didn't know you were here.'

'Where else would I be?'

The same defiant look as that day by the lake, the same rebellious smile as when her feet were balancing on the ice floe.

'Are you hungry?'

They exchanged a long look before shaking their heads, united in their resistance.

'What are you watching?' she asked.

'Just a film,' said Simon.

Liv stood in the doorway, clasping the door handle and trying to think of something else to say, something that would attract their attention. More than anything she wanted to go into the room and sit with them, retrieve the bottle she could see under the bed and knock back a few large mouthfuls. But it was so apparent there was no place for her, that she wasn't welcome, and all she could do was slowly close the door and return to the silent kitchen.

She lit Vidar's pipe and half-opened the window while she smoked. The wind stirred the trees and carried with it a choir of familiar voices. She could pick out several of her neighbours in the noise and it sounded as if they were close by. She went into the hall and kept the pipe in her mouth while she put on her shoes and jacket, and then took the key from the hook and locked the door on the youngsters. It was the first time she had ever locked the front door and the movement felt stiff and alien, the key unused to the lock. Pulling up her hood she let the voices lead her into the forest.

They had gathered by the lake, Douglas and Eva and Karl-Erik, along with two figures sitting with their backs to her. A fire was crackling and sending sparks into the sky. She stayed on the forest edge for a while to gather her thoughts, but Douglas caught sight of her and beckoned her over. His face was shiny and red in the light from the flames.

'Liv, come and sit with us. You shouldn't be on your own at a time like this.'

Everyone's eyes were on her as she reluctantly approached. Johnny was also there and he stood up to make room for her in the warmth. He tried to take her hand but she ignored him. He folded his arms, tucking his hands in his armpits, and she could see he was hurt. But it couldn't be helped. If she allowed anyone to hold her now she would never let them go. Everything inside her would give way and come pouring out. The entire village would be filled with her shame and relief, and the feeling she still could not express in words. The feeling that it was over now. That life could begin at last.

'Why are you sitting here?' she asked.

'We're trying to work out what the hell is going on in our village,' said Douglas, in a voice that carried over the spluttering flames. His eyes were fixed meaningfully on Johnny. 'A man is dead and someone has to be held responsible.'

Liv looked at their faces, serious and determined in the firelight. Only Serudia showed any sign of sympathy. Her cloudy eyes looked mournful and her lips trembled with emotion. Liv put the pipe in her pocket; she regretted coming. Company had never given her comfort before and it wouldn't now. She could hear Vidar's mocking voice among the spruce trees, heard him curse them one by one with that hate that verged on the insane. Hate was his most passionate emotion.

'The police have searched the entire place,' she said. 'But they haven't given me any answers.'

'They've searched our farm too,' said Douglas, and he spat on the ground. 'It's almost as if they think we've killed one of our own.'

The words jarred inside her head. It astonished her that all of a sudden he was showing such an affinity with Vidar that he called him one of their own, since he certainly hadn't shown such affection while Vidar lived. And Vidar would have protested furiously at that kind of talk, she knew. But now she had been left alone and protests weren't for her. It felt uncomfortable enough to be sitting around a fire among people she had learned to avoid. People who had despised Vidar, never mind what they were saying now.

Karl-Erik raised a hip flask to his lips and took a large swig before passing it round.

Silence spread through the group. Liv felt their enquiring glances as she sat beside Johnny, as if they knew there was something going on between them. The newcomer and Vidar's daughter, that was the kind of thing that got tongues wagging. When the hip flask reached her she took a large gulp and felt the warmth fill her body.

She saw Vidar in the flames, and despite seeing him at the morgue it wasn't the face of his corpse that followed her now. It was his hands, the wedding ring embedded in his liver-spotted skin, and the withered fingers that reached out for her. She recalled the spring when she had learned to ride a bike. She had fallen off and grazed her face, and Vidar had licked his hands and washed her cheeks with his own saliva. Licked her clean the way wild animals do with their young. The wind in the pine canopy carried his voice, drunken and pleading. *If you leave me, I don't know what I'll do.*

The others chatted about the cars that drove through Ödesmark day and night, despite the fact that the winter car-testing season was over. Surely they had something to do with Vidar's death, Eva said. The unknown drivers who didn't belong there.

Liv thought of the car she had seen the morning he disappeared, the black car that had been close to driving into the ditch. Had she mentioned that to the police? She couldn't remember.

It was too hot by the fire. Her collar itched and Johnny insisted on sitting too close. She knew this was how it worked in a normal world, that people sought protection and comfort from others, but closeness had the opposite effect on her. It made her edgy and restless, and caused the itching to flare up. She got up abruptly. The alcohol had reached her bloodstream and made her feel light on her feet.

'I left Simon and Felicia back at the house,' she said. 'I shouldn't have done that.'

It was an excuse no one could object to. The chilly air cooled her scorched cheeks as she headed for the forest. Plunging in among the trees was like diving deep into a cold well. She stood for a while and filled her lungs, noticing the talking grow louder behind her, their cries chasing after her in the darkness. She shouldn't be alone, they shouted, not at a time like this. There was a desperate ring to their voices that made her go faster.

The forest was filled with pale apparitions in the beam of the headlights. The gravel road twisted unpredictably through the blackness, forcing Liam to hold the wheel with both hands. He wanted to call his mum, to hear her say Vanja was asleep and all was fine, but there was no reception. I've got to get home, he repeated to Gabriel, but Gabriel wasn't listening. He was slumped in the passenger seat, smoking and silent, lifting a hand now and then to show Liam which direction to take. When Liam asked where they were going there was no answer. He felt a growing paranoia that he was on his way to his own execution, but he tried to shake it off, persuading himself it was ridiculous.

'What did you say to Juha?' he asked eventually.

'Nothing you need worry about.'

'He's unreliable. If he decides to talk, we're done for.'

Gabriel blew smoke in his face.

'Juha won't talk.'

'And how do you know that?'

'The guy lives in a fucking hovel, for God's sake. He'd die rather than talk to the cops. And let's be honest, who would listen to him?'

The gravel road became uneven tarmac, and the potholes and juddering made Liam's head ache. He bit the inside of his cheek until he felt the taste of blood on his tongue. He sensed water beside the car now, an opening in the trees in which the crescent moon was reflected. They didn't encounter another vehicle – nobody was out driving at night – but now he recognized where they were. Only five more kilometres and he would be home in Kallbodan. All he needed to do was keep calm, focus on the road and not cause a fight. Soon he would be at home with Vanja. He could already see her snuggled down in his old childhood bedroom, surrounded by threadbare soft toys and his mum's stones. He would make up a bed for himself on the floor and sleep to the sound of her breathing.

But Gabriel slapped his shoulder, refusing to leave him alone.

'Stop at this lay-by up ahead.'

'Why?'

'Stop, I said.'

The wheel became slippery under his hands. Stopping was the last thing he wanted to do, but if he didn't there would be trouble. Liam slowed down and tried to hide the desperate feeling of apprehension racing through his body.

The lay-by had an oblong wooden building with toilets and a map of the area at one end. They had spent a lot of time here when they were younger, spraying graffiti on the walls and giving misleading directions to lost tourists. A few years earlier a foreign berry-picker had been shot here. Rumours about the incident had spread wildly but the police never found the perpetrator.

A light came on when Liam swung in and parked. One of the toilet doors was open and swinging on its hinges. A shiver ran down his back.

'I've got to get home,' he said. 'Mum will be starting to wonder where the hell I've got to.'

'Let her wonder.'

Gabriel held the pack of cigarettes under Liam's chin, forcing them on him. The scar on his lip shone in the dim light but his eyes were empty, as empty as the night outside. Liam put a cigarette in his mouth and switched off the engine. He was weighed down by a feeling of doom as he got out of the car. He heard the river rushing beside them, swollen and full of life.

A narrow path led to the building and Gabriel nodded to him to go first. As Gabriel followed he tossed his head, and the bones in his neck cracked. The sound made Liam shudder. He stopped at the bench by the toilets. A roll of wet toilet paper lay on the ground and there was a stink of piss in the air. He didn't want to sit down. His lip stung where Gabriel had hit him and the swelling made it difficult to smoke. He wondered how he would explain it to his mum and Vanja. To Niila and the customers.

Gabriel leaned against the dirty wall, a dark gleam in his eye.

'Remember that berry-picker who got his head blown off here?' he asked.

'Yeah, obviously.'

'Christ,' said Gabriel. 'Brain matter all over the wall. That's a sight you never forget as long as you live.'

His head began to pound. There were rumours it was a drugs deal that had gone wrong and that was why the picker had lost his life, but this was the first time Gabriel had hinted that he'd had anything to do with it. That he had been there. Liam smoked his cigarette and tried not to show the turmoil that was taking over his body.

'What are we doing out here, anyway?' he said, and spat. 'It's bloody freezing.'

Gabriel's teeth glinted in the darkness.

'I just want you to know I've got my eye on you,' he said. 'Many eyes. I don't care if you are my brother – one foot wrong and you're in big trouble. Get it?'

Perhaps it was the fear, or the tiredness, but Liam felt the laughter bubble up in his throat and heard it ring out before he could stop himself. A hoarse, nervous laugh. He flicked the half-smoked cigarette in Gabriel's direction, hoping it would burn him. Gabriel lurched forward but Liam grabbed his neck in the crook of his arm. Then they were lying on the damp ground, punching and pulling at each other as they had done so many times before. He knew how Gabriel fought; he wouldn't hesitate to use teeth or any kind of weapon, so long as he got the upper hand. The drugs had weakened him but his lack of inhibition made him unpredictable.

Liam found himself on his back with Gabriel's hands round his throat. The cold from the wet earth seeped through his clothes and skin and right into his bones. He couldn't breathe, couldn't see properly. Gabriel's shadow and the tree canopy flickered above him. There was a gurgling sound that could only be coming from him. He saw Vanja, her gappy smile as bright as the sunshine. With a roar he managed to wrench Gabriel off him and get on his feet. He aimed a kick at Gabriel's chest that made him tumble into the bushes. The anger raged inside him. They had fought many times before, given each other concussion and broken fingers, but he couldn't ever remember feeling such fury. He saw Gabriel stand up, shake, and brush himself down. He was bleeding freely from a cut on his temple but it didn't seem to bother him. Instead, he smiled into the darkness.

'I swear you're getting more like Dad every day,' Liam said, wiping his mouth.

'Go to hell.'

Liam put a hand to his aching throat and spat. He kept his distance but he was still trembling with anger. Gabriel lit another cigarette and began walking towards the car, signalling that the fighting was over for now. He opened the door on the driver's side and nodded at Liam.

'I've got my eye on you,' he said. 'Don't forget.'

Then he slammed the door shut and started the engine. Liam stood in the darkness and the smell of piss and watched him drive away.

∗

She was almost back home before she noticed someone was following her. She heard the breathing, hoarse and laboured, long before she saw him, and sank onto the veranda to wait for her stalker to appear. Karl-Erik staggered out from between the trees. He stood with his hands on his knees for some time before regaining enough energy to straighten up and look her in the face.

'Anyone would think you were running for your life,' he said. 'You're faster than a bloody ferret.'

'What do you want?'

'I only wanted to make sure you got home safely.'

Karl-Erik leaned heavily on the veranda railing and the rotten wood groaned loudly under his weight. In the darkness he looked younger, the wrinkles smoothed out and his eyes bright. Liv looked down, scowling, and tried to control her breathing. For a moment she had imagined it was Vidar who was chasing her.

'Vidar is dead,' said Karl-Erik, as if he could read her thoughts. 'Nothing will be the same again.'

'I saw him at the morgue. I saw him with my own eyes. But it still feels like he's just gone for a walk, as if he'll come strolling out of the bushes any minute.'

'It'll take time for the truth to sink in. You have to get over the shock first.'

She didn't dare tell him how empty she felt, how unreal it all was in spite of her seeing the corpse. Vidar like an anaemic doll, laid out in front of her. She hadn't cried yet, not when Hassan gave her the news nor later at the morgue. The only thing she felt was a growing sense of relief inside, and skin that had stopped itching.

Karl-Erik put one foot on the step and leaned his weight on it. She wondered if she should invite him in. It was probably time to start behaving like other people, now Vidar had gone. It might be best to make friends with the village before she left it, but she always felt wary when Karl-Erik was around. It reminded her of the anxiety Vidar gave her, a feeling of wanting to crawl out of your own skin.

'We've got to stick together now,' he said. 'Whether we want to or not.'

'How are we related? Remind me,' she asked, although she knew.

Karl-Erik didn't answer immediately and at first she thought he hadn't heard. He was staring at the door behind her.

'Vidar's mother and my mother were half-sisters. They had the same father. But they didn't know each other, as far as I can make out. Your grandmother was illegitimate. She was never allowed to come to my mother's home.'

'Is that why you and Dad never got on?'

'Oh no, our crap went deeper than that.'

'What was it about?'

'It's a long story and I'm tired. But drop in one day if you feel like it, and I'll tell you more.'

The sombre note in his voice made her get up and reach for

the door, and the old boards creaked under her. She wanted to ask why Vidar had called him a bad loser, to find out what had been lost, but it felt as if he was standing out there in the darkness, listening to them. As if he might still vent his rage on her if she said too much.

'One thing you should know,' said Karl-Erik, pointing at her. 'Blood ties don't make a family — shame does. It's shame that binds us together.'

He was looking straight at her and it was a few moments before she could catch her breath again, before her body could act normally. Somehow the words branded her, came too close to home. She wrapped her arms around her body, trying to cover herself.

'I don't know what you're talking about.'

Karl-Erik gave a sad smile.

'I think you do.'

A gust of wind carried with it the others' voices and the smell of their fire. Karl-Erik leaned closer and whispered, as if he was afraid his voice would also carry too far on the night air.

'How much do you really know about that man?'

'Who?'

'Your tenant. Johnny, or whatever his name is.'

'You wouldn't know he was there. He works, pays his rent and keeps to himself most of the time. I've nothing against him.'

Karl-Erik looked thoughtful and scratched his beard. It seemed as if he was going to argue but instead he took his foot off the step and got out the hip flask. He took a few mouthfuls without taking his eyes off her.

'You must be careful who you let in,' he whispered again. 'None of us is safe now. All we can do is keep our eyes and ears open and not trust a blasted soul. Not even each other.'

✳

Liam stumbled through the pitch-black forest. The moon had disappeared behind a cloud and hail whipped his battered face as he ran. His trainers squelched and the freezing cold jeans clung to his legs, but despite that he was sweating. This wasn't the first time Gabriel had abandoned him in the middle of nowhere, but he swore it would be the last.

The farmhouses were silent and in darkness by the time he reached Kallbodan. The dogs barked long before they saw him and his mum was standing at the window, looking out into the darkness as he ran into the yard. When he stepped into the hall she was there already.

'Oh my God, what's happened?'

'It was Gabriel,' was all he said.

That was enough. She didn't ask any more questions, didn't want to know. Instead, she reached out for his wet clothes and draped a bath towel around him, as she had done many times before. She led him to the kitchen and took a moose steak from the freezer to put on his swollen lip. He asked about Vanja although he knew she would have gone to bed much earlier. His mum lit the wood burner and he sat on the chair closest to the flames, feeling the warmth spread through his frozen joints, making them ache. Perhaps it had something to do with his silence, or the way he was breathing, because his mum stood behind him, wrapped her thin arms around his chest and rested her cheek against his. He didn't try to stop her although she was holding him so tightly it hurt his aching body.

'Gabriel took my car,' he said. 'Can I borrow yours tomorrow to get to work?'

'You know you can.'

'Thanks.'

'You know what I've said,' she whispered. 'Just because you're brothers doesn't mean you have to spend time together.'

After he had recovered he crept upstairs. Vanja lay fast asleep in his old bedroom, hugging a toy rabbit that had once been his. He fetched a quilt and a pillow and made a bed for himself on the floor. Anxiety tormented him as he lay listening to the breathing of his sleeping daughter. He thought of all the evenings he hadn't come home, all the days he had been dead to the world while Vanja sat with his mum and waited for him to wake up. Her joy when he finally did, as if he was the best dad in the world, despite everything. He tried to console himself by thinking he had changed his ways, that it was a long time since he'd missed a bedtime or spent a whole day sleeping, but the shame and the realization that he didn't deserve her gave him no peace.

Thoughts swirled in his head. All the nights people phoned, needing dope. He always met customers down by the road, never let them near the house, never let them see Vanja. But those days were over. He'd stopped keeping the goods at home. People soon figured that out and now they called Gabriel instead. He was the one who ran the cannabis farm, took care of everything. Liam had less and less to do with it as the months passed, tried to cut himself off from his former life one day at a time. The money had dried up, but that didn't matter. The dirty money ran through his fingers anyway, it was never enough for anything. And he was clean these days. He might take something for his nerves occasionally, but not like before.

Both the police and social services had been watching him. If he didn't get his life in order they would take Vanja away from him. It was only a matter of time. If it hadn't been for his mum they would have done it long ago but she had always been there, propping him up, stepping in when he wasn't there, when he went off the rails. He didn't know why she did it, or even how she coped. He only knew it was thanks to her that he still had Vanja. But not even his mum could save him now, if the truth about the night in Ödesmark got out. The game would be up then, his daughter would grow up without him. Silent tears ran down his cheeks when he thought about it. How bloody close he was to losing her.

＊

Liv knew the key to Vidar's secrets was in his bedroom, but she didn't know where to start looking. She could sense his disapproval burning her fingers as she rifled through his abandoned possessions, a feeling of doing something forbidden, pulling out his boxes and poking among everything hiding there. Cheap pipe tobacco, a large collection of Sami knives, a stainless-steel watch he had stopped wearing long ago, and everywhere visible trails left in the dust by police officers carrying out their search. A hopeless feeling that she wouldn't find anything they had already got their hands on.

Vidar was still present in the room. No matter how much fresh air she let in, the sweet sickly odour of him lingered in the faded wallpaper. She filled a bucket with hot soapy water and began scrubbing the walls and the floor, leaving the window wide open as she worked to let in the smell of the forest.

When she pulled out the bedside table she discovered his diary that had fallen down in the dust behind it. The black diary that Vidar carried around like a bible, but that no one was allowed to touch. He bought a new one every year and kept the old ones in a box in the cellar. When she was younger she had secretly read them from time to time but she soon realized that when you had read one, you had read them all. So barren was his life.

She put down the floor cloth and began leafing through the diaries, hearing Vidar's protests in the silence. The pages were covered in brief notes of everything he had done each day: gave Liv a lift to work, smoked the salmon, repaired the hinge on the outhouse door, collected Liv. Taking and collecting Liv were the most frequently occurring entries, the rest of the daily activities had to be fitted around them. On some days that was all he did. It was a miserable existence, captured in spidery, old-fashioned handwriting.

Here and there he had even made notes that proved his continual need for control.

Liv left home 01.16, back 04.32.

Liv went jogging, gone over three hours.

Simon's bike outside Modig's farm 21.22.
Liv left home 00.12, back 03.31.
Saw two men on our land 02.13.

That last entry caught her attention. He had mentioned wolves on their land, not men. The observation was dated 25 April, one week before he disappeared. She put the diary down and held her head in her hands. She should have understood. Vidar always called men something else – they were monsters, dogs, vultures. Never people.

She began to tap in Hassan's number but regretted it halfway through. Vidar's notes were too shameful, they revealed too much about their life, his obsessions. They were a logbook of a sick existence and were not for other people's eyes.

✳

Vanja was leaning over him when he woke up. Her eyes were so close to his they melted into one.

'Your mouth is all black,' she whispered.

'I fell over and hurt myself, that's all.'

'It looks really scary.'

He gently touched his face. The blood had coagulated in a great scab on his lower lip. His head thudded as he sat up and it felt as if his entire body would explode. Vanja laid her hands gently on his cheeks.

'Shall I kiss it better?'

'Yes, you do that.'

She pursed her lips as if she was about to blow out candles on a birthday cake. Liam shut his eyes and let her plant a kiss on his face. He sat absolutely still and swallowed hard to stop the tears that were stinging his eyes. He wondered what he was going to say to Niila at work, what the customers would think when they saw him. He was worried he'd get fired.

A man's voice downstairs made them both jump. Vanja's eyes widened.

'Gabriel's here,' she said.

'Sounds like it.'

Before he had time to react she had let go of him and was running on her bare feet to the stairs. She ran down them, although she knew she shouldn't, and he was too groggy to remind her. His head and heart thumped in tandem when he got up from his makeshift bed. He shuffled into the bathroom where his mum had hung his clothes to dry. He dressed quickly and splashed cold water over his aching face. In his inside pocket he found the bag Gabriel had given him and took out a benzo to dissolve under his tongue. Then he stood for a while with his hands on the washbasin, collecting his thoughts.

Gabriel was sitting in their dad's old chair when Liam came down to the kitchen, and the restlessness in his body was making the table judder. The room smelled of jam-making and his mother was backed against the work surface, as if there was a strange animal in her kitchen rather than her own son. Vanja was sitting on Gabriel's lap, glowing in the sunlight, vibrating in time to his insanity. He ran his eyes over Liam, taking in the filthy clothes from the night before and the split lip.

'Shit, looks like you had a rough night.'

'What are you doing here?'

Gabriel twisted Vanja's plait round his hand like a rope and stared at him challengingly. Liam took a couple of reluctant steps into the room. His mum's herb tea was steaming in a teapot on the table next to the home-made rye bread, and she began nervously laying out cups and food. Her jewellery clicked and rattled, like a prisoner's chains. Her voice sounded small when she finally made her excuses and went out to the dogs, eager to get away. Gabriel had the same effect on her as their father. He filled the whole house with dread.

When the door had slammed shut behind her Gabriel gestured to Liam.

'Sit down.'

'I haven't got time. I've got to get to work.'

Gabriel rested his chin on Vanja's head and locked her in his veiny arms as if he was planning to squeeze her to death.

'Sit down, I said.'

His voice was totally calm; only his eyes betrayed his anger. Liam looked at the clock. He could spare ten minutes, no more. Gabriel whispered something in Vanja's ear that made her laugh. She began to spread a sandwich for him, with plenty of cheese and ham and sliced cucumber. *Piteå-Tidningen* lay open on the table in front of them and Gabriel pushed it towards Liam, tapping his knuckles on the headline. The black letters seemed to scream at him:

Missing man found in well.

The room spun. Gabriel leaned across the table and fixed him with his eyes.

'A well, eh? How the hell do you explain that?'

*

Liv sat in the front pew and tried to conjure up a few tears. The church was packed. People had made the pilgrimage from the villages, from Moskosel, Arvidsjaur and Järvträsk. The air was thick with perfume and aftershave and all the rest. Curiosity and questions. She felt their stares on the back of her neck. They had all heard about Vidar but no one knew him. They were here to see the daughter and the grandson. She felt like a fox forced from its den, afraid and naked in the daylight. Her arm was around Simon, who she wanted to shield from the inquisitiveness and the intrusive eyes. Felicia was sitting on his other side, their fingers intertwined. They were always together now, they never let go. Liv's hand brushed against Felicia's hair as it rested on Simon's shoulder. It was softer than she had expected, not at all as stiff or artificial as it looked. Her make-up had run, black streaks revealing her emotion. But they weren't real tears, Liv thought. The girl was clever at playing along.

Liv felt still and blank inside. The police were also there; she had caught sight of Hassan on her way to her seat. Dark shirt and tie, no uniform on an occasion like this, but she understood why he was there. She couldn't shake off the knowledge that Vidar's murderer could be present in the overcrowded church. Perhaps he was sitting on one of the hard pews, studying the result of his work. In front of her was the simple wooden coffin with flowers that had already begun to wilt. Eva and Douglas had arranged everything, insisting that Vidar had to have a proper funeral. Liv herself had protested, saying he wouldn't have wanted to throw away money on such inessentials. When I'm dead you can throw me on a bonfire, he said, more than once. I don't want any trappings. He would have gone through the roof if he had been able to see them now, all these people gathered together to mourn his fate. She could hear Vidar's protests as the priest droned on, his gruff voice so clear inside her now: *Confounded vultures, the lot of them. Now I can't even be allowed to die in peace.*

She threw a look over her shoulder and saw the mass of people jammed together in the pews. Others without a seat were standing with their backs to the yellow wall. She caught sight of Johnny among the people who were standing. He was bigger than she had realized in the widow's house. He towered over the congregation like a pine tree and seemed to be looking straight at her, seeking contact. She continued scanning the familiar faces. They were all there, the neighbours and the customers from the filling station, all wearing masks of grief.

Simon put his mouth to her ear.

'Nobody gave a toss about Grandad when he was alive,' he whispered. 'So why are they here now?'

Over coffee they came up to offer their condolences. A chorus of voices, all saying the same thing. What had happened was incredible, frightening, awful. Vidar was tricky, unpleasant even, but no one deserved such a fate. A few shared anecdotes from when they were young, from the days when Vidar grabbed everything life had to offer, when he made business deals and chased women. Stories that gave rise to hollow laughter, fruitless attempts to liven up the atmosphere, to make him a person they could remember with warmth. But Liv didn't laugh or cry. She merely sat watching the clock, wondering how soon she could say thank you and go home without seeming ungrateful or attracting too much attention.

Douglas, Eva and Karl-Erik gathered around her and Simon and tried to divert the attention. She hadn't expected that, not after the walls Vidar had put up over the years. Now they had collapsed in one night. Serudia was also sitting there, drinking coffee from her saucer, and when no one was listening she leaned over and laid her hand on Liv's.

'I can't trust my memory these days,' she said. 'But one thing I know for certain – there are cloudberries growing in the place where I found Vidar's hat.'

'There aren't any cloudberries now, the snow has only just melted.'

'You know what I mean. That hat of his was lying in the middle of the cloudberry patch.'

They were whispering about her. Liv made out parts of sentences, felt the scorching stares. Mute accusations that stung her skin.

'This is a funeral,' she heard Douglas say several times. 'This isn't the right place for gossip or speculation. We must let the police do their job.'

She sat for a long time on the toilet, her head in her hands. Voices cawed around her like birds. The floor swayed under her feet when she made her way back to her table, to the neighbours. Johnny sat apart from the others; she could see

225

his face shining through the room, a strange gleam in his eyes when they met hers. Simon's hair was like sunshine on the chair beside her empty seat. They seemed so far away, there were so many bodies keeping them apart, a sea of black polyester and accusing looks. Liv edged her way through the smartly dressed people. Her dress clung like a slippery skin to her body and her hair felt damp. Only her mouth was dry. Her tongue had stuck to the roof of her mouth and she couldn't answer people's questions, even if she wanted to. A hot rage welled up inside her, and she wanted to wrench off the white paper tablecloths, spill hot coffee on their self-righteous knees, and fill their best shoes with crushed porcelain. She wanted to put a shard to her own throat, in front of them all, but the most she could do was lift her head and meet their gaze, one by one. They fell silent as she passed, as if someone was walking alongside and lowering the volume. And she knew they were all thinking the same thing, although nobody dared to say it within earshot. Their conviction so unmistakable in their tense shoulders and pinched mouths that they might just as well have trumpeted out their innermost belief: that she had killed her own father.

WINTER 2002

She ignores all the signs, her tender breasts and her sense of smell that has become so acute she can hardly go anywhere. Everything stinks — people's breath, petrol fumes from the snowmobiles that drive through the village, and the sweet odour of butchery from the neighbours' farm where the animals lie stacked in neat pieces in the yard. Nothing escapes her.

She hides her expanding body under layers of loose-fitting clothes, grateful for the cold and the midwinter darkness. When she can no longer disguise her stomach she stops going to school. She lies in her room feeling the baby move, squirming like a worm inside her, an enormous parasite sucking all the life out of her.

When her father comes in she pulls the covers to her chin, but he doesn't dare look at her anyway. His eyes hover somewhere above her head. Three times a day he brings her food — black pudding, liver, bone-marrow broth — food rich in iron and fat that will make her strong enough to give birth to a new life. The child wakes when she eats. It kicks and turns, as if it hungers for something.

Her father doesn't want her to leave the farmstead during the last few months. She has to be content to stand at the edge of the forest and breathe in the scent of snow and the stillness, but she feels his stares from the house and they give her body no peace. She opens the window instead and listens to the whispering of the falling snow and the wind in the spruce trees. The village is enveloped in darkness. People and the normal world feel distant. Her father repels anyone who tries to come too close. He says they don't need anyone else.

Don't worry, my little cloudberry, we'll manage this together.

At the end the child is so heavy she hasn't the strength to go out anyway, and stops halfway down the stairs to get her breath. When her father shouts at her to stay in her room, she obeys. She lies in her childhood bed with the pink sheets and looks at her bulging stomach. She can make out the child's foot when he kicks, because she already knows it is a boy – a future man and a monster. She dreads the day when it will force its way out of her, when she will have to meet him.

She thinks of the cars and the men, their cold hands under her jacket, and the neon lights of the filling station. A feeling of melting ice as they enter her, goosebumps and chattering teeth when they leave. Memories of the lone wolf are the only things that make her feel warm. Sometimes at night she stands at the window, looking out for him. She senses the wild smell and exhilaration of his nearness in her blood. His passenger seat is the closest to freedom she has ever come.

Death mingled under the fluorescent lights. Black suits and dresses crowded between the shelves, an icy satisfaction on people's faces. Outside the filling station shop there was the threat of rain. The sky hung like a dirty sheet over everything, as washed-out as the people coming in and out of the doors, bringing the damp in with them. They had just buried Vidar Björnlund and no one could talk about anything else. Liam stood behind the counter absorbing everything that came out of their mouths.

'I thought she was going to faint, poor girl.'

'What'll happen to the lad? He'll come off worst in this mess.'

'I don't like to speak ill of the dead, but Vidar got what he deserved. He's given me the creeps ever since that wife of his died.'

There was a great deal of speculation about how Vidar had been killed. A man with stubbly hair and a bushy beard leaned over the counter and whispered to Liam that he knew how it happened. He'd heard it from a reliable source.

'First he had his head blown off and then they drove over him with a quad bike and crushed every bone in his body. He was like a sack of potatoes when they got him out of the well!'

They were so wrapped up in their talk about the dead man that they didn't notice Liam's split lip and cut cheek. Niila was the only one to ask and Liam had blurted out something about hockey training, even though he had never played hockey in his life. Even though he had dreamed of nothing else since he was little.

During his break he was so exhausted he had to lean against the stinking skip to stop himself collapsing. The bag of tablets Gabriel had given him grew emptier by the day. He didn't want to take them but he couldn't stop himself. He needed something for the stress. His nerves were so fragile that every little noise made him jump. He had taken two benzos before his shift but they'd had no effect, his head was still full of paranoia. He kept an eye out for Gabriel while he smoked, always afraid his brother would come gliding out of the darkness and torment him with more problems, more demands, more lies.

Liam knew it was Gabriel who had moved the body, although he denied it. He had sat at their mum's table playing the innocent, saying it wasn't him. It was impossible to reach him these days, ever since that night on the marsh. Gabriel was in worse shape than their father had ever been. The drugs let him live in his own reality, let him believe his own lies. And the only thing Liam could do was keep his distance and not allow himself to be dragged even deeper into the shit than he already was.

He had just stubbed out his cigarette when the stockroom door opened and Liv Björnlund appeared. She was wearing a black dress that hung on her. Her face was pale and grim.

'What happened to you?' she asked.

'Clumsy tackle at hockey practice.'

'Can you spare one?'

He tried to control his trembling hands as he fumbled with the packet. She didn't have a lighter either and when he held up the flame to her face he could see she was as exhausted as he was. Her face was full of tired shadows and lines. But he didn't notice any signs of crying.

'It was my dad's funeral today.'

'I heard. I'm sorry.'

'Niila doesn't want me to work this month. He says people are too nosy, they won't leave me alone. He says you can work my shifts.'

'Only until you're back. Then it'll be like normal again.'

She stared out into the twilight, as if she was afraid somebody was standing out there, listening. She took short, hard drags of her cigarette, hunching over.

'Don't say anything to Niila, but I don't think I will be coming back.'

'Why not?'

'I'm finished here. Dad's gone and there's no reason for me to stay. I'll sell the house and take my son and move somewhere far away.'

There was an excitement in her voice that hadn't been there before, a light in her eyes as she pushed her hair out of her face and looked at him. This was better than anything he had dared hope for. If she and the boy left there would be no daily reminders. It would all soon be forgotten.

'I've got to go back in before Niila comes looking for me.'

'I hear you've got a daughter?'

'That's right.'

'Niila says that's why you work here. For her sake.'

Liam lowered his head and looked down at their shoes. Unmatched socks protruded from the tops of her black ankle boots, one white and one black.

'I've promised her a house.'

'Oh, that's cool.'

She extinguished the cigarette under her boot. Liam reached for the stockroom door and held it open for her, nodding at her to go first. She stopped in the doorway, leaned close to him and whispered:

'Do you know something more important than giving her a house?'

'What?'

'Making sure she's strong enough to leave it one day.'

Vidar had been shot dead before being dumped in the well. The newspaper hoardings screamed it at them as they drove through the community. And everywhere, people's eyes bored into them. Simon sat next to her with his hood up, trying to hide the fact that he was crying. She wanted to comfort him, to say something about Grandad not suffering at least, that it must have gone so fast he hadn't felt anything. But the words felt awkward in her mouth and when they reached the village they sat in silence, connected by the new darkness surrounding them.

Standing by the barrier at the foot of their drive were two strangers, a man and a woman. Journalists, judging from the camera and fat microphone. Liv recognized them. They had been huddling outside the church too, like a pair of starving crows.

Simon put a hand on the door as she slowed down.

'Shall I tell them to go to hell?'

'No, we won't give them a thing.'

She got out and raised the barrier so he didn't have to. How are you, Liv? asked the female reporter. Her voice was gentle, almost pleading, but Liv drew her head inside her hood and refused to look at the woman. Somehow she managed to lift the barrier and drive them to safety. Once indoors she pulled down the blinds to block out any curiosity lurking out there. The looks that tore her apart.

She waited until darkness had fallen over the village before daring to venture outside. She was sitting on a veranda chair with Vidar's pipe in her mouth, staring at the forest, when Hassan called to say he was on his way. The reporters had gone when she went down to raise the barrier and let him in.

'Anyone would think you'd moved in,' she said, as he climbed out of the car.

'Don't tell my girlfriend. She thinks I'm away too much already.'

He sat down beside her. Liv sucked on the pipe, studying his face to see if she could find out why he had come. She offered him the pipe but he shook his head.

'How are things?' he asked.

'They've been better.'

She waited for Hassan to say something. The impatience crawled in her body, the feeling that he was pretending to care simply so he could keep an eye on her.

The *Piteå-Tidningen* lay on the veranda table where it had been thrown. She stabbed a finger at the black headline.

'It says here he was shot.'

Hassan sighed heavily.

'That's right.'

'So why do we have to read about it in the paper? Why couldn't we have heard it from you?'

'Because it was a leak. They weren't supposed to write about how he died. The investigation is still at a sensitive stage.'

'Have you any idea who's behind it?'

'No one I can discuss with you, not as things stand.'

He looked genuinely regretful. He turned so he could see her better. Liv kept her eyes on the forest, watching the trees merge together in the darkness.

'You all think I shot him, don't you? That's why you're searching here, and that's why you haven't told me anything.'

Hassan dragged a hand over his face, distorting his handsome features.

'You can't investigate a murder without looking at the people who were closest to the victim. That's just the way it is. We can't apologize for doing our job. All I can say is that you mustn't take it personally. This is normal procedure.'

The pipe went out exactly as the horizon swallowed the last of the sun. A damp chill rose out of the darkness. Liv shuddered but didn't want to go back indoors. Everything in there felt foreign now, opened up and on display. Hassan leaned closer, speaking softly:

'Believe it or not I'm on your side, Liv. I want you to know that, even if I can't reveal exactly what we're thinking or why we're doing what we're doing. We're here for your sake and for Vidar's. Nobody deserves such an ending.'

Her eyes streamed in the wind and she didn't bother to wipe them in case he mistook it for crying. For love.

'I know you and Vidar were very close,' he went on. 'This is an incredibly hard time for you and Simon, and I want you to know that I'm here if you need anything. Not just as a police officer, but as another human being.'

'What makes you think we were very close?'

The question took him by surprise and she could see it puzzled him. He ran a hand through his thick hair.

'Well, otherwise you wouldn't still be living under the same roof, would you? And he wouldn't be carrying a photograph of you.'

Hassan fumbled with his jacket, muttering something about Vidar's clothes and evidence, and pulled out a small plastic bag. He handed it to her. The photograph had been in Vidar's shirt pocket when he was found. Liv held the bag but didn't bother to look. She already knew.

'That's not me in the picture, it's Mum.'

'Wow, you don't say. You're so alike. I could have sworn it was you!'

The photograph was thumbed and worn, Kristina young and smiling, her hair loose. Only her eyes revealed the solemnity she hid inside, the darkness that would soon demand its right. Liv handed back the photograph. Vidar had carried pictures of Kristina around with him for as long as she could remember. When she was small she had liked looking at them, staring for a long time at the beautiful face without ever having enough.

But that all changed as she grew older and it was only herself she saw.

'She took her own life when I was just a few months old.'

'It must have been really tough,' Hassan said. 'Growing up without a mother.'

Liv stood up and whistled for the dog. Her body ached with exhaustion, every step hurt. She stopped at the front door and gave him a final look.

'People say it was Dad's fault she did it. They say he loved her to death.'

*

All the rumours made his head spin and led his thoughts to the photographs he'd taken on his phone. Liam waited until darkness had fallen and the dogs were silent. Vanja was sleeping with her face to the wall, and the cracks in the wallpaper fanned out like a spider's web above the little body. He sat in the light of the computer, looking at the images that soon covered the whole screen. Vidar's back, bent over the ground. His hands deep in the steaming earth, as if he was looking for something.

Liam had copied the pictures to his computer before deleting them from his phone. He didn't feel safe having them there either, but he couldn't bring himself to delete them entirely. Something inside him protested each time he tried. He had to look, had to understand what happened that night, even if it made him feel ill.

Most of the pictures he had taken were of the house and its surroundings. The solitary window shining in the night and the paths offering escape routes in the moonlight. The three doors leading into the house, one at the front, one at the back and a cellar door on the side. The apple tree that could act as a ladder if anyone needed to jump from the second floor or the roof. The Volvo parked to one side, its nose buried in blackcurrant bushes, its rusty wheel trims like gold in the dawn light.

The blurry images moments before it happened. The old man with his face looking down at the ground. His fragile shadow between the spruce trees as the sky grew light and the first rays of the sun fell over the ground. The shadow of the moose tower falling over him. He had kept clear of the path, almost as if he was also silently creeping up on something.

Liam turned up the brightness and zoomed in. Everything was so much clearer on the computer screen. The memories rushed back, the screech of the birds and the smell of explosive. The cold sweat down his naked back made him shiver but he couldn't stop looking.

Vanja moved in the bed and he stiffened on his chair. A milky light had already begun to fill the room, casting a sickly lustre over her sleeping face.

He turned back to the screen. Vidar was kneeling with his hands in the earth. Something in the left-hand corner grabbed Liam's attention. He zoomed in, squinted at the screen and at a shadow that seemed out of place. Something light was shining in the shadows of the moose tower, clothing of some kind, perhaps. A jacket worn by someone hiding up there. Could it be Gabriel? No, he had been on the other side. Liam zoomed in until everything became a grainy confusion of pixels. He increased the brightness and the contrast but all he could see was the hazy blue contour. He couldn't even be certain that someone was actually standing there. It could easily be his tiredness playing tricks on him.

Vanja made a faint sound and he clicked the pictures away. In the light of the computer he watched her turn over, her plait dangling over the edge of the bed, but she didn't wake up. Sleep was holding her in such a tight embrace it was hard to see if she was actually breathing. He walked quietly over to her on stiff legs and rested a hand between her shoulder blades to assure himself there was life in her. Just like he had done when she was a newborn and the fear of losing her was so overpowering that he could hardly sleep at night.

He curled up on the mattress, pulled both the duvet and a blanket over him, but felt cold anyway. He shivered until sleep swept him into nightmares and Gabriel's cough filled the room.

The neighbouring village was sleeping more soundly than Ödesmark. Empty barns and gaping windows of weather-beaten houses watched as they drove past. Liv was slumped in her seat, all the time thinking someone was standing behind the dark glass, on the lookout for her. Simon was driving, he needed the practice. The sad shadows under his eyes made him look older, more grown up. When they passed some swings he slowed down, but it was a long time since children's laughter had been heard on these farms. Liv tried to swallow her unease.

'If the police are there we'll turn back straight away,' she said.

'We can't do that, they'll hear us coming.'

'I can't cope with the way they look at me.'

The police had accounted for the last few days of Vidar's life, but they still didn't appear to believe her when she said he didn't have either friends or enemies. Solitude had become his security and the only people he could tolerate were his immediate family. He had always kept himself clear of debt. The police had searched the house and the car and taken the guns from the cabinet in the cellar. But worse than the questions and the intrusion were the looks that tried to see right inside her. They wanted to get under her skin and root around. Their eyes drilled holes into her.

When they passed Big-Henrik's farm he was standing by the barn. He glared at them, his fleece jacket bright like a winter sun in the bad light. Simon raised his hand but received only a black look in return.

'Screw you, then.'

'Nobody wants to know us now,' said Liv. 'We bring bad luck wherever we go.'

'Nobody wanted to know us before, either.'

They saw the cordoned-off area from a distance. Wheel tracks criss-crossed the gravel road and police tape flapped in the bushes. Beyond the perimeter of the garden with its weeds was the felled part of the forest, looking like a disease in the dull green surroundings. There was no life, only shadows moving slowly across the ground in the moonlight. Simon drove so close the bumper touched the tape.

'There's nobody here,' he said.

'Where do you think the well is?'

'It's got to be here somewhere. Shit, it's so overgrown. If they hadn't been logging, they'd never have found him.'

Maybe it was the approaching storm or the desolation, but suddenly tears were choking her. Tears that had been noticeable by their absence ever since she had been informed of the death. Liv blinked and blinked and the tears found their way out through her nose instead. She licked the salt and reached for the door. She didn't have the peace to grieve.

The police had trampled paths that ran like small black streams all over the ground and converged at the well that lay inside a ring of naked birches, its mouth open to the first heavy drops of rain. They stopped in front of the moss-covered stones and without hesitating Liv lifted the lid.

She wondered if he had been thrown in head first. The well was deep and dry, and when she leaned over the stones she could hear an odd rushing sound, a whisper from the depths of the earth. Close by were dark patches where the blood had left its mark on the lichen and the stones. Liv turned her head away and saw Simon staring over the tree stumps, as if he was searching for an explanation among the harvested trees.

'Some people are saying Juha is behind it,' he said.

'Juha Bjerke? Who says that?'

'A farmhand at Modig's. She says she's seen Juha sneaking around the village a lot lately. Seems like he hunts here, though he hasn't got a licence. And it wouldn't be the first time he thought a man was an animal.'

Liv shook her head.

'People always blame Juha as soon as something happens. I doubt he's got anything to do with it.'

She hoped Simon wouldn't hear the trembling in her voice. She hadn't seen Juha Bjerke for many years, but she could still bring to mind his shaggy beard, the hunted look in his eyes. It was a long time ago now but she would never forget how they drove around in his old car while autumn flamed outside the windows, talking about freedom, smoking weed. It had been a good time, filled with hope, before Vidar interfered and destroyed everything. She didn't know what he had said to get rid of Juha. All she knew was that the lone wolf from the North Forest had never come to pick her up again.

'Do you know Juha?' Simon asked.

'I wouldn't say that. Everyone knows who he is, don't they?'

'You're crap at lying.'

Only to you, she wanted to say. I can never lie to you. She walked a few times around the well and the overgrown brambles. If it was true Vidar had been shot, it hadn't happened here. There wasn't enough blood, only the few patches around the lid. The only explanation was that he had been dragged here to be hidden, dragged from a place where the cloudberries grow, if she was to believe what Serudia said. Here around the well no cloudberries had ever grown. The ground was far too dry.

A cigarette end was hiding under the low bushes. Liv held it up to the light. Marlboro Red, half-smoked and looking as though someone had crushed it under their shoe.

'What have you got there?'

'Nothing.'

She quickly closed her fingers around the cigarette and slipped it into her pocket.

'Let's go. I don't want to stay here any longer.'

Big-Henrik wasn't standing outside his barn as they passed, but she could make out his shadow behind the curtain. Without thinking she put a hand on Simon's.

'Pull in here.'

'Why?'

'I want to know what's going on in this bloody village.'

*

Gabriel wasn't answering when he phoned, and when he drove to the flat it was Johanna who opened. She was wearing Gabriel's clothes and her dark hair was hanging over her face. A black eye was visible between the strands.

'Gabriel isn't home.'

'Can I come in and wait? It's important.'

'He says I mustn't let you in.'

'Do you know where he is?'

She shook her head, biting her lip. Liam could see she knew more than she was letting on but he didn't want to argue with her. She had enough to deal with already.

'If you see him, tell him I was here, yeah?'

She began to close the door, leaving it open just wide enough for her healthy eye to look out.

'He worries about you,' she said, in her drawling voice. 'He says you're losing your head.'

Liam smiled.

'It was there last time I looked.'

He found him at Frasses. Gabriel was sitting alone at an outside table, cramming chips into his mouth. His cheeks bulged. He didn't react when Liam got out of the car and only looked up when Liam sat down opposite him. In the sunlight the lazy side of Gabriel's face looked as if it was drooping more than usual, and tomato ketchup dribbled out of the corner of his mouth. He pushed his food away and wiped his hands on his jeans.

'I lose my appetite just looking at you.'

'I can only say it's mutual.'

'So what do you want?'

'Can we go for a drive? There's something I want to show you.'

'I can't. I'm waiting for someone.'

'Ten minutes, that's all. I'll drop you back when we're done. It's important.'

The lake lay shiny and desolate. Nobody was swimming there yet; it was still too cold. A shimmer of green covered the birches but summer still felt a long way off. Gabriel opened the window and lit a joint. He coughed and smoked in turns, and avoided eye contact with Liam. The scream of a bird made them both jump, their nerves constantly on edge and their bodies ready to run.

He's afraid as well, thought Liam. We're afraid of each other.

Gone was the time when they sought comfort together, as they did during the endless nights when darkness lay like a suffocating blanket over the house that reverberated with tears and fighting. It was always Liam who crept into Gabriel's bed, never the other way round. Gabriel used to hold his hands over Liam's ears so he didn't have to hear what was going on downstairs, everything that was smashed and could never be mended. Sometimes, when it was at its worst, Gabriel would sing and make the air vibrate under the covers. He sang until Liam fell asleep.

Liam took a puff of the joint to bridge the gap between them, and then tapped the keys on his phone.

'I don't think we were alone,' he said eventually. 'Someone else could have been there.'

'Don't start.'

Liam held his phone to Gabriel's face, showing him the picture of the old man on his knees and the rising sun throwing a warm glow over the forest. Gabriel drew deeply on the joint and held the smoke in his lungs as he spoke.

'I thought I told you to delete that crap.'

'I know, but have a look at this. On the left, in the corner.'

'So what am I looking at?'

Liam pushed the phone closer. It wasn't that clear on such a small screen but it was possible to make out the blue shadow hovering behind Vidar.

'There, among the trees. See the shadow?'

Gabriel exhaled and peered at the screen.

'I can't see a fucking thing except a picture you should have deleted long ago.'

He stubbed out the joint in an empty Coke can, leaned back in his seat and looked at Liam from under his heavy eyelids. Small twitches in his face indicated the anger simmering under the surface. He rapped a knuckle on Liam's forehead.

'Sometimes I wonder if there's anyone at home in there,' he

said. 'You don't listen, you don't do as you're told. What am I going to do with you? Maybe I should have let Juha deal with you, so I don't have to.'

Liam leaned back, pretending not to hear. He scrutinized the picture again, suddenly doubting his own senses. It could be the wind in the trees that made him see things that weren't there, that captured the light and gave the world different colours and shapes. Maybe Gabriel was right. Maybe his overstressed brain was fooling him, looking for other alternatives. Looking for a way out.

Before he had time to react Gabriel snatched the phone from his hand and got out of the car. Liam watched as he held it over his head and then hurled it as hard as he could onto the tarmac and stamped on it. Over and over again he stamped until only fragments remained. The rage turned his face into a white mask. When he had finished, he picked up the pieces and threw them far out into the lake.

Liam sat immobile and let it happen. He watched the rings form on the water and felt the ground shift under him, the crack as the earth slowly swelled and opened. Waiting for him.

✳

A thin cat was sitting in Big-Henrik's porch, looking at them reproachfully as they got out of the car. No one opened when Liv rang the doorbell, but she could hear someone moving behind the door.

'You might as well open it,' she called. 'I know you're at home.'

Simon had already started to walk back to the car when the door creaked and Big-Henrik's face appeared in the opening.

Liv was no taller than his chest and his enormous bulk filled the doorway. Despite that he didn't lift his face from her shoes.

'What do you want?'

'We want to come in and talk to you.'

'What do you want to talk about?'

'I'm sure you can work that out for yourself.'

Big-Henrik shuffled his feet. A memory from when she was a schoolgirl flashed through Liv's mind: a cold January with snow weighing down the branches, the school bus with a puncture, and she and Big-Henrik walking together in the tracks from a snowmobile, chatting all the way to Ödesmark, despite the fact that they had never seen each other before. Where the snow was deepest he went ahead so she could step into his footprints. The next day it was as if it had never happened, nothing that betrayed the time they had spent together. It was the same now, the wrinkled face that pretended not to know her.

'You might as well come in.'

The house was big and quiet and sparsely furnished. Big-Henrik showed them into the kitchen and offered them a seat. A random pattern of coffee rings on the wax tablecloth showed which side of the table was his. He lived alone now, after his mother's death. Of all the siblings only Big-Henrik had stayed in the village.

'You'll be wanting coffee, I suppose?'

Without waiting for an answer, he fed the stove with a large log and began spooning coffee into a jug.

'Don't go to any trouble for us.'

She made an effort to sound friendly; she didn't want to put him on the defensive. Simon sat next to her, biting his nails. Big-Henrik brought out fine china cups with gilt edges. He had a bald patch on the top of his head which he kept scratching.

'Damned awful, what happened,' he said. 'I was at the funeral. Nicely done, I thought.'

'The Modigs helped us, otherwise there wouldn't have been a funeral at all.'

Big-Henrik gestured towards the window.

'It's hard to get it into your head, him lying out there, only a stone's throw away. It scares me stiff to think about it.'

'So you haven't seen anything?'

His eyelids flickered.

'I've already told the police everything I know. How Vidar got into my well is beyond my understanding.'

'You haven't seen anyone drive past, someone who has no business here?'

'Nobody drives past my house these days. The forestry company comes in from the other side, they've carved out their own road. No one has any reason to come past here. Not until this disaster happened. Now the road's all churned up by the police and the newspaper people, and all those other nosy devils.'

The bald patch on his head shone as he poured the coffee. Simon leaned his elbows on the table, staring closely at the big man as he sipped the hot liquid. Liv couldn't bring herself to drink anything. Her stomach was in turmoil.

'I guess there's a lot of talk going around? I'm sure you've heard a few rumours.'

The fine china looked comical in Big-Henrik's great paws, as if he was playing with a doll's tea set.

'I might have heard a thing or two, but I don't know if it's anything you'll want to hear.'

'Forget about us. We only want to know what people are saying.'

Big-Henrik sighed and put his hand to his face, looking from one to the other.

'Well, I'm sorry if this sounds hard, but there's many of us around here who wanted to put a bullet in Vidar Björnlund's head. A lot of anger has built up through the years. In a way it's a wonder it took so long.'

Simon put his cup down with a crash. Liv could see his pulse beating above his collar.

'Anyone in particular you're thinking of?' she asked.

'I'm not going to drop someone in it, because I've heard it from more than one person. People didn't care for that dad of yours, and you know it. Vidar prospered on other people's unhappiness. He tricked honest folk out of their land only to sell it on to the forestry companies and other outsiders. There were families who lost everything overnight, and you don't forget that kind of thing. Those wounds still hurt.'

'Dad hasn't done any business for over twenty years.'

'That may be so, but he left a trail of turmoil in his wake. Now they've got permission to fell North Forest too, after all these years, even though it's proper ancient forest. And it was none other than Vidar who got that ball rolling, when he bought up Bjerke's land and sold it on.'

Now it was Liv's turn to look down at the tablecloth. She felt Simon's eyes on her. She wasn't certain how much he had heard about that old stuff, about everything that had happened before he was born. The kind of things neither of them were responsible for now, a lifetime later. She knew there had been people who were angry with Vidar, but it was all so long ago and should be forgotten.

'Is it money you're after?' she asked.

'You've never been right in the head, you.'

'Name your price, anything at all. I'll pay whatever you want, if only you'll tell me who killed Dad.'

He raised his head now and looked straight at her. The huge body shook with anger as he leaned across the table.

'I remember when you used to stand on the main road with your thumb in the air, trying to get away from here. You jumped into the first best set of wheels that came along, but you never got anywhere. And now it's too late. You've turned into your father. You think everything comes down to money.'

She stood up so abruptly her coffee spilled on the table. The old shame flared up inside her as she hurried through the dingy hall and out into the dusk that fell from nowhere and wrapped its chill around her as she ran to the car. She had already started the engine and made a turn in the gravel by the time Simon caught up with her. He slid into the passenger seat and struggled with his safety belt, and it took a while before he found his voice.

'What was all that about?'

Liv reached out for his hand.

'It doesn't matter. Whatever happened before you were born doesn't matter.'

EARLY SPRING 2003

The child's cries pierce her but she can't summon the energy to get out of bed. The cot becomes a cage in the moonlight, a prison significantly smaller than her own. The dilapidated walls of the house cannot keep a child's cries inside. She imagines them carrying over the village and scaring the birds from the trees.

It is her father who lifts the tiny child and holds him to his own chest, rocking him in the dark room with a protective hand over the bare head. All night he paces like that, untiring in his love. Every few hours he walks quietly into her room. The girl pretends to be asleep when his shadow falls over her.

He needs feeding.

I'm sleeping.

You don't want him to die, do you?

He tries to frighten her but her body doesn't react to fear any more. It is as if all her insides leaked out when she gave birth, leaving her empty and echoing. She has neither stomach nor heart, no blood to carry the terror.

She hoped they would take the child away from her after the birth, that the midwife and the nurses would see the situation and take pity on her. But they didn't see and they didn't take pity.

Her father sits her up in bed and lifts her top, revealing the swollen breasts. The child is unbearably heavy in her arms.

She sits in the dark and watches it latch on. Her nipples sting in the greedy little mouth, and when he finally lets go the fragile skin has cracked and started to bleed.

She sits with her eyes tightly closed while her father praises her.

Now he'll be big and strong, you'll see.

Snow weighs down the spruce trees and nothing is breathing. There is only the baby's wailing, vibrating over the hushed whiteness. The girl puts the pillow over her face, pretending she is also buried in the cold. She sees the child's reflection in the dark window, the wrinkly face and the toothless mouth wailing for everything she's unable to give him. A harsh light fills the room but she can't welcome the new day. All she can do is slide her hand under the mattress and grasp the knife that is waiting there. She runs the sharp blade over the soft white flesh of her lower arm. There is always a way out, even if it doesn't lead anywhere.

Kristina's black eyes watched her from across the room. She walked over, freed the photograph from its tarnished frame and sat holding it for a long time, running her finger over the grainy face. It was so like her own she could be looking in a mirror. Only the hair was different, Kristina's thick and black as tar, making her pale eyes shine like stars.

Liv turned the photo over and noticed some numbers in the top right-hand corner. At first she thought it was a date but that couldn't be right, there were too many, eleven in all. It was Vidar's writing, spidery and sloping. She looked at the closed wardrobe door. Behind it was the safe, still locked and taunting her in the darkness. The police had said they would send out a technician to open it, but that would take time. Unsteadily, she got to her feet and called Simon.

She had forgotten Felicia was there. They came sauntering down the stairs, both of them, with dishevelled hair and rosy cheeks, as if they had been caught out.

'What's all the shouting about?'

Liv hesitated and looked at Felicia. The girl smiled at her. The wild blue hair made her look like an elf, something out of a fairy story. Finally, she held up the photo of Kristina.

'I think I've found the code to the safe.'

Simon took the photo from her and studied the numbers. A smattering of inflamed spots covered his shoulders. Liv could hear Vidar's rasping voice inside her head. *Put a jumper on, boy, so we don't have to look at you.*

'Come on, let's try,' he said.

The wardrobe door swung open with a heavy sigh. It looked very dark and bare inside now that she had got rid of Vidar's clothes. All that remained were a few hangers that rustled in the draught, and the black eye of the safe. It was fixed to the bottom and couldn't be moved. Liv had seen the bundles of notes inside it when she was very small, but that was long ago and she couldn't rely on that memory now.

Liv and Felicia leaned over Simon's shoulders as he started turning the combination lock. Every click reverberated in Liv like a pistol shot. Felicia noticed and put her hand on Liv's back, patting her awkwardly. She gave off a faint whiff of alcohol, or perhaps it was only perfume, Liv couldn't be sure. She had a tiger's face tattooed on her upper arm. Its cunning mouth gaped wide and the enormous teeth shone realistically in its jaws.

'Do you know what's kept in there?' she asked.

Liv shook her head.

'I haven't seen Dad open it since I was a kid. In the days when he still trusted me.'

'My dad's just the same,' said Felicia. 'He literally sleeps with his wallet under his pillow every night.'

There was laughter in her voice as she said it, but her hand felt cold on Liv's back. Simon crouched down. Trickles of sweat spread down his back and he smelled as if he had been running through a rain-filled forest. His hand was carefully cupped over the dial. There were eleven resounding clicks before the safe door swung open. It happened so suddenly they all stepped back, as if they were expecting Vidar to be sitting in there, reaching out for them. There it was, the black opening that had mocked her for as long as she could remember. She thought of Juha, how she had always imagined he would be the one standing there, opening the safe door to get at the money. But there were no bundles of notes or treasure, only dust swirling in the dark opening.

Simon turned round.

'There's nothing here. It's empty.'

She was so astonished she was shaking.

'He must have another hiding place. Or else he put it in the bank after all, for safety's sake. But I find that hard to believe.'

Vidar had never completely trusted banks. He always said you had to have a treasure chest as well. Just in case.

Simon put his hand inside the safe, ran it over the shiny shelves and stopped when something rattled under his fingers. Gently he lifted his find to the light. Liv held her breath. Her head swam with memories when she saw the necklace. The scent of freedom and dried meat washed over her. The broken chain and heart were tarnished by time, but there was no doubt it was the same necklace Juha had given her once, a long time ago.

'What's this?' Simon asked.

'It's mine.'

'What's it doing in the safe?'

'I don't know.'

But she did know. The necklace was a message to her, a reminder that she had gone behind his back that autumn with Juha. Their naive plans to take the money and run – the youthful stupidity and ultimate betrayal. That was why Vidar had emptied the safe. Even though they never got round to putting their plan into action he had never forgiven her. She could hear his curses ringing in her head as she reached for the necklace. The fear in her as profound as if he was still alive.

*

Liam sat in the staffroom scrolling through houses on a property website. They were too expensive, all of them, and he didn't want to live in the kind of run-down places that were all he could afford. His dream was a little red house by the water, with the forest behind and his own garden. Far away from his mum's dogs, from Gabriel, from the old life. He would make an effort with the neighbours, invite them in for coffee and a chat, behave like proper people. If only he had the chance.

The new telephone was bigger than the one Gabriel had smashed and the screen was much clearer. When Niila came into the room and stood looking over Liam's shoulder, they watched the red-painted dreams roll by on the display.

'It's cheaper to buy land and build your own. If you know what you're doing, I mean.'

'I haven't got a clue how to build a house.'

'Your dad didn't teach you?'

'He died when I was thirteen.'

All his dad had taught him was how to break things. There were more holes in his mum's walls than she had pictures to cover them, but that was nothing he could say out loud. Niila patted his shoulder and Liam stiffened at his touch.

'I can teach you, if that's the route you want to go down. I built my own house and my brother's. It's bloody hard work but the feeling when it's finished is unbeatable, knowing you've built your own home. Stays with you for a long time.'

Liam swallowed and felt his throat start to ache. He wasn't used to people offering him help; he didn't know what to say and sat there like an idiot, coughing to disguise his feelings. Perhaps Niila picked up on that because he didn't say any more. He just gave his half-smile and filled their coffee cups before disappearing back into the shop.

Liam had only just furtively put a tablet under his tongue when the entry keypad began clicking again. He thought Niila had forgotten something, but instead it was Liv Björnlund who came into the room. The door slammed loudly behind her and the sound rang around the walls as they looked at each other.

'Is there any coffee?' she asked.

'I think so.'

A bitter taste filled his mouth as she walked over to the machine and poured some coffee into a mug. He hurriedly swallowed the tablet and tried not to gag. His phone was still on the table in front of him but the screen had timed out. She wouldn't see his dream house.

'Are you working?' he asked.

'No, Niila doesn't think I'm ready to stand on the stage again.'

'What stage?'

She sat down opposite him. Her top half was swamped in a

red flannel shirt with threadbare patches on the elbows and dark coffee stains down the front. Like a little girl who has borrowed her father's clothes.

'The till is like a stage, haven't you noticed? Everyone looks in that direction. And you have to stand there and repeat the same tired old sentences day in and day out.'

Liam looked at her, blinking. He thought he was the only one who felt watched. Who was acting.

'I know what you mean.'

She smiled. Strands of matted hair fell over her face but her eyes were shining underneath. He could glimpse the child she had once been, before her shoulders stooped and the shadows had spread across her face.

'I'm only here to collect some forms from Niila,' she said. 'Seeing as he insists I take sick leave.'

'And you'd rather work?'

She shrugged.

'At least you hear what people are saying, all the rumours and speculation. You don't get that sitting at home.'

'It's only a load of bollocks, anyway,' Liam said. 'You're better off without it.'

She tilted her head to one side and looked at him intently.

'Can you tell me what you've heard?'

'About what?'

'My dad. Me. I know people talk. Everyone who comes in here has a theory about what happened. It would be strange otherwise.'

Liam finished his coffee and glanced at the clock. Three minutes, that was all, until he had to be behind the till again.

'I don't listen to gossip.'

'Come off it, you don't have to spare my feelings. They blame me, don't they? They think I killed my own father.'

'If I were you, I wouldn't give a shit what people think.'

The daylight fell on her face and her eyes were so startlingly blue he had to look away.

'You think I did it too, don't you?'

He got up to rinse out his mug and felt her eyes following him, waiting expectantly. He tried to smile at her over his shoulder in the comforting way he used for Vanja when she was worried about something. He smiled despite his guilty conscience that sat like a weight in his belly. It was his fault she was sitting there suffering. He was the one who had barged into her world and caused chaos.

Before leaving the room he touched her shoulder and coughed to find his voice.

'I think Niila is right. You should go home and rest.'

She couldn't rest, couldn't cope with the hiatus. She had to be on the move and wouldn't let herself sit still and think. She leaned her forehead against the window and looked at the mutilated rowan tree. The black branches fanned out like finger joints in the slumbering grass. She would burn them together with last autumn's leaves and rip out the stump by the roots. Exactly as she had promised herself all these years.

The house smelled of cleaning fluid. Surfaces shone where the sun streamed in, the floor was swept and scrubbed and the dog had left pawmarks over the wet boards. The door to

Vidar's room was wide open. The room was now as empty and soulless as the man who had used it.

The windows on the ground floor were open and the spring air blew in, sweeping away all the old bitterness. There was nothing left of Vidar, not even his smell. She had gathered his clothes together in a pile on the driveway, a jumble of fleece, down and flannel. Yellowing old underpants and socks full of holes. It looked as if a huge mottled animal was crouching in the grass. Everything would be burned eventually, in a bonfire of memories.

A peal of Felicia's laughter floated down from an upstairs window. Liv had expected Simon to protest about the clear-out, saying he wanted Vidar's room to stay exactly as it had always been, but he hadn't said a word. Maybe he understood her, maybe he also thought it was easier to breathe now. Either that or he was simply consumed by the girl with the blue hair.

It was the laughter that drove her away, the sudden loneliness among the shining surfaces. All at once the scrubbed house felt alien. She stood in front of the cracked mirror and combed her hair with her fingers, splashed her armpits with cold water and pinched her cheeks. Then she called to the youngsters, telling them she would be gone for a while. *Bye*, came their voices, eager to see the back of her. Their laughter followed her onto the driveway.

She ran past the pile of Vidar's old rags and in among the pines where the last remnants of winter were evaporating in the warmth. Water bubbled in the ground and the birds had found their voices after a long silence. She felt spring fill her too, felt the sun warm her skin and make everything erupt and simmer inside her. There was no room for thoughts of Vidar and darkness.

She took a short cut over the marshland, keen to get to Widow Johansson's house. Now it was her turn to laugh, to disappear for a while. But she hadn't gone far over the spongy ground before something flashed in the sunshine and made her slow down. It was a piece of metal, reflecting the light. She zigzagged nearer, jumping between tufts of grass and moss-covered stumps until she was bending over the shining object. She caught her breath when she saw what it was. The glass had broken and the metal was twisted, but there was no mistaking what it was. Vidar's glasses. He was practically blind without them. Carefully she lifted the broken frames out of the water and held them cautiously between her thumb and index finger as if they were a dead animal she preferred not to touch. She put them in the inside pocket of her jacket and splashed around the spot where she had found them, searching for something more, an explanation. But there was only moss and mud and the wet breath of the ground rising to the sky. She recalled Vidar sitting at the kitchen window with the binoculars aimed into the darkness, convinced there was a wolf prowling around on his land.

A few metres away were the tracks of a quad bike, two dark ruts disappearing in among the pine trees. In the other direction stood the lookout tower, casting a mournful shadow over everything, and she could almost hear the shot echo over the village, feel the draught from the bullet and see the birds take off from the trees. That was how it had happened. Serudia was right. It was here he had died, in the middle of the cloudberry patch.

Swollen water drops hung like jewels from the branches, burst and rained down on her as she forced her way through the low branches. The spruces snagged her hair and she felt the eyes of the wild creatures staring at her from their hiding places. It was ironic to think of all the witnesses that had kept Vidar company at the moment of his death. The ravens circling between the trees, dreaming of the soft body parts, the lips and the eyes. Predators in the distance that had lifted their noses to the sky and inhaled that first aroma of death, when the body was still fresh and filled with blood. Perhaps that was why he had been dragged to the well, not merely to be hidden but to prevent him being torn to pieces on his own land. A final gesture of mercy?

The ground squelched under her feet as she aimed for the lookout tower. Vidar's glasses had been lying beside a fallen pine tree and she supported herself against the darkened wood as she tried to judge the distance to the tower. Vidar didn't stand a chance. His murderer must have lured him into the forest that morning, made him walk right into the trap. She could see it all so clearly.

The quad bike had scored deep grooves in the terrain, but black water had seeped from the ground and blotted out the tyre prints. The tracks were everywhere and nowhere. She was careful to step in the same water so her own footprints would also be blurred by the mud. Low clouds came from nowhere and crowded out the sun. She was bent so low over the ground she was almost crawling over the last bit, looking for something, anything. By the time she reached the tower's precarious ladder her clothes were dripping with water and the cold had penetrated the layers and made her teeth chatter. She heard Vidar's hoarse voice like a mantra in her head as she climbed the ladder. *No mosquitoes yet,* he sang. *No flowers yet on the cloudberry bushes. Soon we will make love again in the meadow, soon our child will come.*

The tower was empty apart from pine needles and cones that had been driven in through the generous cracks. She sank to her knees and ran the palms of her hands over the uneven floor, searching for cigarette ends or anything else a possible gunman could have left behind, but there was nothing. She stuck her hand under the loose plank on the wall and dug about in the small hiding place until she felt the plastic under her fingers. She was astonished it was still there. With bated breath she worked the plastic bags out of their hole. Once they had been blue, she was sure, but the colour had bleached with the years. The old notes were discoloured and crinkled at the edges, and they had stuck together, making it impossible for her to count them. A powerful sob rose up in her chest and she dropped the bundles back into the bags and pushed them back under the plank. She didn't want to remember.

The blackened planks creaked worryingly as she crawled to the firing slot. A sudden shower fell over the marsh, landing on the moss in hushed whispers. When she was younger he had promised to teach her how to hunt. Every autumn when he set off into the forest he repeated the same old song, that next year she would definitely go with him. But next year came and she wasn't allowed to go anywhere near the rifle.

The moose on the wall stared at her through the coils of smoke and seemed to be grinning slyly. The curtains were closed but still the sun leaked into the room, exposing the dust and their pale winter bodies. Johnny's hand rested on her hip, light as a feather. It would have been peaceful except he insisted on talking about Vidar, filling the moment with the dead man's ghost.

'How's the investigation going?' he wanted to know. 'Have you heard any more?'

'The police say they're making progress, but I don't know what that means.'

'Have they got a suspect?'

'Not that they've told me.'

'Rumours are flying round like crazy at the sawmill. It's buzzing like a beehive in the coffee room.'

'I can imagine.'

She laid her hand on his chest, her fingers in the coarse hair. His heart was beating fast underneath.

'They talk about you a lot,' he said hesitantly.

'And what do they say?'

'That you're the one who stands to gain from all this.'

She drew back her hand and stared at the moose head for a few seconds. Then she got out of bed and started looking for her clothes, holding an arm in front to cover herself. Sometimes she could feel the presence of the elderly widow in the room, the rank smell of old age that lingered in the walls. She knew people were talking, they always had. For as long as she could remember gossip had circulated about little victim Liv Björnlund and her miserly father.

'Did that piss you off? I'm only saying what I heard.'

'People are full of bullshit. I don't care what they say.'

'Don't go, please.'

She found her jumper and pulled it quickly over her forehead. Her jacket was on the chest of drawers and in the inside pocket were the frames of Vidar's glasses. She felt the sharp steel against her chest as she pulled up the zip. Johnny lit another cigarette, his eyes dark and staring in the glow. Slowly she walked over to his bedside table, bent down and picked one of the cigarette butts out of the ashtray. She studied it.

'What are you doing?'

'Do you know how to hunt?'

'No. Should I?'

'You've never held a gun?'

'Only when I did my military service, but that was a long time ago.'

'Can you shoot or not?'

'I don't know about that,' he smiled. 'I guess I'm not completely hopeless.'

She dropped the butt into the ashtray and reached for her jeans. They hung loosely around her waist now. The weight had fallen from her over the past year or so. Everything had started falling away, even her own body. The dogs began barking outside as she dressed. A car was driving up the road and she walked quietly over to the window and looked through the blind.

'It's the police.'

Johnny hurriedly stubbed out his cigarette and grabbed his clothes, pulled the cover clumsily over the crumpled sheets and the depressions in the bed where their bodies had been. Soon impatient knockings started vibrating through the old house. Liv stood pressed against the wall in the shadow of the moose head.

'I don't want them to see me. Not here.'

Johnny disappeared into the hall and came back with her shoes.

'Go out through the window,' he whispered, and pulled the bedroom door closed.

She heard them step into the hall and then a woman's voice filled the house. They wanted to have a little chat, she said. About his neighbours the Björnlunds and the dreadful thing that had happened in the village. Johnny invited them into the kitchen; chair legs scraped on the floor and water gushed from the tap. Liv crept behind the curtain and undid the window latch. Dead flies lay with their legs in the air between the double glazing and delicate spider's webs full of black bugs stuck to her jacket and hair. The sun had gone down outside and the dark embrace of the forest waited only a few steps away. She lifted first one leg over the sill and then the other, and Johnny's dogs came and sniffed inquisitively at her shoes as they hung suspended in the air. When she let go and started to run they followed, chasing her far out onto the marsh where she stumbled in the water and fell to the ground. She shut her eyes and let the coldness soak into her clothes. The foul smell from the dogs' jaws made her bare her own teeth, challenging them to finish her off, rip her to shreds and let her be sucked up by the moss and the black water of the marsh. But they left her there, sinking into the mud.

*

A red Ford had been parked by the pumps for some time without filling up and the driver was making no move to get out. Liam kept the car in sight as the customers came and went, suddenly petrified it had something to do with Gabriel or the cops. Irritatingly enough the driver was hidden behind one of the pumps. Liam's imagination ran wild, even if he knew plain-clothes officers usually rode around in more recent Volvo V70s, and he hadn't spotted any extra rear lights or visible antennae. Nothing to indicate it was the cops. Quite the reverse, because the motor was in pretty bad shape. Most likely it belonged to some loser Gabriel hung out with, someone who would take Liam's place behind the wheel.

The after-work rush came and went, and by the time the queue had dwindled the red car had gone. Liam tried to shake off the paranoia. When his shift was over he got a coffee from the machine and put his head round the office door to say goodbye to Niila before going out through the stockroom. The light bulb above the door needed replacing so he lit his way with his phone to avoid stepping out into total darkness, just in case Gabriel was lurking outside in the shadows.

But this time it wasn't Gabriel waiting for him, it was the red Ford. The stockroom door closed behind him with a loud bang and he couldn't go back into the shop, even if he had wanted to. Coffee spilt from the mug and he stood with his back to the door, watching as a woman with dark blonde hair got out of the car and smiled at him. She had a red coat and red lips that had stained her teeth.

'Liam Lilja?'

'Who's asking?'

Thoughts whirled in his head as she approached. She seemed too frivolous to be a cop but at the same time too smartly dressed to be running errands for Gabriel.

'Malin Sigurdsdotter,' she said. 'Journalist at *Norrlands-Posten.*'

A journalist. He should have realized. Niila had warned him about the vultures that would flock around Liv's tragedy. Say nothing, he'd told him. The most important thing now is for Liv and the lad to have some peace and quiet.

Malin Sigurdsdotter pulled her hand from her glove and held it out to greet him. She clasped his fingers and gave him a powerful handshake, her smile wide and red. Liam wondered if he should smile back, if he should at least pretend to be obliging, or whether it was safest to ignore her. He pulled back his hand, took a mouthful of coffee and started to walk to his own car. He didn't want her to see the panic that was starting to take hold of him.

She strode after him, asking about the job, about the atmosphere among his colleagues, about Liv.

'I've got nothing to say. I'm new here. I don't know anything about anything.'

He slid into the driver's seat and put the mug in the cup holder. The journalist leaned through the door, unwilling to let him drive off.

'They say Liv Björnlund got fired because her dad was murdered, and you've been given her job. Is that right?'

Liam snorted.

'No, that's not right.'

He began to close the door, forcing her to retreat. A sense of burning irritation spread to his fingertips as he started the engine and gripped the wheel. He reversed without looking at the journalist, acting as if she didn't exist. An unsettled feeling stayed with him all the way home. Everybody seemed to think he had taken Liv's place, and that irritated him. Maybe because there was some truth in it.

✳

Liv ran through the forest. Tree roots kept tripping her up and she fell hard onto the wet ground over and over again, only to clamber back to her feet and continue running. She couldn't move fast enough. The dog barked somewhere in the darkness, an urgent baying, the kind only heard during hunting. When she reached Björngården she saw a police patrol car parked beside the garage. Through the window she could see Simon's blond head and the broad figure of Hassan. It was as if the police had invaded every house in the village. The thought of turning round and running away flashed through her mind, but it was too late and she had nowhere to go. Nowhere to hide.

She was met by their laughter as she walked into the hall. Hassan's shoes stood neatly on the mat, mockingly polished and shiny beside her own shabby boots. They were sitting in an aroma of coffee with a plate of biscuits between them, and if it hadn't been for the police uniform it would have looked like an everyday coffee with friends. She stood in the doorway and saw the shock in their eyes when they caught sight of her.

'What have you done?' Simon asked. 'You look totally crazy.'

She became aware of her soaking clothes, her hands black with soil.

'I took a shortcut over the marsh, that's all.'

She looked at Hassan.

'What are you doing here?' Her voice was hard, almost hostile, but Hassan only smiled.

'I know you're getting sick of the sight of me, but basically I'm here with some good news. I was just telling Simon that we've recently made good progress in the investigation. I'm afraid I can't go into the details – all I can say is that we've found definite evidence close to the well where Vidar was found, and I'm convinced we'll find the answer we're looking for soon.'

Liv patted her chest pocket and felt the hard edges of Vidar's frames underneath. She paused.

'I found something that might be important to the investigation.'

'What? Tell me.'

'I came across Dad's glasses, just a stone's throw from the moose lookout tower. He was blind without his glasses. Never went anywhere without them, ever.'

Carefully she took the glasses from her pocket, walked over and gave them to Hassan. The old scratched frames caught the light.

'I think that's where he was murdered,' she went on. 'Out on the marsh. Serudia suggested the same thing, but I didn't understand at the time. She said she found Dad's bloodstained hat where the cloudberries grow.'

Hassan got out a pair of thin blue rubber gloves and put them on before picking up the frames and examining them closely.

'Can you show me where you found them?'

'I think so. They were down a ways from the lookout tower.'

'And you're perfectly sure they're Vidar's?'

Both Liv and Simon nodded. There was no doubt. They sat in silence and watched Hassan as he gently put the damaged glasses in a paper bag and marked it with the date. It was a strange experience seeing Vidar's belongings treated that way, like a badly wrapped present. Things lost their power without him. Became less real.

SPRING 2003

The child is an exotic flower that grows in the darkness between them. Spring arrives with new hope and fills the rooms with a special light. The father and the girl stand over the child, searching for themselves in his crinkled face and filled with the pure naked fear that only love brings.

Every visit to the clinic sends her anxiety levels soaring. The girl carries the child against her narrow shoulder, feels him growing bigger and heavier every day. He eats and sleeps and cries and reaches out for her with his strong little fingers. Even so, she stands over him every morning and watches the soft, growing body, strokes the downy head and searches the blank eyes for signs of the monster living in there. The conviction that he is carrying some invisible sickness tears her apart, because she knows something is wrong. He isn't like other children. He should never have been conceived.

'There's nothing wrong with the lad,' her father says. 'Anyone can see that.'

But on her way to the clinic her neck is always moist with sweat despite the frost that still sparkles on the trees. As always, her father waits in the car park while she goes through the doors with the child in her arms. His stare burns into her back as the heavy doors shut behind her. Harsh sunlight follows them into the waiting room and blinds her as she faces the doctor. The girl sits on the edge of the seat and watches them weigh and measure the child. There is a halo of spring light around his fragile head and the doctor speaks to her with a smile in her voice.

'What a beautiful little fellow.'

He is growing exactly as he should, there is nothing to be concerned about. If the doctor glimpses the monster, she doesn't mention it. It's the girl she worries about.

'You have got someone to help you, haven't you? It's important you get some rest in between.'

'I'm doing all right.'

'And the boy's father? You still have no idea who he is?'

'No. I don't know him.'

The lies are a big warm blanket she wraps around herself and the child, a powerful web of self-preservation keeping people at a distance. And in the car park her father sits with his head in his hands, rocking backwards and forwards.

The morning was bright and alive as she made her way through the village. She took an overgrown detour past Serudia's house to avoid meeting the old woman. She could hear the birds screeching from far off as she pulsed through the undergrowth.

Karl-Erik's house was on a hill. The farm had been passed down through the generations, but unlike Björngården it had been well looked after. The house shone red through the spruce trees. She had vague memories from her childhood of sitting in a sun-warmed kitchen, dunking almond biscuits in her coffee while Vidar and Karl-Erik exchanged a few words round the back of the house. That's what Vidar called it. Even when Karl-Erik hurled a bottle after him, making him run away down the hill, he still called it that: exchanging a few words. But the older she grew, the more Vidar warned her about Karl-Erik, saying he wasn't in his right mind and he had a tendency to lose his head when he was among women. *It's not for nothing he's a bachelor.*

Karl-Erik's face looked swollen in the daylight, his grey skin covered in open black pores.

'Oh, it's you, Liv. Come in, come in.'

The house was in even better condition on the inside, with a renovated kitchen and new flooring that made her walk carefully in her socks and speak in a low voice as if she was in a church. Karl-Erik put a cafetière on the table between them and asked if she wanted milk with her coffee. When he ducked behind the fridge door she heard him swallow a couple of mouthfuls of something hidden there.

'Perhaps you want something stronger?'

'Just coffee, thanks.'

She looked around the room, pausing at a group of pictures hanging over the kitchen bench, pencil sketches of dead trees spreading their naked branches towards a blurry grey sky. It seemed to be the same tree in every picture, but from different angles. The rowan tree where Kristina had hanged herself. The realization sent a shudder down her back.

Karl-Erik pulled the tab on a can of beer and the noise made her jump.

'How are things with you and Simon?'

'Not too bad. We're coping.'

'The police are here almost every day, asking questions. But they never seem to get anywhere. Or maybe you know more than I do?'

Liv shook her head, thought of the marsh and Vidar's glasses, but she didn't want to talk about what she knew. Not to Karl-Erik.

'It's not good enough,' he said. 'You're Vidar's family and they tell you nothing. A damned scandal, that's what it is.'

He drank the beer and smothered a belch. His lethargic movements told her this wasn't his first beer of the day. His watery eyes stared at her and made her want to turn and run.

'I never understood why you stayed with Vidar,' he said. 'I always thought you'd get out and see the world. Or at least get a place of your own.'

She regretted turning down the offer of something stronger if these were the kind of questions he was going to ask. His kitchen table looked as new as the floor, the wood shiny and free of scratches. No blemishes to stare at.

'I'm here because I want to talk about you and Dad,' she said. 'The disagreement you had.'

Karl-Erik crushed the beer can and took another from the fridge. The cheeks above his beard shone bright red.

'We shouldn't speak ill of the dead but I'll tell you the same as I told that police officer. I'm not grieving for Vidar, far from it. At last we can breathe freely in this village. If I knew who was behind it I'd give him a pat on the back.'

The anger flared up in her, hot and unexpected, and her jumper clung to her back. The dead trees on the wall seemed to be moving, mocking her.

'Why do you say that?'

'Wait here.'

Karl-Erik disappeared into an adjacent room and she heard him pull out drawers and slam things about. Her eyes fell on a knife lying on the work surface. It had a sheath of dark leather and an engraved reindeer-horn handle and was astonishingly similar to the one Vidar used to carry on his belt. She stood up to get a closer look and ran her fingers over the crafted leather as she listened for Karl-Erik. She pulled the knife from the sheath and held it up to the light and started feeling uneasy as she studied the exquisite details.

When Karl-Erik returned she held out the knife, pointing the blade at him.

'This looks like Dad's knife.'

Karl-Erik leaned against the door frame, squinting at her and the knife.

'I've had that knife since I was a boy. It was a present from Uncle Henrik. He used to carve them for me and Vidar, so it's no surprise your dad had one like it. But that knife is mine, I give you my word.'

He had a photograph album under his arm and he put it gently on the table.

'Come and sit down,' he said. 'Have a look at these old photos and you might understand a thing or two.'

Reluctantly she replaced the knife and sat down. When she didn't make any attempt to open the album he stood behind her and began leafing through the pages with a shaky hand. They were full of old pictures from the time when Karl-Erik's narrow cheeks were edged with sideburns. He was smiling so much she hardly recognized him, but there was no mistaking the woman in the picture. Hair like oil and an expression that made everything inside her stop. The same look she saw in the mirror every morning.

It took a while before she understood. Karl-Erik's arm around Kristina, their heads close together. In one of the photographs they were swimming naked together as the sun set on the other side of the lake. On another they were wearing cross-country skis and matching hats and winter jackets. They were so young, both of them. Simon's age, still only children. In some of the other pictures there were other people, but the only person she recognized was Vidar. He was sitting apart, smiling and laughing, and he was young, too. And he wasn't the one with his arm around Kristina.

She looked at Karl-Erik. His lips were like a bleeding wound in his beard.

'So you and Mum were together?'

'Kristina was my first great love. The only woman I have ever loved.'

His voice was quite sober as he spoke. Clear and steady. His face radiated pain.

'But what happened?'

'You know very well what happened. Vidar took her from me. And then my world fell apart.'

✳

'Daddy, can you do a fishbone braid?'

'A fish what?'

'A fishbone braid. One of those fat plaits that looks like a fish bone.'

'Sounds weird.'

'It's really, really hard to do, but Jamila's mummy can do them because she's a hairdresser.'

'I'm sure I can learn.'

Vanja smiled at him from the back seat.

'Jamila says mummies can do hair better than daddies but I said that's not true because my daddy can do all the hairstyles on YouTube.'

Liam laughed.

'Well, I can always try.'

The pride in her voice touched him. It was a feeling he thought he would never get used to, that there was someone in the world who believed in him and who only saw the good in him.

He didn't notice the patrol car until it was too late. It was parked in his mum's drive and the dogs were going mad behind the bars. There were so few visitors they weren't used to them, least of all the dogs. He considered doing a U-turn and disappearing onto the main road again, but he knew it was too late. They had already seen him.

Vanja tapped her finger on the window.

'The police are here.'

'I can see.'

'Do you think they're looking for Gabriel?'

'I don't know. Let's go in and find out.'

He was weak at the knees as he walked round the car to unclick Vanja's seat belt. She must have picked up on his fear because she fell silent and insisted he give her a piggyback. Her small arms clung tightly round his neck and he wanted nothing more than to run off into the bushes with her and vanish.

His fear was so strong it made him feel nauseous as he walked through the doorway. It was all over now, he knew. His mistakes had caught up with him. His attempts to create a normal life wouldn't save any of them now, he had waited too long. They would take Vanja away from him, he wouldn't be her daddy any longer. Someone else would carry her and braid her hair and be overjoyed by her laughter. Someone who deserved it.

His pulse raced and he felt dizzy. But whatever happened he mustn't lose control, he mustn't frighten Vanja. He would ask his mum to take her to another room before they arrested him, so she didn't have to see what kind of person her daddy really was.

His mum met them in the hall. Her hair smelled of saffron as she held them to her.

'He's been here for over an hour,' she whispered. 'But he won't say what it's about.'

Hassan was sitting on his dad's chair, drinking tea from a gilt-edged cup his mum had bought in Marrakech. She had gone there after their dad's funeral in a belated attempt to find herself. Liam leaned against the door frame with Vanja still hanging round his neck, wide-eyed and with her cheek pressed to his.

'So here you are,' said Hassan. 'I'd almost given up hope.'

'What do you want?'

'Right now I'd like to know who this little monkey is on your back.'

Vanja leaned over Liam's shoulder.

'I'm not a monkey.'

'No? Who are you, then?'

'I'm Vanja.'

'Vanja?' Hassan stared. 'Last time I saw you, you were this tiny.'

He measured an imaginary baby between his hands.

'Do you know me?'

'No, but I know your dad. Sometimes when he's been up to mischief I'm the one who has to come and give him a good telling-off.'

Hassan winked at Vanja. Liam lowered her gently to the floor and asked if she wanted to go out for a while and look at the dogs. She pulled a face and gave Liam and

Hassan a long look before finally going outside with her grandmother.

Liam waited until the door had closed behind them before turning to the police officer. He convinced himself it was a good sign that Hassan was here alone. If they had planned to arrest him there would have been more of them.

'That is someone you can be proud of,' said Hassan.

'What do you want?'

'Sit down, let's have a chat.'

Liam walked slowly across the floor and sat down without taking off his jacket, even though the air in the kitchen was sweet and stifling. Hassan spooned sugar into his tea and looked at Liam with an expression that revealed nothing.

'Incredible,' he said. 'You look like a whole new person. I hardly recognized you.'

'It's that why you're here? To comment on my appearance?'

'No, it's just that you're looking good and that makes me happy. Obviously you're sorting yourself out.'

'I'm trying.'

He watched Vanja and his mum through the window. The gate to the dog pound creaked and the wind played with their hair as they waded through the sea of eager dogs. Soon they would be visiting him behind bars too. The thought pained him.

'I heard you've started work at the filling station.'

'That's right.'

'Niila says you're doing Liv Björnlund's shift.'

Liam felt the chair disappear from under him when he heard her name. The cracks in the floor widened.

'Only until things calm down a bit for her.'

'Did you know each other from before, you and Liv?'

'I've bought things from her in the shop, that's all.'

'Has she told you anything about her father's death?'

'Only that he was murdered.'

Hassan slurped his tea. A piece of rock quartz stood on the table between them, catching the light. Liam knew his mum had put it there in an attempt to protect him. The sight was a comfort even if he had no faith whatsoever in her stones.

'She didn't say anything else?'

It suddenly occurred to Liam that he wasn't the one Hassan was after, it was Liv. So not only did people in the village think she was behind Vidar's death, the police did too. He picked up the crystal from the table and held it tightly, feeling the relief flood through him.

'She asked me the other day if I thought she'd done it.'

'Done what?'

'You know, killed her own father.'

'And what did you say?'

'I told her to go home and rest.'

Hassan's stare was unrelenting.

'So you don't think Liv Björnlund had anything to do with her father's death?'

The crystal embedded itself into his palms. This was his chance. He knew what Gabriel would have done if he had been sitting here: taken the opportunity to pour suspicion over her until he was blue in the face. His conscience never got in the way when it came to saving his own skin.

Vanja's laughter came through the window and Liam felt the stone cut into his skin.

'Liv Björnlund is bloody weird,' he said. 'But she's no murderer.'

✳

They drove towards the coast and Simon sat next to her, looking at his phone. Their solicitor, Ljuslinder, had called, asking them to come and discuss Vidar's will. Liv didn't even know there was a will. The news shook her. She was worried about his final decisions and whether they were yet another attempt to get at her.

They left the windless forest behind them and drove until they could see the sky reflected in the sea. Simon's hair had grown so long he could sweep it back into a little ponytail on his neck, revealing a red mark under his ear that she hadn't seen before. She realized it bore the trace of Felicia's lips. That childish need to leave an impression, to try to embed themselves into each other, like the blade of a knife on bark. That wasn't love, but she couldn't say it. That was the kind of thing only life could reveal.

And in reality she was glad he had someone at last. The gentle, lonely boy with his downcast eyes had gone. The one who spent breaktime kicking a ball against the fence because none of the other kids wanted to play with him. The one who always sat at the front of the bus so the driver could intervene if someone bullied him. The one who wanted Barbie dolls and My Little Pony for Christmas, so he could give them to the girls. The girls who were sometimes kind, kinder than the boys. They made him necklaces that he had to hide under his jumper when he came home so Vidar wouldn't see. But in the end he did, of course. Vidar had reached out and torn the necklace from him, and the kitchen floor had become a sea of shimmering beads. Liv could still remember the terrible sound of a world crashing down.

'Are you sad?' she asked.

He nodded and looked out of the window, away from her. She saw him wipe his eyes, not wanting her to see the tears.

The town shone in the spring sunshine. People undid their jackets and screwed up their pale winter faces in the bright light. The river ran through it all like a huge artery, lined with the green haze of birch trees. Liv steered through junctions and roundabouts, her knuckles white. She wasn't used to traffic and the cars seemed to be coming from all directions.

'Are *you* sad?' Simon asked, when they parked at last.

She had brought Vidar's pipe with her and she sat clumsily filling it with tobacco.

'Of course I'm sad.'

'But it doesn't show. You don't cry.'

'I can't cry. I don't think I know how to.'

'I've never seen you cry in my entire life.'

She smiled. There was so much he hadn't seen, so much he didn't know, about her and the nights and the strangers' cars. The gravel like rain against the chassis while the men's hands groped her skin. The liberation when they forced themselves, their tongues, inside her. And then the emptiness when it was over. On the way home it was always Vidar sitting behind the wheel, refusing to look at her. That's when the crying started. Only then. She stroked her boy's hair, his stubbly chin.

'My tears disappeared when I had you.'

They were early. The meeting was for ten and it wasn't even half past nine. Liv got out and leaned against the bonnet, lighting the pipe and smacking her lips as she sucked in the smoke the way Vidar used to do. The memories lay like a weight across her chest and she saw him everywhere. His contorted hands on the kitchen table in the morning, the same hands that let go of the parcel rack when she was learning to cycle. It wasn't until she was getting near the main road that she noticed he was no longer running after her, that he was only a small dot in the distance. That's when the bike started to wobble and soon she was lying on the gravel with grazed knees and tears of betrayal making her eyes sting. His eyes as he looked at her over the top of his glasses. We must stick together, you and me, he had said. If we leave each other all hell breaks loose.

Simon got out and joined her. When he reached for the pipe she didn't protest. Their shoulders touched as they stood blowing smoke rings towards the shining rooftops, and neither of them cried.

Inside the solicitor's office it felt as if everyone was staring at them. Liv's boots were unsteady when she walked across the patterned carpet and Ljuslinder showed them into his office. His eyes were red-rimmed and his hands clammy, his head was bald and shiny with sweat. Nasal hair hung down and mingled with his bushy moustache as he spoke. The office was dusty and stank of rotten fruit.

'My sincerest condolences for what has happened. Vidar was a good man. This is dreadful. *Dreadful.*'

A cloud of banana flies hovered above the waste-paper basket and stole her attention while Ljuslinder licked his finger and leafed through his papers. He had known Vidar for over twenty years and it had been a genuine honour to have worked for such a charismatic man, he said. Liv sat on the edge of her chair and tried to decide whether he was being honest or ingratiating. It surprised her that Vidar had chosen to trust solicitors and banks instead of his own family, but she understood it was all to do with control. He would have the final word, whatever happened.

Ljuslinder slid a sheet of paper across the table. His fingers had left a damp mark in the margin. His nasal voice droned through the room. Vidar's will had been drawn up the same year Simon was born and there was absolutely nothing remarkable or unusual about it.

'Vidar simply wanted to ensure that his grandchild would also inherit after his death. Without a will it is the children who inherit first, of course, and in that case the whole amount would have gone to you, Liv. But Vidar's wish was that you inherit half each and in so doing divide everything equally. In his eyes that was a fairer solution.'

Liv looked at her son and felt a lightness fill her chest, and she heard herself laugh out loud. She had expected something very different, something nasty and deliberately hurtful, a last attempt to control her. Anything at all, but not this.

Simon looked bewildered and blinked as Ljuslinder read out the details. The amount sounded vulgar coming from his mouth, incomprehensible. An amount that could change everything. Liv found it hard to take the words in, she saw only the nasal hair and the flies and Vidar's shadow looming over them. She envisaged him pacing up and down with the newborn baby boy in his arms, one hand cupped like a shield over the velvety head. Stolen glances at her as if he was afraid she would take the child away from him. He had loved the boy from the very first moment, long before she could bring herself to do it.

She drove too fast on the way home, ignoring the flashes of the speed cameras and the breaks in the wildlife fencing. Clouds raced across the sky and the spring winds made the ocean of forest storm around them. The old Volvo lurched over the cracks in the road.

'We can buy a new car,' Simon said.

'We can buy new everything.'

The thought should have made her happy, the knowledge that the meagre life she had lived with Vidar was over at last. Now there was no need to worry about anything, not the car or the chainsaw, not the dilapidated house. The world was at their feet, every decision was theirs. But still she couldn't relax. She felt pressure in her chest when she thought of their new freedom. It seemed so alien, almost threatening. Perhaps Simon felt the same because he sat staring into the forest, chewing his cheek.

'I want to do something good with the money,' he said.

'Such as?'

'I want to help Felicia's family. They're going to lose everything – the cows, the lot. And the bank won't give them another loan. If they don't get help they're finished.'

The wind forced the car closer to the ditch and Liv's hands ached on the wheel.

'I don't think you should get mixed up in Modig's affairs.'

'Why not?'

'It's kind of you to want to help, but you're so young and it's never a good idea to bring money into relationships. It can only end badly.'

'Oh yeah? And what do you know about relationships? You've never had a proper relationship. Not that I've seen, anyhow.'

The patronizing tone reminded her of Vidar, as did the dark look in his eyes. It struck her that death didn't matter. Not as long as the old man lived on in them.

Liv was woken by Simon skipping outside and it was as if the heart of the house was beating harder than ever. The light behind the curtains spoke of warmth and rebirth, and all of a sudden she knew it was time. The impulse was so strong she didn't think to put on clothes, and wearing only the T-shirt she slept in she went out to the woodshed and fetched a can of petrol. In a fury she drenched Vidar's possessions, the threadbare clothes that looked harmless enough now, lying there soaking wet and waiting for the match. The fire took hold with a fierce crackle. The weather was calm and the flames shot up hungrily. She imagined the smoke was full of him as it rose to the sky, the same foul smell as the one that came from his throat when he bent over her. It spat and roared and she didn't hear Simon coming closer. Suddenly there he was, sweaty and out of breath. She was afraid he would protest, that he would cry like he did at the morgue when it all became a reality. But he merely stood still beside her and stared at the leaping flames.

'I'm thinking of selling the place before summer,' she said.

'Why?'

'Because we're free now. We don't have to be here any longer.'

They had to shout to make themselves heard over the flames.

'But I want to stay here,' Simon said. 'I don't want to sell.'

'You always said you wanted to live in a town.'

'That was before, when Grandad was here. When he was in charge. We can make the decisions now.'

He didn't get any further because just then a couple of patrol cars came along the road. No sirens or blue light, but driving fast. Far too fast. Liv turned her head to watch as they passed her driveway and carried on into the village. Her stomach began to churn.

'Where do you think they're going?' Simon asked.

'No idea. We'll have to wait and see.'

'I'll shoot over to Felicia's. They might know.'

Liv stayed by the fire and watched him disappear into the forest. She wanted to call out and ask him to stay, but couldn't formulate the words. The loneliness scared her; it was when Vidar came back. His shadow moved out of the corner of her eye as if nothing had changed. As if he was still alive.

She went back into the kitchen and sat by the window, watching the flames climbing higher. The dog sat at her feet and every time it pricked up its ears her heart beat faster. She sat the way Vidar used to sit, hunched behind the curtain, her eyes on the road and the bonfire. A feeling of being watched came over her, the same as when she stood behind the till at the filling station with everyone's eyes on her. She convinced herself that someone was standing out there, their body concealed among the trees and her head in the line of sight.

It took a while for the police to come back. The cars were moving slower now but despite that she couldn't see who was driving, whether one of them was Hassan or not. She held her breath as they passed the barrier, afraid they would turn into her drive, but they drove on and disappeared around the hill.

Shortly afterwards Karl-Erik drew up at the barrier and sounded the horn. The new car shone like a salmon in the sunshine as she walked down to let him in. He swerved clumsily past the bonfire and made ruts in the gravel as he braked in front of the veranda. He threw nervous looks about him as he climbed out, almost as if he thought someone would jump out at him, and his gaze stopped at the smoking heap.

'I believe the police have driven off with your tenant.'

'Really?'

'I passed them just now, two police cars. Johnny Westberg in the back of one, looking unhappy.'

Liv peered down towards the road, trying to hide the turmoil she was feeling inside.

'I don't know anything about it.'

'What are you burning?'

'Just some of Dad's stuff.'

Karl-Erik nodded as if he understood. She saw traces of Vidar in his face, a family likeness in the tired furrows. He slid a veiny hand inside his jacket and her first thought was that he was going to get out a hip flask and take a swig, the way he had when their paths crossed in the forest, as if the very sight of another person drove him to drink. But instead he took out a bracelet and handed it to her. It was a black leather strip with plaited pewter thread and a reindeer-horn button that felt cool to the touch.

'It was Kristina's. I don't know if it's your size but never mind, you should be the one to have it.'

The leather was soft and well-worn, the pewter thread discoloured by time, but the craftsmanship was exquisite. Without a word she put it around her wrist and let Karl-Erik fasten the button. She noticed his hands were also stiff, but not as bad as Vidar's had been. The bracelet fitted perfectly. She could feel her own pulse beating beneath it.

'Where's that lad of yours?'

'He's at the Modigs'.'

Karl-Erik spat on the ground.

'I reckoned Douglas had got his claws into him.'

'What do you mean?'

'Douglas is running around bragging about how they're going to take over the whole village, his lass and that lad of yours. Been behaving like he's won the lottery ever since Vidar died.'

Liv put her hand over the bracelet. She felt the warmth from the fire and breathed the acrid smoke deep into her lungs, trying not to think of Johnny in the patrol car or Douglas's heavy arm around her son, the abandoned glasses on the marsh. Everything was spinning too fast. She heard Vidar's warning echo inside her: *the day you rely on another person is the day you lose yourself.*

She walked the dog before locking it in alone and setting off into the bushes. The evening sun lit up the path but she didn't need light to find her way. The village was quiet around her, only the smell of Modig's cows filtered across the marsh, along with intermittent barking. Otherwise there was no sign of life.

Widow Johansson's house stood abandoned beside the marshland. All the lights were off and no dogs came over the gravel to meet her. The only sound was the slap of plastic in the wind and when she got closer she saw the police tape across the door and a notice warning that the area was cordoned off. Liv reached across the tape and felt the door. It was locked. For the first time since Johnny had moved in, it was locked.

She stood outside the kitchen window and shone her phone's torch into the darkness. Everything looked the same inside: the abandoned washing-up on the draining board, a couple of burned-down candles on the table, a box of matches. The widow's embroidery stared back at her from the wall. She walked round the house and peered into the bedroom window where the moose head hung as if nothing had happened. The duvet was in a twisted heap on the floor as if he had been dragged from sleep when the police arrived. She switched off the torch and hugged her phone to her chest. She didn't want to see any more.

She was sitting in the darkened kitchen when Simon came home. Felicia was with him and their voices were excited as they stamped spring mud from their shoes and hung up their jackets. When they came into the kitchen you could tell from their faces that something significant had happened, and she couldn't stop them telling her, even if she didn't want to hear. She wasn't certain she could cope with what they had to say.

'The police have arrested Johnny Westberg,' Simon said. 'We saw them taking him away.'

'We asked what he'd done but they wouldn't tell us,' Felicia added.

'It's him, right? He's the one who murdered Grandad.'

Simon was red in the face and spittle flew as he spoke. Liv could only shake her head.

'I don't think we should jump to any hasty conclusions before we know more.'

'You love him, don't you? That's why you're defending him!'

'I'm not defending anyone, but we can't judge anyone before we know what's happened.'

Simon slammed his hand hard into the wall, so hard he made a hole. He looked, horrified, at the damage and then at her, before running upstairs and disappearing into his room. Felicia blinked dumbly at Liv before recovering and hurrying after him. Liv stayed where she was. She felt the loneliness surge through her veins, left with only the gaping black hole in the wall.

SUMMER 2003

The child is sleeping in her arms. She holds her thick cardigan over the neat little face to protect it from the sun and the wind and the passing cars. Fragile greenery bends over the gravel road and the smell of summer hangs in the cool air. It's early but the sun is beating steadily down on the dusty gravel and reflecting in the car windows, making it impossible for her to see who is driving. She stands in the ditch with the child in her arms as the cars pass one by one. A bag full of nappies hangs over one shoulder and the strap is slowly eating into her skin. Her arms ache with the child's weight. He is growing fast, his light eyes seeing more and more every day. She must hurry, time has already started running away from them.

A black car appears on the crest of the hill, its bonnet shiny like oil in the sunshine. The girl with the child takes a deep breath and steps out into the road, lifts her free hand and smiles so hard her cheeks ache. It is only when the car slows down that she sees it is a woman behind the wheel. She pulls back her hand but it's too late, the woman has stopped and wound down the window and is looking at her over the top of her sunglasses.

'Where are you heading?'

The girl rests her hand on the child's soft neck. She usually avoids women, they see too much, their eyes bore into everything. They're not like the men, who only see what they want to see and get trapped in their own fantasies. Women have a grasp on reality.

'Just to Arvidsjaur.'

'You've taken more than you can carry, I can see that. Jump in and I'll give you a lift!'

The woman's hair is dyed a claret red and choppy curls frame her face, a face that trembles with curiosity when the girl at last opens the door and sinks down into the seat. The woman removes her sunglasses and rearranges her cardigan, looking in adoration at the sleeping child.

'Oh,' she says. 'And who have we here?'

'I didn't bring the baby seat, I'm afraid.'

'Then I will drive carefully, with such a precious load.'

The woman offers her chocolate toffees, and coffee from a thermos. It smells wonderful but the girl is afraid she will spill it on the sleeping child, so she refuses. She hugs the soft body to her chest and stares at the road ahead as the woman looks her up and down.

'Where shall I drop you?'

'Wherever it suits you.'

The sun is climbing in the sky and the leaves take on an unearthly light. The girl points to the beauty of the countryside to deter the questions. It's a kind of superpower she has developed over the years, gliding away from people's curiosity and all the traps they try to set for her. The woman isn't smiling now. The chocolate toffee bulges in her cheek.

'Does he hit you?' she asks suddenly. 'Is your life in danger?'

'Nobody hits me.'

'It's Friday today. The police station is open until three.'

'Right.'

'What if I drop you off there? So they can help you.'

The girl's heart beats so hard in her chest she is afraid it will wake the child. She bites the inside of her cheek until the taste of blood fills her mouth. This is the last time she'll get a lift from a woman. As they pass the church her free hand is on the door handle. If it hadn't been for the child she would have opened it and run, but now she hesitates, afraid of hurting him. It is for his sake she is here, so that no harm will come to him.

Summer has invaded the streets. There are people everywhere and the air quivers with sun-soaked tarmac and happiness. The girl stares hungrily at them, at their smiles and their suntanned legs. The woman parks outside a low red building and strokes the child's sleeping cheek with her finger.

'I'll come in with you.'

'There's no need.'

Quickly she takes the child and the bag and gets out of the car. She walks slowly towards the closed doors and doesn't turn round until she reaches the steps. The woman waves at her before putting the car into gear and heading off. It amazes her that she drives away so fast, that she doesn't insist. There is a sign on the door saying *Back soon* and when she feels the handle it's locked. The relief goes to her legs and she sinks to the step and stays there. The child's mouth opens and searches for her. She sits on the steps of the police station with her face to the sun and her eyes closed as she breastfeeds the child. All of a sudden she is utterly exhausted.

The breeze carries with it the stench of death. The birches surrounding the building rustle as she gets to her feet and follows the smell round the corner of the building. Three rubbish sacks are lined up in the shade and a cloud of flies swarms around the black plastic. With one hand over the child's head she leans over and parts the top of the first sack. A reindeer head stares up at her, flies crawling over its unseeing eyes. Part of its tongue is hanging out of the lifeless mouth. The girl recoils and covers the child with her cardigan. A sound escapes her mouth and rebounds among the trees.

'Reindeer theft,' says a voice beside her.

A young policeman with spots on his chin has appeared from nowhere. She hugs the child tighter.

'But who does that kind of thing?'

'Well, a lot of crazy things happen when hate takes over.'

He is carrying a takeaway food bag and the hair on his neck is damp. His uniform looks warm. The girl holds her breath and the only sounds are the gurgling of the child and the buzzing of flies over the animal corpses. The mutilated reindeer send her a warning, a cold shudder down her backbone.

'Anything I can help you with?' asks the officer. 'Are you here to report something?'

He gesticulates to her to follow him into the station. The girl checks for an escape route as he unlocks the door. The child burps up a string of warm milk over her shoulder and she studies the shiny red neck of the police officer as she tries to gather her thoughts. It's harder to lie to men in uniform; they are trained to sniff out the truth and the truth is dangerous. She must never tell anyone. Otherwise they will take the child away from her.

The man in the uniform holds the door open for her and a

dark oily patch spreads over the bag in his hand. She walks into the cool air, the smell of death still in her nostrils. She smiles broadly to hide the fear that is thudding and twisting inside her.

'I don't want to make a report, I just need to borrow the phone to ring my dad. We've kind of lost each other.'

The police officer leans towards the child and his face wrinkles in a grin.

'Of course you can. Dads are important, we mustn't lose them.'

When Hassan arrived at the house Vidar's possessions lay in a charred heap. He came alone, and she was grateful for that. She hadn't slept a wink and her head was heavy from insomnia.

'What have you been burning?'

'Just a few of Dad's old things.'

He blinked at the blackened remains.

'Isn't that a bit drastic? There are second-hand shops, you know.'

'It was rubbish, nothing you could sell.'

'Some people will buy anything.'

'Dad wouldn't have liked someone running around in his things. He'd rather see them burn.'

The floorboards creaked under him as he walked into the hall, and the dog huddled in its corner, its ears flat against its head. Liv wondered whether it was the uniform or the sheer size of Hassan that scared the dog, or whether it sensed the gravity of the situation. Hassan crouched down and held out his hand, waiting patiently until the dog decided to approach him.

'Coffee?'

'Please.'

She went into the kitchen and spooned coffee into the jug without keeping count as she waited for him to say something.

But he stayed where he was, scratching the dog, fawning and chatting to it in a silly voice that would have made her laugh under normal circumstances.

Later, as they sat opposite each other at the table, his eyes kept returning to the charred heap outside, as if it somehow had the answer.

'I hope you saved a few mementoes, at least.'

'I've got more than enough memories.'

He smiled grimly.

'How are you keeping?'

'I'm alive.'

'And Simon? How's he coping with it all?'

'It's tough on him but he disappears to his girlfriend's house most of the time. He's there now.'

'Felicia Modig?'

'Uh-huh.'

She wondered how he knew that Simon and Felicia were seeing each other, whether Simon had told him or he had found out some other way. Presumably he knew all about them by now, from all the gossip the village had to offer.

'I understand you're also in a relationship with someone in the village,' Hassan said. 'That you and Johnny Westberg are together?'

'I wouldn't call it together. We have sex sometimes.'

Her face was on fire as he watched her. She couldn't look at him.

'According to him, it's more than that. He says you've been together since last autumn and that he's in love with you.'

301

'He's entitled to his opinion.'

'How would you describe your relationship?'

'Same as I did just now — we have sex from time to time. It's never been anything else and I don't know what it's got to do with the police.'

Hassan leaned back in his chair, studying her face, searching for something. She reached for Vidar's pipe and the pouch of tobacco that lay on the windowsill, needing something to do with her hands.

'Johnny Westberg was detained yesterday,' Hassan said.

'So I heard.'

'We have reasonable cause to suspect him of your father's murder, and that is the highest degree of suspicion. The evidence against him is strong.'

The loose tobacco slid through her fingers and rained down on her untouched coffee. Pictures of Johnny flashed through her mind: the scar on his throat that shone in the dim light, the darkness in his eyes when he said it wasn't right that she had to sneak around on account of her own father. The sudden admission that Vidar had tried to evict him only a few days before everything happened. The anxiety in his voice had distressed her deeply. She envisaged Vidar's body in the morgue, the soft white fingers, the forehead now perfectly smooth. She tried to imagine it: Johnny shooting her father, throwing the lifeless old body into the well. The thought made her gag. She gripped the pipe hard but couldn't bring herself to light it. Hassan refused to take his eyes off her, looking for something in her face, some kind of emotional reaction that would give him a lead.

'So far he's denied it. But he has also told us that Vidar didn't like him and that you had to keep your relationship under wraps. He says you ran home to him at night, after Vidar had fallen asleep. That you had to sneak around like a couple of teenagers.'

'Dad didn't like anyone except his own. Me and Simon.'

'Johnny says you were with him the night Vidar died.'

The pipe in her hand moved in time to her pulse. It was true, she had been at Johnny's briefly. She never stayed longer than a few hours. Her fear of Vidar was too great, the worry that he would discover them. Maybe he had done that, discovered them. Maybe he had followed her and waited until she left before revealing himself. In her mind she pictured the two men confronting each other in the moonlight. The thought made her freeze.

'I was only there for a few hours.'

'At what time?'

'Between midnight and two, maybe not quite as long. I never stayed long.'

'Why haven't you mentioned this before?'

'I didn't think it was important.'

Hassan looked at her as if they no longer knew each other.

'Can you tell me how you met, you and Johnny?'

'It was last autumn. He came to the farm wanting the key to old Widow Johansson's house. I don't know what the date was, but the first snow had fallen, I'm sure of that. We said hello, that's all. Dad dealt with the practical details.'

'You didn't have any contact before that, online or anything?'

'No. Dad took care of all that. He wanted to let the house instead of selling it. He thought it was safest that way. But I don't know how he got hold of Johnny. All he told me was that he'd found someone who wanted to live in the Johanssons' house. Shortly after that Johnny was here, standing on the doorstep and asking for the key. I'd never seen him before.'

'When did the sexual relationship start?'

'Not long afterwards.'

'Who took the initiative?'

She looked out at the forest, billowing in the spring wind.

'I jogged past the widow's house one evening and saw him sitting there. He looked so alone in the old place. I asked if he had any coffee and he made me some. That's how it started.'

It was true, all of it, but even so she felt like a liar. Perhaps it was the shock, being unable to comprehend anything, having a head full of grey fog. How well did she know Johnny, really? She had warded off any of his attempts to get closer, and that had frustrated him. He had never shown any signs of violence but she had sensed his disappointment every time she left him to run home, even though he pleaded with her to stay. A dark shadow fell across his face every time they had to part. She thought it was all her fault, she should have been more careful. Ever since she had been old enough to hear, Vidar had warned her against the outside world, against the monsters slinking around their property, waiting to strike. If you got involved with them you were in trouble.

There was a look of resignation on Hassan's face. He hadn't touched his coffee either.

'I understand you inherited a large amount of money after your father's death.'

'You could say that.'

'Did you ever talk about money, you and Johnny?'

She shook her head and her hair fell across her cheeks. She never talked about money with anyone, not if she could avoid it. To be honest, the very word made her want to choke. Money was ugly and evil, put walls between people and deprived them of their common sense. She could still hear Vidar's warnings, the pessimism he had imprinted in her since she was a child. *Money is the main reason people kill each other*, he used to say. *You must never mention our fortune, my little cloudberry. Not if you value life.*

*

Liam could see the children playing through the window. It looked as if they were dancing in a circle with Vanja in the middle, spinning round and round, her skirt like a yellow umbrella. He knew she was laughing even if he couldn't hear it, her infectious laugh that not even the most cold-hearted bastard could resist. He lived for that laugh.

He left his jacket in the car, wanting the staff to see his work shirt. He wore the blue garment proudly, like a flag. He wanted them to see he was serious, that he was getting his life in order. They could keep any queries and concerned looks to themselves.

His phone vibrated in his pocket as he walked up the gravel path. Probably Mum wanting him to buy dog food – she could be as desperate as a punter as far as the dogs were concerned.

One more two-kilo sack will be enough, she always said, otherwise I'll have to take the salmon out of the freezer.

But it wasn't his mum, it was Gabriel, and it sounded like he was running. He was panting loudly.

'Get here now, bro. Everything's been trashed!'

'I can't. I'm at the school.'

'And I'm at the greenhouse. You've got to get here quick!'

'What's happened?'

But the line broke before Gabriel could answer. Liam stood on the well-raked gravel path outside the school and tried to call back but all he got was the ringtone. Usually Gabriel didn't ask for help, he gave the orders. Liam felt the panic spread through his body. Vanja had caught sight of him and stopped dancing. She was standing with her head pressed against the glass door and looking at him, wide-eyed and serious. The plait lay fat and tousled over one thin shoulder, and her cheeks were flushed. Liam slid the phone back into his pocket and forced a wide smile as he hurried towards her. She pushed open the door and met him on the threshold, studying his face for a few seconds before allowing him to pick her up. Her chin was very warm against his.

The teachers flocked around them while Vanja struggled into her outdoor clothes. Their oily, well-meaning smiles made his skin creep. They wanted to know how he was getting on at the filling station, whether he had found an apartment. Marcus, the youngest, had a cousin in Abborrträsk with a house to sell, if he wanted one. His phone vibrated manically in his pocket and by the time they were ready to leave Gabriel had sent two messages. *Hurry up*, they said, *it's wrecked!*

'Are we going to buy dog food?' Vanja asked.

'We've got to go and see Uncle Gabriel first.'

'Has he taken drugs?'

'No, no, he just wants to talk.'

Vanja sat in silence as he strapped her in. It was impossible to fool her these days, maybe it always had been. He gritted his teeth as he drove. Really he should leave Gabriel to deal with his own shit, but he couldn't turn his back on him, not yet. Too much was at stake. Now that he was finally on the right path he had to keep an eye on Gabriel so he didn't cause any more damage. So he didn't try to sabotage everything Liam was trying to build up.

Spring was in full swing outside the smeared windows. There was water everywhere, it steamed and sprayed and left a dirty film over cars and road signs. Vanja's boots dangled like yellow suns over the edge of the seat.

'Grandma says Gabriel was super-smart before he started taking drugs. Smarter than you, even.'

'Does she?'

'She says the drugs have fried his brain.'

Vanja spread her fingers and made a buzzing noise. The phone vibrated in his pocket again but Liam left it there. It felt as though water was rushing through him, too, in cold dirty streams. It gathered in his throat, stung his eyes and threatened to choke him.

'Do you think it hurts, Daddy?'

'What?'

'When your brain fries.'

Liam wound down the window and spat.

'Yes, I think so. I think it hurts a lot.'

'But why do people eat drugs if it hurts them?'

'Because sometimes it hurts more to stop doing it.'

✳

The bundle of papers landed on the table with a dull thud. Repayment demands and letters from the Debt Enforcement Agency, creased and coffee-stained. Hassan tapped a knuckle against the rows of figures and the frown turned his face into someone else's, someone older and wearier. She turned her head towards the treetops outside. She didn't want to see the letters, didn't want to know.

Hassan slowly pushed them over the table, bringing her back to reality.

'How well would you say you know Johnny Westberg?'

'In actual fact I don't know him at all. I only know he comes from down south and works at the sawmill in Glommersträsk.'

'It never occurred to you to apply for a credit check on your new tenant?'

'Dad looked after all that. And I doubt he would have paid for that kind of thing. He'd rather make up his own mind.'

'Did Johnny have a problem paying the rent?'

'Not that I know. It wasn't much, after all. The place had stood empty for ten years. We were just glad someone wanted to live there.'

'It's a pity you didn't run a credit check because then you would have seen that Johnny Westberg has debts of over two million kronor. He's been living on the poverty line for almost three years, a situation that has clearly been very tough for him. He has tried to take his life several times. The scar on his neck is the result of his latest attempt and according to his medical record he almost succeeded.'

The scar on his neck. Liv could feel the raised surface under her fingertips, the white strip of skin that was so much softer than the rest of him. She had been close to asking how he got it but something held her back. Simply sensing someone else's darkness was enough to make her back off. She had plenty of her own.

'I had no idea. We never talked about his past.'

'It's become apparent that Johnny had dealings with the criminal underworld in an attempt to clear his debts, but that only made the situation worse. Clearly the threats from these new acquaintances drove him north. And I don't think it's chance that he rented somewhere from you. We confiscated his laptop and found hundreds of Google searches he made about Vidar's fortune, both before he moved to Ödesmark and after. Everything points to the fact that he had his eyes on your money from the very beginning.'

Liv could hear Vidar's mocking voice from the shadows. *What have I always told you? The only people you can trust are your own. The rest are only beggars and vultures.* This was what he had warned her about for as long as she could remember. The evil and greed that lay in wait on the other side of the forest.

She thought of Johnny, of his face in the glow of a cigarette, the vulnerability she glimpsed sometimes in his shy expression. Johnny had never hinted that he was in need of money. She was the one who had sought him out from the very beginning. Everything was her initiative.

'If it's money he's after, he's hidden it well.'

'Johnny Westberg is a desperate man,' said Hassan. 'And desperate people do stupid things. So far he has denied being involved in the crime, but I doubt he'll be able to keep up the pretence for much longer.'

A hard patter of rain against the window made them both jump. A storm had swept in over the village without them noticing. Soon they had to raise their voices to make themselves heard.

'If it was money he was after, couldn't he just have robbed us? Why would he want to kill Dad?'

'Perhaps that wasn't intentional. It could have been a fateful act in the heat of the moment.'

Liv put a clenched fist to her mouth. Nausea started to rise up inside her. She thought about what Johnny had told her, that Vidar had been to see him and told him to move out. Perhaps that was the trigger. She wanted to tell Hassan about it, but couldn't. There was so much inside her that threatened to pour out, so much she mustn't say. Her hand was a shield for her mouth, her jaws tightly clenched.

Hassan leaned closer, searching her face.

'Did you tell Vidar about your relationship?'

'I didn't need to,' she whispered. 'He found out anyway.'

'And what did he say after he found out?'

'He said the same thing he always said whenever I met anyone.'

'And what was that?'

'That they'll end up hurting me.'

✳

He had sworn never to let Vanja come anywhere near the cannabis farm, but something in Gabriel's voice told him to make an exception. Just this once.

It was an abandoned summer house beside a river, with boarded-up windows and overgrown vegetation obscuring the walls. Wheel tracks in the grass were the only sign that anyone ever visited the place. Gabriel's car was parked well in among the trees and the door on the driver's side banged in the wind, but there was no sign of him.

'What a horrible house,' said Vanja.

'It's a bit run-down, that's all. Stay here, I'll be back soon.'

The wind battered the trees and when Liam stepped out of the car the air was filled with the unmistakable smell of the plants growing inside. He looked round, scanning the turbulent forest. It was a long way to the nearest house and people were only there over the summer, if at all. As he waded through the undergrowth he was hit by a feeling that something was terribly wrong. The farm had been his idea when Vanja was tiny and he hadn't been ready to leave the drugs alone. Growing his own meant he wouldn't have to do deals with a load of idiots. At least, that was the plan. Until Gabriel got involved and wanted to scale things up so they could sell the weed as well. Liam had done all the dirty work, sowing the seeds and experimenting with grow lights and air filters until everything worked and the plants began to thrive. It turned out he had a talent for it. Maybe he had inherited his mum's green fingers, her affinity with all living things.

Over the last year he had tried to abandon the whole bloody thing, told Gabriel to run it himself, said it was too risky. But Gabriel was clever at luring him back in. He always knew which buttons to press.

As he approached the door he realized what was wrong. It was too dark in there, the lights were off. The lilac glow had been replaced by utter darkness. He looked back and saw Vanja's wide eyes behind the windscreen. The plait was in her mouth, a habit she had when she became nervous, sucking and chewing her hair until it hung in damp strands. He had tried to frighten her by saying she would end up with a tummy full of hair and have to have an operation if she didn't stop, but she carried on and he knew it was his fault. He caused the anxiety in their life.

Gabriel's hoarse cough sounded from inside the house. Liam pushed open the door and walked into a scene of destruction.

The ground was covered in earth and broken glass. The plants were gone; someone had been there and torn them from the pots. Only the weakest remained, lying in wilted heaps among the wreckage. The grow lamps were smashed and the plastic wall linings had been torn down and were lying in black shreds over it all.

The hum of the fans had gone silent. They had stopped turning and everything was destroyed. It was as if a tornado had ripped through the house.

Gabriel was crouching in the middle of the chaos, searching among the rubbish.

'Well, well, you've got here at last. What took you so long?'

'What the hell's happened here?'

'It's Juha, I know it. He wants to punish us for the Vidar thing. About half the plants are gone and the rest will die. And every fucking lamp is broken. He's trashed it all.'

Gabriel picked up a plant pot and hurled it so hard at the wall that several fragments embedded themselves in the dark wood. Liam stayed by the door, trying to collect his thoughts and work out how much had been lost. In all honesty he didn't care, not now. All he felt was relief the police weren't there, waiting to arrest them. He didn't give a toss about the cannabis farm, it might as well be gone for good.

Shards of glass crackled under Gabriel's boots as he moved about the room. His face was ashen.

'Come on,' he said. 'Let's find Juha.'

'I've got Vanja with me. I can't go anywhere.'

'I forgot what a total dickhead you've become. Never mind, I'll do it myself.'

'What are you going to do?'

Gabriel kicked a broken lamp and a shower of splintered glass flew across the room.

'Juha won't be able to roll a joint by the time I'm finished with him, just you wait. I'll see to it he goes the same way as old man Björnlund.'

*

Douglas Modig filled the schnapps glasses to the brim and raised his own, slopping the alcohol over the top. He put his free arm around Liv and leaned his sweaty cheek against her forehead as he made a toast.

'To the police,' he said. 'For a job well done. With Vidar's murderer under lock and key we can start getting over this tragedy at long last.'

Liv looked down at the slices of reindeer meat on her plate. The fat had set into a yellow film and she hadn't managed to take a single mouthful. It had been a mistake coming here, to the Modigs' house. It felt as though she had betrayed Vidar simply by stepping over the threshold. And she didn't like the way Douglas and Eva looked at her, as if she was a riddle they'd given up trying to solve.

It was for Simon's sake she had come. He was sitting opposite her and wasn't eating like he usually did, merely prodding the food with his fork. But he was used to being here in the Modigs' house, she could see that. He downed his schnapps in one and Liv wondered how often he drank when he visited Felicia, because this wasn't the first time.

'I thought it was odd he didn't have anything with him,' Eva said. 'When I went to see him last winter he was surrounded by old Widow Johansson's things. Not a stick of furniture of his own. It looked really sad.'

'Yes, dammit,' said Douglas. 'We felt sorry for the bastard to start with. He was badly prepared for life up here – moved here midwinter without so much as a stick of wood for the stove. We gave the poor guy logs so he wouldn't freeze to death before he'd got himself settled in. And then you find out he's a cold-blooded murderer. It makes my flesh go cold.'

Liv felt the old itching on her arms. The food became a blur on her plate. It was a pity to see such good meat going to waste but she couldn't even lift her fork. The conversation turned all the time to Johnny Westberg and she knew they were waiting for her to say something. When she didn't, Douglas hugged her to him again.

'So what have you got to say about it, Liv? I understand you used to see each other, you and Johnny. That you had something going on.'

Liv pushed the plate of untouched reindeer meat away from her and glanced at Simon.

'No,' she said. 'There was nothing going on. I went there sometimes to check on the house, that's all.'

Douglas gave her a smile of disbelief.

'I'm surprised Vidar didn't suspect something,' he said, sticking a toothpick under his lip. 'You couldn't fool him.'

His cheeks were red, his eyes shining with excitement. Like a child at Christmas, Liv thought. It was so obvious he was enjoying this. But whether it was Vidar's death that got him worked up, or the general commotion in a village where usually nothing ever happened, was hard to tell. Every time he leaned closer she wanted to scream.

By the time Eva finally stood up to clear the table Douglas had already poured out more schnapps. Liv swallowed one mouthful, then another. It burned pleasantly all the way down to her stomach. She noticed Simon's hand resting on Felicia's thigh under the table.

Eva whistled as she made the coffee. She brought out ice cream and cloudberry jam, and as she did so she smiled knowingly at Simon.

'Don't worry,' she said to him. 'I've got sorbet for you. I know you're scared of the fat.'

Perhaps it was the motherliness in her voice, or the way

she caressed the top of his head, but suddenly Liv couldn't breathe. He was only seventeen. They should have asked her permission before offering him alcohol. One whole schnapps glass, and then another. Sorbet instead of ice cream. Eva knew nothing about his fears. It wasn't fat he was scared of, it was Vidar's scorn at the table. Comments about watching what he ate, that he'd never get a woman if he was fat as well as ugly. That's what was going round in his head. Eva and Douglas knew nothing about her boy, yet they behaved as if he was theirs.

Everything went still when Liv got up. Simon stared at her, the colour in his cheeks rose and he pulled a face, warning her to behave before she embarrassed them.

'I'm going now,' she said. 'You'll have to excuse me but I don't feel well.'

Douglas reached out to her, trying to make her stay, but Liv hurried into the hall where she fumbled blindly among the outdoor clothes. She found her shoes but Eva had to help her on with her jacket, pulling up the zip as if she was a child. Liv had already opened the door and stood facing the cool night, filling her lungs. The cows lowed in the barn and she staggered out into the darkness, excusing herself for a second time before shutting the door and hurrying away. Back to her own home. She took a shortcut through the forest and turned round to see if Simon was following her. But behind her was only darkness.

SUMMER 2008

The child's laughter makes her heart swell. The boy is standing in the water and the sunshine, blinding her with his chubby body and his face glowing with happiness. His joy is infectious, it slides under her skin and breathes new life into her. It's like taking off a blindfold and rediscovering the world – the forest exploding in delicate greenery and dragonfly rings on the water where her boy is practising his first swimming strokes. The world is beautiful, thanks to him.

She doesn't see the man wading through the rosebay willow-herb, swatting at flies. The smell of manure reaches her first, and when he sits down beside her it's so overpowering she has to breathe through her mouth. She says hello without taking her eyes off the boy in the water, an edge to her voice to let him know he is an intruder. This is their paradise, their beautiful moment on earth.

'Do you want a cup?'

A thermos of coffee appears and he insists she takes it, along with a thick slice of cheese that lies sweating between them on the bench. There is a predator's gleam in his eyes when he looks at the child, and every muscle in her body knots up and hurts.

The man dips his cheese in his coffee and grins.

'That's a fine lad you've got.'

The boy is holding a net which he sweeps under the water, hunting for tadpoles and perch. The movement makes him unsteady and he almost falls, but regains his balance at the last moment. He screams and laughs at the same time. The man beside her laughs too, it's impossible not to. The coffee slops over the mug and lies steaming on the grass. He shouts something to the boy, something about him needing a proper fishing rod. It's hot, sweat trickles down her spine and she knows what he's after. She sees the way he shields his eyes from the sun and peers hard to study the boy. The curls and the chubby cheeks.

'You couldn't say he's like you to look at,' he says.

'No, luckily.'

He chuckles. The coffee burns her throat and tastes of manure. She already knows what he's going to say next, she can practically hear the words taking shape in his mouth.

'Who's his father?'

'No one you know.'

'But you must know people are curious.'

'As if I care.'

He pulls his T-shirt over his head and uses it to dry his armpits. His belly quivers over his belt and on his chest is a tattoo she hasn't seen before, his daughter's name printed in swirling letters. He breaks off another piece of cheese and puts it in his mouth, pulling a face at the boy who pulls a face back, as if they are having their own conversation and she is not a part of it.

The air buzzes with flies. They sit in black clusters on his filthy boots and try to get to the sweat in her hair. She finishes the coffee and calls to the boy that it's time to go home, but he's staring under the water and pretends not to hear. The man leans back and pats his white distended gut.

'People have even asked if he's mine.'

'Really?'

'But I have to be honest and say how it is. That it's been a few years since you and I were together, so he can't be mine. Even if I wish he was.'

'I didn't think you were interested in village gossip.'

'People want to get to the bottom of things. It can't be helped, it's the way we're made.'

She stands up and calls the boy again. He has thrown his net into the grass and is standing with his fat little hands cupped under the water. The man behind her coughs. He won't give in.

'It wasn't your dad, was it, forcing himself on you?'

She doesn't say it loudly but the words seem to echo across the water even so.

'You can rot in hell.'

Her heart is thudding in her ears as she hurries to the water and picks up the boy. The bucket of frogspawn thumps against her back as she carries him away.

The yard was in darkness and the only thing moving was the dog. It stood at the end of its chain, eyes fixed on the house as it growled softly, as if something dangerous and alien was hiding inside.

When Liv put the key in the lock she discovered the door was already open. On the doorstep she was met by a strange smell, something sour that made her stomach turn. She took the shoe horn from the shelf and held it in front of her like a weapon as she followed the smell into the kitchen. She saw a shadowy figure by the window, sitting in the chair that had been Vidar's. She felt the fear rise in her throat as she reached for the light switch. A man she didn't recognize was revealed in the sharp light. Liv put two fingers under the dog's collar to stop it going any closer.

'Who are you?'

'Come on, Liv. Don't you recognize me?'

His greying hair fell below his sinewy shoulders and merged with a beard that had been left to grow for many years. It was evident his face had aged before his body, the skin weathered and lined by the changing seasons. A familiar light in his eyes made her gasp.

'Juha?'

'It's been a few years.'

She remembered the autumn they'd had together, the

shady lay-by where Juha waited for her while the leaves showered down on the roof and winter approached. His hair had been darker then, his skin healthier, and he had filled her with such hope that her chest ached when she thought about it.

'You can't just walk into my home. You scared me half to death.'

'I heard what happened to Vidar. I'm sorry for your loss.'

'You're not sorry at all.'

There was the hint of a smile but it wasn't the same smile she remembered. This one was mournful and full of gaps. She let go of the dog and it nosed its way towards him. He had a better way with animals than humans, apparently. She studied the scruffy clothes he was wearing – a green fleece jacket and dark padded trousers, stained by the forest and open fires. Two knives hung from his belt, but it didn't look as if he was carrying any other weapons.

Liv stayed by the sink, keeping her distance. She checked for signs of Simon through the window. The man by the table didn't take his eyes off her. She held his gaze, challenging him.

'You're sitting in Dad's chair.'

'But he doesn't need it any more, does he?'

Juha winked at her. In the light of the kitchen lamp she could still see the man who had slept with his head in her lap. There was a feeling that time hadn't moved on at all.

'I waited for you in the lay-by,' she said. 'A whole winter, I waited. But you never came.'

'Vidar told me to stay away.'

'And you listened to him?'

'He could be very persuasive, your father.'

'I missed you.'

The smile died. He put a hand over his eyes and gave a soft moan. Liv didn't move, didn't want to get too close. Her nose had become accustomed to him, just as it always had. She couldn't smell him now. There was dirt under his nails and in the furrows on his hands, as if he had dug his way up from underground. For almost twenty years he had avoided her, kept away, but now here he was, suddenly, sitting at her table as if he had also been waiting for her.

Slowly he looked up again and his eyes fastened on the photograph of Simon hanging on the wall.

'Is that your lad?'

'Yes.'

'He's more like Vidar than you.'

'Go to hell.'

Juha held up two dirty palms.

'Believe me, I'm not here to argue with you. You still shimmer like a lake in winter, Liv, and that makes me glad. I know I'm on the late side, I should have come a long time ago. But I'm here now and I think we can help each other.'

'I doubt it.'

He kept glancing out into the darkness pressing up against the window, as if he was afraid someone was out there, listening. She fetched the bottle of Vidar's vodka and poured a little for each of them. Juha drank gratefully and the alcohol shone on his cracked lips.

'Dammit,' he said. 'It feels like only yesterday we were driving around together.'

Liv sipped her vodka, not wanting to say it felt like a lifetime to her.

'Do you remember what I told you about Vidar and the land?' Juha asked.

'You said your parents sold everything to Dad after your brother died.'

'That's how it started. Neither of them was in any shape to think clearly when the deal was made. My brother was barely cold in his grave when Vidar turned up. No one could stand the sight of me so I was sleeping in the Merc. And they still can't stand the sight of me. Mum's in the hospital at Skellefte and she told the staff that whatever happens they mustn't let me in. Her only living son.'

Once he had started talking he couldn't stop. Liv stood by the sink while Vidar's homebrew warmed her from the inside and gave oxygen to the rage that was also smouldering in there. A whole winter she had waited for Juha. And now here he was, old and worn out and full of the same old injustices. It occurred to her that she wasn't the only one who was stuck; there were others who were much worse off. She slammed down her glass, to shut him up.

'None of this has anything to do with me.'

That threw Juha. He ground his teeth as he looked at her.

'There's one more thing you might not know.'

'And that is?'

'We made a deal with each other, me and Vidar, after he found us together. He promised I could go on living in North

Forest. As long as I kept away from you I could go on living there. For almost twenty years he kept his promise, but in March I got a letter from the forestry company.'

He took a sheet of paper from his inside pocket and unfolded it slowly.

'They're felling the lot. They want me out by midsummer.'

His face twitched with emotion as he looked at Liv, as if he was on the point of bursting into tears or screams or even something worse. The sight of it inflamed her rage. So that's why he abandoned her. A simple promise from Vidar was all it took.

'I've got nothing to do with Dad's business deals. You know that.'

'But you inherited his money, didn't you?'

'Is that why you're here, because you want money?'

He grimaced as if the words hurt him, and his eyes streamed. In his grief he was more like the young man he had been, the man she had loved like a brother. She had believed in him that autumn, put her hope in his solitariness that was so like her own. But he had chosen the land over her.

'I only want to take back what belongs to me,' he said. 'And I know you can help me.'

'I don't think so.'

He wiped his face with the back of his hand. His eyes flickered from wall to wall and found it hard to meet hers.

'The police have got the wrong man. I know who did away with Vidar and it wasn't that chancer they're writing about in the papers.'

'How can you know that?'

'I'm a recluse, Liv. I don't live among folk. The only people who'll have anything to do with me are small-time thieves and others who've lost their way, and that's the truth. The unloved tribe who live in the shadows, just like me. We know about everything that happens in the dark, whether we want to or not. That's our curse.'

He pointed into the night.

'I know who killed Vidar,' he went on. 'And it wasn't this gold digger who rented your house. The police have got the wrong man.'

'Maybe you should be talking to the police instead of me.'

'I don't give a damn about the police. It's you I want to help, don't you get it? I thought about you so much as the years went by, Liv. I want you to know that. And you deserve the truth, if nothing else. All I want is the land Vidar promised me and then I'll tell you who did it.'

Liv gripped the edge of the sink so hard her fingers hurt.

'I can't give you any land and you know it. Dad sold it all.'

'Give me the cash he got for North Forest and we're quits.'

Juha put a cigarette in his mouth without asking. The smoke curled out of his nose and mouth while he waited for her to say something. When she didn't, he rapped an impatient finger on the table.

'Put everything right, Liv. That's all I'm asking. Then you get your dad's killer on a plate.'

*

Liam stood by the container, smoking and trying to read the evening papers in the wind. The hoardings had thick black headlines about the forty-two-year-old who had been arrested for the murder of the millionaire from Ödesmark. The man was described as an outsider with massive gambling debts. They speculated that it was the dream of a new start that had driven him north, and it was Old Man Björnlund's money that made him choose Ödesmark in particular. Vidar Björnlund's name had featured on the lists of the richest men in the county, something the accused man would have been very well aware of. The forty-two-year-old had rented one of Björnlund's houses and found work at the sawmill in Glommersträsk. His colleagues said he was a quiet man who kept to himself most of the time, but apart from that there was nothing wrong with him and he had been good at his job. The police were reticent about the motive for the murder, but everything indicated that it was about money.

'You mustn't believe all you read.'

The voice came from nowhere. When Liam lowered the paper there she was, pale and hollow-eyed, but looking determined.

'I don't.'

Liv reached for his cigarette, put it into her mouth and inhaled deeply while keeping her eyes fixed on his. Liam folded the newspaper and put it under his arm. He lit another cigarette in an attempt to keep the distance between them, glanced at the clock and saw that his break was almost over. Niila would be sticking his head out any minute, wondering where he was.

'The police have got the wrong man,' she said.

'That wouldn't surprise me.'

A faint smile spread across her face. She was standing too close and they had to turn their heads to avoid breathing smoke onto each other. When the door swung open and Niila appeared they sprang apart as if they had been caught out.

Liam stood behind the till and watched as Liv and Niila disappeared into the office. He smoothed out the newspaper and put it back on the stand. The customers always headed for the papers as soon as they came through the door. The headlines about Ödesmark were more important than milk or tobacco. They stood there, flicking through the pages and humming, while Liam kept an eye on the office door. His body couldn't relax when she was around. He paced in circles behind the till like a caged animal and his jaw tightened whenever a customer tried to talk to him. He could see the dead man in their faces, and wondered what she meant about the police having the wrong man. And how much she actually knew.

When she finally came out of the office all she did was nod in his direction before disappearing through the stockroom door.

Tension gripped his body. Something about the way she looked at him made everything fall away, as if she could see right through the mask he was trying to hide behind. Niila came out of the office, stood beside Liam and spoke in a low voice.

'We must keep an eye on her,' he said. 'I'm afraid she's starting to crack up.'

'What do you mean?'

'She says she's going to find her father's murderer herself.'

The next time he took a break she was still there. As soon as Liam pushed open the stockroom and lit up, there she was again, in the shadows, almost as if she had been waiting for him.

'My car won't start. Have you got any jump leads?'

He didn't understand what she meant at first and stared at her mouth like an idiot. Perhaps he had been expecting something else, something terrible. Every time she confronted him he thought it was all over.

He shook himself.

'Jump leads. Yes, sure.'

He didn't have to move his car; her battered old vehicle was parked alongside it. He took the cables from the boot and lifted the bonnet. She stood beside him, continually running a fluttering hand through her hair. It made him nervous.

'This old crate has seen better days,' he said.

'I will buy a new car, I just haven't got round to it yet.'

'You've had enough to think of.'

'Dad always said buying a new car is like using money to wipe your backside.'

It sounded amusing when she said it, as if she was imitating her father. Liam gave a laugh and when he glanced at her he saw she was smiling. The smile made him feel calmer. Heavy clouds gathered over their heads and she shone her torch as he attached the cables.

'Do you know who Juha Bjerke is?' she asked unexpectedly.

Liam fumbled with the battery clips.

'That lone wolf in North Forest? Everyone knows who he is.'

'He came to visit me yesterday.'

'Oh yeah?'

'He says the police have got the wrong man. He says he knows who murdered Dad.'

'No shit.'

'But he wants paying before he'll tell me.'

Liam straightened up slowly. His head was buzzing.

'You can start the engine now.'

She switched off the torch and got into the battered car. The door played up and wouldn't close, but on the third attempt it slammed shut, and when at last she turned on the ignition the engine started and he could see her smiling through the dirty window. He smiled back, but his heart was beating so hard he could scarcely breathe. She wound down the window and thanked him, and he gathered up the jump leads and held them tightly to his chest.

'Juha Bjerke is mad,' he said. 'I wouldn't give much for his opinions.'

It was late, but Gabriel answered after the first ring. The night was his time for being awake.

'Something's happened,' Liam said.

'OK.'

'It's our friend in the forest. I think he's about to squeal.'

There was a moment of heavy silence before Gabriel swore.

'I'll be over.'

Liam couldn't sit still while he waited. He walked round and round the confined space, stopping now and then by the window to check the road. He could see the shadowy figures of the dogs down in the pen. Vanja was wrapped in a deep sleep with one of the smaller dogs beside her, a shaggy little thing that lifted its head and watched him with wary eyes as he paced the room.

He saw the lights through the trees before he heard the car, and went downstairs as quietly as he could, leaving Vanja asleep in the warmth. The dogs' tails clapped eagerly against the railings when Gabriel turned into the driveway. A light went on in the big house and Liam could see his mother's inquisitive eyes behind the plants. She was like the dogs, awake and prepared. Nothing slipped past her.

There was a loud commotion as Gabriel got out of the car. Liam roared at the dogs to be quiet, afraid they would drag Vanja from her sleep. They sat down on the rough fabric of the sofa that had sunk into the grass. Their dad had dragged it out of the sitting room when the cancer came. That first winter of his illness it had been buried under the snow, but as soon as early spring arrived he scraped off the snow, laid reindeer skins over the cushions and dug a hole for the fire. Then he sat there until he died.

Gabriel turned up his collar and coughed down into his jumper to deaden the sound of his rattling lungs. The orange fleece gave off a sweet smell of hash.

'I saw Jennifer yesterday,' he said. 'She asked about you.'

'And?'

'I showed her some pictures of Vanja, how big she's grown, but I shouldn't have done that. She went mental. Started screaming, pulling her hair. She tore out these great lumps of it.'

'I thought she was in Stockholm.'

'Yeah, well, she's back. She wanted to do a deal but I sent her packing. I told her I wasn't selling to her any more.'

Liam spat into the grass. The gravel road curved like a snake in the moonlight and he half-expected Jennifer to come walking along in the dark, with her colourless eyes and her huge Vanja belly. That was still the way he saw her, pregnant with their child. The pregnancy was unexpected and they didn't plan to keep the baby, but Jennifer had missed all her appointments at the clinic and soon you could see the bump and feel the child moving inside it, and Liam had never been so terrified in the whole of his life as he was the summer Vanja was born. He hadn't been sober one single day, the fear had made sure of that. And Jennifer was even worse; she knocked back tablets and homebrew in secret. She didn't come home at night even though her body was so clumsy it made her waddle as she walked. As the due date approached Liam had to kick down three front doors in his search for her. The night Vanja was born he was under arrest, alone with a police officer who brewed coffee and offered him smuggled cigarettes. Liam had paced the windowless room, repeating that they wouldn't get a child but a monster, because neither of them could stay clean and whatever was growing inside Jennifer had never even been given a proper chance. When he was freed the following morning, his mother was standing there, red and wrinkled from crying, telling him he had become father to a little girl. An absolutely perfect little girl.

He took a sidelong glance at the garage door, to make sure Vanja wasn't standing there, listening.

'Jennifer knows the terms. If she gets clean, she gets to see Vanja as much as she likes. I won't stand in her way.'

'She'll never get clean. You should have seen the mess, hair all over the hall. It was like two cats had been in a fight.'

Gabriel smirked. They could see their mum in the window. She had lit a candle and the flame flickered as she moved behind the curtain.

'You wanted to talk about Juha,' said Gabriel. 'What's he done now?'

Liam hesitated. It was always risky telling Gabriel things. He was a puppet on strings as far as his emotional life was concerned, controlled by the impulses and rage that continually simmered under his skin. But Liam had to tell him, before everything got worse.

'He called on Vidar Björnlund's daughter and told her the police have got the wrong man. He says he knows who really killed Vidar.'

'Is he blaming us?'

'He hasn't said so yet. He wants paying before he tells.'

Gabriel's jaw worked and the glow from his cigarette darted like a firefly in the night.

'For someone who lives in a hovel he's fucking greedy.'

'She hasn't paid him yet, but you can tell she's interested. She wants to save her boyfriend, him with the debts.'

'What, the guy they've arrested is her boyfriend?'

'That's what people say.'

Gabriel laughed hoarsely.

'You don't have to worry, I've already taken care of Juha. I've just come from there.'

He held a hand up to Liam's face, revealing a couple of bloody knuckles. The darkness hid the rest of him, but he shone his phone so Liam could see the fresh bloodstains spreading over his clothes and arms, and up his face. It looked like he had butchered an animal.

'Christ, what have you done?'

'You told me to take care of Juha, right? So I took a trip to North Forest to get the plants and have a little chat with our lone wolf. He won't be troubling us any more.'

SUMMER 2009

The child grows older and there is no room for thoughts about leaving. Springs and summers have come and gone but the girl no longer prowls the road with her thumb in the air. The men in the cars are a shadow play in her memory. She sees them sometimes, in the darkness that settles over the village, but she no longer thinks they can save her.

Her father sits behind the wheel now, giving her a lift to the village and the neon lights of the filling station where she stands among people, day after day, almost as if she belongs there. It was the owner, Niila, who gave her the job, one winter when she was standing with Simon on her hip, waiting for Vidar to fill the car outside. Perhaps he felt sorry for her standing there, so young and with a child of her own to look after.

'We could do with some new blood here in the shop,' he said. 'If you're interested.'

At first she stood absolutely still as if she hadn't heard, but then she quickly said yes, before her father was able to interfere. By the time he came in through the door she and Niila had already shaken hands on it.

Now she stands on the stage under the harsh lights and smiles at people's curiosity. They pay for their petrol and their milk and can't resist dropping a question into the small talk. Their eyes gleam and their lips purse when they ask about the child. They study every detail of the boy's face when he visits the girl at work and stands with his hand in hers. People look for the answers in his beautiful childish features. It's odd, they say, it's as if the boy came from nowhere. You'd almost think he fell from heaven like an angel.

She forgets all about the bundle of notes decomposing between the worn slats in the moose lookout tower. The lies, those black lies, keep her there, her love for the child stronger than any of the dreams she once had. The father sits on his chair in the kitchen and sees everything before it has happened. He leads the way through the forest, showing the boy everything that will be his one day.

If you leave me I'll drown myself, he says at regular intervals, and love and threats become the tapestry that enfolds them and holds them tight. The village is a black hole that sucks them in and will never let them leave. Every morning the same view from the window on the first floor, the dark rowan tree and the wall of forest. Outside the door is the red mat, running like an umbilical cord to the boy's room. Now she is no longer alone with her father, and never will be.

It was many years since she'd spent time with Juha Bjerke, but the memories were still strong inside her. The smell of wildness and the sense of freedom were in her blood. She had only seen his pitiful home on one occasion, but there was something about the fear that reinforced her memories and she let them lead her into the sunless forest. The narrow road wound through the backwoods, past forgotten farmhouses whose empty windows stared blankly after her. The evening sun burned in the rear-view mirror and forest shadows reached out to the car, and she was on the point of giving up and turning round when she saw the timber cabin wedged between the pines, exactly as she remembered it. His car was also there, and she could still feel the rough seat cover irritating her legs and smell the marijuana, hear her voice begging and pleading to be taken away.

She tried not to look at the animal carcasses hanging from the trees, but she couldn't avoid hearing the creaking ropes and the flies' buzzing dance around death. The pelts of two roe deer were stretched between the trees like enormous wings in the twilight, and she could hear the brook murmuring in the undergrowth. Yet she wasn't afraid as she approached Juha's home. She had already stood face to face with his madness and she knew he wished her no harm.

Shrill barking met her tentative knock on the door, but no

Juha. In the end she banged her fist so hard the skull above the door rattled on its hook.

'Juha!' she called. 'It's me. Liv Björnlund. I've come with the money!'

The bundle of notes chafed inside her jacket. It was more money than she had ever carried in her entire life. She hadn't been able to bring herself to touch a single krona of the inheritance, despite everything they needed — new car, new roof, new lives. The money scared her. The sudden freedom had a paralysing effect and she couldn't think what to do with it. Not until now, when suddenly she was standing outside Juha Bjerke's house, willing to pay for the name of her father's murderer. The idea might be futile but she convinced herself that if only she could find out the truth the nightmare would end and life begin.

She felt the door and it slid slowly open. The dog was waiting inside, a shaggy wolf-like creature that would not allow itself to be patted and followed her movements closely as she stepped into the cabin. Hot stale air met her and she smelled the man long before she saw him. Grey light fell through the doorway, revealing pieces of simple wooden furniture that were shadows in the dim interior. There were hunting trophies everywhere — horns, skulls and skins. It was like stepping into a crypt, a place decorated with death.

Juha lay on a bunk at the back of the cabin, a thin bundle that neither moved nor spoke. If it hadn't been for the unmistakable smell she would not have noticed him.

'Juha, it's me. Liv. Are you awake?'

There was not so much as a sigh in reply.

'Are you alive?'

She left the door half-open and took a couple of wary steps into the room. Gusts of fresh air wafted around the clutter inside and ash, pine needles and dead leaves whirled around her boots. The cabin was like an extension of the forest, more a camp than a proper home.

Either he was dead or it was a trap. A man who lived in the wild would never sleep that soundly and let the world fade away around him. He couldn't afford to do that.

A low protest came from the dog's mouth as she approached the bunk, but it kept its distance. She called Juha's name again. Intense fear washed over her when he didn't answer. Not until she was standing over him did she hear his breathing. A sickening smell of blood rose up from him, sweet and metallic. Memories from butchering hunted animals came to mind, the cold film on Vidar's eyes as he sliced through the animal's body, and the hot steam given off by the fresh incision.

Gently she placed a hand on Juha's shoulder and he moaned under her touch. His contorted face shone with coagulated blood and his beard lay in matted clumps on his chest. His hand came from nowhere and gripped her wrist with a strength that proved there was still life in him. His voice was a thin whisper.

'He tried to kill me.'

'Who tried to kill you?'

'The Devil himself, I'm afraid.'

Liv eyed the front door.

'Is he still here?'

'I heard him drive away. I didn't fight back so he got bored in the end. He thought it was all over.'

Juha let go of Liv and tried to heave himself up, but the effort made him cough so violently that he fell back against the reindeer skins. It sounded as if something had come loose inside him. Liv looked around the room. If she wanted to find out the truth she had to first help Juha Bjerke.

'You must go to hospital.'

'Like hell I will. I'd rather die here and now.'

He grimaced and pointed to a bottle on the mantelpiece.

'Give me a drink, that's all I need.'

'Your cuts need cleaning up.'

'No, dammit, just give me the bottle.'

She ignored his protests, left him in the cabin and found her way to the stream to fetch fresh water to clean his injuries. There was nothing else available so she ripped off a piece of her T-shirt and used that to wash him. Gently but with great difficulty she pulled off his clothes, the fleece top and the padded waistcoat, the long underpants. The pain brought him out in a sweat, but even so he tried to make light of it.

'This is what you really came to see.'

She washed off a layer of dirt to reveal the bruises underneath. There was a swelling over his shoulder and he yelled when she touched it. But his face was worse; there were inflamed cuts on his lips and both eyebrows, and the blood had set on his cheeks and chin and far down his throat. It came off in flakes like bark as she wiped him with the cloth. The dog sat beside them and insisted on licking the injured body with the tender earnestness of a bitch removing the amniotic sack of her newly born puppy. Liv didn't prevent it because she saw it made Juha feel better. The dog had a soothing effect on him.

When he was more or less clean she poured a few drops of homebrew into a plastic mug and held it out to him. She also rolled a clumsy joint and put it between his lips. After he had downed the alcohol and taken a few rattling puffs he was strong enough to pull himself into a sitting position. Liv opened her jacket, giving him a view of the bundle of cash.

'Tell me what you know about Dad's killer and the money's yours.'

'I don't want your money any more.'

A few teeth were missing from his upper jaw and he slurred his words as he spoke. Liv closed her jacket again. The adrenalin and stuffy air were making her feel nauseous.

'I want to confess my sins,' Juha said. 'That's all I want.'

Something in his voice made her blood run cold. Liv went to the front door, stuck her face through the gap and breathed in the smell of impending rain. He didn't appear to be thinking clearly. She wondered if he'd received a blow to the head. Concussion, perhaps.

'I only want to know what happened to Dad.'

'It's a long sorry tale, I'm afraid. And one that will stay between us because I won't be talking to the police. What I've got to say is for your ears alone.'

'Out with it, then.'

Juha nodded, preparing himself.

'It all started with the letter I got from the forestry company. I had a shock when it came, driving me off my land after all these years, the same land where my brother's buried. It was damned hard to take in. Vidar swore blind I could stay here. As long as I kept my hands off you, nothing would change. That's what he said. But when I went to see him last spring he laughed in my face and said it wasn't him who made the decisions. Turned out his promises were all hot air.'

He was taken over by a fit of coughing. Liv stayed by the door and looked at the frail body of the man shuddering in the half-light. She felt a growing fear in her chest.

'It was you, wasn't it? You killed Dad.'

'If I'd had the courage to kill Vidar I would have done it long ago, but I'm too much of a coward for that kind of heroic deed. I already have one human life on my conscience and that's more than I can live with.'

'You said you wanted to confess your sins.'

His chin and beard shone with the phlegm he had coughed up. He picked up his fleece from the floor and wiped his face with it, squeezing his eyes shut to gather his thoughts.

'There are two brothers,' he said at last. 'One of them worthless and the other a devil. They come here with weed and coffee so I don't have to drive to the village for anything. Convenient for a recluse like me. They're young and fit and greedy for what life has to offer, unlike yours truly. So I decided to send them in Vidar's direction, as soon as I heard about the forest. It was my way of getting revenge once and for all.'

Liv recoiled.

'You asked them to kill him?'

Juha drew deeply on the joint and waved away the accusation.

'No, dammit, of course not. I never wanted him dead. They

were only meant to take back some of the money he stole over all these years. Money that lay rotting in that dump you call a home. Money that belongs to me and all the other poor souls he fooled. Vidar had lined his pockets at other people's expense for too long. It was time he had a taste of his own medicine.'

Liv clung to the door frame. A wave of heat made her face flush, despite the cold air on her back.

'But I should have known better than to trust those two,' Juha continued. 'The one I called worthless, his finger slipped on the trigger and killed Vidar. And now they decide I'm going the same way because I know too much. But you can't get rid of me that easily.'

'What are those brothers called?'

Juha hesitated for a long time, his eyelids so heavy she could hardly see his expression.

'Lilja is the name,' he said at last. 'Liam and Gabriel. The family's got a place in Kallbodan. Their dad died of cancer and their mum is some kind of hippie who rescues dogs. You can't miss the house, there are mongrels everywhere.'

'Liam? Did you say Liam?'

'Yes. Why, do you know him?'

Liv gulped. Her head was spinning. Liam at the filling station. That damaged guy who dreamed about buying a house. Who could hardly look her in the face. She took the bundle of money from her jacket and held it out to Juha, but he shook his head.

'I don't want your money. Just put it right, that's all. That's all I want.'

She faltered. The money dug into her skin. Swiftly she reached out and put it on the table. Then she slipped out through the door, leaving him there.

The gravel road ran like a meandering stream through the forest. A hushed rain spread its glossy filter over the world. Vidar's rasping voice echoed through her head as she drove, warning and reprimanding her. A shadow of his self-satisfied smile hovered in the windscreen and she switched on the wipers to get rid of it. He hadn't mentioned anything about selling North Forest, or that Juha would be driven from his land after all this time. Juha was no liar and if he said Liam and his brother had come to Ödesmark to rob them, then that was the truth. She'd known there was something odd about Liam the very first time she saw him at the till. The apprehension that made his face twitch whenever he saw her and his body tense up as soon as she came near. It was no coincidence he had been drawn to the filling station, to her. Everything was a part of something bigger, something she didn't understand but that Vidar had warned her about long before he died.

She heard the dogs before she saw the house. It was an isolated place in the same sorry state as Björngården. A dog pen ran along one side of their garden and she could see eager tails wagging behind the bars. When she stopped the car her fingers were clenched rigidly round the wheel. The smell of Juha lingered in her nostrils and when she looked down at her clothes she saw they were flecked with his blood. She glanced in the rear-view mirror and discovered red streaks on her face, too. Ancient warpaint, staring back at her. She licked her fingers and tried to rub away the worst of it. Her eyes were bloodshot from fear. She tried not to think too much but let herself be steered by instinct instead. A voice inside her said she ought to phone Hassan, inform him of what she was about to do. But he would advise her against it, she knew. In one of the windows a face had appeared, a woman with frizzy hair and a wild look in her eyes. Liv climbed out of the car, her blood pounding in her head. Barking followed her up the path and reached a peak when she rapped her knuckles on the door, the other hand resting on a knife.

It was the woman who opened. She was wearing a long dress that came to the floor and had a tattooed eye between her collar bones that stared back at Liv.

'Can I help you?'

She wasn't much older than Liv but the years had etched bitter lines around her mouth and made her look worn out. Liv held out a hand and introduced herself.

'I'd like to talk to your sons.'

'Are you from the police?'

'I work at the filling station, with Liam.'

'Has he done something stupid?'

'I just want to talk to him, that's all.'

The woman had a necklace of shining stones that she was twisting so tightly around her hand that her fingers went white. She nodded towards a building across from the house.

'You'll find Liam in the garage.'

Liv turned around and caught sight of a decaying sofa half-buried in the bushes. A single window shone behind it, but no one was looking out.

'Thanks,' she said, but the woman had already shut the door.

The howling rose again as she walked past. Greedy predator eyes followed her from behind the bars. It was like moving through a prison corridor, accosted by hungry looks.

She stopped outside the garage and walked up the stairs to a front door. An orange sign with lightning flashes and the words *Keep out* stared back at her. She heard voices inside, the high laughter of a child that made her take her hand off her knife. The warning sign shook on its nail when she knocked. A little girl opened. She had a thick plait and inquisitive eyes.

'Who are you?'

Liv searched for words, thrown off her guard by the child. She folded her arms across her body to hide the bloodstains on her clothes.

'Is your daddy home?'

Liam was sitting inside in the dim light, and he looked shocked to see her there. He seemed younger without his work shirt. The dark hoodie he had on drowned him, and he was more like a big brother than a dad, someone who was playing at being a grown-up.

'What are you doing here?'

Perhaps there was something in his voice because the little girl scuttled into the room and hid behind his back. The sight took Liv back in time, to the policeman's dark trousers and Vidar's hand fumbling for hers under the kitchen table. The fateful feeling that her existence was like the spring ice, ready to crack. Two more steps and she would be sucked down into the deep water.

'Juha Bjerke sent me. I need to talk to you. About Dad.'

She saw he understood. His Adam's apple bobbed up and down when he swallowed. He picked up the girl in his arms and sat her on his lap, and she buried her face in his throat.

'Vanja, run over to Grandma for a little while, so we grown-ups can have a chat.'

The girl sat upright, her cheeks rosy like apples.

'Shall I ask Grandma to make some coffee?'

'That would be nice.'

'And warm buns?'

'If she's got any.'

He followed the girl to the door and they stood and watched as she ran to the big house. Liam was breathing fast. Liv was aware of her knife again and gripped the handle, ready to put it to his neck if necessary. He made a gesture towards the room.

'Would you like something to drink? I've got beer or juice.'

'No, nothing for me, thanks.'

She stood with her back to the door as he walked around the room. He took a beer from the fridge and sat down at the table. The round surface was littered with crayons and drawing paper and the works of art were in various stages of completion. One of them had *Vanja* ♥ *Daddy* written in wobbly letters. Liam nodded at the table.

'Come in and sit down.'

'I'm fine standing here.'

✳

She didn't dare enter the room and kept her eyes on him as if any second he would attack. A hand behind her back made

347

it obvious she was hiding a weapon of some sort, a pistol or a knife. It didn't scare him.

'You looked for a job at the filling station just so you could get at me,' she said.

'I looked for a job because I wanted to start a new life.'

'I saw your car outside on the road that night.'

Her hair was hanging in wet strands over her face and there were dark patches on her clothes, as if she had been crawling in mud. Or blood. Her look seemed to penetrate his skin, making the shame itch all over him. Liam cracked open a can and took a swig of beer.

'I don't know what you're talking about.'

'Come off it. Juha has already told me everything. And I saw you. So did Dad. He said wolves were prowling around the house, but he meant you. He found you out and that's why you killed him.'

His fingers tingled and the beer can burned in his hand. If Gabriel had been there he would have thrown it at her, tipped over the table and shouted that she didn't know what she was talking about. He would have put his hands round her throat and held her up so her toes were off the ground. Liam might have done the same thing not so very long ago, at a time when he was controlled by his impulses. But now he sat as still as he could while the beer and the nervousness bubbled in his stomach.

'Juha is good at making up stories.'

'So are you, obviously. Both me and Niila believed your little sob story about a new life, we swallowed it hook, line and sinker. I even felt sorry for you the first time I saw you at the filling station. You seemed so lost, so unsure. Now I know why.'

'I've got nothing to do with the death of your dad.'

He looked her straight in the eyes, his voice calm and steady, used to it after a lifetime of lying. Perhaps he could convince her that this was all a mistake, before it was too late.

Her face was as immobile as a doll's, revealing nothing. Her right hand was still behind her back, the other on the door handle, but her chest was heaving as if she was already running. Liam wondered if she had called the police, if they were on their way right now. Maybe they had already picked up Gabriel, maybe he was giving them his cobbled-together version in an interview room somewhere. Whatever happened it would be word against word. The only thing he could do was convince them, and convince her.

Liv took a step into the room. Her courage impressed him. The fact that she had come alone.

'An innocent man has been arrested,' she said. 'And I'm not giving up until I know what really happened.'

Liam finished his beer and opened another as his brain ticked over. Vanja's drawings were on the table, pleading with him: a sun with rays reaching down to the grass, people with wide smiles, and butterflies with starry wings. And in the middle her name, *Vanja ♥ Daddy*.

Tears stung his eyelids. The woman in front of him was also someone's daughter. A dead man's daughter. An enormous weariness washed over him as he looked at her. Every muscle in his body gave up and stopped fighting. He simply couldn't lie any longer, he hadn't the energy.

'I was there,' he said, finally.

'What?'

'I wasn't the one who shot him, but I saw him fall. I was there.'

Words began pouring out of him and he couldn't stop them. Liv held her breath as he described how they had parked by the lake and stood in the shadow of the trees, looking at the pale light from their window and the movements inside the run-down house. He described how they had bided their time to make certain there would be no mistakes. Even so, they had deviated from their plan when they followed Vidar into the forest. That had been Gabriel's idea. In actual fact they had arrived too late. The sun was getting ready to rise and night was almost over. He told her how they had separated and how he had lost Gabriel. His ears burned as he told her, his mouth so dry the words got stuck. He drank his beer and avoided looking at her as he described the forest and the marsh, everything suddenly very clear in front of him. The waterlogged ground blushing in the dawn light, the mist clinging to the trees. The old man's body swaying like a windblown tree seconds before he fell. The mute shock when the shot was fired, an eternal silence before the birds filled the sky.

'No one was meant to die. That wasn't the intention. Basically, something went very wrong out there. My brother does things sometimes, without thinking.'

The crying was strangling him, words came out jumbled, he gulped and gulped and something in her eyes scared him. Vanja's pictures fluttered when she approached the table.

'So it was your brother who did it?'

'I thought so at first, but now I'm not so sure. I think there was someone else out there that morning, someone who was there to kill him.'

Liam caught sight of the knife in her hand, her white fingers round the shaft. Her fear mirrored his own. He tried not to think about the police, about what would happen next. He only tried to give her the truth.

'I've got something I want to show you.'

Without waiting for a reply he got up and fetched his laptop. His hands shook when he tapped in the password and opened the hidden file of pictures. Gabriel would murder him if he found out, but that didn't matter now. Nothing mattered. Liam wasn't worried about his brother or the police. All he knew was that everything he had held inside had to come out. The burden would kill him otherwise.

He turned the screen so she could see. There was a swish as she pulled the knife out of its sheath. Slowly she walked to the table. She smelled of rain and sweat and her hair was dripping. Liam swallowed some beer and pretended not to see the knife, but in reality he kept it in the corner of his eye at all times, ready to twist it out of her hand if necessary.

He heard her gasp for breath as he opened the pictures. Her home flickered past on the screen, the lonely window and the doors, the black opening in the forest where the tracks criss-crossed. When he got to the pictures of the old man her body started shaking.

'I don't know how he got into that well,' Liam said. 'Because he was shot on the marsh.'

'I know,' she said, and her voice came from deep down inside her. 'I know where he died.'

They saw Vidar's frail body bent as if in prayer over the ground, his hands tearing at the wet earth.

'He was digging for something out there,' Liam said. 'But I don't know what it was.'

'He dropped his glasses,' she whispered. 'That's what he was looking for.'

Liam put the arrow in the left-hand corner and zoomed in. He studied the blurry trees and the warm dawn sky as if for the first time. He pointed at the screen.

'Gabriel was somewhere on the other side. I'm not really sure where.'

He moved his finger to the light patch hovering among the trees.

'I might be imagining it, but it looks like someone else was there. A person in a blue jacket. Can you see?'

Liv leaned closer to the screen, her fingers pressed to her mouth, her face so white it frightened him. He stood up and tried to make her sit in the chair before she fainted, but she pushed him away and came dangerously close to grazing him with the knife. Her eyes didn't leave the screen. She stared at the unclear contours and the blue shadow, as if from a jacket or a jumper, that didn't belong in the green of the pine needles. It could be an illusion, but the longer he looked the more certain he became that someone was there.

'I can't see anything,' she said, standing up.

Liam felt the disappointment like a blow to his stomach.

'Can't you see it could be someone? Someone in a blue jacket?'

But she couldn't see. She only shook her head and began to move away from him, quickly, towards the door. The rain thundered on the roof and the single window and she pulled up her hood for protection. Her thin body was lost in the shiny fabric. Liam suddenly stopped. If the picture hadn't been in front of him he wouldn't have noticed, but now the similarity was so obvious it cried out to him. He looked from the screen to Liv's jacket and back again. The colour blue hit him in the eye.

*

The rain collected in glistening death traps on the road. She drove fast, even though the car skidded dangerously on the curves and the windscreen wipers couldn't keep up. The downpour was so heavy she couldn't distinguish the sky from the forest; everything blurred into one, a dark tunnel without an end. She shook with weeping, salty tears coursing down her cheeks and chin. She didn't see the sign for the village, knowing only that it was there. An invisible cord ran between her and her childhood home, preventing her from getting lost. Preventing her from leaving. The road was covered in mud which stuck to the tyres. In the glow of the full-beam headlights the rain was falling like white spears from the sky, a declaration of war to anyone who dared set foot out of doors. She didn't expect to meet any oncoming vehicles, or any people. Which was why she came alarmingly close to running him over.

He was walking in the middle of the road, his body bowed against the storm, and she braked so hard the mud flew up into his face. She dipped the headlights so he could see it was her, and dried the tears from her face with her wet jacket so he wouldn't see the state she was in, how close she was to tipping over the edge. As he slid into the passenger seat she threw her arms around him, saturating her own clothes in the cold water that ran from his. She felt him shivering and grabbed the dog blanket from the back seat and draped it over his shoulders. He was still her child, her boy. No one would take him from her.

'What are you doing out here?'

'I had this row with Felicia. I didn't want to stay any longer.'

She started the car and carried on down the village road, feeling as if her heart was exploding in her chest. When she reached the barrier and the drive that led up to Björngården she chose to go on. Simon was restless in his seat, misting the window with his heavy breathing.

'What are you doing? You've missed the driveway.'

'We can drive for a while.'

'What, now? It's torrential out there!'

'I just want to talk to you.'

He pulled a face but didn't protest. When they came out onto the main road the rain had eased and she could see the sign and the large boulder where she used to huddle in the summertime, waiting for the perfect car. The one that would sweep her out of there.

'What did you argue about?'

'What?'

'You and Felicia.'

'I don't know.'

'You don't know?'

'I don't want to talk about it.'

Liv glanced at him. He seemed more angry than sad. It was rainwater running down his face, not tears. A sudden feeling of hopefulness unfurled inside her. This was their chance to get away, their very last chance. She was the one behind the wheel now.

'When I was younger I used to hitch a lift on this road, have I told you that? I wanted to get away no matter what. I didn't even care who picked me up, I was so desperate.'

'So why did you come back, if you wanted to get away so badly?'

'Dad always found me. It didn't matter how far I went, he was always sitting there in the Volvo, waiting. Then you came along. And then I didn't want to run away any more.'

Simon ran a finger over the window, drawing a circle in the condensation.

'It's dangerous, hitching lifts. You could have died.'

It was the same overbearing tone Vidar used to use. She wondered if he was aware how alike they were, more and more every day, and how that frightened her. She pulled into a lay-by and swung round, back towards Ödesmark, the decisiveness beating in her chest.

'When we get home I want you to pack a bag.'

'Why?'

'We're getting out of here. Once and for all.'

She lit the pipe and studied her reflection in the black window. Darkness thickened outside but there was still plenty of time. Liam wouldn't put the police on to her, he had too much to lose. Images of Johnny in a cell floated across her mind, but she blew the smoke between her teeth and dismissed them. Freedom craved its victims, its blood.

Simon's movements upstairs made the house shake to its foundations. He slammed doors and flushed the toilet, but he didn't come down, not until she called up to him.

'Have you packed?'

'I don't plan on going anywhere.'

'You've got no choice. If I tell you to pack, you pack.'

Perhaps he heard in her voice that she was serious, because he came sloping down the stairs. His hair was still damp and he was wearing his jogging bottoms to clearly signal his intention of staying at home. He stared at her bag perched on the table, a few changes of clothes, that was all. The necessities. She would leave the rest.

'It's the middle of the night. Can't we wait until it gets light?'

'We haven't got time to wait.'

'What's the rush?'

His shadow fell across the room, towering over her. She realized he scared her, that she was afraid of her own son. She could see the pulse beating in his throat, the anxiety in his body. She nodded towards the chair where the jacket was hanging, the blue material shining in the dim light.

'Sit down,' she ordered.

Reluctantly, he pulled out the chair. He rested his head in his hands, knotting his fingers around his hair as if he was about to pull it out by the roots. Under the new layer of muscles and masculinity she could still detect her boy. He became clearer now, with his trembling lips and the tears in his voice.

'I don't get it. Why do we have to leave? We're free now. Grandad's gone.'

'Put the jacket on.'

'What?'

'The jacket on your chair. Put it on.'

He raised his head and looked straight at her, his eyes filled with fear. Slowly and without taking his eyes from her face he lifted the jacket from the chair and slid it over his arms. It was too small for him; the fabric pulled across his shoulders and the arms didn't reach to his wrists. The shabby garment seemed to crush all the air out of him. His breathing was fast and strained.

'Happy now?'

She shook her head.

'I want to know what you were doing with my jacket the morning your grandad was shot.'

He hid his face in his hands, disappearing inside himself for a long time before he started to explain.

EARLY MORNING, 2 MAY

The old hands force their way into his sleep, stiff claws grasping him, rough and impatient under the covers. The room is thick with darkness and his grandfather's breath. It's a while before he can make out the ageing face.

'What are you doing, Grandad?'

'Get up, lad. We're in a hurry.'

He's got the rifle with him. The boy sees the black barrel and shrinks back against the pillow. He gets the idea his grandfather is going to shoot him, that everything has finally gone crazy, that it's over now. He wants to call for his mother but his grandfather reads his thoughts and clamps a hard fist over his mouth. The fingers smell of explosives.

'The wolves are prowling about outside. It's time to get the bastards.'

'But it's the middle of the night.'

'It'll be sunrise any minute. Come on!'

His grandfather holds out the rifle. His useless hands can't hold the weapon any longer, let alone fire it. The boy understands why he has been woken before the crack of dawn. It's so that he can be the executioner. He wants to protest but there is something in his grandfather's voice that makes him obey. It doesn't sound cracked now, his voice. The thirst for blood appears to have a healing effect on him. The old man stands at the window and peers out through a gap in the blinds while the boy gets dressed. His grandfather's lungs wheeze as he breathes.

He moves silently in front of the boy down the stairs, his stiff joints creaking along with the wooden boards. They have grown old together, his grandfather and the house; they are well past their prime. Down in the hall the boy hesitates, tying the shoelaces slowly, his own and his grandfather's, and then he stands for a long time pretending to search for his hat. He hears the wind scrape at the outside walls and fears the darkness and the cold on the other side. Finally he drags his mother's jacket from its hook. It's the warmest one. His grandfather becomes impatient, pushes the boy in front of him like a disobedient animal.

The cold wind hits him in the face when he opens the door. A blood-red streak is visible in the sky to the east, but daylight seems far away. His grandfather points down towards the lake.

'You take the east side, I'll take the west. Then we'll meet on the marsh.'

His claw-like hand pats the rifle with brisk tenderness.

'Don't hesitate this time, do you hear? Shoot to kill.'

That's the last thing he says before disappearing. The boy shuts the door behind him, tiptoes through the house to the veranda door at the back, and opens it as quietly as he can before stepping out into the cold. It isn't the first time they have gone their separate ways; his grandfather likes to have eyes in several places at once. The wind tugs at the boy as he walks quietly towards the forest edge, and he listens out for noises that jar, that are out of place, but all he can hear is the sighing of the trees and the dog standing in the hall, whining after them. Grandfather never leaves it behind. He must really think there are wolves out there that could rip the dog to shreds if they aren't careful. The boy glances up at his mother's window before he goes. The white curtains are moving like ghosts in the dull light. He knows the way she sleeps, with her face to the door and the knife under the mattress. Her secrets follow him into the undergrowth.

A monster lives inside him. It doesn't show on the outside but people sense it even so. He usually stands in front of the mirror, looking deep into his eyes, and if he stands there long enough he sees a glimmer of the monster. People always say he's the spitting image of his grandfather, almost as though they want to tease him. He convinces himself that they know all about it. When he was younger he was happy when people said they looked alike, then the words made him feel bigger. But that was before he realized what a dark place the world is, what people can do to each other.

A milky fog drifts between the pines and all he can hear is his own blood roaring in his head. He feels the monster moving about, wanting to escape. His fingers lock around the rifle and his arms ache with its weight. Dawn is filling the forest, the spruces reach out for him, slapping and tearing, but the pain drives him on. It incites the monster.

He gets there first. The marsh spreads out like a fleshy steaming wound in the pale light. He splashes around the edge and checks for his grandfather on the other side, but he isn't there yet. Age has settled like weights around Vidar's joints and made him clumsy and slow. In reality they don't have to do as Vidar says any longer. He said that to his mum last Christmas when she padded in with presents for him in the morning. That Grandad was too old to control their lives. Now they could do as they liked. But she only smiled the smile that meant he must keep quiet, because Grandad can hear everything even when you whisper or form the words silently. He floats above them like an all-powerful god, and although he is ageing before their eyes they doubt he will ever die.

The moose lookout tower takes shape among the trees. A lonely snowdrift clings on in the shade of the darkened wood. He hangs the rifle over his shoulder and reaches out for the ladder. The rungs are damp, with patches of peeling lichen, and his shoes slip dangerously on the slippery surface. The thought is an innocent one at first, that he will only keep a lookout for his grandfather. It's not until he is sitting there with the rifle barrel in the opening that he realizes he now has his chance. To be free.

The insight vibrates through his body. He finds it hard to hold the rifle still. He has the sun at his back as his grandfather steps out onto the marsh. The man moves clumsily in the undergrowth, like a wounded animal. The boy is about to commit an act of mercy. He will put an end to suffering, his and theirs. He sees his grandfather fall to his knees, sees him bend over the wet ground. He has dropped his glasses, his eyes are black notches when at last he gets to his feet and turns his face to the sun and the boy.

The boy has thought this thought so many times, that everything would be better if only his grandfather would die. If they could get free. Everything would be so much easier then, when he didn't control every step they took.

The bullet hits his grandfather with such force he is thrown backwards. The sky is filled with black birds and they squawk in the boy's ears when he takes aim again. It was his grandfather who taught him to shoot and he would be proud of him if he wasn't the one lying there, thrashing in the moss like a fish. It doesn't look real; everything is happening as if in a dream. Through the opening he sees his grandfather's body fall still and begin to sink under the moss. The ground is trying to pull him down, in a hurry to bury him. Everything seems to flicker.

The boy slings the rifle across his back and scrambles down the ladder. He stands for a few moments looking at the immobile heap out on the marsh, trying to comprehend the fact that it is his grandfather lying there. Then he seems to hear voices, the howling of wolves. They are chasing him. He turns and runs, as fast as he can, back to the house. He hides the weapon in the woodshed and sneaks up to his room. His mother's door is still closed and suddenly he longs to be in there with her. He wants to burst in and tell her everything. It's over now, he will say, and she will understand exactly what he means. She will lift the duvet and make room for him, stroke her fingertips over his eyelids as she did when he was little, and whisper that there isn't a monster inside him any more. They have driven it away.

But he doesn't dare. The hinges creak as he walks stealthily to his own room. He takes off the cold wet clothes and crawls down under the duvet and lies there, looking up at the ceiling. He tries to convince himself it was all a dream, but his heart is still pounding wildly. He can't fool his own body. Time passes, the room grows light and shifts colour. He hears his mother stirring, her sleepy footsteps on the stairs. The sun is shining brightly through the blinds and the first thing she does is call for his grandad, and the loneliness in her voice travels all the way up to the boy. He holds his hands to his ears and shuts his eyes. Pretends he can't hear.

The house and the familiar rooms seemed immediately alien. A numbness in her chest made her struggle to find the feelings. She must be feeling something. Simon's eyes sought hers, his voice was hoarse after his confession and his exhausted body slumped over the table. Liv ran her fingers through his damp hair. He looked away.

'You sent me to school but I didn't go. I ran back to the marsh and saw him lying there. Those ravens had already been at him. When I got there he didn't have any eyes.'

He swayed on the chair, the moonlight falling over his bloodless face, and Liv was afraid he would faint. She went round the table and lifted him gently to his feet. She led him into the sitting room and helped him lie down on the sofa. Then she sat on the floor beside his head, stroking his pale cheeks and trying to stifle the nausea that was rising in her throat. She didn't want to hear any more.

'You should rest.'

But he carried on, unable to stop the words once he had started.

'I don't know why I did it, I just knew I had to.'

He clamped his fingers round her wrist and drew her close to him. His wild look reminded her of Vidar.

'He wanted me to be like you, Mum, but I couldn't. I'll never be like you.'

She rested her face on his chest, heard the strong beating of his heart. Her boy. Something was moving inside him, she knew that. Something wild and foreign had taken control of his body, something she had only sensed through the years but which had now surfaced. Slowly the room grew light, and soon they would be able to see each other clearly. Soon they would be unable to hide.

'It's my fault Johnny's in prison, Mum,' he said.

'No, it isn't. It's the police's fault.'

'No, it's mine. I set him up.'

'What do you mean?'

'I pretended to go to school the next morning like I said, but I kind of ended up at Widow Johansson's house. I stood in the bushes and watched Johnny leave for the sawmill, and that's when I decided. I got the rifle out of our woodshed and hid it in his cellar. The door was open and literally all I had to do was walk in. I cleaned the rifle so it didn't have my fingerprints on it, then I left it there with the rest of the cartridges. Grandad never bothered registering the gun so I knew I didn't have to think about that. The rifle could easily have belonged to the Johanssons. Or Johnny. It didn't have to be ours.'

His skin felt feverish to her touch. She wanted him to stop talking, tried to hush him up. The words made them both feel sick. His voice had almost gone, but even so he persisted.

'Do you remember the break-in at school last Christmas?'

She nodded.

'The burglars left fag ends behind, that's how the police caught them. Their DNA was on them. That's how I got the idea. So I took some of the fag ends out of Johnny's ashtray and put them in a plastic bag. The key to the quad bike was hanging in his hall. That's what I used to move Grandad. I thought I'd take him far away, to the lime works maybe, but I was scared someone would see me. I only got as far as the next village. To the well. Then I left Johnny's fag ends there. That's how I set him up.'

It was all too much. Liv staggered to the bathroom and vomited violently into the rusty handbasin. Afterwards she stood looking at herself in the cracked mirror. She didn't recognize her own face. By the time she got back the morning had made its way into the sitting room and Simon's closed eyelids were bathed in a sickly light.

She sat in the armchair beside her sleeping boy until the sun poured into the room. She went to the kitchen and brewed some coffee, but when the steaming cup stood on the table she couldn't drink it. She no longer saw Vidar in the shadows, or heard his voice. Her subconscious had finally accepted the fact that he was dead.

She put the bags in the car. The morning grass had turned into a sea of dandelions. Her attention was caught by the red petrol can in the garage and she looked at the house and the thirsty old boards. She could already picture them contorted by the flames, could hear the groan when everything collapsed. She carried the can to the wall of the house. Her shoulder ached as she peered in at her sleeping child. It had never shown on him. For all of his short life she'd wondered where the monster was hiding. It had never been visible in him. Every doctor had insisted he was a perfectly healthy little boy. He had followed all the curves, grown and thrived as he should. If there was anything stirring inside him, it couldn't be seen with the naked eye.

She unscrewed the lid of the petrol can and held her breath in the fumes. Her head was buzzing, she couldn't get her thoughts in order. She would burn down the house and drive her son to safety. Take the guilt on herself and confirm the suspicions of the villagers. It was her jacket in the photograph, after all. She was the one who had never managed to break away from Vidar. Simon was only a boy, a child. But she stayed sitting beside the petrol can with her face to the sun. However much she wanted to, she couldn't bring herself to set the house alight.

In her head it was Simon's face she saw, a young Simon with round cheeks and his whole body full of laughter. It was her fault, it was as if she had failed. She was the one who had filled him with her demons and taken his laughter away from him. Slowly the realization grew stronger. A fire wouldn't offer a solution, neither would lying. All lies had to offer was yet another prison. And if she took the blame Simon would never be free. The lies would follow him like a cold shadow through life, growing bigger and heavier with the years until he was unable to bear the burden of it. That's what happened with the darkest secrets, she knew. They destroyed you slowly from the inside, until there were nothing but fragments left. The only thing that could save him was the truth. If he was ever to have a chance to live she must let him make amends for his crime. Otherwise he would never be a human being.

The birds screeched after her as she made her way back into the house. She could hear Simon's regular breathing in the sitting room while she tapped in the number, her lips close to the phone as she whispered: 'Come as quickly as you can. We need help.'

It was almost an hour before Hassan drew up on the gravel. The sight of the patrol car outside the house was as unreal now as it had been that morning when he came to tell her Vidar was dead. She waited until he was standing on the veranda steps before going to wake Simon. She stroked her thumb over his eyelids and saw them flicker as he came to life.

'Hassan's here.'

He hauled himself up.

'Why?'

'It's time to tell the truth now.'

She thought he would get angry, that he would push her away and head for the door, run down to his cellar and take cover among his exercise equipment. But he threw his arms around her and hugged her tightly and desperately, as he hadn't done since he was a little boy. She felt the fear pulsing through him. Hassan called out to them from the front door.

Simon opened. He walked onto the veranda, holding out his hands to the police officer, revealing his thick wrists.

'It's me you're looking for.'

The police station looked the same as it had the day she stood on the steps with Simon in her arms. She put her hands on the red sun-warmed brick, her head bowed. She had been forced to come out to get some air. Now only dandelions leaned against the wall. There were no black sacks this time. No dead reindeer.

'You did the right thing by phoning.'

Hassan's hand was between her shoulder blades; she hadn't heard him come out. He stroked her back. Her legs shook and it was an effort simply to stand upright.

'It should be me sitting in there.'

'Why do you say that?'

'I should have protected him, given him a future. Instead I let him grow up in Ödesmark with Vidar, even though I know what it does to a person.'

'You could never have known it would end like this.'

She supported herself against him as they turned to go back in. She scanned the car park to make sure Vidar wasn't still sitting there, waiting to drive them home to Ödesmark.

Hassan gently sat her down on a chair in the corridor.

'Don't leave me.'

'I'm not leaving you, I'm just getting some coffee.'

She didn't dare look at the other police officers. Their uniforms creaked along the shiny corridors. The strip lighting stung her eyes like winter sun. Hassan placed a mug of steaming coffee in her hands and then stood beside her, diverting her thoughts with small talk. She had to wait outside while Simon gave his statement. When he came out he was wearing handcuffs. He would be taken to the town where the prison was, and when they faced each other to say goodbye she saw his eyes were clear with relief. She was the only one crying. She put her arms around his neck and he pressed his cheek hard against hers. He couldn't use his arms to hug her back.

Summer sparkled over the village and the air was heavy with foliage and sun-warmed forest. Liv sat on the veranda steps with the key in her hand, waiting. The sun burned her face and horseflies buzzed around her, hunting for blood. She didn't want to sit in the deserted house a minute longer. The silence in there almost choked her, and she kept finding herself listening for the sound of Simon's skipping rope against the cellar floor and the old man's shuffling footsteps on the stairs. It didn't matter that one of them was dead and the other locked up; they were still alive between these walls and gave her no peace.

She told Simon about it when he phoned.

'I can still hear you hitting the punchbag every morning.'

'Sell the dump,' he told her.

'I will.'

'You're the one behind the wheel now and don't forget it.'

It was so lively around him, shouting and laughter, that sometimes she imagined he was already in town and waiting for her. The town where no one knew their name.

Johnny had tried to take her away. Shortly after he had been freed by the police he was standing in her doorway, telling her to pack a bag. She had expected him to be angry with her because of what Simon had done, for all the days he had spent in jail, but he merely wrapped her in his arms and said he was going to take her with him. Away from everything they didn't want to remember. And she had come dangerously close to agreeing, despite the fact that he couldn't be trusted. It had seemed so easy, to sink into the passenger seat and let someone else do the steering as the unfamiliar roads stretched out in front of her. But she knew it was wrong. That wasn't the way it was supposed to be. If she was going to get away she had to do it single-handed.

At long last she heard the car on the gravel. A cloud of dust rose up between the trees and soon she saw him. He was wearing sunglasses and the girl was in the back seat, and they both smiled and waved. She stood up on her aching legs and went to meet them as they climbed out. The girl had the remains of an ice cream around her mouth and her lips were dark from the chocolate. In her hand she had a colour chart which she held to the peeling walls, blue-green shades that glowed in competition with the sky.

Liam pushed his sunglasses up over his forehead. His eyes were tired underneath but they brightened up when she handed him the key.

'This doesn't feel right,' he said.

'What doesn't?'

'That you won't take any money.'

She dismissed that.

'I should be paying you for taking the place off my hands.'

'Look, Daddy – this colour will be super-cool!'

The girl held up the chart like a fan and pointed to one of the squares, a pale turquoise colour.

'Yes, that's lovely,' Liam said.

He had the key in his hand but still he hesitated on the gravel. Liv took a few steps towards her car, keen to get away.

'Just call if there's a problem. You've got my number.'

'I read he's getting a short sentence because of his age. And the circumstances.'

She stopped, her shame burning along with the sun. The horseflies were drawn to her perspiring skin and she tried to swat them away.

'I hope so,' she said. 'I don't know what the papers are saying but he's not a monster. He's only a boy.'

'There aren't any monsters,' the girl said. 'There are only people.'

She had his eyes, large and light blue. She waved the chart about and stared up at Liv in curiosity.

'What have you done to your neck?'

Liv put her fingers to the scarred skin. The heat had made her forget and she had put on a thin strappy top which didn't hide anything.

'I used to scratch myself so much it left scars.'

The girl pulled a face.

'That must have hurt a lot.'

'It did hurt. But I'm better now. It doesn't itch any more.'

They smiled at each other. Liam rested his hands on the girl's shoulders. She found it hard to stand still, and her growing body hopped and fidgeted. Liv threw a last look at her childhood home, pausing at the dingy kitchen curtains where Vidar used to sit peering out at the village. Now there was only stillness and peace. They waved after her as she drove away.

In her rear-view mirror she saw them wave and then turn and walk towards Björngården, the girl's plait a string of gold in the sunlight. Another girl and another father, a completely different story that would slowly paint over the old one. In the colours of the Northern Lights.

Acknowledgements

To my editors Helena Ljungström and Anna Andersson, thank you for your patience, enthusiasm and the ability to bring out the very, very best in my writing. It is a true joy working with you. A huge thank-you also to Martin Ahlström, Göran Wiberg, Thérèse Cederblad, Bo Bergman and everyone at Albert Bonniers Förlag.

To my agent Julia Angelin, thank you for your fantastic involvement and sterling work with my books. Massive thanks also to Marilinn Klevhamre, Anna Carlander, Josephine Oxelheim and all at Salomonsson Agency – you are stars. You make dreams become a reality.

To Niklas Natt och Dag, my warmest thanks for reading the manuscript. Your sound discernment has been invaluable. It is an honour to call you my friend.

To Daniel Svärd, thank you for giving me the opportunity to share your experience of reading my manuscript, chapter by chapter, and making it possible for me to see the text with completely new eyes.

To Kenneth Vikström, thank you for so generously sharing with me your knowledge about police procedures. Your help has been incredibly valuable during the process of writing.

To my husband Robert Jackson, thank you for always believing in me. I love you.